THE
TSARINA'S
DAUGHTER

ALSO BY ELLEN ALPSTEN

Tsarina

THE
TSARINA'S
DAUGHTER

A NOVEL

ELLEN ALPSTEN

ST. MARTIN'S
GRIFFIN
NEW YORK

First published in the United States by St. Martin's Griffin, an imprint of St. Martin's Publishing Group

www.stmartins.com

Map by Emily Maffei

Designed by Meryl Sussman Levavi

Library of Congress Cataloging-in-Publication Data

Names: Alpsten, Ellen, 1971– author.
Title: The tsarina's daughter : a novel / Ellen Alpsten.
Description: First U.S. edition. | New York : St. Martin's Griffin, 2022. |
Identifiers: LCCN 2021044948 | ISBN 9781250214416 (trade paperback) |
    ISBN 9781250214409 (hardcover) | ISBN 9781250214423 (ebook)
Subjects: LCSH: Elizabeth, Empress of Russia, 1709–1762—Fiction. |
    Russia—History—1689-1801—Fiction. | LCGFT: Biographical fiction. |
    Historical fiction. | Novels.
Classification: LCC PR9110.9.A47 T735 2022 | DDC 823/.92—dc23
LC record available at https://lccn.loc.gov/2021044948

Our books may be purchased in bulk for promotional, educational, or business use. Please contact your local bookseller or the Macmillan Corporate and Premium Sales Department at 1-800-221-7945, extension 5442, or by email at MacmillanSpecialMarkets@macmillan.com.

Originally published in 2021 in the United Kingdom by Bloomsbury Publishing

First U.S. Edition: 2022

1   3   5   7   9   10   8   6   4   2

In your end lies your beginning. No man shall disappoint you as a woman will. An angel will speak to you. The lightest load will be your greatest burden.

Prophecy of the Golosov Ravine

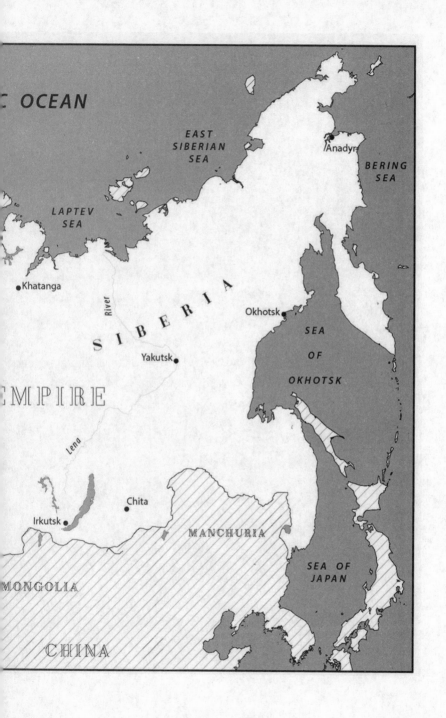

CAST OF CHARACTERS

ELIZABETH'S FAMILY

Elizabeth Petrovna Romanova / Lizenka, daughter of Tsar Peter the Great and Catherine I

Tsar Alexis Mikhailovich Romanov of All the Russias, the second Romanov Tsar; Elizabeth's grandfather

Tsar Peter the Great of All the Russias, also known as Peter Alexeyevich Romanov, *batjushka* Tsar, Peter I; Elizabeth's father

Catherine Alexeyevna, Elizabeth's mother. A former serf, once the mistress and then the wife of Peter the Great, later Tsaritsa, Tsarina Catherine I of All the Russias

Evdokia Lopukhina, Peter the Great's first wife, formerly Tsaritsa of All the Russias; mother of Tsarevich Alexey

Tsarevich Alexey, Peter the Great and Evdokia's son and his original heir; Elizabeth's half-brother

Peter Alexeyevich Romanov / Petrushka, Alexey and Sophie Charlotte's son, later Tsar Peter II; Elizabeth's nephew

Anna Petrovna Romanova / Anoushka, daughter of Peter the Great and Catherine I; Elizabeth's sister and mother of Karl Peter

Karl, Duke of Holstein, husband of Anna Petrovna; father of Karl Peter

Regent Sophia, Peter the Great's half-sister; Elizabeth's aunt

Tsar Ivan V, Peter the Great's half-brother; Elizabeth's uncle

Tsaritsa Praskovia Ivanovna Saltykova / Pasha, Ivan's widow; Elizabeth's aunt

Tsarevna Ekaterina Ivanovna, daughter to Tsar Ivan V; Elizabeth's cousin

Charles Leopold, Duke of Mecklenburg, husband of Tsarevna Ekaterina Ivanovna and father of Christine, the Regent Anna Leopoldovna of All the Russias

Christine, Elizabeth's cousin, born Elisabeth Katharina Christine, Princess of Mecklenburg, daughter of Ekaterina Ivanovna, later adopted by Tsarina Anna I and styled Crown Princess, Tsesarevna and Regent Anna Leopoldovna of All the Russias

Anthony, Duke of Brunswick, husband of the Regent Anna Leopoldovna; father to Tsar Ivan VI

Tsar Ivan VI, the infant son of Regent Anna Leopoldovna (Christine), Elizabeth's cousin. Later dubbed Ivan Antonov, prisoner number one of Russia.

Tsarevna Anna Ivanovna, daughter to Tsar Ivan V, Duchess of Courland, later Tsarina Anna I of All the Russias; Elizabeth's cousin

Duke of Courland, husband of Tsarevna Anna Ivanovna

Augustus, Prince of Holstein, cousin of Karl, Duke of Holstein; fiancé of Elizabeth Petrovna

AT THE RUSSIAN IMPERIAL COURT

Prince Alexander Danilovich Menshikov, a general in Peter's army and his trusted friend; also known as Alekasha

Princess Maria Menshikova, daughter of Menshikov and fiancée of Tsar Peter II

Feofan Prokopovich, Archbishop of Novgorod, confessor and adviser of Peter the Great, Catherine I, and Elizabeth Petrovna

Prince Alexis Grigoryevich Dolgoruky, godfather to Peter Alexeyevich Romanov (Peter II)

Princess Katja Alexeyevna Dolgoruky, daughter of Prince Alexis Dolgoruky, later engaged to Peter II

Count Peter Andreyevich Tolstoy, courtier and confidant of Peter the Great and Catherine I

Alexander Borisovich Buturlin, an officer of the Preobrazhensky
Regiment, lover and supporter of Elizabeth Petrovna
Ernst Biren, Count de Biron, a groom and stable boy, also known as
de Biron, Duke Biron of Courland, Regent of Russia; lover and
adviser to Anna I
Margarete de Biron of Courland, de Biron's wife
Charles, Peter, and Hedwig de Biron, the Biron children
General Ushakov, Head of the Secret Office of Investigation
Maja, maid to the Ivanovna family
Lt. Semyon Mordvinov, a sailor who carries letters between
Anoushka and Lizenka
Prince Avram Volynsky, Russian Ambassador to Persia
Prince Antioch Kantemir of Moldova, Russian Ambassador to
London

THE EUROPEANS

Augustus the Strong, Elector of Saxony, Peter the Great's ally and
interim King of Poland
King Louis XV of France
Maria Leszczyńska, daughter of Stanislas Leszczyński, King of Po-
land, princess of Poland; wife of Louis XV and Queen of France
Jean-Jacques Campredon, French Ambassador to Russia
Duke of Liria, Spanish Ambassador to Russia
Jan d'Acosta, a Portuguese Jew, jester to Peter the Great, Catherine I,
Peter II, Anna I, and finally Elizabeth
Jakob Schwartz, an Austrian spy, cellist, music and dance teacher
Jean-Armand de Lestocq, French aristocrat; Elizabeth's physician
**Andrej Ivanovich, Count Ostermann, original German name
Heinrich Johann Friedrich Ostermann,** Chancellor and Vice
Chancellor of Peter the Great, Catherine I, Anna I, and the
Regent Anna Leopoldovna
Liebman, a Jew and Court Jeweler to Tsarina Anna I
Count Moritz Karl von Lynar, Saxon envoy and lover of the Regent
Anna Leopoldovna

Julie von Mengden, Baltic baroness, Ostermann's niece; Imperial nurse to Ivan VI and lover of the Regent Anna Leopoldovna

Count Alessandro Melissimo, an Austrian diplomat and fiancé of Katja Dolgoruky

T'o-Shih, head of Chinese mission

AT KOLOMENSKOYE

Illinchaya, the childhood nurse of Anoushka and Lizenka

AT THE PECHARSKY MONASTERY

Abbess Agatha, a friend of Catherine I

Alexis Razum/Razumovsky, a Ukrainian shepherd and soloist with the Imperial Choir of Anna I; Elizabeth's lover

THE
TSARINA'S
DAUGHTER

PROLOGUE

IN THE WINTER PALACE, ST. NICHOLAS'S DAY
DECEMBER 6, 1741

Ivan is innocent—my little cousin is a baby, and as pure as only a one-year-old can be. But tonight, at my order, the infant Tsar will be declared guilty as charged.

I fight the urge to pick him up and kiss him; it would only make things worse. Beyond his nursery door there is a low buzzing sound, like that of angry bees ready to swarm the Winter Palace. Soldiers' boots scrape and shuffle. Spurs clink like stubby vodka glasses, and bayonets are being fixed to muskets. These are the sounds of things to come. The thought spikes my heart with dread.

There is no other choice. It is Ivan or me. Only one of us can rule Russia; the other one is condemned to a living death. Reigning Russia is a right that has to be earned as much as inherited: he and my cousin, the Regent, doom the country to an eternity under the foreign yoke. Under their rule the realm will be lost, the invisible holy bond between Tsar and people irretrievably severed.

I, Elizabeth, am the only surviving child of Peter the Great's fifteen sons and daughters. Tonight, if I hesitate too long, I might become the last of the siblings to die.

Curse the Romanovs! In vain I try to bar from my thoughts the prophecy that has blighted my life. Puddles form on the parquet floor as slush drips from my boots; their worn thigh-high leather is soaked from my dash across St. Petersburg. Despite my being an Imperial Princess—the Tsarevna Elizabeth Petrovna Romanova—no footman had hooked a bearskin across my lap to protect me against the icy wind and driving snow while I sat snug in a sled; I had no muff to raise to my face in that special graceful gesture of the St. Petersburg ladies, the *damy*. My dash toward my date with destiny had been clandestine: snowfall veiled the flickering lights of the lanterns and shrouded the city. Mortal fear drove me on, hurrying over bridges, dodging patrolled barriers—the *shlagbaumy*—and furtively crossing the empty prospects, where my hasty passage left a momentary trace of warmth in the frosty air.

This was a night of momentous decision-making that I would have to live with forever. An anointed and crowned Tsar may not be killed, even once he is deposed, as it sets a dangerous precedent. Yet he may not live either—at least not in the minds of the Russian people or according to the diplomatic dispatches sent all over Europe.

What then is to become of the boy?

I feel for Ivan's limp little hand. I simply cannot resist—never could—nuzzling his chubby, rosy fingers, which are still too small to bear the Imperial seal. We call this game a butterfly's kiss; it makes him giggle and squeal, and me dissolve with tenderness. I drink in his scent, the talcum powder blended in Grasse for his sole use—vanilla and bergamot, the Tsar's perfume—carefully recording it to last me a lifetime. The men outside fall quiet. They are waiting for the decision that will both save and damn me. The thought sears my soul.

In Ivan's nursery the lined French damask drapes are drawn. Thick, pot-bellied clouds hide the December new moon and stars, giving this hour a dense and dreadful darkness. During the day the seagulls' cries freeze on their beaks; the chill of night grates skin raw. Any light is as scarce and dear as everything else in St. Petersburg. The candle-sellers' shops, which smell of beeswax, flax, and sulfur, do brisk business with both Yuletide and Epiphany approaching. On the opposite quay the shutters on the flat façades of the city's palaces and houses are closed, the windows behind them dark. They are swathed in the same brooding silence as the Winter Palace. I am in my father's house, but this does not mean that I am safe. Far from it—it means quite the opposite. The Winter Palace's myriad corridors, hundreds of rooms, and dozens of staircases can be as welcoming as a lover's embrace or as dangerous as a snake pit.

It is Ivan or me: fate has mercilessly driven us toward this moment. The courtiers shun me: no one would bet a kopeck on my future. Will I be sent to a remote convent, even though I do not have an ounce of nun's flesh about me, as the Spanish envoy, the Duke of Liria, so memorably recorded? I had once been forced to see such an unfortunate woman in her cell; as intended, the sight instilled a terror that would last me a lifetime. Her shorn head was covered in chilblains, and her eyes shone with madness. A hunchbacked dwarf, whose tongue had been torn out, was her sole companion, both shuffling about in rotten straw like pigs in their sties. Or perhaps there is a sled waiting for me, destination Siberia? I know about this voyage of no return; I have heard the cries, seen the dread, and smelled the fear of the banished culprits, be they simple peasants or even the Tsar's best friend. By the first anniversary of their sentence, all had succumbed to the harsh conditions of the East. Maybe a dark cell in the Trubetzkoi Bastion, the place nobody ever leaves in one piece, will swallow me; or things will be simpler, and I am fated to end up facedown in the Neva, drifting between the thick floes of ice, my body crushed and shredded by their sheer force.

The soldiers' impatience is palpable. Just one more breath! Ivan's wet nurse is asleep, slumped on her stool, resting amid his toys: the scattered pieces of a *Matryoshka* doll, wooden boats, a mechanical silver bear that opens its jaws and raises its paws when wound up, and a globe inlaid with Indian ivory and Belgian *émail*. One of the nurse's pale breasts is still bare from the last feeding; she was chosen for her ample alabaster bosom in Moscow's raucous German Quarter. Ivan is well cared for: Romanov men are of weaker stock than Romanov women, even if no one ever dares to say so. I celebrated his first year as a time of wonder, offering my little cousin a cross studded with rubies and emeralds for his christening, a gift fit for a Tsar, and put myself in debt to raise an ebony colt in my stables as his Yuletide present.

Ivan's breathing is growing heavier. The regiment outside his door weighs on his dreams. As I touch his sides, his warmth sends a jolt through my fingers, hitting a Gold in my heart. Oh, to hold him one more time and feel his delightful weight in my arms. I pull my hands back, folding them, though the time for prayers has passed. No pilgrimage can ever absolve me from this sin, even if I slide across the whole of Russia on my knees. Ivan's lashes flutter, his chin wobbles, he smacks his pink and shiny lips. I cannot bear to see him cry, despite the saying of Russian serfs: "Another man's tears are only water."

The lightest load will be your greatest burden. The last prophecy is coming to pass. Spare me, I inwardly plead—but I know this is my path, and I will have to walk it to the end, over the pieces of my broken heart. Ivan slides back into slumber; long, dark lashes cast shadows on his round cheeks, and his tiny fists open, showing pink, unlined palms. The sight stabs me. Not even the most adept fortune-teller could imagine what the future has in store for Ivan. It is a thought that I refrain from following to its conclusion.

Beyond the door utter silence reigns. Is this the calm before the storm my father taught me to fear when we sailed the slate-colored waters of the Bay of Finland? His fleet had been rolling at anchor in the far distance, masts rising like a marine forest. "This is forever Russia," he had proudly announced. "No Romanov must ever surrender what has been gained by spilling Russian blood." In order to strengthen Russia, Father had spared no one. My elder half-brother Alexey, his son and heir, had paid the ultimate price for doubting Russia's path to progress.

Steps approach. My time with Ivan, and life as we know it, is over. I wish this were not necessary. The knock on the nursery door is a token rasp of knuckles; so light, it belies its true purpose. It is time to act. Russia will tolerate no further excuses. The soldiers' nerves are as taut as the spring in a bear trap. I have promised them the world: on a night like this, destinies are forged, fortunes made and lost.

"Elizabeth Petrovna Romanova?" I hear the captain of the Imperial Preobrazhensky Regiment addressing me. His son is my godchild, but can I trust him completely for all that? I feel as if I am drowning and shield Ivan's cradle with my body. In the gilt-framed mirrors I see my face floating ghostly pale above the dark green uniform jacket; my ash-blond curly hair has slid down from beneath a fur cap. On a simple leather thong around my neck hangs the diamond-studded icon of St. Nicholas that is priceless to me. They will have to prise it from my dead body to take it from me.

I am almost thirty-two years old. Tonight I shall not betray my blood.

"I am ready," I say, my voice trembling, bracing myself, as the door bursts open and the soldiers swarm in.

Everything comes at a price.

1

EIGHTEEN YEARS EARLIER—SPRING 1723

We had gone to Mother's palace in Kolomenskoye, as always when we needed safety, solace, and strength. Ever since my elder half-brother, the Tsarevich Alexey, died, Mother had struggled to give Father, Tsar Peter the Great of All the Russias, an heir to the world's largest and wealthiest realm. A couple of weeks prior to our departure, she had been delivered of yet another still-born son.

It was a relief to leave St. Petersburg shortly after Easter: I had hardly known my half-brother, as Alexey had been eighteen years older than I. Mother's recent misfortune weighed on me more heavily. Still, we had celebrated Easter, the most joyous and sacred of Russian holidays, as usual by handing out brightly painted eggs to all the courtiers and wishing them well: Christ had risen. While our own plates remained as good as untouched, we watched them feast on *kulich*—a sweet, yeasty, dome-shaped bread—and *pashka*—a custard made of cheese curd, almonds, and dried fruit.

When I stepped out of the Winter Palace shortly after dawn, I felt like drinking in the cool spring air, to chase away any memory of the long, stuffy, dark months of winter and the atmosphere of dread and sorrow that still lingered inside. Morning slid into the dawn light as smooth as a dove's wing, offering us a first glimpse of the sunrises of summer: a hazy blend of mauve, mustard, and mother-of-pearl. The *ottepel*, or great thaw, had begun, and already winter's stark handover from day to night was beginning to fade, the harsh contrasts softening. No change in Russia comes about easily, not even the shift in the seasons. The *ottepel*'s strength shocked us anew, year after year, as it made rivers swell and tore open the earth. Our jaded spirits lifted as snow and ice receded, the light lingering longer day upon day for the span of a cockerel's crow. Sunshine warmed the frozen earth and thawed the frost and rime from our veins, stirring the blood, quickening the heartbeat. The spring winds scattered seeds over the land, bringing with them the promise of fertility; they blew the cobwebs from our minds, rousing Russia from its drowsy stupor.

My sister Anoushka was older than I by a year, and we knew Mother's palace of Kolomenskoye well. We had spent the first years of our lives there, before our parents were married, and before each of us was proclaimed Tsarevna, Imperial Princess. Mother, the Tsaritsa, had always accompanied Father wherever he went, be it in the field of the Great Northern War against Sweden—a struggle for Russia's survival that had weighed on our country for almost two decades—or on his travels to the West and all over Europe.

Despite being the Tsar's daughters, at Kolomenskoye we roamed as freely as peasant children. Our nurse Illinchaya let us run barefoot in the red dust beneath the poplar trees, wearing loose plain dresses, and fed us soups and stews, staples of a Russian peasant kitchen. Under her watchful eye, we visited the dovecotes of the Tsar's falconer and reared kittens in spring, picked berries in the forest or swam in clear lakes in summer. In autumn we foraged for mushrooms or played hide-and-seek in gigantic heaps of rustling leaves. In winter we went ice-skating and tobogganing or built igloos and once even a portly snow woman, which looked suspiciously like Illinchaya herself. She had laughed so much at the sight; she coughed and wheezed. In the evening she climbed into bed with us—"Come here, my little doves, and tuck your beaks beneath my wings!"—and told us old Russian fairy tales, all set in Kolomenskoye, which we were told teemed with evil spirits, beautiful maidens who were abducted, and strong young men who saved them. "This is old earth. I have seen these things happen myself," Illinchaya declared and crossed herself with three fingers, signifying the Holy Trinity of the Russian Orthodox Church.

"I did not get to say goodbye to Father," I said as Anoushka and I walked to the carriage. She shook her head at me in a silent warning, her gaze searching the windows of the Tsar's apartment in the upper reaches of the Winter Palace. The curtains were still drawn; Father slept on after emptying at least two or three bottles of vodka on his own the evening before. A chamberlain's bare belly would serve as his pillow. Only the warmth of flesh on flesh kept his demons at bay: he'd feared sleep ever since Alexey's death.

"Nobody has seen Father since Mother was brought to bed last, Lizenka," Anoushka reminded me, calling me by my pet name. "He had hoped so much for a son. Russia needs an heir. The Old Believers blight his life."

The Old Believers hated the Tsar for his reforms and the change he had brought to Russian life: Father had twisted the country about like a doll's head, making his people turn from the East to the West. The Tsarevich himself had been the leader of the Old Believers. When my half-brother had been accused of high treason and sentenced to death, the unthinkable had happened. Driven mad by disappointment and fear for the future of his realm, Father had executed his only son and heir with his own hands. Ever since, all mention of Alexey was forbidden.

"I need him," I said, my voice small. Could I not simply sneak up into Father's rooms and take my leave? No.

"Russia needs him more. Careful, Lizenka. Think of how he treats little Petrushka."

Petrushka was Alexey's young son. Father had removed the boy—his only grandson—from his and our lives, tearing our nephew from the family as he would twist a tick from behind his mongrel dog's ear. Petrushka should not be a pawn in the Old Believers' hands. Any chance of him, a traitor's son, ever ruling, had to be eradicated. No wonder that nightmares plagued Father: the wardens in the Trubetzkoi Bastion, where Alexey had died, swore that the Tsarevich's soul had fled his body in the shape of a crow. After that the Tsar had called open season on the hapless birds all over his Empire. Farmers caught, killed, plucked, and roasted them for reward. None of this helped: silently, at night, the bird would slip into Father's bedchamber. In the cool shadow of its ebony wings, the blood on the Tsar's hands never dried. It could be horrid to witness Father in the grip of this delusion: he roused the Winter Palace with his screams. Only Mother could soothe him then.

"Let us hope he will be better when we see him in June, to celebrate his name day," I said. I was still not quite able to link the terrifying authority of the Tsar, who was tortured by his deeds, to the warm and embracing father on whose knees I loved to climb so that his dark, bristly mustache tickled me—"Come here and pull my whiskers, Lizenka!" He had taught me how to lathe a timber plank—"If my hands are busy I have the best ideas!"—and to tack a boat, the power of the wind delighting him: "Keep your head down and hold the rudder tight!"

"Come time, he will accept God's will, as always. Now do not dawdle. Get in." Anoushka pushed me inside the carriage, a gaily painted little house on wheels. Mattresses layered with thick polar bear skins and embroidered velvet cushions had been spread copiously for our comfort, but I loathed the journey: several *arshin* of ice and snow melting in the thaw had turned the roads to bog. Kolomenskoye lay a good six hundred *versty* away from St. Petersburg, which would take us only three or four days in the freeze while sitting in big, comfortable sleds, instead of the two weeks it would do now. The rivers were swollen and the barges leaky, while the roads were pockmarked with treacherous potholes and deep, muddy ruts. Inside the carriage we bumped into each other like hams dangling in the flue of a smokehouse. Normally these mishaps would make us laugh aloud, shoving each other even harder, breathless with mirth after taking tumbles. Now, though, we sat up again, resuming our former places, sighing but otherwise silent. Father had sent his favorite Portuguese dwarf, d'Acosta, along to amuse us. But after an ill-judged jest in which the imp had shoved a cushion underneath his shirt, moaning and arching his back like a woman suffering from birth pangs, Mother's lady-in-waiting had slapped and gagged him. Now d'Acosta cowered in a corner, bound like a chicken for market, cheeks bulging and eyes watering. By the third day the gag was no longer necessary: he sat as silent and sullen as any of us—Mother, her lady-in-waiting, Anoushka, and me.

As any dacha along the road still lay deserted, we slept in inns. D'Acosta relished using his whip to chase grown men off the top of the gigantic flat oven—whose steady heat warmed the room, roasted the pork and poultry, dried the clothes, and served the innkeeper's family for a bed at night—clearing space for our party. We rarely had our own rooms but stretched out on the rough benches or on bedding rolled over the soiled straw.

"Why can't we sleep beneath the stars and cook on an open fire? That is what spring means to me," I whispered to Anoushka one night, curling up close, my body pressed tightly against hers.

"You will have to wait for Kolomenskoye for that," was the answer. "Mother needs to rest and try to forget her cares. Once she is more settled, you can do whatever you want."

"I wish!" I giggled, then lay in silence, hoping to feel less sick in a while after yet another supper of kasha—a salted millet porridge greasy with bacon—or some fermented cabbage, the sauerkraut that innkeepers invariably offered us. At the end of winter, the storerooms and larders were emptying fast, and people scraped the barrel literally. For me this was yet another reason to look forward to the bounty of spring. It provided Russians with delicacies such as fish, pork, poultry, caviar, mushrooms, berries, and honey, while new crops of rye, wheat, barley, and millet allowed for our variety of breads, little pastries, *pierogi, pelmeni,* and pancakes such as *blintshiki.* At least we moved on quickly: in an inn we could easily change horses. D'Acosta took his pick from the stables, never paying.

What belonged to any Russian, first and foremost belonged to the Tsar.

"After everything that has happened, this will be good for us," I said, as the six strong horses harnessed in single file before our carriage crossed the orchards and the vast park surrounding Kolomenskoye. An endless number of carts followed. They were laden with stout chests secured with chains and locks, holding all our belongings: furniture, rugs, china, crystal, bedding, and chandeliers. The Tsar's palaces stood empty during his absence, as the risk of fire ravishing them, or else thieves burgling them while the guards lay in a drunken stupor, was too great to leave them fully furnished. Next to our wagon train roamed livestock—cows, goats, chickens, and sheep—to supplement the provisions in Kolomenskoye's kitchen. Red dust billowed underfoot, suffusing the last pale rays of the setting sun. Our throats were parched as the dust passed easily through the mica panes of the ancient carriage's doors, settling in our pores, eyes, mouths. I hoped Illinchaya, who now acted as a housekeeper for the palace, still had some of last year's elderflower cordial left to blend with fresh cool water from the estate's spring. It was so deliciously refreshing I would have liked to bathe in it.

"Why are you saying this?" Mother looked worn, I noticed, from her recent blood loss, exhaustion from the journey, and more. Her slanted green eyes lacked fire; her full lips seemed bloodless. Her maid had struggled to coif her dark tresses, which hung limp and dull.

I sat up defiantly. "We have to heal and not silence our sorrows. Feofan Prokopovich told me that grief swallows the soul. And isn't he the Archbishop of Novgorod and the wisest priest in Russia, who always gives Father the best counsel?"

"Lizenka is right," Anoushka chimed in. "We must not fear. We know how much Father loves us all, despite what he did to—"

Mother pressed a warning finger to her lips, reminding us that

Father had forbidden us to speak Alexey's name ever again. "Silence protects, too," she said. "Least said, soonest mended." Then, though, her eyes lit up. "Feofan Prokopovich has told me something, too."

"What did he say?" I asked.

"Come the day of reckoning, I shall have given the Tsar an heir for Russia." She crossed her arms defiantly, her fingers brushing the deep scars on her lower inner arms. When I had first seen these gashes some weeks ago, after Feofan Prokopovich had hastily blessed and buried my stillborn brother's small corpse—much too small to go into the earth like that, alone—the wounds' frightening precision had terrified me. "Why could God not leave me this son?" Mother had wailed, lying in her bed. "Why did he not take another . . . Anoushka, or you, Lizenka? You are only girls." Her lady-in-waiting had ushered me out, whispering: "It is unbearable. The Tsaritsa has lost so much blood that the doctor has forbidden her any further pregnancies. There will be no son. Pray for Her Majesty, Tsarevna Elizabeth."

"As you say, Feofan is the wisest man in Russia. So, all hope is not lost for me," said Mother, pushing Anoushka and me into an answer that would ease this greatest of her worries.

"Of course not. You will give Father an heir. We will not stop believing this, whatever happens," Anoushka said.

"You know what Father says: never give up!" I added.

"My girls. I love your spirit," Mother said, a hint of pride in her brittle voice.

"Guess where we get it from," I said, and gently took hold of her hands so that they no longer cradled her empty womb.

The carriage rattled on toward the palace: finally we had arrived! The poplar trees growing all around Kolomenskoye were in blossom. Wind-borne seeds—*pukh*—billowed in clouds like snow in spring and hazed the air. They settled like a halo over Mother and Anoushka's dark tresses as I poked my head out of the window and quickly ducked back: the horses kicked up mud and loose stones that could take out an unwary traveler's eye.

"I can see Kolomenskoye," I shouted, delighted. "God, it's been so long. Look! Just look!"

Anoushka and I scuffled for the best view: Moscow was a jumble of brightly painted wooden houses of every size crammed around its thousand churches and their spires. The city coiled around its dark and brooding heart, the Kremlin. Somewhere a church bell was always giving tongue in Russia's former capital, calling for hours of devotion in a long service or else honoring a saint, rendering conversation impossible. The city had grown as rampant as a weed over the centuries, the stronghold of Rus, the territory from which our great country grew. By contrast, in St. Petersburg—Father's shiny new "paradise"—every street and canal had been carefully planned, copying the best features of cities he had seen and admired on his travels in the West. The Italian envoy called it "a kind of bastard architecture, which steals from the Italian, the French, and the Dutch." Palaces, mansions, and houses with elegant flat façades were strung like pearls along the Neva's embankments and the dozen man-made waterways. Crossing the city's streets on a stormy day was like a steeplechase: the wind dislodged any loose tiles, sending them crashing down, narrowly missing people, or not, as they ran for their lives, tripping and falling on the uneven, sloppily laid cobblestones.

Kolomenskoye, however, arose as if from an ancient dream: my grandfather Tsar Alexis, the second Tsar of All the Russias in the Romanov line, had built this palatial hunting lodge above the River Moskva. It sat on a ridge like the colorful crest of an undulating wave of green parkland, forests, brooks, and ravines. The ground floor, with its stables, storerooms, and pantries, was built from timber and now-crumbling wattle and daub—a mix of bleached clay, sand, and dung. Behind its tiny windows—mere unglazed gaps—the servants would huddle together with the livestock, bodies and breath mingling. Bundles of boiled moss still filled cracks in the rendering here and there, but the flaking patches of tar would not keep out the cockroaches this summer. Also the walls urgently needed new whitewash to prevent wasps building their nests on them. On the first floor, where we would live, light and a steady stream of drafts flooded the palace from its countless big, ill-fitting windows with proper glass panes, the timber surrounds brightly painted. Yet Kolomenskoye's roof was the house's crowning, messy glory, despite its myriad missing slates. It was inspired by the different shapes and styles of roofs throughout All the Russias: be it rising like a staircase, bulging out like onion-shaped Byzantine cupolas, lying hipped and deep-drawn like a Polish cap, or, in a finishing touch, piercing the late-afternoon sky with sharp spires as pointy as needles.

Even Mother pressed herself up to the window: "I love this place especially," she said. "It was my first proper home. When your father gave it to me, I was not yet even his wife. He wanted to reward me for your safe arrival, Anoushka. And just a year later, you were born here, Lizenka, on the day of the big parade after Poltava—"

"—when Father and Russia celebrated his victory over the Swedish devils, under the December stars, with my feet coming first, and Illinchaya, who brought you chicken broth to help you recover your strength, paled with fear at this sign, while Father threatened to flog and flay her, but you pleaded for her life, saying she should not be punished for helping you survive such a difficult birth," I rattled off. I had heard the story so often that I knew it by heart.

For the first time in what felt like an eternity, we all laughed together—even the dwarf d'Acosta forgot all the callous jesting, slapping, and gagging—just as the carriage pulled up in Kolomenskoye's graveled courtyard.

2

Clouds of flies descended upon the ponies' sweaty bodies and steaming heads, settling in black, shiny clusters around their eyes and nostrils. Stable boys swatted them away before lifting off the animals' heavy tack and leading them away to be rubbed dry, fed, and watered. The coachman wiped his face and eyes clean before climbing off his box; with a sigh, he curled up his stiff body beneath the carriage door, and we followed Mother in treading on his back. Once on firm ground, Mother's lady-in-waiting steadied her by her elbow, while Anoushka and I stretched our arms and stamped our feet. Servants hurried toward us from the house, and supplicants already hung around the high porticoed entrance, chanting their vows of submission and reaching out to press upon Mother scrolls containing petitions, which they had paid someone good money to write for them.

It was customary for the Tsar and his family to hold public audience upon their arrival in any of the palaces they owned throughout the realm: here they sat in judgment over neighborhood issues, such as boundary disputes or alleged theft of livestock, listened to suspicions about the involvement of sorcery in the cases of fire or famine, granted or refused demands for bigger estates, together with the serfs—unfree peasants—attached to them. We heard the people crying out for Mother to heed them: "Tsaritsa!" "Little Mother, listen to me!" "No, not him! He's a scoundrel. Me first! My eternal devotion—"

"Take the scrolls," Mother ordered her lady-in-waiting. "I shall decide upon them later, once you have read them to me. Believe me, I know how they feel." Despite Mother's rise from illegitimate Baltic serf girl to Russian Tsaritsa, she was still illiterate. Father and she had met in his military camp when she was a Russian prisoner of war. We loved to pester her with questions about that moment—*What did you wear when you met Father? What were his first words to you? When did you know that he loved you?*—though her answers remained evasive. The lady-in-waiting collected the petitions from pleadingly outstretched, unwashed hands, gathering them in her bunched-up skirt. Before d'Acosta followed her in, he imitated the supplicants, bowing and cowering, then showing them his tongue and cartwheeling inside the house.

Anoushka and I lingered while our carriage and the carts were unpacked. The servants moved about like an army of ants—the maids with their arms laden with covered baskets and the men loading the chests onto their backs, muscles straining underneath the threadbare linen of their shirts. The afternoon sun warmed my face, and my body steadied itself after the lurching carriage ride. Now that Mother was safely inside the house, I felt myself bubbling over with joy and anticipation, as if a lid had been lifted from a pot of boiling broth.

"Where is Illinchaya?" Anoushka looked out for our childhood nurse. "Do you think she will already have heated the bathwater?" She tugged on her Persian shawl of soft, embroidered cashmere that was looped around her narrow shoulders and over her flat chest. Illinchaya had on Father's orders always treated us children to a weekly bath: the copper tub had been filled with steaming water scented with rose oil, and we battered each other mercilessly with sponges, splashing and screaming, playing Russian and Swede meeting on the battlefield of Poltava. As Illinchaya was nowhere to be seen as yet, Anoushka turned to check on her case of books: spring brought a bevy of merchant ships to St. Petersburg, laden stem to stern with exciting wares such as china, fabric, and, yes, novels.

I answered: "Of course she has. And I hope she has made her special stew—cauldrons of it! Kolomenskoye bacon is better than anywhere else, and Illinchaya is not as stingy with it as Father's cook. She cuts it nice and thick. Will you come with me to the stables first? A cat is bound to have had a litter. Perhaps there is a kitten I can take to bed with me."

"I will have no smelly little thing in my bed. And you'd better stop this nonsense," Anoushka warned me, but laughed all the same. "Very soon you will have to tend to someone other than a kitten in your bed. Do you think the King of France will enjoy sharing his silken sheets with a hissing, scratching ball of fur?"

The King of France. I rolled these words in my mind like marbles, feeling myself blushing, which enhanced my already high color. Father had offered Versailles my hand in marriage when I was a child. It seemed a perfect match—young King Louis XV and I were of similar age—but France would give no firm answer, letting us wait and hope. This silence worried me less than what the jester d'Acosta had told me: the dwarf swore that Louis wore more paint than any lady at my parents' court, as well as acres of lace in his jabot. I checked my unlaced, dusty cotton dress, which was crumpled from the journey and fell loose and comfortable to my feet, but clung flatteringly in all the right places thanks to my ample cleavage. Surely it would not withstand the scrutiny of the young King of France and his Versailles courtiers, who were said to change their clothes five times a day. Why not swap tailors if they were so unhappy? At least the cornflower-blue dress flattered my eyes and my blonde curls, which were braided and wrapped around my head for travel. My maid kept my hair shiny and luscious by a regular treatment with egg yolk, camomile, and beer. That was not my only beauty remedy: a blend of *kefir* from the steppes and preserved lemons, which Mother ordered from Italy, ensured that our skin was soft and clear. Perhaps Louis would not need quite so much face paint if he tried it, too?

"Better a small and smelly kitten than a big, hairy man. I would

be scared to death to be in bed with him if he were like that," I giggled nervously. "What might he wear?"

"A nightshirt?" Anoushka guessed.

"What? Like mine? Silken and lacy?"

"Well, it might be a *different* nightshirt. Men are *different,* aren't
they?"

I hesitated. "They ought to be. But different in what way?"

"I don't know," Anoushka admitted.

"Well, I shall stick to kittens until Father has a firm answer from
Versailles." I shrugged, pretending not to care. In truth the years of
silence that had passed since my portrait had been sent to France
were insulting, although the painter Caravaque, who also took
Anoushka's likeness, had been beside himself with compliments:
"*Mon Dieu.* Your eyes are as lively as a bird's!" "That skin, that bust,
that golden hair—just marvelous! *Merveilleux!*" We had copied him
while skipping through the corridors, chanting *MonDieuMerveil-
leux.* Even the French envoy to Russia, de Campredon, was in favor
of the match: in his letters, which the Secret Office of Investigation
read and resealed, he described me as "Christianity's most lovely
princess," possessing "the warmth that made the Tsar marry her
mother"—which was to me a rather puzzling comment.

Anoushka's smile lit up her normally serious face: "No news is
good news. In the end, the beautiful princess always gets her knight
in shining armor."

I was grateful for her uplifting words. What should I do without her once I left for France? "In your books, yes. But does it happen for real?"

"You surely don't doubt it. Things tend to go your way, Lizenka.
Almost magically so. You know that. I can read your thoughts."

"Ah. So what is it I am thinking right now then?"

"You are wondering if Grisha the blacksmith's big bellows are
still in the stables. The ones we used as a seesaw?"

I held up my hands. "You have won. But I can't play on them
on my own."

"Are you trying to corrupt my immortal soul?"

"Yes, sinful as I am," I giggled, and snapped my fingers at her maids. "Take the Tsarevna Anoushka's books to our rooms. The latest love story from Italy must wait. First there is some urgent bouncing on bellows to be done."

"It will destroy my hairdo," Anoushka moaned.

I lunged to ruffle up her dark straight hair, which had been braided and rolled in coils at the sides of her head. "There. No need to worry now. All done." I kissed her cheek and pulled her along.

We crossed the vast vegetable garden that lay between the kitchen and the stables. Onions, leeks, turnips, beetroots, and cabbages grew among a lavish carpet of weeds that spoke of seasons of casual neglect: everywhere clover and daisies blossomed already, and the bees were busily taking advantage of each minute of the longer days, gathering pollen for the delicious Kolomenskoye honey I loved to spoon in thick dollops on my kasha. I breathed in deeply, enjoying the fresh air. Come spring in St. Petersburg, the Neva flooded its banks, and all the blossoms of the scented plants that Father had ordered far and wide, from France to Persia, could not blot out the musty smell that reigned once the water receded. It blended with the whiff of rotten market leftovers and clotted blood on the gallows, which, as a warning to the Russian people, were habitually situated on all the busiest squares and crossroads.

"What is this?" I asked, stopping at a big stone just outside the kitchen door. At the back entrance to the palace, the cook welcomed deliveries during the day, while at night thieves among the household servants sold off their loot.

"That is where the kitchen maids whet their knives. Look, the stone is all chipped and pockmarked," Anoushka told me.

"I know that," I said impatiently. "But why is there a plate with a pancake and sour milk set on top of it?"

"Already hungry again? Hold yourself back," Anoushka teased me and pinched my plump waist. The thick pancake was dripping with honey; just add a sprinkle of nuts, and it would be perfect for me after the long hours on the road!

"You should have some, beanpole!" I countered, and we started to tussle together, giggling.

"Yes, girls, hold yourselves back! This is an offering." Mother appeared on the kitchen threshold; her pale cheeks were already flushed with faint color now that the endless lurching was over. She lacked all airs and graces, moving about as casually as if she were still a serf living in a tiny Baltic *izba*, owning nothing but the clothes on her body. "Don't you know that the Domovoi rules the woods of Kolomenskoye?"

"The Domovoi?" I asked, still eyeing the pancake, and remembered one of Illinchaya's fairy stories. "The spirit of the woods?"

"Yes. His heart breaks with every tree that is felled. Imagine the forest that had to give way for Tsar Alexis to build Kolomenskoye here. Illinchaya wants the Domovoi appeased," Mother said. She was smiling at the housekeeper's belief in old myths and fairy tales. Seeing her like this, my mood soared: Mother would surely be able to heal here, and she might even have another son, despite the doctor's gloomy verdict.

"Indeed! I appease all spirits!" Illinchaya appeared behind Mother. "Kolomenskoye is old earth and alive with them." My heart leaped when I saw her. Despite the years that had passed since our last meeting, in which Anoushka and I had turned from little girls to young women, our childhood nurse seemed unchanged. Her cheeks were red-veined, and her broad face flushed; she seemed out of breath from climbing just two or three shallow steps. Her clothing brazenly defied Father's laws. He had ordered all Russians to dress in the style of the West, even though such clothes were tight and uncomfortable, and their thin, cheap cloth not woven to withstand our weather. Illinchaya wore a long-sleeved linen blouse and a traditional apron dress, the wide, warmly quilted *sarafan*, which she had adorned with intricate floral embroidery. The patterns were like a secret language in Russia. The women of each family had their own, filling long winter evenings with perfecting that beautiful craft, while sitting around the warm oven chatting.

"Old earth alive with spirits?" Anoushka said, her face flushed. "Oh, I remember your fairy tales about the witch Baba Yaga, whose house is built from chicken bones! It rests on three pillars and spins with the sun. Then there are the Leshy, mischievous rascals, who lead people astray with their prophecies."

"These are not fairy tales." Illinchaya frowned.

"Old earth? What rubbish," laughed d'Acosta, suddenly appearing from behind Mother, as always sliding in and out of places in the blink of an eye. "Silly superstitions, invented to torment the peasants so as to squeeze the last kopeck from them." He raised his caterpillar eyebrows at Illinchaya and made the coins rattle in his pockets, like a bear-baiter taking wagers at a spring fair.

"Silence, imp," Illinchaya scolded. "I must properly greet the Tsarevny!" She curtsied deeply to us, kissing our fingers, and pressing the back of our hands to her forehead while murmuring blessings; the ruffled cap covering her white-blonde hair brushed my wrist. She rose, smiling broadly, showing her dozen or so remaining teeth. "Anoushka Petrovna and Elizabeth Petrovna: welcome back to Kolomenskoye. It is for the saddest reason that you come—may God have mercy on another of your brothers' little soul—but the house, and all of us, greet you with love and loyalty."

Anoushka and I swapped a quick glance—normally, no one dared spell out Mother's misfortune in having buried five sons altogether, some straight after birth, others living just a couple of years. Yet Illinchaya's years of service and utter lack of malice excused a lot, and so we rushed forward to embrace her.

She clapped her calloused hands and spread her strong arms, exclaiming: "Finally! The day you moved away from Kolomenskoye to be grown up and important, you took my soul with you. Oh, I might burst with joy!" Then she clamped us in an embrace like a vice, and we had to struggle free, giggling, as we had done as little girls when her affection had grown too much for us to bear. Illinchaya dabbed at her narrow light-blue eyes, which spouted tears. Like many Russians of Finnish descent, she was almost uncannily pale and fair. "How tall and beautiful you are. If my eyes do not recognize you any longer, my heart always will. Soon, I pray, I will cook a feast for your weddings."

"Oh, I wish that could be so," Anoushka said, shyly eyeing Mother, who smiled enigmatically and answered: "Who knows what the future holds for my lucky girls."

At that I could not stop my eyes from welling up with tears. Mother turned to me, surprised: "What is it, Lizenka?"

Anoushka put her arm around my shoulders, full of silent understanding.

"I am just so glad that we are all together. All will be well again. I know it," I cried, before we began to sob and embrace: Anoushka and me, Tsarevny of All the Russias; our mother the Tsaritsa; and Illinchaya the cook, holding each other close, while d'Acosta sank onto the stone next to the pancake, lamenting out loud in the fashion of his Mediterranean people, bleating away, all snot and tears, his funny little face scrunched up.

Already the magic of Kolomenskoye's old earth wove a bond of ease and simplicity between us, a thousand threads to its loom, sanctified by our shared sorrow and suffering. Our tears were as much an offering to peace and friendship as the pancakes on the whetting stone had been. Mother was right: we were lucky to be back here. For how often in life do pancakes, honey, and sour milk suffice to appease an evil spirit?

3

W e settled for the spring in Kolomenskoye. Even if half of the corridors had been hastily blocked off upon our arrival, as the beams beneath them would not carry our weight, the palace had not changed. It was so large that we all lost ourselves in its more than two hundred fifty, not needing to see another soul for days on end. Illinchaya swore that the woodworms were by now so big and mighty that she heard them chewing at night: "Stop telling whoppers, Illinchaya. We are not children anymore," I scolded her.

Room by room, we regained possession, filling our grandfather's hunting lodge with our youthfulness and joy. We slid down the big staircase, sitting or lying on mattresses, pretending they were toboggans, and loved how the steps made our teeth chatter. We chased our spinning tops down the corridors, placing bets on their speed. Anoushka dusted off her doll's house: a master cabinetmaker from Nuremberg had copied the Summer Palace's sunburst splendor in every detail, down to its paneled walls shaded in the Neva's icy green and the honey-colored, patterned parquet flooring. She would move about her families of dolls, their porcelain faces blank and their lower limbs rigid. The dolls' beautiful dresses, once fashioned according to the latest European tailoring, were long gone—mice had probably bolstered their nests with them—so Anoushka pinned sun-bleached scraps of fabric that Illinchaya gave her into their soft bodies. I watched her, fascinated:

she applied the same thought and care I would to my tack and saddle, seeing them properly soaped and waxed for the next day's ride.

One last room we had not so far revisited was the Great Hall, my grandfather's Throne Room. As we slipped into its vast space, one leaf of the high double doors creaking on its hinges, I halted on the threshold, staring in awe. The midday light filtered moodily through the stained-glass panes; every inch of the intricate wood paneling on the walls and ceilings had once been gaily painted, but the colors had faded. It felt as if I had shrunk and stepped into a former favorite toy, the kaleidoscope that Father's envoy to Persia, Prince Avram Volynsky, had once given me.

"Look, Anoushka. It is still here," I said in a hushed voice, pointing to the only piece of furniture always to have remained in situ in Kolomenskoye: my grandfather's ebony throne. Its back was high, and each arm ended in a mighty carved lion's head. Like the rest of the palace, the throne had gently gathered the dust of decades since Grandfather Alexis's death and our moving away.

"Come," I told Anoushka, and we slid over the parquet, as if skidding on a frozen lake, to reach the throne. The lions' jaws were closed but their gold-leaf manes flamed, and their eyes were inlaid with rubies. The gems had promised our Grandfather a sound mind, helping him to make wise decisions. Their crimson fire gleamed at Anoushka and me. I stepped up, polishing the jewels with my sleeve, before moving a secret lever behind one head. "Waaaah!" I roared as the beasts opened their jaws in a creaky, rusty motion. Anoushka jumped, and I giggled. The mechanism had probably scared witless the peasants who came to see Grandfather.

I stepped back next to her and stood facing the throne. "Go on. Sit on it." I gave Anoushka a little shove. "You are the elder."

"I'd never dare. What if Father found out?"

"He would laugh," I said, trying to sound convinced.

"Is that so? Why don't you sit on it then?"

I checked the throne on its dais. The red velvet canopy above it was musty, flecked with spiders' webs, and it had been attacked by moths. The high ebony chairback was intricately carved, and a footstool of embossed silver lay carelessly toppled, as if our grandfather had just risen to go hunting with his falcons, a favorite pastime. Even as little girls growing up here, carefree and far removed from all pomp and protocol, we had never dared to climb onto the dais and sit on the throne. I swallowed hard.

"All right then," I said. My palms were clammy as I took a step forward. The chair seemed to grow in size and towered over us, its dark outlines a dire warning not to trespass on a Tsar's power.

"Lizenka!" Anoushka seized my elbow. "Don't. This is not for us."

"Of course not," I said and stood still. "No woman has ever ruled Russia, and no woman ever will. Do you remember what Illinchaya told us about father's evil half-sister Sophia? The one who acted as Regent for Father and mad Uncle Ivan when they were Tsars as boys, and too young and too ill to reign? Even she never dared take the throne."

"I do. I also remember that Illinchaya did not call our uncle *mad* Ivan." Anoushka grinned.

True: naughty, outspoken Illinchaya had called my father's elder half-brother, who had been stricken by a terrible illness since his birth, "Ivan the Idiot." Such lack of respect could earn our nursemaid anything from a thorough flogging to being flayed alive, depending on the mood of the judge interpreting the Tsar's laws. Oh, I could not wait to sit in her kitchen again and listen to stories from the past about our family, as we had done as children.

"Father must never hear that. Ivan and he were Tsars together, ruling Russia, whether Ivan was mad or an idiot or both—or neither," I said. After Ivan's death, Father had locked up his usurping half-sister Sofia, but he took generous and loving care of Ivan's widow Praskovia, whom we called our Aunt Pasha, and her daughters, our much older cousins Ekaterina and Anna Ivanovna. Once we had left Kolomenskoye we had even lived for a couple of years with Aunt Pasha in Izmailov Palace. Father's wish was clear, and it was our command: the family, as the country, should stand united. Russia needed a single, strong, and anointed ruler, instead of being torn apart by siblings squabbling for the throne.

I glanced at the throne once more, as if the shadows around it could eavesdrop and betray me. "But Anoushka, I wonder . . . Alexey is dead," I whispered and hastily crossed myself with three fingers, "and Aunt Pasha and Tsar Ivan had only daughters, Ekaterina, and Anna, who are married off and far away." I crossed myself again, averting the evil eye from my cousins.

"Yes?" Anoushka probed me.

"So, if Mother should bear no more sons, who then would inherit Father's throne?"

Anoushka turned to check that we were truly on our own. Any allusion to Father dying one day was high treason, and our half-brother Alexey's fate served as a dire warning to everyone—even us! No one was safe from the Tsar's wrath. "You know what Father made Feofan Prokopovich declare. A Tsar would rather leave Russia to a worthy stranger than to his own unworthy child."

"How about a worthy grandson, little Petrushka? He is—you know—whose son after all." I barely stopped short of mentioning our half-brother Alexey's name, as Father had commanded. "He's almost ten years old, the sole surviving Romanov male, and a suitable heir for both Father and Russia."

"Poor little Petrushka will never reign. Father can hardly bear to see him live and grow up. Mother had to beg for sour-faced Count Ostermann to be his tutor. Father only agreed because he hoped to keep the Old Believers at bay."

"Poor Petrushka, having that gouty German as a tutor."

"He is better than the tutors we had," Anoushka laughed. "Learning is a privilege."

"Speak for yourself. I, for my part, learned a lot."

"Like what? Surprise me! German, French, and Italian? Embroidery? Handwriting?"

"Well, no, not exactly. But I can catch and fillet a fish, shoot my crossbow like a Tatar, and ride faster than any Cossack."

"All enviable skills for the wife of a king," she laughed. "Versailles will be so impressed when you arrive on horseback, sitting astride and dressed as a man, as you always do."

"Hush! That is a secret." My mood darkened. "I wonder what it will be like. I mean, moving to Versailles . . . or anywhere at all really. I can't bear the thought of leaving Russia, nor of leaving you."

"Don't worry about me," she replied, a bit too quickly, raising her chin. "I, too, will make a glorious match." It was clear that she had thought about this many times before. Then her expression softened. "Are you afraid?"

"Afraid? I am terrified!"

"I feel the same. There is nowhere like here. Perhaps we can ask our cousins Anna and Ekaterina Ivanovna what it is like to be a married Tsarevna and live abroad?"

"If we ever see them again. They live so far away and are so much older," I said.

"Do you think they ever mind?" Anoushka asked.

"Mind what?"

"Well, that Mother, you, and I are now the first ladies in Russia, even though mad Ivan was Father's elder brother and a reigning Tsar, too."

I hesitated. "No. I think they ought to be content with their lot." Aunt Pasha's daughters had been the first Russian Tsarevny ever to be married. Prior to Father's travels to the West, a Tsar's daughters and sisters remained unmarried, living in the *terem*—the women's quarters of a Russian house—or the Kremlin. Only their brothers and fathers would ever see them, as any lower-born Russian was perceived as a subject, while a foreign prince was deemed a heathen. I had been an infant when Anna Ivanovna got married to the Duke of Courland, a small Baltic state. Yet at Ekaterina's wedding to the German Duke of Mecklenburg, Anoushka and I had been maids of honor. Father had given both his nieces astounding dowries of three hundred thousand roubles and had himself led them up the aisle. The Tsar's best friend from childhood days, Prince Alexander Danilovich Menshikov, had footed the festivities' outrageous bill, adding a chapel to his Moscow palace and transforming its Great Hall into a blooming indoor garden. Flowers and fruit had been brought in from the Crimea, and thousands of bottles of champagne had been sabered. Father had been so delighted with the success of the feast that the following day, he had married off hundreds of dwarves to each other in a ceremony mirroring Ekaterina's. Both the matches our Ivanovna cousins made had brought Russia wedding contracts that were much to Father's liking.

Anoushka chuckled. "They ought to be happy with what they have? Lizenka! No man ever is, and a woman even less so."

"Better not ask them then if they want any more," I giggled. I, too, should further Russia's fortunes. "If I can neither embroider nor write beautifully, perhaps King Louis will be happy that I dance well?" I whirled a couple of steps, pulling her along, before I stopped and held her by both hands. "I dread being separated from you, Anoushka."

It was midday. Shifting clouds outside cast shadows on her face as she said: "I feel the same. Though now I want to fetch my book and read in the kitchen before lunch. Shall I see you there? Illinchaya is preparing a *solyanka*."

The thought of a cauldron full of the sweet and sour stew of beef, sausage, and pickled vegetables made my mouth water. "Then I might be there before you," I said as she slid away almost soundlessly over the dull parquet. The door fell shut behind her with a thud, an echo lapping after it in tiny waves, before it lost itself in the Great Hall's vast space.

I held my breath, listening to Anoushka's steps disappear, until I was sure that she was truly gone.

Then I turned to Grandfather Alexis's throne.

4

My skin prickled. Blood rushed through my veins. I got goose bumps. The lions' ruby eyes were watching me. I stood still for a while, yet the throne's majesty and supreme confidence lured me closer. In Versailles I would sit on a throne next to my husband, ruling France. What else could my birth under the December stars, feet first, on the day of the celebration of Father's biggest ever victory, have portended? I would be a great queen. What did Herr Schwartz, my Viennese dance teacher, always say in his harsh and edgy-sounding Russian, before setting down the dainty feet that did not quite match his bear-like body? "Practice makes perfect." Indeed. And, after all, nobody would ever know. So . . .

The throne reeled me in. I edged toward it, my heart pounding, breath quickening. I turned to look over my shoulder, as if my steps might have alerted someone. For a moment I thought I heard the drumbeat, which had once announced my grandfather's sitting in state in this hall, followed by the regimented steps of his hundreds of grim-faced Cossack guards, wielding shiny axes, their white leather uniforms studded with gold and silver. People had slid up to Tsar Alexis on their knees, prostrating themselves, never daring to raise their face toward their *batjushka* Tsar, their little father. I seemed to hear those soft shuffling sounds now—but, no, it was just my pulse racing. Once we received Versailles's answer, I would leave Russia, God's most blessed country. I needed to prepare. My feet felt as if they were weighed down, yet the steps leading up to the throne were surprisingly shallow. I took a deep breath: there, I had done it. I was on the dais and shoving the silver footstool aside so that I could stand comfortably, spread my wide skirt. The crimson of the velvet seat cushion was almost obscured by dust, the gold galloon tassel torn and frayed. It had once been meticulously quilted. I turned my back on the throne; my trembling hands rested on the lions' manes as I slowly, very slowly—shaking with fear and excitement and imagining fanfares and oaths of allegiance—lowered myself onto the seat. I first balanced on its very edge, squeezing my eyes shut, as my mouth went dry, and the blood pounded in my ears. The earth might open and swallow me. The sky could crack and fall in on my head, crushing me like an ant, if lightning did not strike me down first.

Time crept by.

My breathing steadied.

Nothing happened.

I shuffled backward until I felt the carved backrest edging uncomfortably into my spine. I first squinted through my lashes, seeing the hall as if between bars, before fully opening my eyes. Light fell through the stained glass, pooling on the parquet like water and tinting the wood all the colors of the rainbow. Dust flecks danced in the air. A sunny silence reigned. All was as it had ever been. I relaxed my shoulders, breathed out, and sank into the cushioned seat, even bouncing up and down a bit. There! I clenched my fists. I had done it. I sat on the throne of All the Russias. A giggle rose in my throat. How different things looked from up here: if the hues of the stained-glass windows gleamed more intensely, and the design of the painted wood paneling was more startling and evident, the lions' heads looked much more worn, viewed from close. My finger traced the line of their manes' stylized curls, where the gold leaf had worn thin.

Outside, in the corridor, footsteps were approaching.

"Lizenka? Are you still here?" Anoushka called. The handle of the big door moved. I jumped up as if the throne had scalded me.

"I am coming." I leaped clear, making the cushion slip, and jumped off the dais to run across the Great Hall. Only once I had reached the safety of the doorway did I halt, my breath catching, and turn back to meet the lions' ruby gaze. I stuck out my tongue at them and wiggled my fingers in my ears: "Whaaaaa!"

Then I slipped out into the corridor.

Anoushka read while walking, frowning at the latest twist in her novel. I skipped along, running rings around her, smiling to myself at the memory of my secret adventure.

5

"What is your plan for the afternoon?" Illinchaya asked as she helped herself to a bowl of *solyanka*. We had finished our meal on our own, as Mother still spent most of her time in her rooms. Our gold plate and porcelain—beautiful, intricately patterned blue-and-white Meissen, of which thankfully not too much had been smashed on the road—sat as awkwardly on the scrubbed wooden surface of the kitchen table as a rich lady visiting a poor relation. Our Murano goblets were filled with elderflower cordial and clear water. Both Anoushka and I left wine, beer, and vodka until dinnertime.

The vast vaulted kitchen was warm from two fires, crackling at either end of the room. Chickens, geese, and piglets ran freely, and the maids' chatter, while they prepared the evening meal, filleting a huge sturgeon and buttering the copper tins for honeyed *medovik* tart, made our ears burn. Illinchaya stirred the *solyanka*, fishing for the last pieces of cured beef, slices of kielbasa sausage, as well as the capers, onion slices, and pickles, before she poured herself some *kvass* from a jug. A second cup of the bitter, cheap drink of fermented yeast she placed in front of d'Acosta. The jester slurped from it, eyes closed in delight, while Illinchaya preferred to dip a slice of crusty unleavened bread in her *kvass*. It gave her a swift boost; judging from the flush on her fair skin, it was not her first of the day.

"Mother is asleep," I said, fidgeting with impatience. I still felt the lions' heads beneath my palms and the ebony carvings of the backrest pressing against my spine. Noon had passed; the day stretched ahead of us like dough.

"Best not to disturb her," Illinchaya said, talking, chewing, and gulping, all at the same time, which was frightful to watch. "She has much to recover from."

Anoushka suggested: "We might go to see the dovecotes and the falcons. Perhaps Lizenka can choose a fledgling to train?" In the grounds of Kolomenskoye, a hundred thousand doves were kept in cotes dating from the days of Grandfather Alexis; they were bred as fodder for his birds of prey. The ceremony with which he had surrounded the falcons surprised foreign envoys and made his family gently tease him. But falconry was not a pastime that Father enjoyed, so who knew what was left of the cotes and nests? Possibly by now all the birds had had their necks wrung so that they could be plucked and roasted.

"That's a good idea. The falconer still lives there. Do you remember, Evgeni with the ginger hair? Though nowadays he is more salt and pepper, as are we all." Illinchaya chuckled and took a deep sip of the *kvass*. D'Acosta imitated her, smacking his lips, and screwing up his face in mockery, as she winked and said: "Just don't lose your way—you might end up in the sacred oak grove or beyond."

"Silence, woman," d'Acosta ordered, suddenly stern, sitting up straight.

"Where?" I asked.

"The sacred oak grove?" Anoushka chimed in.

Illinchaya blushed, with an effect like throwing a raw crayfish into a boiling pot of broth: the fine translucent flesh turned bright red. "Just some fairy-tale nonsense," she mumbled.

"You said those were no fairy tales," I answered, sliding toward her and topping up her bowl of *kvass* generously once more. "Tell us. Come on. Father never mentioned a sacred oak grove."

"For good reason. Enough of this," d'Acosta said, pushing his bowl of *kvass* away, but Illinchaya could not resist our cajoling. "Ah, well," she started as if implying, *There is a lot your father never mentioned to you.* Of course, saying that out loud could result in her having molten metal poured down her throat. "Why not? You are not children any more. I have kept the secret long enough, as the Tsar ordered."

D'Acosta's frown deepened. "Since when has that order been rescinded?"

I could hardly sit still. "What secret?"

D'Acosta sat back, his lips thin and disapproving, as Illinchaya spoke after sucking again at the soggy, intoxicating crust of her sourdough bread. Anoushka and I listened with bated breath. "The sacred oak grove lies deep in the grounds of Kolomenskoye. Beyond it opens the Golosov Ravine." Illinchaya was loving the feeling of our attention fixed on her. Her words gave me goose bumps, and Anoushka, too, crossed her arms, as if to warm herself from a chill of foreboding. From all her reading, her imagination was teeming, and most nights, at dream time, when both heroes and villains came to life for her, she slipped into my bed for comfort, and we fell asleep together.

"The Golosov Ravine," I repeated, tasting the words. "I have never heard of it."

"It's cursed," Illinchaya warned. "Whoever walks into it one day, returns a century later. Tsar Ivan Grozny is said to have sent a troop of Tatar soldiers in there to explore. They came out a hundred years later, unchanged, just in time to salute your grandfather, Tsar Alexis."

"But why did Ivan the Terrible send those soldiers into the Golosov Ravine?" I wondered.

Illinchaya's eyes opened as big as saucers. "The ravine answers your every question."

"Any question at all?" My heart thumped.

She nodded. "There you will learn your fate. But everything comes at a price."

I cleared my throat. "What sort of price?"

"Tsarevna. Please do not insist on asking such questions, I beg you," d'Acosta said, squirming on his seat.

"I thought you said it was all silly superstition, d'Acosta?" I teased, and Illinchaya shrugged, loftily ignoring the little man, as so many people did.

"Who knows whom, or what, the Tatars encountered in that ravine?" said Illinchaya.

"Was it the witch Baba Yaga, who ate their children, or the Domovoi lobbing timber at them?" I could not help it, I giggled.

Illinchaya shrugged grumpily. "Whomever. In any case, they were lucky to return at all."

Anoushka shivered, as if our nanny's words crawled like a spider's legs on her skin.

D'Acosta leaped off his seat. "Enough of this! No, Tsarevny, go and see the falcons, please. Evgeni told me that he has hundreds of fledglings, so take your pick. The Tsar will have our hide if anything happens to you."

"Quiet, d'Acosta, or I'll lock you in the chicken coop. There you can cluck and fret all day long." Illinchaya rolled her eyes at him before she was required at the kitchen door: peasants had called, carrying baskets filled with jars of last autumn's pickles and preserves to sell to the Imperial household.

I pulled Anoushka to her feet. "You are right. Let us go and see the fledglings." D'Acosta's gaze followed us as we left. In the dusky cool of the corridor, Anoushka laced her fingers with mine, setting off for Evgeni and the dovecotes.

"Wrong direction," I said. "We want to go out toward the forest and the Golosov Ravine."

"But—you heard what Illinchaya said. It steals your life. What if we never come back?" My sister's voice was shaky.

"Scaredy-cat. Don't believe old women's tales." In truth I would not want to go there on my own and hoped that Anoushka's curiosity would get the better of her. "I am as good as engaged. Don't you want to know what fate has in store for you, as the Tsar's elder daughter?"

Still, she shook her head, hesitant.

I crossed my arms, tapped my foot. "Fine. As you wish. I shall go on my own. But I will neither tell you whom I met in the ravine nor what I asked them. You can suit yourself!"

"Lizenka," she pleaded, holding me back. "I will not let you go alone. You are right: I *do* want to know my destiny. How could I not?"

I took her hand again, feeling ashamed. No illicit sitting on whichever throne in the world justified harassing my own sister. "Anoushka Petrovna Romanova," I said solemnly, clasping her fingers close to my heart. "You shall learn all about your glorious destiny, I promise! And now let us be off, before the snoop d'Acosta has the idea of accompanying us to see the falcons. That would not be fun, would it?"

We first walked, then skipped, and finally ran, giddy and laughing, all the way down to the tall gate out to the garden. It was bolted: "One, two, three," I counted, and together we lifted the iron bar. It was much heavier than expected and slipped from our fingers, crashing on the flagstones. Anoushka pulled me back just in time, otherwise it would have squashed my toes. We stared at each other, wide-eyed, listening to the fading echo, but so soon after lunchtime everyone else was dozing. We pushed open one side of the large double gates—they were only ever both opened to allow the Tsar's carriage to pass—and slipped out into the grounds. The gravel crunched beneath my silk slippers as we stole away.

"Shouldn't we get boots and capes? We'll catch a cold." Anoushka shivered in the afternoon chill.

"Hush now. Who cares about capes and colds when you are about to know your fate?" I ducked into a thicket, and Anoushka followed, her cheeks flushed, blue eyes sparkling, and her dark braids loosening.

When I turned to look back over my shoulder, Kolomenskoye had disappeared from view.

6

The foresters here did their work sloppily: much too soon the garden turned into a wilderness with no path to be seen. The dense, thorny undergrowth tore at my skirt, and any grass was still drenched in dew, the new blades sharp. Above our heads the treetops met, intertwined branches locking out the daylight. Roots as gnarly as Illinchaya's fingers reached for our feet. All around us, the dark, moist green breathed. Branches cracked under nobody's step, the unexpected sound sending birds flapping and shrieking for cover. We chased on, jumping and stumbling. My blood raced, my heart pounded, breathing hurt. Anoushka grabbed my hand, holding me back: "Is this the right way?" We looked around. The bushes closed behind us like barriers; no twig was broken, no moss torn, no earth furrowed by our steps. Everything looked just as it had before. Had we already left the boundaries of Kolomenskoye, and missed the sacred oak grove as well as the ravine?

"If we turn around now, nobody will ever know we left. We would be back for dinner," Anoushka suggested.

"No. Look at the clearing over there," I said, my voice sounding small despite my best efforts to seem confident. "That must be the sacred oak grove. The Golosov Ravine is right behind it." I felt her hesitate and added: "You do not want to turn back, now that we have come so far?"

She shook her head, and we walked on until we stood in the oak grove. Mottled rays of late sunshine slipped through the branches and leaves, shading the moss in hues of gold, amber, and rust. While many of the trees had fallen and lay tossed about as if part of a giants' game, some were still standing. I arched my neck, trying to see their tops, but the light blinded me. Their trunks were thick enough to carve out an entire cradle from.

"Let us take a break here." I leaned against a wide stump. Each ring in a felled tree's trunk marked a year in the passage of time; the span in between was a trace determined by seasons of precipitation or drought, just as wrinkles mirrored years of ease or concern in a human face. There were too many rings to count. My finger stopped tracing them: strange, dark-red glistening stains blurred the rings, like blood oozing from the wood. I suddenly understood: these trees had been felled! The destruction of this formerly peaceful spot had been man's work. The Domovoi ought to be furious, however many pancakes Illinchaya left for him.

The leaf fall of countless autumns crunched beneath my feet, releasing a musty scent. Elsewhere the meadows were full of clover, daisies, bluebells, and buttercups, but here no young shoots pushed through. The wind turned chilly, and Anoushka stood looking undecided. I said: "Let us press on. Even drunk, Illinchaya will notice if we are not back for supper, and d'Acosta will raise the alarm. That would worry Mother out of her mind."

As we left, it felt as if myriad eyes followed our every move.

A couple of steps farther on, the ground fell away sharply beneath our feet. The birds, which had been singing before, happy about the longer twilight, had fallen silent. Large trees drooped over the ravine's edge, roofing the gulf with their dark canopies; overgrown branches were gnarled and twisted. Weeping willows cascaded down the slope, and holly bushes reared up to meet them, thorny and thick, their leaves a dark, waxy green. Boulders broke through the thick undergrowth like the teeth of an old wolf. Deep down in the ravine, water gushed.

"Here we go. The Golosov Ravine. Are you ready?" I asked.

"Yes. Well. Kind of. You?"

"Sure." I shrugged. "I shall ask about my betrothal to the King of France. And you?"

"I want to know if I will have children. Best would be a whole tribe of them, boys and girls. A big, loving family."

"Don't tell me. Save it for whomever we meet down there." I winked at her.

"Oh, God. I wish I were at home, curled up next to the oven reading." Anoushka cast a doubtful glance at the thicket ahead of us.

"Do you really prefer a book over life? Are we truly sisters, or is one of us a changeling from the German Quarter?"

"All right." She half-heartedly hitched up her skirt. "How do we get down there?"

"Like this, Tsarevna," I replied, and twisted my dress hem into a big knot around my knees. "Come. Nobody will ever know," I assured her, and grabbed a branch for support, carefully placing my feet at the start of the steep descent into the ravine.

7

We slid on the wet, muddy ground, grazing our hands and knees, tearing and sullying our wide-skirted house-dresses, smearing our faces with mud, and scratching our cheeks and foreheads. At first I laughed when I fell, even pulling Anoushka along for a tumble. Soon enough, though, we were both panting and gasping when we scrambled up again, our legs and arms trembling from exhaustion.

"Enough now, Lizenka," she scolded, catching her breath, just as we arrived at the bottom of the ravine. We stepped out of the thicket. Wet black sand and gravel formed a shoreline of sorts. Water roared: about twenty *arshin* away from us a waterfall cascaded down the cliff face, foaming in a pool before it raced toward us, the speed of its passing filling our ears. It was impossible to tell how deep it ran, as slate darkened the river bottom. I pointed downstream, mouthing: "This way." We held hands; the sharp gravel cut through the soles of our slippers, and the spray soaked us, drawing patterns on my muddied sleeves. My sister almost banged into me as I stopped in my tracks: "Look, Anoushka." My voice was clipped with fear. Ahead of us a woman crouched in the sand—or it seemed like a woman, until I took a closer look.

"What is this?" I whispered, clutching Anoushka's hand.

"It's an evil spirit. A Leshy. Illinchaya did not lie," my sister answered, terrified.

A Leshy spirit. Illinchaya had warned us about these forest

dwellers, who were mischievous at best, abusing their power of prophecy, deliberately leading people astray.

The Leshy looked as much a part of this landscape as the leaves, the gravel, and the river, and it was shrouded in furs. A fire smoldered in front of its den, which was built of woven branches and mud. The flames gave off a dense smoke; the wood must be too green and wet. The being rose. At its feet rock pools swirled as though filled with hot water, the vapor from them reeking like the Devil's wind. It closed its eyes, breathing with flared nostrils as if to take in our scent. We were on its territory.

The being suddenly opened its eyes wide, revealing their brightness. We stood petrified while it advanced, and I realized that the Leshy wore no covering at all: only the spirit's own thick, long hair spilled over its body, like mottled gray-and-white fur with leaves and dirt clinging to it. What was this creature living on? Ribs poked at its hide, and long bones showed through the flesh of the upper arms and shanks. The Leshy spirit smiled, revealing a set of gleaming fangs.

Anoushka wanted to hold me back, but I urged: "Leshy or not, we have not come here for nothing, have we?"

The Leshy beckoned, as if it sensed our hesitation. "Welcome, Tsarevny," it growled.

"How do you know who we are?" I dared another step forward but froze when the Leshy started to chuckle, her mirth rising to laughter. It sounded like a howl, and we were showered in tiny flecks of spittle. Then the creature fell silent, its gaze gleaming. "I also know what you want to know," it said. I noticed its probing eyes were a strange shade of mustard, like a stale apple.

"Go on, Tsarevny. Ask me what you want to know. You first." The spirit pointed at Anoushka before rattling some little bones in the hollow of its cupped hands. My sister's curiosity got the better of her.

"All right then," she said, licking her dry lips. "Will I marry? And will I bear an heir, a strong son?"

The Leshy cowered low on its haunches and sucked in the rising steam, nostrils wide. Its eyes rolled up, showing their whites, as the creature tossed the bones high in the air. Its body went rigid; then, as the bones fell in a random pattern, it slackened.

"Yes," the Leshy said thoughtfully while studying them.

Anoushka clenched her fists triumphantly. "Yes! Will I give life?"

"A life you will give indeed," the Leshy repeated, then looked at me. "Your turn, Wolverine."

The name caught me off guard. "Wolverine?"

"That is what you are, born feet first, under the December stars. The worst signs for a woman. Let us hope you make the best of them. You have a flair for drama, haven't you, beautiful Tsarevna?"

"How do you know all that?" I asked.

"How should I not know?" the Leshy retorted. "Kolomenskoye is my land."

I cleared my throat. "All right then. Will I be a mother, too?"

The creature's eyes locked with mine. "As ever putting the cart in front of the horse, young Elizabeth," it said, sounding surly. "You will be a mother, but you will have no child."

I frowned. "What does that mean?"

"I only answer. I don't explain."

"Will I marry a king and rule together with my husband?" The words tumbled from my mouth. Suddenly I, too, did not wish to spend a minute longer than necessary down here, in this sickening stench, encountering the unknown. The Leshy sucked in the geyser's stench, eyes dulling and lids fluttering. Its whole body swayed. I jumped as the spirit spoke again: its voice sounded as deep as a bronze bell.

"Better rule marriage out," it slurred.

"Nonsense," I said. "I am about to be engaged to the King of France. I will have a husband who reigns."

"A husband to rein you in," the creature chuckled. On the geyser's surface, a bubble burst. The rising fumes made the Leshy tremble, and its claws clenched the little bones.

"Lizenka," Anoushka cried out as the Leshy's lips began to foam and spew out words, making a prediction. *"In your end lies your beginning. No man shall disappoint you as a woman will. An angel will speak to you. The lightest load will be your greatest burden."* It reared up and then turned rigid before collapsing, heaving. Its silver hair parted, showing bald patches of raw-looking skin.

Anoushka seized my hand, wide-eyed with dread: "Come!" We turned to run away, but the Leshy lunged, grabbing hold of my skirt. It wrapped the fabric twice around its fists and pulled with all its might. Its eyes were lit with fury. The Leshy bared its fangs, looking ready to slash my skin and drink my blood, just like the Caucasus bats Illinchaya had told us about. "What about my reward?" it snarled.

Anoushka patted the sides of her skirt, but in vain. "I am sorry." We never carried any money—what on earth for? The Leshy hissed and reeled me in further. Its fury reeked, blending with the sulfur smell. "Ah! The fine young Tsarevny. Never carry roubles, eh? What is ours is yours, as it ever was, and in the end we all pay for your mischief. But you are mistaken." The spirit tugged my dress sharply, almost making me stumble. "Very well, Tsarevny. You shall give me something else."

"Just tell me what it is. I'll give it to you," I screamed, beside myself with fear, digging my feet into the shoreline. The Leshy tore at my skirt while Anoushka yanked at my arm, screaming as well: it hurt so much, I thought they would rip me apart.

"I want your soul," the spirit howled. "That is my just reward." The strength in its skeletal hands was shocking. My feet slid closer and closer to it. "No, please, don't," I begged. One more breath, and I would be in its claws—forever.

"Lizenka!" Anoushka wailed.

Her fear gave me a jolt of unexpected strength. I had made her come here; I was responsible for bringing her home unscathed. I half turned to swing a punch, raised one leg and kicked the Leshy sideways. It shouted as it tumbled over. I kicked it wherever I could reach while the beast sprawled at my feet: on the chin, in the teeth, its hollow chest, the stark ribs—even the concave stomach beneath. I kicked and kicked as hard as I could until the Leshy howled with pain and rage, writhing in the gravel that grazed its sallow skin, finally letting go of me.

"Run, Anoushka!" I panted, grabbing my sister's hand. We darted off, the sharp gravel tearing into our soles. I turned to look back while running; the Leshy stumbled to its feet, shaking its fists at us. "Curse the Romanovs!" it screamed. "Your sons shall bleed." At least it was not pursuing us but instead sank back, slumping in the sand, tears and snot streaming down its face. Then the water's thunder swallowed up its cries. We had reached the spot where we had stepped onto the shore. I grabbed whatever branch I could get hold of, not caring if it was thorny, and pulled myself up, sensing Anoushka close behind me, coughing and gasping for breath.

When we stood at the edge of the sacred oak grove, the branches closed behind us, cutting off any sign of the ravine as if we had never been there. The evening chill fell, and the clearing was shrouded by a hazy purple dusk. Every bone in my body hurt, as if battered against the ravine's boulders; my spirit felt shredded. I almost choked on sobs while looking around.

8

How much time had passed? According to Illinchaya, the Tatar troop had wandered about for more than a century. I knew better than to doubt her stories any longer. A dull twilight reigned in the forest, heralding the approach of the White Nights. The sky was mauve, like a bruise, as the shadows of the sacred oak grove drew closer. Anoushka sank to the ground, hunching down next to a stump. Darkness rose like a wave. I raised my arms in vain. It enclosed me like a fly caught beneath a cup. I was terrified. What if the Leshy had kept my soul after all?

"What now?" Anoushka sounded exhausted. "Do you know the way back?"

I sat down next to her, leaning against the same thick tree trunk, burying my head in my arms. It still rang with the Leshy's spiteful words: *You will be a mother, but you will have no child. Better rule marriage out. A husband to rein you in.* And then her prophecy: *In your end lies your beginning. No man shall disappoint you as a woman will. An angel will speak to you. The lightest load will be your greatest burden.*

What had I been thinking, seeking her out?

"I don't know the way back," I admitted.

This was all my fault. We clung to each other, forsaken amid the towering trees. The daylight dimmed further, but even when night fell at last, we stayed awake, shivering and trying to keep each other warm. Anoushka rested her head on my shoulder. I kissed her forehead. When Kolomenskoye would miss us was anyone's guess. I prepared to look the last minutes of my life straight in the eye.

My limbs were stiff from the cold, and finally I found an uncomfortable slumber when torchlight fell upon the forest. Flames tore into the inky blackness, and a man's voice shouted, ragged with relief: "There they are!" It was Evgeni the falconer. Behind him more and more people stepped into the clearing. They whistled, clapped, and cheered; hunting horns were blown in a signal that was passed back to the palace. Anoushka stumbled to her feet, and I followed. We both cried with relief, embracing each other.

"We have found the Tsarevny!" Evgeni rushed toward us, wrapping us in blankets. D'Acosta followed him, and hot *chai* laced with honey and vodka was forced down my throat. I had been lifted onto a mule—a tufty reindeer skin made the wooden saddle more comfortable—when Illinchaya crashed through the thicket like a mother bear looking for her cubs, shouting: "Lizenka! Anoushka! Your Highnesses! My little sunshine Tsarevny!" She smothered us in her fat arms, and tears spouted from her pale eyes. "My doves! Never do that again. You frightened me to death. Oh, my God, this is all my fault."

"Are you still awake?" Anoushka whispered when finally we lay in our beds, bellies filled with hot kasha made as each of us preferred it—mine sweetened with honey and berries, while Anoushka's was savory with added bacon pieces.

"How could I not be?" I said and sat up, pulling my knees beneath my chin. "I don't dare close my eyes. Come over here. Please." I folded back my blanket.

Anoushka tiptoed over the wooden floor and climbed into my high bedstead. We snuggled up close beneath the blankets and furs. Legs, feet, and fingers were in a tangle, glad of each other's warmth. All candles were carefully snuffed every evening—a fire would roar through the building's maze of wooden corridors as through a chimney, and in every room several buckets of sand and water stood at the ready. Anoushka breathed evenly, wide awake.

Finally I dared to ask: "How do you think it feels if someone takes your soul?"

"At worst, as if someone is tearing you into a thousand pieces," she guessed after a while.

"And at best?"

I sensed her chewing her lip: "Lonely?"

"We will never be lonely," I said, pressing myself against her bony body, delighted when she embraced me back. Then she sat up. "But what if the Leshy has done it—taken our souls—and we haven't noticed yet?" Anoushka's dark hair fell straight over the delicate broderie anglaise of her nightshirt. "It's too horrible. We must never tell Mother or Father what happened today," she decided after thinking for a moment. "*Never*. Father would be furious. Who knows how he would punish us for our disobedience? Think what happened to Alexey. And Mother . . ." Her voice trailed off.

"You are right." While I felt that I could weather Father's fury, in this case Mother could not bear another tragedy.

Anoushka continued: "And we'd best not mention it to each other either. As Mother says: least said, soonest mended." She lay back down, seemingly relieved. I wished I could do the same. What *if* Father had given the Leshy his soul; would we do so as well, in due course? *Lonely at best.* For as long as I had lived, someone had always been by my side: Anoushka, of course, and our aunt Pasha when Mother followed Father wherever he went, and in more recent years, our parents. I stared into the dark room. *One in a field is not a warrior*, my father would sigh when overwhelmed by the task before him.

"*Schastye*," I murmured: the Russian word for "happiness" implied being undivided, part of something bigger.

"Mmh? What?" Anoushka asked drowsily, but a moment later I heard her deep, steady breathing. How could she sleep? I crossed my hands and soundlessly prayed to my patron saint, Elizabeth.

Still, sleep would not come for long hours. Finally, as the first light crept into our room, the milky hue of the morning light dappling the wall, I, too, fell into an exhausted slumber.

Yet if Mother never learned of our encounter with the Leshy, someone else certainly did.

9

A good two weeks later I heard the stable door opening shortly before dawn. Who was there, a horse thief? I should catch the knave! I rolled from my bedstead and tiptoed over to the big window overlooking the garden, the stables, and the forest beyond. Where horizon and heavens met lay the Golosov Ravine. I averted my eyes and looked down into the garden and inner courtyard instead.

Two strangers looking like Cossack heyducks—mercenaries and renegade bandits—dragged a woman's plump body into the merciless morning light. They dropped her in the dust only to string her up as hunters would a deer: binding her hands and feet over a big stick, which they shouldered. When they set off, the woman's head lolled back. The ruffled linen cap slipped, and I could see her face. I recoiled, cupping my mouth, fighting to suppress a scream. Illinchaya's eyes stared unblinkingly into the clean sky, reflecting its pale blue. Her face was black-tinged and swollen; her hands and feet, too, had ballooned, looking like bear paws. I gagged: Illinchaya had been strung upside down in the stable until the blood flow made her brain burst. What other crime would have warranted this ultimate punishment for unruly servants but disobeying the Tsar's orders? She had told us about the Golosov Ravine, against Father's command. Or rather, I had made her tell us. I bit the back of my hand to strangle a sob so as not to wake Anoushka.

Outside the men stumbled toward the fringes of the forest with their load. Illinchaya's arm came loose from its tie and hung limp.

Her plump fingers, which had braided my unruly blonde curls when I was a child, and had stirred my kasha just yesterday, trailed through the dust. I choked on my own dread. Did Kolomenskoye have a graveyard behind the chapel, where I had worshipped as a child? But no priest joined the two heyducks as they moved toward the forest. The woods closed behind them like a green wall; they would dump Illinchaya's body there as food for the wild animals.

The morning light took on a bitter hue. I tore the window open. All was silent, and cold air drifted in as I stood there, shivering and staring, blinded by tears. When I wanted to return to my bed, I tasted bile.

I might as well have strung up Illinchaya with my own hands.

When we came downstairs, a messenger who had arrived from St. Petersburg the evening before—a tall, burly new man—lingered in the kitchen while we silently spooned our *kasha*. One of the maids cooked our millet porridge for us, oversalting it for Anoushka and not adding enough honey for me, while we listened to d'Acosta reading us Father's latest summons. We were to join him as soon as possible in Peterhof, our summer palace on the Gulf of Finland, about twenty *versty* outside St. Petersburg.

While our maids were busy packing up our belongings, which had barely left the travel chests, d'Acosta had already climbed up and down on the coach box, swinging about like one of my monkeys, making Mother laugh as she got inside the carriage. Anoushka stood outside the house, frowning. "I wonder where Illinchaya is." She shielded her eyes against the sunlight, searching the bustling courtyard. "She would never let us go without saying goodbye, would she?"

All the blood seemed to have flowed from my head, and my heart raced. I had brought the Leshy's curse upon Illinchaya by coaxing her to tell us about the ravine. How could I admit this to Anoushka or to anyone? Nobody but me was to blame for our visit to the sacred oak grove—and beyond. My bookish and well-behaved sister would never have pushed to go there. I flushed with shame, remembering how intoxicated I had felt after sitting on the Lion Throne: silly me!

As the carriage jerked into motion and the whimsical splendor of Kolomenskoye disappeared, Mother's lady-in-waiting read her a second note from Father. Mother smiled at me, and her voice was warm when she said: "We ought to hurry, Lizenka. Father has a special announcement to make. Might he have had word from Versailles?"

10

"If this is what it will be like in France, I shall be happy to live there." I shielded my eyes, looking out over the grounds of Peterhof.

"Versailles is much more beautiful than this, I hear," Anoushka answered.

"I can't believe that," I said, as the beauty of Peterhof seeped into my spirit and my soul, purifying me. Our large Imperial barge had made slow and steady progress from the Neva estuary, and the boat had been well stocked with delicacies and chilled vodka; musicians had played while we lay on cushions beneath a large parasol, eating, drinking, and chatting when I could convince Anoushka to put her book down, tickling her in persuasion if need be. In the end she had been so exasperated by the constant disruptions that she had read me the story. One of the frequent rain showers in the area had soaked the poor musicians, who played on. Even Mother laughed at the sight.

We found Peterhof's park bursting with blossom. We gazed in wonder along the sea channel where two hundred gilded statues lined a white gravel path leading up to the Grand Cascade with its sixty-four sparkling fountains. Light bounced off the water, making each drop sparkle. The earth excavated for the ponds and canals had been used to erect several rings of ramparts three *arshin* high, which shielded the fruit trees from the harsh sea winds. In the orchard I spotted lilacs, jasmine, and rhododendrons blossoming. The ground of the surrounding forest glowed indigo with thousands of blueberries waiting to be picked, their fullness interspersed with the crimson sweetness of wild strawberries. Anoushka and I would balance the berries on our fingertips, feeding each other, pretending to be robin fledglings picking at food.

In Peterhof, Father blended impressions he had gathered of the West, recreating what he had most admired there. No wonder that Peterhof was said to rival Versailles: countless huge windows in the graceful buttercup-and-*smetana*-colored façade overlooked the vast parkland, where fountains sparkled brightly enough to rival the sunshine. Everything here promised a future of dazzling days, bright and golden.

This comforting thought chased away any last lingering impressions of our gloomy visit to the Golosov Ravine. What remained was the memory of Illinchaya's love for us. I prayed for her every night, when I settled down to sleep in the small pavilion known as Mon Plaisir—a long low building that Father had designed himself, which had just been completed. Its unique blend of Russian bathhouse and Dutch red brick, set amid tree-lined canals, as well as its pantry full of incredible inventions, was so typical of him that I knew I should always sense his presence there.

In Mon Plaisir not even the Leshy and its prophecy could do me any harm.

"Lizenka, little sunshine. Anoushka, my dove! Why are you sitting here idly while your mother toils?"

"Father!" Both Anoushka and I jumped up from the game of chess we were playing in the snug Chinese Cabinet of Mon Plaisir. Here our parents displayed the imported Eastern porcelain service they were so proud of—trade with China was notoriously difficult—and Russian artisans had toiled for months to master the art of lacquering black panels in red frames that were adorned with Chinese-style miniature paintings, to give it a suitable setting. We toppled the chessboard and sent the pawns we had taken prisoner flying.

"Tsarevny!" called Father and I flew toward him: a moment with him alone was valuable by dint of its rarity. He wore the old green-velvet dressing gown that hung off his giant frame—he stood almost three *arshin* tall in his boots—even though it was frayed at the hems and the cloth was threadbare and shiny along the pockets and seams. His dark, curly hair, which was threaded with gray, looked tousled, as if he had just stepped off a boat or had a morning in bed—which never happened. The Tsar rose long before sunrise, firing off a volley of letters: correspondence abroad to his ambassadors, agents, and foreign rulers; new laws and commands—the *ukazy*—went to his generals, admirals, and the rural administrators—the *voyvody*—all over Russia. There was no exception to that rule, wherever he was, and however late and wildly he had feasted the evening before.

He held me tight, rocking me and growling like an old bear. I barely refrained from pulling his mustache, as I would have done as a little girl, treating it like cat's whiskers. Instead I buried my face in his chest, sucking in the scent of tobacco, leather, smoke, and the Tsar's special perfume of vanilla and bergamot, which was mixed in Grasse for his sole use. That scent was as particular to him as sunrise was to the morning. His tall body was a curious blend of narrow shoulders, strong arms, yet surprisingly dainty hands, which had easily held in check Finette, his nervy Arab steed, on every battlefield, over a paunch grown soft due to countless years of feasting and his love of food—slow-cooked pork and sauerkraut was a firm favorite—and drink. He had invented his own huge chalice, the eagle cup, in order to down more vodka at his notorious "all-drunk, all-jesting synod."

I looked up at him: his face was puffy—the dewiness of youth depicted in his official portraits was long gone; his cheeks had turned to jowls, and the once noble nose had grown bulbous—but his blue eyes gleamed bright and clear, despite the dark shadows underneath them. He smiled at me momentarily. His expression was never still; he frowned a bit, nose twitching, lips smacking together or forming a silent whistle while his chin wagged. This was how I had always known him.

"Have you slept, Father?" I asked, concerned for him, as I knew about his nightmares.

He kissed my forehead. "Sweet Lizenka. Always worried for your *batjushka*. I did! Peterhof and Mon Plaisir do your little father wonders." I felt relieved, yet astounded by his way of putting things behind him and moving on. If Alexey's death and the lack of an heir still tormented him, he would not let on. Anoushka stepped up to us and now he embraced us both, kissing our heads in turn and laughing, while he said: "Other people shoot the messenger, but you kiss him. I like this! Listen to me: are you ready for a feast? I have given the cook leave. Your mother is preparing breakfast in the pantry."

He walked ahead on long, thin legs, his feet shuffling in felt slippers. Yet even while walking, he seemed to be tapping a rhythm, and already he impatiently clutched a bundle of papers, even starting to read them on his way to the pantry. His time and attention were the most valuable present he could give.

"Just in time," Mother said, her face glowing as we entered the pantry. She wiped her hands on a clean, beautifully lace-trimmed apron, and the warmth of the oven made her cheeks blush and her eyes shine. She, too, had recovered from the strain of the past. "Anoushka, fetch water for the samovar," Mother ordered.

"I will have *kvass*," said Father, who preferred the yeasty drink of the peasants to *chai* laced with vodka. He sank into an armchair sturdy enough to take his weight and lit his ivory pipe, rustling through his papers—Vice Chancellor Count Ostermann had concluded the Treaty of Nystad, which put an end to the two decades of the Great Northern War—and studying drawings for new uniforms or palaces, as well as the order of the new "Table of Ranks," which restructured Russian society, establishing such new Western-sounding titles as Prince and Count. As my sister busied herself at the big stone sink—the tap was fed from the Sheaf

Fountain, and we marveled at it: running water!—Father turned papers this way and that, before scattering them on the floor.

Anoushka set the samovar to simmer and boil. I gawped at everything Mother had prepared: soft-boiled eggs and fresh gray caviar were heaped in dainty mother-of-pearl bowls; smoked trout lay on pewter platters, and she had added pickled whortleberries to venison pâté before piling gherkins and Baltic herring marinated in *smetana*, apples, and onions onto plates.

"Lizenka, help me with the bread. It won't butter itself, will it?" Mother said, but I made a mess of my duty, as I could not resist eating half of it while I worked. I chewed hungrily and admired the blue-and-white patterned Delft tiles, which had just been placed on the walls. Each portrayed unknown flowers, animals, and landscapes. I had never traveled abroad—as no Russian would, unless under duress. No Russian but Father, who had left his realm for three years of travel in his younger days. Now he got up from his chair again, stepped carelessly on his papers, and embraced Mother.

She laughed. "*Starik!* If you hold me like this, we will never eat."

Father snatched a herring and ate it as an alley cat would, holding it upside down by its tail, marinade dripping, its scaly head disappearing first into his mouth. "Let us sit down then," he decided.

"Will you tell us your important announcement now?" I asked, burning with impatience and curiosity, sidling up to him on the bench, which was fashioned after the simple furnishing of a Russian peasant's *izba*. They all had a "beautiful," or red, corner.

"No, later. In my study. Petrushka, Ostermann, and Menshikov are to join us there."

Anoushka and I stared at each other. Petrushka was to join us! This was unheard of. Normally the Tsar abhorred the sight of his only grandson and would happily have seen the earth open and swallow him up without trace. We had not seen our young nephew since Alexey's death five years ago. The poor boy grew up far from us: he was being punished every day of his life for having had our half-brother Alexey as his father. This announcement had to be important indeed—even Father's closest friend, Prince Menshi-kov, and his most respected adviser, Count Ostermann, were to attend.

It had to be about my engagement to Louis, King of France! *Later,* Father had said. How should I contain myself? It was im-possible. Finally all my dreams were to come true. But I had to pretend to be calm and prove myself worthy of the honor that Father would bestow on me. I was to be betrothed to the King of France. Until then I was bursting with love and pride. In Mon Plaisir, we were not the Imperial Romanovs ruling Russia; we were simply a family at ease.

11

Anoushka and I were walking on toward the Grand Palace, crossing the checkered floor of the terrace, when I heard a boy's voice calling out to us, tripping over the words in his excitement. "Lizenka! Anoushka!"

I turned. "It's Petrushka! He has arrived!"

Anoushka and I swapped apprehensive glances. We stood surrounded by splendor, swathed in finery, smothered with love and attention. How should we greet the boy who was despised by his own grandfather? Before I knew it, I'd opened my arms wide to him, because nobody else ever did.

"I'll catch you, little bear," I said, calling him by his childhood nickname.

"Yes! Lizenka! I knew it." The gangly boy at the other end of the terrace tore himself away from the stooped figure of his tutor, Vice Chancellor Count Ostermann. The German followed at a slower pace, in his usual lopsided gait, steadying himself with a cane made of ebony, its ivory handle adorned with rubies.

Petrushka's narrow little face was lit by joy as he flew toward me, his long hair fanning out behind him like a dark halo. I opened my arms wide and caught him. He cheered, and I drank in the sight of the freckles on his long thin nose, the light in his amber eyes.

"Got you, Petrushka," I gasped. My nephew had grown heavy since I had last seen him—or since anyone had last seen him. He pressed into me, melting into my embrace, wanting to imprint my tenderness on his body, desperately seeking any sign of affection.

At eleven years old he stood almost as tall as I did. When he looked at me, he resembled Alexey so much that my heart clenched with worry. Had anyone prepared Father for this similarity? I feared it might give him one of the dreadful fits that only Mother could soothe.

Petrushka sighed with delight. "I am so happy to be here," he said, tilting back his head, his pale skin almost translucent under the bright summer light. "St. Petersburg is plagued by flies, and the drying swamp reeks. The Winter Palace is unbearably stuffy. I can hardly breathe when I have to sit there and study."

I felt sad for him, remembering the closeness and comfort of our morning in the pantry of Mon Plaisir. Petrushka had never known the like: a loving sister, a caring mother, a doting father. "It is wonderful to see you," I said, kissing his cheek, wanting to make up for the solitude and rejection he suffered. "Let us have some fun together. Tomorrow we can ride in the morning and sail after lunch. The network of canals here is terrific. You will be captain of a boat in no time at all."

"Really? Captain of a boat? Grandfather will like that, won't he?" The hope in his voice pained me. Father would never like anything about Petrushka, especially not if he were growing into Alexey's spitting image. "You're sure you're not just taunting me?" the boy asked me, his gaze suspicious. "Can I trust you?"

"Of course! Why ever not?"

"Count Ostermann tells me to trust only him."

Perhaps the prickly Vice Chancellor gave good advice after all. Even Father and Mother never made the priest's son from German Bochum the target of their many practical jokes. Officials who delayed his requests by just a day too long found themselves demoted to Siberia, close to the Arctic Circle, where they bemoaned a year filled with days of either utter darkness or everlasting daylight. De Campredon, the French envoy, had once sent him a year's supply of the finest cognac; it had been disdainfully returned, unopened, and worse still, with one bottle broken.

"Well, you brought him along to Peterhof. That's very studious of you."

"He brought me along. I will tell you a secret. In truth Ostermann is just like the fish in Grandfather's pond," he whispered, looking over to the ponds where the white-and-orange-flecked backs of giant ornamental carp broke the water's surface.

"Don't whisper," I whispered back. "It's rude. I fear that Ostermann would never do our bidding as those fish do. Last year Anoushka and I trained them to come and feed when we ring a silver bell."

"That is wondrous!" Petrushka marveled. "Can we do that later, together?"

"We can do whatever you wish while I am here," I said carefully, as—who knew?—I might be asked to leave for Versailles soon. I should be busy, I thought, my heart leaping: preparing a royal trousseau fit to impress the Bourbon Court was no mean feat. Making Petrushka empty promises would be callous, given the loneliness and rejection that engulfed him. "But why is Ostermann like our fish?"

"Just look at those protruding eyes and his waxy skin. Also he is just as warm and funny."

"But does he taste as good? Shall I take a nibble?"

"Please do." Petrushka grinned. I loved to see him like this, smiling with unabashed glee. It was too rare a sight.

"My boy," Ostermann said as he stepped up to us: Father had awarded Petrushka no title at birth, neither Tsarevich nor Prince of Russia. The German's impatience was palpable for once: it was so rare for the Tsar to summon his only grandchild and sole male Romanov heir that his guardian would not wish there to be any delay.

"Welcome, Count Ostermann. Thank you for the good care you take of our nephew." Anoushka smiled at Ostermann. "I suppose in Father's new Russia, learning never stops."

"Whatever it takes to please His Majesty the Tsar," Ostermann answered, bowing. Petrushka's continued survival depended on Father's scant mercy toward the boy. The Vice Chancellor was well turned out, his thin body clad in the red jacket and soft kidskin breeches of the Imperial Guard, though he never had marched in any field of battle and moved only by sedan chair, carriage, or sled. A good dozen honorary medals gleamed on his narrow chest. Pride of place, however, belonged to the brooch bearing my father's portrait, which pinned down the blue sash of the Order of St. Andrew, Russia's highest honor; the diamonds framing it flamed imperiously in the sun. Was he dressed up like this to celebrate my engagement? I would never know, as he kept his eyes carefully lowered; according to him, the gaze was the traitor of our thoughts and feelings. That lesson seemed lost on Petrushka, who beamed at me, his expression open and trusting, while Ostermann ruffled the boy's thin dark hair, his fingers short and surprisingly gnarled. "Shall we go? The Tsar awaits," he said.

Petrushka gave me a last rueful smile, straightened his dark, unadorned little waistcoat, and took Ostermann's hand to head toward the Grand Palace.

I watched them leave. In Ostermann's gray eyes I had spotted that most unusual thing at court: true love and tenderness for this child. "I am surprised that Father asks Petrushka to witness my betrothal to the King of France," I said to Anoushka, who had watched in silence.

"Oh, Lizenka. Please do not be disappointed if there is another reason why Father has asked us here."

"Why? What else could it be?"

"You yourself wondered only weeks ago who Father's heir would be. It was in Grandfather Alexis's throne room. The same day that we . . ." She halted, unable to say more. I pleadingly rested my finger on my lips.

"Don't," I begged.

All light and sunshine seeped from the day around us. "Oh,

God. I have not slept well ever since," she said, tears welling up and the words tumbling from her mouth.

I fought back tears. "I am so sorry. It was all my fault."

"No. You must not think that, ever. It was fate. Hush now." Anoushka took a deep breath, gathering herself. "But really: suddenly Petrushka appears in Peterhof. Can't you guess what that means? Who if not he should inherit the throne once Father . . ." She stopped short of committing a crime tantamount to blasphemy: alluding to the Tsar's mortality.

Of course. Father was finally doing what was only right: welcoming little Petrushka to the family—his family!—and recognizing his claim to the throne. I took a deep breath, chasing away my disappointment, feeling a wave of tenderness: Petrushka was blood of my blood, flesh of my flesh. I should support him wherever possible. "Well, what a reason to celebrate and be merry. In a couple of moments, Russia might have a new heir."

Anoushka smiled. "That's what I love so much about you. Your heart is as big as your mouth."

"That big?"

"Bigger still." She opened her arms to me. "The best things will come to you, little sister sunshine."

I wove Anoushka's arm around my waist while wrapping my own around her shoulders. Together, we followed Petrushka and Count Ostermann inside the Grand Palace to hear Father's big announcement. More than even the most advantageous engagement, Russia needed an official heir, a Tsarevich.

12

In the Grand Palace light poured through the two-tiered windows of the Portrait Hall, warming its glacial majesty and making the gilt stucco embellishment gleam like sunrise. The fifty-foot-high, stark white walls were enlivened by the myriad paintings Father had acquired from Italy: they hung frame to frame from floor to ceiling, where I admired the recently finished work of another French master. A fresco showed the four seasons flowing from a Greek god's bountiful hands. Fortune's cornucopia doused and drenched me: whatever awaited me in Father's study, I would do Russia justice. If I had pitied Petrushka before, I now felt proud of my young nephew.

A sea breeze filled Father's wood-paneled study, even though its four latticed windows gave on to the quiet of the Upper Garden. It was undisturbed by even the sound of lapping waters, allowing him to concentrate. The study's paneling was carved with depictions of all that captivated and inspired him: trophies and arms, globes as well as astronomical and nautical instruments, the signs of the zodiac—I spotted my own, Capricorn—and musical motifs, together with flower garlands, scallop shells, and foliate scrolls. Both worlds, the natural and the intangible, were celebrated side by side.

"Welcome, Tsarevny," Father said, leaning on his desk. He wore the green uniform jacket of the Imperial Preobrazhensky Regiment and the blue sash of the Order of St. Andrew on his chest. While the gold buttons shone as much as the gold galloon of his epaulettes and the military medals he had been awarded for bravery in the field, he wore his old boots, which he had earned the money to pay for by working in a Dutch shipyard as a young man. Their tips and soles had been mended dozens of times. He paused a moment, his face set. The air thickened with his authority. The change in him from the humorous, loving father we had seen in the pantry just a couple of hours ago, to absolute monarch and incalculable and unpredictable Tsar here in his Grand Palace, was awe-inspiring. His whole being was infused with his Divine calling as ruler of Russia. Anoushka and I curtsied, my gaze skimming his desk, looking for correspondence bearing the Bourbon coat-of-arms. But I only saw the usual array of scrolls, papers, and open books, next to all sorts of interesting objects, ranging from nautical instruments, which he ordered from England, to strangely shaped shells he gathered during his morning walks along the shore. A frayed wig lay crumpled up next to a half-empty jug of *kvass,* an oily film on its surface. His precious Augsburg bronze table clock with its curious horizontally placed dial—making it look like a compass even when Father was not at sea—ticked steadily. It was a symbol of the philosophy he lived by; lost time, like death, could not be reversed.

Mother stepped closer to Father. She was swathed in a purple silk gown, lace foaming at her cleavage and sleeves. A diamond headband studded with amethysts sparkled as brightly as her eyes. Her shiny curls, which she wore pinned half up, half down, tumbled onto her shoulders in a luscious wave. If Father mostly looked down-at-the-heels, he preferred his ladies to be elegantly turned out and expensively adorned.

"Ready?" he asked her tenderly, before turning to glance at Feofan Prokopovich, the Archbishop of Novgorod and Father's most trusted adviser. I smiled at him: he had baptized both Anoushka and me and had married our parents. Feofan Prokopovich always found a way of supporting even Father's most daring dreams. He returned my smile warmly and touched his golden cross, which covered his chest from his collarbone to his belt and was studded with pearls, crystal, rubies, and emeralds—the *panagia*—yet his dark brown eyes, assessing Anoushka and me, were as alert as spiders in their nest of wrinkles.

"Petrushka, this is an important moment for you and for us, as it is for All the Russias," Father said in a clipped voice but without turning to look at his grandson.

Petrushka stood and smiled at him, his gaze open, and then he bowed, shyly and sweetly, prompted by Ostermann, who seemed determined that his charge should make a good impression. As he straightened up, the Vice Chancellor clasped Petrushka's still childishly bony shoulder. What had he told the boy to prepare him for this moment? Inheriting the world's largest and wealthiest realm ought to come as no surprise. If Petrushka's face was even paler than before, Ostermann's pride to be witnessing this moment after long years of carefully instructing his charge was palpable. I gathered my thoughts, ready for the elevation of my young nephew to heir of All the Russias.

Father cleared his throat and unearthed a freshly sealed *ukazy* from the mayhem on his desk. No chamberlain was allowed to impose what he took to be order there. Ink glistened on the crisp paper and the Imperial seal had been forced deeply into an oozing mass of crimson sealing wax. His hands trembled ever so slightly when the door opened one more time.

I looked up.

The most favored of all my father's courtiers entered the room: Prince Alexander Danilovich Menshikov. "I beg your pardon for being late," he murmured, bowing to us carefully so as not to make his wig slip. It was as high, white, and curly as a French grandee's. Nothing in his appearance, from the abundant fine lace of his jabot, the brocade jacket with aquamarine buttons, the fabric stiff from gold embroidery—according to Mother, a serf household could live a dozen years on the proceeds of one thread—his ivory silk trousers, and his shoes of polished black calfskin with huge ornamented silver buckles, gave away his humble background. Like Mother, he had risen from dirt-poor beginnings to the most dizzying heights of power. Father and he had met as young boys in the Moscow suburb of Preobrazhensky, which means "transformation" in Russian. It was an auspicious meeting: Menshikov, who peddled his pie-baker father's pastries in the suburb's freezing streets, and the young Tsar, who was shunned by his half-sister, the Regent Sophia, became firm friends. Menshikov accompanied Father on his early travels to Germany, the Netherlands, and England, and finally gained his lifelong admiration for conquering the swampy wilderness around Lake Ladoga, then home to only bears and wolves, where Father founded St. Petersburg. The Tsar's trusted friend Alekasha could do no wrong—rising from abject squalor to Grand Master of the Teutonic Knights, Field Marshal, Senator, and hereditary Prince of Russia, as well as of the Holy Roman Empire.

Father grinned: "Lateness is not a problem but speak once more without permission and I'll train my whip on you, Alekasha." He threateningly wagged his *dubina*, the omnipresent knout dangling at his side, at Menshikov, then winked at his friend and blew him a kiss. Their tiffs fizzled out as quickly as they flared up. Mother, too, gave Menshikov a warm smile. He had spotted her beauty when she had been taken as a prisoner of war by the Russians and had placed her in the Tsar's path.

"I shall gladly take any beating if it is for the glory of Russia," Menshikov chuckled, and casually took a place by the fireside. Petrushka stared at both father and him: the boy was not accustomed to their banter. Court life was a dark and dangerous maze; I should help my nephew understand the forces at work here, I decided. Menshikov leaned against the vast fireplace next to Ostermann, who ignored him, a slight that Menshikov returned. He winked at Petrushka but did not greet him further. Instead he slapped his soft, cognac-colored riding gloves impatiently against one broad peasant palm, as if he had just got off his horse from

Oranienbaum, his neighboring estate, which rivaled Peterhof in beauty, elegance, and luxury.

Father closed his eyes as if pained. Feofan Prokopovich clutched the *panagia* hanging on his breast and soundlessly recited a prayer. I smiled at Petrushka, readying myself to drop into the perfect curtsy my music teacher, the bear-sized yet nimble Herr Schwartz, had taught me.

"Anna Petrovna Romanova. Elizabeth Petrovna Romanova. My daughters, Tsarevny of All the Russias. Our time is an era of great change for which we must be ready. Your nephew and our grandson, Petrushka, is only a boy." Ostermann shifted, barely able to master his impatience to hear the words he longed for, though they had so far been left unsaid: Petrushka, however shunned, was the sole surviving male Romanov heir.

Yet Father kept his eyes fixed on his daughters. "The way from the playroom to the throne is fraught with peril, treason, and hardship. I have sought counsel from God before taking this enormous decision." He nodded to Feofan Prokopovich, and Ostermann laid his other hand on Petrushka's shoulder as well, fingers splayed protectively.

Father stepped around his desk, but instead of going to Petrushka, he placed his hands flat on Anoushka's and my foreheads: heat emanated from his calloused palm. Mother folded her hands in prayer and closed her eyes while Feofan chanted, praising the Lord and the Tsar's decision, his voice as solemn as a bronze bell. A shiver chased down my spine as Father announced: "My daughters, I herewith declare you Crown Princesses of All the Russias—Tsesarevny. Serve the realm. If Russia is not great, we are nothing."

Sweat prickled on my neck as heat rose from deep inside me. This was impossible; my nephew, the last male Romanov, stood just an *arshin* away from us with no title conferred on him. I felt like embracing Petrushka to console him. He should know himself loved, despite everything. Had Father truly brought him here for the sole purpose of witnessing our elevation? Was he mocking us as well, turning the world on its head as he loved to do? Menshikov stared: his gaze sought out Anoushka and me, seeing us in a new light, before his eyes moved on to Petrushka, taking him in as if for the first time. He seemed as surprised as we were, and he disliked being surprised. Petrushka winced as Ostermann's fingers clenched his shoulders before he could mouth an objection. Instead, his little face darkened; his gaze fixed on Father with disappointment and rage.

Feofan gave his feline smile, caressing his gray beard as if it were one of his many Persian cats. Once more he had encouraged my father to express his most daring dreams, going against all custom and tradition. No wonder the Old Believers and the white clergy, the simple country priests, hated him for his courage and progressive thinking. I sought Father's eyes. Now that it was done, he beamed at Anoushka and me, looking elated. Behind him, beneath his desk, I caught a movement: the dwarf d'Acosta lay there curled up like a kitten, his eyes squeezed shut and fists pressed to his ears.

I drew a breath that sounded like a hiccup. Feofan Prokopovich stepped forward, his smile warm and his gaze deep as he drew the Sign of the Cross on our foreheads. "May God's will guide you and His wisdom give you good counsel, Tsesarevny," he said, addressing us by our new title, his dark eyes fathomless.

Ostermann's hands fell slack. Petrushka's lips were pinched into a thin line and his amber gaze lit with rage. Once more he had been cruelly punished for being Alexey's son. In Father's eyes no water in the world would wash him clean of that sin.

"But is the eldest male inheriting the crown *not* God's will?" Anoushka dared to ask, casting a confused glance at our little nephew.

Feofan calmly said: "God's will *is* the Tsar's will. Only He knows the secrets of a ruler's soul."

Mother rushed forward, smothering us in her embrace. "My

daughters are Tsesarevny of All the Russias," she marveled. Warmth and pride rose from deep inside me. Father had trusted us with this enormous honor. I understood him. Russia needed to be able to take its pick from a multitude of heirs. Who knew what fate had in store for Petrushka? D'Acosta left his hiding place, took Petrushka's hand and drew the boy toward us. Petrushka made a perfect bow. His voice faltered as he said: "My sincere congratulations, Tsesarevny Elizabeth and Anoushka."

I embraced him, but he would not return my show of affection. Petrushka stood stiffly, arms hanging, fists clenched. "Don't you ever dare stop calling me Lizenka," I said. My feelings for him had not changed. "I won't," he whispered, tears welling in his eyes.

Menshikov pushed himself upright, clearly wishing to be part of this process. He was seething that Father had left him out of the decision-making. "Don't we have any champagne to celebrate with? That slimy *kvass* on your desk will not do, *minher* Peter. It's worse than horse piss," he said, hiding his humiliation behind a joke. Father grinned at him as Menshikov addressed some additional words to him in Dutch, which was their secret language, reminding him of their youth.

"Ostermann, you may take the boy back to St. Petersburg," ordered Father, not even looking at Petrushka. He had neither touched the boy nor directly spoken to him. But Petrushka would have none of it. Instead of bowing and leaving, he wriggled out of Ostermann's grasp.

"No! I do not want to return to that stuffy place. What are you punishing me for? I have done nothing wrong. If my father was a traitor, I am not!" Tears overwhelmed him, and I bit my lip. "Grandfather, please, allow me to stay. I want to feed the fish with Aunt Lizenka. She said I could be captain of a boat—"

Father turned his back on him, ignoring Petrushka's plea. Ostermann seized the boy, clutching both his upper arms. "I, too, have a fishpond in my garden. And we can study the world's most famous seafarers in our lessons—"

"No! Lizenka is *fun*! I want to be with her." Petrushka fought him.

I shook my head at him, just enough for him to notice: he was making things worse for himself. He ceased struggling, hanging limp in Ostermann's grip, looking at me with utter despair. Father stood tall, towering over the boy, his eyes glacial. If he had once vilified his half-sister Sophia, a woman, for assuming the Regency in his and his half-brother's name, today he had elevated Anoushka and me beyond our imagining. Then, he turned to stare out of the window. His shoulders were slumped, weighed down by questions. He looked out as if expecting the answers to arrive by messenger.

Ostermann grimaced, straightened his gouty leg, and bowed, before bundling a still-protesting Petrushka out of the door. We waited until it had closed and the sound of their footsteps had faded.

"*Starik*," Mother whispered—*old man*, her nickname for him—as she stepped up to Father. She laid his hand on her belly in a movement that made me blush. "God may still grant us a son." She smiled hopefully. Father nodded curtly. We lowered our eyes. Was she really still hoping for it to happen? Even we knew it would not.

"Indeed," my father said. "Tsesarevny, you are not to rule Russia. But you can pass on the right to its crown by marriage and childbirth."

"Marriage? Has there been word from France?" I asked. "Now that I am a Tsesarevna, Versailles has all the more reason to accept my hand, doesn't it?"

My parents swapped glances. Prokopovich piously folded his hands.

Better rule marriage out, the Leshy spirit's taunting words rang in my mind.

"Good things take a while to happen," my father said casually, yet his face twitched. He was furious about Versailles's delaying tactics. Mother raised her eyebrows in a silent warning to me: better leave it there, or one of his fits might be the result. "The King of France—or another good husband who reigns over a powerful country," she said soothingly.

A husband to rein you in.

Father cast her a grateful glance—she alone knew how to handle his epileptic fits—and clapped his hands. The doors were flung open. "Come now," he said, "let us celebrate my new heirs. I have one last surprise for you today. Somebody who is a fount of wisdom when it comes to life as a married Tsarevna!"

13

"Aunt Pasha!" I called delightedly as Tsar Ivan's widow, the Tsaritsa Praskovia, pushed her way into the little study. Since her husband's death almost thirty years ago, she had worn only soot-colored clothes. When I had been a child, I had thought she looked like one of Father's ships in full sail, all rigged out in black. An opaque dark veil covered her raven hair, which was frosted with gray and adorned with strings of charcoal-tinted pearls, each as large as a chickpea. Her dark train, too, was embroidered with a shower of black pearls and jet crystals, but even their luster did not lighten her appearance. She was well known to Anoushka and me: Aunt Pasha had taken care of us in her beautiful countryside palace of Izmailov near Moscow each time Mother had followed Father, be it on travels in Europe or into battle.

Time had not changed our aunt, perhaps because Father looked after her so generously. Once her daughters, the Tsarevny Anna and Ekaterina Ivanovna, had been so splendidly married off to their German dukes, Father kept Aunt Pasha in great comfort: nothing benefits a woman's looks more than a full purse and a well-stocked pantry. Her round face was hardly wrinkled, and her sour-cherry eyes twinkled as she assessed us as cunningly as when she had caught us as children playing dress-up with her precious costume chest. While Aunt Pasha had had her own company of actors, we had not been supposed to stage plays of our own.

Now she curtsied deeply to us. "Tsarevny! Elizabeth and Anoushka—my little sunshine nieces," she cooed.

"Please do not, Aunt Pasha. Rise." I stepped forward to help her up and spotted a woman standing on the threshold directly behind her. I looked at her, surprised. Her richly embroidered dress—its cyclamen color seemed oddly familiar; was that not one of my St. Petersburg castoffs?—hung slack on her thin frame, and her scalp showed bald patches where whole clumps of her straggly black hair had been torn out. The skin about her blackbird eyes looked bruised and her face marked, as if from a bad fall. Anoushka, too, had noticed her and sharply drew in her breath as the stranger's pinched lips parted in a mockery of a smile, which made us both recoil. We bumped into Mother, who stood behind us like a wall, forcing us toward the stranger. A couple of her teeth were missing, as if knocked out.

"How you have grown, Cousins Elizabeth and Anoushka," the stranger said to us.

14

Anoushka and I swapped a quick glance, in which surprise, doubt, and apprehension mingled. Cousins? The woman was clearly mad. In her house in Izmailov, Aunt Pasha surrounded herself with a court of holy men, fools, scoundrels, beggars, gypsies, and other waifs and strays. She fed, clothed, and housed them, as had been the tradition in olden days. Normally they fled in terror and hid at the thought of having to meet Father; this woman might be an exception to the rule, coming to Peterhof to seek him out. The poor creature looked as if she had tumbled from a carriage, become caught in the reins, and been dragged along. I was ready to greet her with pity and kindness when I met her stare, which was inky with jealous hostility. She took it all in—my primrose-yellow silk dress, cut according to the latest French fashion, its stomacher tight and sparkling with pearls and crystals, and the skirt deliciously, exaggeratedly full. Ounces of gold and silver had been added to the thread, which dainty hands had fed through the precious gown in thin needles to embroider it all over; intricate patterns of pearls and crystals gleamed like a sprinkle of sunlight. Many *arshin* of Lyons lace adorned the hem and sleeves, as well as my full cleavage.

"Look who is back from her Duchy in Mecklenburg: my daughter, your darling cousin Ekaterina Ivanovna," Aunt Pasha said.

Anoushka and I swapped a shocked look. So this was one of our cousins Ivanovna, whose good luck and fortune as a married Tsarevna Anoushka and I had envied just weeks ago!

Before we could greet her, Ekaterina turned away, her voice chiding: "Come now, meet the family. For God's sake—do not claw at my skirts. Your fingers are grimy." Behind her scant figure, a pale young girl was hiding, clutching the stiff fabric of Ekaterina's dress—yes, it was one of my castoffs!—with really rather grubby little hands. Her slanted dark eyes were set in a curiously round, plain face. She cowered like the mouse I kept in my bedroom, only my pet was better fed and cared for. The girl stared, taking it all in: my giant of a father, leaning against the windowsill, where the rays of the afternoon sun framed him like a halo; my mother, sparkling like a jewel casket; Aunt Pasha, who opened her arms welcomingly, beaming a wide smile; Menshikov's relaxed demeanor; and finally Feofan Prokopovich, who bowed his head in a polite greeting.

Ekaterina pulled the child close. They both curtsied deeply, which revealed the bald patches on her scalp. "I am back, dearest Father-uncle, as my husband left much to be desired." She ever so slightly, cunningly, offered her maimed face to the bright light. My father chewed his lip, weighing her brutally mutilated looks. Her hair should grow again. His cook would fatten her up. Possibly those missing teeth could be fixed: the German Quarter in Moscow was home to an ivory carver, if not two.

"Welcome back, Ekaterina Ivanovna, my niece. And who is this?" Father openly appraised the child, who returned his gaze dully.

"This? This is the son and heir I failed to give my husband, the Duke, much to his displeasure," Ekaterina said. "Meet my daughter Christine, Princess of Mecklenburg. I hope for her to be brought up here in Russia as a Romanov."

Aunt Pasha smiled at my mother, but her eyebrows were raised expectantly. Even as a Tsar's widow, she still had to make sure to bring in her harvest and hustle for what she thought was her due.

Mother took the cue: "Dearest Pasha, you have looked after Anoushka and Lizenka so well whenever I accompanied the Tsar. We are so grateful for all the kindness you have shown them—and me. Princess Christine is most welcome here. She is a Romanov and will be treated like my daughters' younger sister."

Anoushka and I stooped, kissing the child on both cheeks; her skin and hair smelled of the cheap camphor soap used to keep nits at bay. Christine's dark features placed her clearly within Aunt Pasha's side of the family, the Saltykovs. I cast about for something friendly to say to Ekaterina and noticed another woman sidling up to Aunt Pasha. I almost recoiled but caught myself in time: this was Maja, my aunt's trusted maid. The poor woman was harelipped, a terrible punishment meted out at birth. The skin between her thin upper lip and wide nostrils lay open in an awful gash, showing gums and yellow teeth. Yet Maja was already Aunt Pasha's maid when our uncle Tsar Ivan chose her as his bride, being led by his advisers past a bevy of shy, innocent boyars' daughters in the Kremlin Hall of Facets, as he had been too ill to walk himself.

"Tsarevny," Maja lisped, and curtsied to us.

"Maja." Anoushka smiled at her. "How good to see you. I still remember how you spoiled us with hot chocolate from Spain the first time we arrived in Izmailov as young girls."

"True," I chimed in. "And you took us to the Wolf House to see the polar bear cubs that had been born there, before showing me the shortcut through the Babylon, the maze in Izmailov. What luck to look after three generations of Romanovs, Maja—now that Christine is here."

Maja blushed. "You are too kind, Tsarevny, to remember a humble woman like me at all. It will be my joy to look after Her Highness." She smiled at Christine, who recoiled, looking aghast. "Would you like some chocolate, too?" Maja asked, having suffered much worse reactions a thousand times over, due to her looks. The girl shied away, hiding behind her mother and pointing her fingers in horns, a sign against the Evil Eye. "*Hexe*," she shrieked in German. "*Böse, böse Hexe*."

"What is she saying?" Aunt Pasha frowned.

Ekaterina shrugged. "Nothing but the truth. She is calling Maja an evil witch."

Maja flushed.

"Go," Aunt Pasha said curtly, and the maid fled.

"This is quite a reunion," Mother smoothed things over. "Let us celebrate! The only one missing is your other daughter, dearest Pasha. What a shame not to have Anna Ivanovna here. That is the downside of marrying off your daughters abroad."

"How is Anna doing in her Duchy of Courland?" Father asked, while the dwarf d'Acosta circled Christine and mimicked Maja, pulling up his lip, which made the child giggle. Then he tugged her dress and dashed off, inviting her to a game of "it."

"Why? Does Anna not report regularly to you, the Tsar, as is her duty?" Pasha purred, clearly content to have achieved her goal of placing her granddaughter Christine in the Imperial household.

"She does." Father sighed. "Sometimes, at least. Mostly she asks for a more generous personal purse."

"I apologize for my daughter's rotten behavior. Anna never ceases to shame her house," Aunt Pasha snorted. "She has taken up with a former groom. I have forgotten his name. Brinn or Bronn or something like that. He lives with her in the palace."

Her words shocked me, and Anoushka, too, stared at me, wide-eyed. Not bad enough that Ekaterina had left her husband, her palace, and her Duchy! Aunt Pasha's other daughter, the Duchess of Courland, Anna Ivanovna, "lived" with a groom. The thought of any contact with such hairy, smelly, sweaty, and coarse fellows as grooms was horrid to us. What about her husband, the Duke?

"A groom? It's Anna Ivanovna the Terrible indeed!" d'Acosta chuckled. He had left Christine standing in the middle of their game, panting and red-cheeked. The little man then hopped about, neighing, and clapping his hands to mimic the sound of hooves. The child picked up on the game and followed him around.

"Behave, Christine. Out, creature!" Aunt Pasha thundered, kicking him squarely on his little backside. If she, as Anna Ivanovna's mother, was allowed to chide her wayward daughter in public, a jester and an imp certainly was not. "Go and stuff your ugly face in the kitchens."

D'Acosta was unabashed: he laughed and now pretended to eat, gulping, eyes bulging, cheeks distended. "In Russia we don't need bread and milk. We devour each other instead, blood and bone and all!"

"Enough!" Mother ordered, her tone of voice making d'Acosta retreat anew beneath Father's desk, his vantage point of observation.

"I thought Cousin Anna Ivanovna was *married* to the Duke in Courland?" Anoushka dared to ask. Our Ivanovna cousins' marriages and lives were the only indication of our own likely future that we had. Seeing Ekaterina, and hearing about Anna, tinged my excitement with hesitation, if not serious doubt—and fear.

"Well, yes. Or she was, at least." Mother dabbed her eyes in a show of sympathy. "For three days anyway. Such a terrible, unjust tragedy."

"Ha! I wish I had been so lucky as to enjoy such a brief marriage. Instead I had to suffer almost a decade of—all this." Ekaterina waved one hand to encompass her own battered appearance, blinking away tears.

"What happened after those three days to Anna's Duke?" I asked.

"May God have mercy on his soul." Aunt Pasha crossed herself using three fingers. "He had feasted so much at the wedding that he fell sick when leaving St. Petersburg, three days after the celebrations. He tumbled from the sled, fell headfirst into the snow, and suffocated."

"My God," I gasped. "Why did Anna then not return to live with you, Aunt Pasha?"

"She has to hold Courland for Russia." Father shrugged.

"Also her husband had spent all her dowry already to settle his gambling debts. So who would have her now?" Ekaterina said. "It's a common theme among Germanic dukes. Though mine beats all records. He never returned the dowries he received with his two first wives, whom he divorced, leaving the poor women just as penniless and undesirable as I am today."

"What about the emerald I gave him at your wedding? It was huge—as big as a walnut. And my other gift, the four hundred trained soldiers in uniform?" Menshikov inquired.

"That bauble? He split it into a thousand pieces long since," Ekaterina said. "And the men were sold off as foreign mercenaries."

"You want yourself to be seen as a generous prince, Menshikov, yet you keep accounts like the baker's son you were," Pasha cut in. "Anna is lucky to have Courland for her home. A stable boy or groom or whatever this guy Biren is, is the best she can hope for now, the wretch." She shook her head as if to say: *What did I do wrong?*

"We all make mistakes," Father declared, tired of the bickering. "Welcome back, Ekaterina. My brother's daughters are like my own. Young Christine will be raised as a Romanov. Menshikov, stop squabbling over a handful of heyducks, because that is what your so-called soldiers were. Make yourself useful and get champagne— lots of it. Let us toast Anoushka and Lizenka," he ordered.

"Toasting the girls?" Aunt Pasha asked, eager to please Father. "Do we finally have news from Versailles? I shall be the first to cheer that."

"Not quite yet," I said, blushing.

"Father just made us Tsesarevny." Anoushka smiled. "Even if we will never rule, we will pass on the right to the Russian throne."

"Tsesarevny! Did you come up with this grand new title, Feofan Prokopovich? Trust you and your spin on words. How wonderful!" Aunt Pasha almost suffocated us in her embrace; her gown's scent of myrrh and cloves was intoxicating. She smelled like a week of Yuletide. As I came up for air, I saw Ekaterina Ivanovna snatching her daughter's hand, making the child reel. I sensed my cousin's thoughts, twisting and turning like a caged weasel. What would her life back in Russia be like? I felt pity for her: her bed had been made by others, and she had been forced to lie in it.

Pasha's voice was treacly as she repeated: "Tsesarevny of All the Russias. I must tell Anna Ivanovna that in my next letter. That should shatter the eternal boredom of her life in Courland. Apparently she spends all day lying on a bearskin and lathering herself in butter."

"That would take a lot of butter," Ekaterina giggled.

"Enough. Here is the champagne." Father seized two bottles from Menshikov's hands, and there was more clasped in the crook of his elbows and beneath his armpits. The morning had been too dry for his taste already. Two chamberlains followed, carrying a silver vat large enough for little Christine to bathe in. It was filled with roughly hewn chippings from the Peterhof icehouse and a dozen or so more bottles.

"To my beautiful daughters!" Mother raised her brilliantly colored Murano chalice, which broke the bright light of a Peterhof noon into prisms. The champagne was as frothy as a frivolous joke and tickled my nose when I took a sip. Menshikov burped after emptying a first glass bottoms up and went immediately for a refill. Ekaterina had downed three glasses before I had finished half of mine, and she made two spare, empty goblets discreetly disappear into the folds of my old dress: their gilt rims should fetch a good price in the *gostiny dvor*. Christine was cross-eyed with tiredness, crawling beneath Father's desk to join d'Acosta. Mother and Aunt Pasha chatted of old times. Father leaned by the open window on his own before beckoning me closer to say: "To your health and Russia's glory, my Lizenka, little chicken. Did you know that people in Versailles have more champagne than blood in their veins?"

As we stood there by the vista of the Bay of Finland, my love for him linked the two of us like the opposite ends of a bracelet as if the others were not even present.

Menshikov with his usual jealousy would have none of it. He stepped up to us and raised his glass. "What a decision! Here's to the Tsesarevny. But how come you did not consult me at all?"

"How come I do not thrash you bloody?" Father smacked him playfully with the *dubina*. "Your patronym should be *insolent*, Menshikov."

I toasted them: "To the glory of Russia, always." I felt warm and loved, surrounded by friends and family, happy ever after. Though as I turned back to the room, my eyes met Ekaterina Ivanovna's hungry dark gaze before she quickly averted it. And just like that I remembered Anoushka's question, back in Grandfather Alexis's throne room in Kolomenskoye:

"Do you think they ever mind?"

"Mind what?"

"That we are now the first ladies in Russia, even though mad Ivan was Father's elder brother and a reigning Tsar, too."

Every blessing can be a curse, and too many people wanted what I had: I was the Tsar's daughter.

15

The summer flew by. As the sweet season gave way to falling leaves and chilly winds, we joined Father in Riga, a stronghold of the powerful Hanseatic League and formerly the seat of the Order of the Teutonic Knights. The city was the trump in his newly stacked pack of political cards, the Western Baltics, now part of All the Russias for eternity. In the Great Hall of Dünamünde Fortress, fires roared, servants scuttled from kitchen to table to avoid a beating if the food grew cold, and acrobats somersaulted over the flagstones or juggled with shiny wooden clubs.

"Who is the sour-looking fellow over there?" I asked my mother: opposite us, a young man held himself upright with difficulty; his slight build and pallor singled him out among the red-faced, shouting revelers. He fastidiously avoided flying food and patently disliked having drink spilled over his new, well-tailored clothes. As other men shoved and encouraged him, half jovial, half annoyed, he refused either to link elbows with them or to join in with raucous drinking songs, curtly shaking his head. Everything about his face was thin: his nose, lips, even the lids and lashes of his pale blue eyes, making him look washed out.

"That is Karl, Duke of Holstein," she said. "He might also be heir to the Swedish throne, if things go just a little bit his way." My mother lazily licked her fingers clean of the damson schnapps and honey marinade in which Father's cook had lathered three hundred hares, before slow-roasting them in the colossal fireplaces of the fortress's kitchen. The dark flesh flaked off the bone deliciously.

"After twenty years of the Great Northern War and Russia fighting against Sweden, the heir to its throne is sitting at our table. It's truly an era of great change," I said, choosing some pickled green walnuts from a crystal bowl.

"He might do more than that." Mother raised her glass to him, a gesture he gallantly returned. When he then also toasted me, his pale gaze skimmed my bare shoulders and throat: I wore a beautiful emerald collier with matching earrings. Each gem was as large as an acorn.

I nodded coolly to him. "What else could he ask for?"

"How about a Tsesarevna's hand in marriage?" My mother smiled.

"*A* Tsesarevna?" I teased, as the Duke held out his eagle cup— the chalice that Father had designed for his drinking games, standing an elbow-span high—for a third refill. Did he really have the stomach for this? Possibly one had to be Russian to live, eat, and drink like us. "*Either* of us will do. Anoushka or me?"

"Oh, Lizenka." Mother simply kissed my forehead, leaving me mute with surprise. She must be mistaken. Father would never sell us off as he had our cousins Ekaterina and Anna Ivanovna, to be beaten up and maimed, or widowed and lingering in poverty.

Karl von Holstein bit his fingernails and gulped down his To-kay. A skinny little man with shaky prospects, he was not exactly what I had had in mind when I had dared to climb into the Go-losov Ravine and seek out the Leshy spirit, even if he might one day rule Sweden. Yet such a mismatch might make the evil creature laugh all the harder.

"Well, I will marry the King of France, of course," I observed.

"Hmm. Yes. We shall see. Talks with Versailles are still proceeding," Mother said carefully. "The French have come up with a new obstacle to the match: they object to you keeping your faith. Father will never give in on that. In Versailles too many cooks clearly spoil the broth."

I sullenly sipped my wine. So much for celebrating this Yuletide as the Royal French bride-to-be.

In the hall the musicians played on, battling against the brawling and shouting, while servants skidded in puddles of wine, vodka, and vomit. "Louder, you people!" Father shouted, chucking a pewter goblet at the conductor, hitting the man on the shoulder. "What am I paying you for? I want this to be a civilized dinner, not a herd of pigs around the trough!"

Karl von Holstein rose and came straight to our table, but God, was he plain: he was visibly bowlegged, even in his high, obviously new boots, and his fine linen shirt hung awkwardly from thin, stooped shoulders.

"Tsesarevna," he said in a hard German accent. He fixed his moist gaze on me and then bowed. I kept a straight face. No doubt his palms were sweaty too. "Would you do me the honor of opening the dance with me?"

"What don't I do for Russia?" I said under my breath to Mother, rolling my eyes at Anoushka while I began to get to my feet.

But my sister beat me to it. "Gladly, Your Grace," she cooed, and swiftly gathered up her peach-colored damask skirts. Her cheeks were flushed as she rose and fixed her shiny gaze on Karl.

The Duke of Holstein did not miss a beat but gallantly took Anoushka's outstretched hand and led her into the dance.

16

"Listen to it, Elizabeth!" Anoushka seized my wrist, making me replace my parrot hurriedly on its perch before she pulled me along. "Isn't it just divine? It sounds like, like . . ." She listened rapt with pleasure to the din beneath the Winter Palace's windows, where a concert was in progress. I barely refrained from pressing my hands to my ears. To me it sounded as appealing as little Christine scratching her nails over the windowpanes out of boredom and anger. A thin silver thread of a melody hung suspended in the air.

"Come, let us have a look," I said and opened the window. We both poked our heads outside, the cold air greeting us like a slap. The palace's façade sparkled in the waxen late autumn sun, its frosty rays turning the courtyard's cobblestones to myriad mirrors. We craned our necks: the musicians sat in the main thoroughfare, dwarfed by the soaring building. Icy gusts hit them, cruelly lifting jacket tails, and turning lips blue. The drummer's fingers froze to his sticks; the harpsichord player's fingertips stuck to the ivory keys. He grimaced before playing on, which was too funny for words. Best of all, courtiers, servants, and supplicants, unable to pass by, jammed the passages and walkways all around, while sleds were forced to wait in line, unable to move on. The reluctant observers shouted and shook their fists.

"Move, you morons!"

"I've got a mind to take a whip to you."

"Bloody foreigners, always the worst ideas!"

"How divine—and so romantic, Lizenka," Anoushka sighed before this ill-devised spectacle. "Why would Karl do that? There can only be one reason, can't there? He wants me to be his Duchess of Holstein. And—" she winked at me "—he is not exactly a German farmer! He might one day be King of Sweden. Imagine, then we will both be Queens."

As the music stopped, traffic through the main gateway picked up, people and sleds spilling out onto the vast square in front of the palace. The musicians were served mulled wine as well as *pierogi* filled with dried berries and thick *smetana*: I recognized my mother's wisdom in that gesture, as the men's contented chatter rose to our window. They should return to Holstein having only the best things to say about the Tsarina of All the Russias.

"Such a surprise!" Anoushka's cheeks were flushed from both the cold and her excitement. "Just imagine, if I had not chanced upon you in here, I would not have heard any of it. I had better go to the *banja*. A good whipping with a birch branch will make my skin glow for the ball tonight." She blew me two excited kisses and then left, gracefully maneuvering her wide skirts through the doorway, which Father had had built larger than ever before in Russia to accommodate the Western style of dress.

I waited until the sound of her steps, which gathered pace until she was running like a little girl, had faded away. The concert, a surprise? I retrieved a note from the folds of my dress. My maid had slipped it to me as I returned from my morning ride on the Karelian Plains. I had read it while soaking in my bathtub, the water's heat soothing my aching muscles, its rosewater scent heightening my senses. The elegant, obviously well-bred hand that even I could read well had become smeared with steam and droplets, making the stilted words dissolve before me. But not before I had read the message secretly delivered to me.

Tsesarevna Elizabeth,

It is my pleasure to invite you to a concert of the best music my country has to offer. May each of our days be as sweet as their melodies.

Karl von Holstein

I did not know which pained me more: the fact that the carefully worded message had clearly been dictated to the prince by an overcautious adviser or Anoushka's excitement. Her mood these days was as ebullient and capricious as the hundreds of butterflies that briefly settled to suck nectar from the buddleia bushes in Peterhof.

I flattened Karl's note on the windowsill before folding it into a dart, as an equerry in Kolomenskoye had once taught me to do. It looked like a bird with wings, just magic. I let it fly; it sailed across the room, straight into the fireplace. What a shot! The flames rose, taking hold of the paper. With a pop and a crackle, it curled in futile resistance, glowing blue and then orange before crumbling to ashes.

Anoushka would never know.

17

If Aunt Pasha ever wrote to her daughter Anna Ivanovna, Duchess of Courland, about Anoushka and me being made Tsesarevny, I did not know. Mother and daughter were never to meet again. Aunt Pasha, who habitually slept with her window open, fell ill as a chilly October took hold of St. Petersburg. She at first coughed lightly, then soon brought up blood. As her fever rose, Father ordered Ekaterina back from Izmailov, where she had chosen to live with little Christine. "St. Petersburg," she had decided, thinking of her estranged husband, "is still much too close to Mecklenburg. The brute may reach it in three days' forced march and give me my last hiding." An ebony horsehair wig now hid the bald patches on her scalp, and, to make amends for the match he had forced on her, Father had had fake ivory teeth carved for her, which she squeezed into her gums.

Anna Ivanovna in the Courland capital of Mitau, however, was notified too late. Aunt Pasha dictated a last letter to Anna, her voice rasping and her body wracked by coughing, not wanting to bear a grudge into the afterlife: *My ailments increase hourly; I suffer so greatly that I despair of life. Pray for me, Anna; I have heard that you consider yourself under a curse from me, but I forgive you everything and absolve you from every sin you may have committed before me.*

As Aunt Pasha lay in state, Ekaterina Ivanovna's wailing scared little Christine into hiding in my skirts. I embraced her, wondering how she could still be so scrawny; Father's cook said that she stole the food off everyone's plate, given half a chance. I offered the child my monkeys and parrots to divert her, while Pasha's hare-lipped maid Maja took up position at the foot of her mistress's deathbed. When Christine saw her, she hissed in German: *"Unge-heuer! Fahr zur Hölle!"*

"Hush now," I scolded her, needing no translation: she had called the poor woman a monstrous creature who belonged in Hell. Ekaterina pulled Christine close, eyeing Maja, both of them whispering and pulling faces.

"Shall I send to Izmailov for the Tsaritsa Praskovia's priest to conduct her wake?" I asked Maja, using Aunt Pasha's real name and formal title out of respect.

Maja's face was waxen with grief. "No. I beg to stay with my mistress on my own. She was placed in my care as a toddler. I accompanied her to the Kremlin Hall of Facets, where her beauty bewitched Tsar Ivan. I have assisted at each of her childbeds and dressed her daughters, the Tsarevny Ivanovna, for their own weddings. Now my prayers shall see the Tsaritsa Praskovia into the afterlife."

"So be it." I hesitated. "What will you do after the funeral? Will you join Ekaterina in Izmailov?"

Maja shook her head, snot and tears mingling on her face. Her ragged breathing sounded as if iron chains had wrapped themselves around her heart, which had beaten only for Aunt Pasha and her family. I touched my cheek: I had taken my own beauty for granted as long as I lived. "Bring a jug of vodka and keep it filled. Unleavened bread and salt to ease my aunt's passage," I ordered a page boy. Maja curtsied and kissed my hand before crouching at her mistress's feet, at first crying silently and then wailing in a high, ululating sound that raised the hairs on my neck.

If I had not been able to save our nurse Illinchaya in Kolomenskoye, I could at least help another loyal servant. Following Pasha's funeral in the Saints Peter and Paul Cathedral, I arranged for Maja's journey to Courland, where Aunt Pasha's younger daughter, my cousin Anna Ivanovna, should welcome her.

I was sure never to see the wretched woman again.

18

"Lizenka!" Petrushka called out as I stepped into his little study. Sunshine and fresh air flooded the stuffy room in my wake, and the boy flung down his quill. Count Ostermann peevishly tightened his silk cravat against the draft. "My gout, Tsesarevna," he murmured.

"If anything, springtime is good for your . . . er, gout, Ostermann," I teased. His ailment mysteriously manifested itself only when it suited him, especially in his right hand when asked to sign unwelcome documents. At other times he could write easily enough. I cast an eye over Petrushka's desk, which was covered in dissertations, mostly written in Ostermann's own slanted hand. No Russian ever wrote like this—if he could write at all.

"I have been praying every night that you would come. I have been praying for so long!" Petrushka lunged at me; we had not met since Anoushka's and my elevation to Tsesarevny. I struggled in his almost suffocating embrace, and then held him close, remembering that moment. If Father's hostility must be wounding for him, he showed no bitterness against us. Good. Anoushka and I were young women, ready to further Russia's interests by marrying and giving life to sons. The more heirs the realm had, the better. Only Russia counted.

"Well, here I am. Do you still want to be captain of a boat?"

He nodded.

"We will have to wait until the last ice floes melt, but we can do some training in advance, if you are game?"

"Oh, I am!" Petrushka was taller than me already, but the dark, deep shadows underneath his golden eyes had taken up permanent residence. God, did that boy ever see the sun? Father was too cruel. How could he make a child pay for its father's sins? Giving the boy Ostermann as a tutor had been a gesture of mercy on Mother's part, but the broadest and best education was not worth looking like a maggot. "Enough studying, Ostermann," I decided, ignoring the German's sour look. Surely, he feasted every morning on a bottle of vinegar straight after rising from the hard, folding field bed he slept on.

"I take my orders from the Tsar," he said icily, gathering his papers.

"As you should. You have everything to thank him for," I said and kicked the door to the study shut. Petrushka and I skipped out into the corridor, holding hands, but he was quickly out of breath and coughing. I could not recall having visited this end of the Winter Palace before: the high windows let in drafts, and the floorboards were warped with damp. Why was Petrushka left to linger here; did Father want him to die of consumption? The thought was too horrible to consider.

"Let us race," I said, eager to leave. "Whoever reaches the Tsar's antechambers first, wins."

"I am not admitted there," he said, holding back. "The Tsar has not called for me ever, since . . . Peterhof." He still reeled from the humiliation. I looked at him sympathetically, yet I would not lie to him. The boy expected more from me. Petrushka continued, "The Tsar killed my father because he was a traitor. But my godfather Alexis Dolgoruky told me the truth. My father wanted to save Russia from Grandfather's wicked Western ways."

"Where on earth did you hear that expression? Better listen to Ostermann instead of your godfather Dolgoruky," I warned him. Ever since Alexey's death, Petrushka's godfather had been the most eminent of the Old Believers. How did he gain access to my nephew? "Never—ever—say that again!" I suddenly felt terrified for his young life if somebody heard him speak like this. "Let us go. I will make sure the Tsar doesn't see us." I took his hand. "Ready, steady—go!"

Petrushka shrieked as I set off. He chased behind me. At first our footsteps echoed under a simple stucco ceiling, but after that we slid down the banisters of grand staircases and crossed the chessboard marble floors of vast staterooms. "Come on, let us play hopscotch!" I laughed. We reached the Tsar's antechamber, panting and flushed. Here Father stored the artworks that had been purchased for him, but not yet properly displayed.

"How about a round of *kokolores*?" I eyed the broad windowsills, high skirting boards, and the chairs stacked with canvases. A table piled high with bottles and glasses was surrounded by antique statues; above it hung three sturdy chandeliers. Perfect: they should take my weight.

"I don't know the rules. Is it similar to chess?"

I sighed. "What is Ostermann teaching you? How can you be captain of a boat if you don't know *kokolores*?"

"At the moment I am not even a simple sailor," he said, matter-of-fact. "If Grandfather was allowed, he should cast me overboard, declaring me useless ballast."

"Don't ever say that again!" I was shocked.

My nephew shrugged, tears welling up, his pale face waxen.

I could not help but embrace and kiss him. "Well, knowing *kokolores* might come in handy at any time. The rules are easy. You have to cross the room without touching the floor, as if swinging on the ropes of a ship."

"The whole room?" His eyes lit up.

"Yes. And if you hesitate too long, I will make you cross it twice," I giggled. "Go!" I leaped onto a chair, which skidded on the shiny inlaid parquet, making a painting topple. As I seized the frame, it broke and, with a sharp ripping sound, my hand went straight through the canvas: it was a Dutch painting by an artist with an unpronounceable name, *Van* this or *Ver* that, showing a buxom parlormaid pouring milk from a jug in the hazy morning light. I let my fingers wiggle in rabbit ears above her head, and Petrushka laughed so hard he hiccupped. His turn: he climbed on a chest of drawers and swung from a gilt wall sconce, before reaching for the velvet curtains. He kicked over a statue of a young man, who was naked but for a pair of winged sandals. It smashed to pieces, the severed head's expression one of reproach. Petrushka was catching up with me! I lurched for one of the crystal chandeliers. It creaked and swung as I gained momentum. My feet aimed for the big table, strewn with vodka bottles, glasses, and chewing tobacco. From there I could make it to the door and take the game.

"I'll win, little snail," I laughed, just as brisk footsteps and voices approached, echoing down the corridor. I froze, still hanging from the chandelier. "Silence now," I mouthed. Petrushka cowered on the windowsill, half hidden by the embroidered velvet curtains, pale and witless with fear. What Father might do when he caught him here was anyone's guess. A flogging would be getting off lightly.

I let go, and my soft slippers allowed me to land soundlessly. I crawled underneath the table, motioning Petrushka to join me in the hiding place, just before the door opened. I drew the Persian carpet, which served as a tablecloth, over Petrushka and me, leaving a narrow gap. He snuggled up to me, his scared eyes huge in his narrow face. I held him close as Father, Mother, some guards, and Feofan Prokopovich crossed the room toward Father's study. The Tsar shoved the guards back out into the hall, toward us. "Out! This is not for your grimy ears." Then he turned to Mother: "I have taken a decision that no Tsar before me has. Feofan Prokopovich has once more supported me in my daring." I pulled Petrushka closer. When Father and Feofan were together, not even the sky was the limit for their visionary ideas. He continued to Mother: "I wish to reward you for all and everything you have done for me and for Russia. Listen well, *matka*," he said, calling her by her pet name, before shutting the door to his study.

In our hiding place in the antechamber, Petrushka wrapped his

gangly limbs around me and pressed his nose against my flesh—
had he not been my nephew, it might have felt inappropriate. "You
are so soft and warm," he said incredulously. "How do you do that?"

"A girl's trick," I said, crawling out from under the table.

He followed me but looked forlorn. "Is the *kokolores* over? As
soon as I like something, or somebody, it stops, or they go away."

"I am sorry," I said, eyeing the damage we had done, while
inside the study Mother gasped audibly in surprise, and Father
laughed, the sound full of pride and emotion.

I ached with curiosity. What else apart from his decision to el-
evate Anoushka and me to Tsesarevny had Father come up with?
How exciting to be alive!

"Do you mind?" Petrushka interrupted my thoughts as he
seized the vodka carafe from the table. He raised it to his rosy boy's
lips and gulped, the spirit running over his cheeks.

"Don't, Petrushka." I gently took the half-empty carafe from
him.

"At least now I can face Ostermann again." He swayed and stuck
some of the chewing tobacco beneath his upper lip, noisily sucking
it and casting me a challenging glance. God, where had he learned
this? One could blame Ostermann for many things, but not for encouraging a boy's debauchery. His long, thin fingers, which had
nothing childish about them any more, clutched mine as I walked
him back to his study.

At the door he cupped my face in his hands and pulled it
close to his. I recoiled, surprised, and also because his gums were
stained blood-red. "Promise me, Lizenka," he slurred, his eyes
glazed. "Promise always to love me as no one else does. Promise
never to leave me."

"Well, of course. Whatever else would I do?" I gently freed
myself from his grip. "We'll have so much fun together."

"Like what?"

"Plenty of things! Hunting trips in spring, picnics in summer, foraging for mushrooms in autumn, and ice-skating and sledging in winter. That's just for starters."

"How wonderful!" Petrushka clapped his hands but then stared hard at me. "If you love someone else more than me, I shall punish him."

I caught my breath, shocked at his resemblance to Father when he threatened one of his cronies. Then I said playfully: "Yes. On the stake with the rascal!" I ruffled his hair, pushing him back into the study, though Ostermann had disappeared. Admittedly, as Vice Chancellor of Russia, besides being Petrushka's tutor, he had better things to do than count the flies on the wall.

That afternoon, when I had sought out Petrushka from pity for a lonely child, the Leshy spirit down in the Golosov Ravine must have observed our childish joy through its veil of sulfur stench. Did it foresee the forces that would soon tear apart my family and all our lives? *Curse the Romanovs!* Already as I walked away, wondering what Mother had learned from Father and which other changes were afoot in a realm so in want of an heir, I had dismissed Petrushka's threat.

19

Only a couple of days later, I chanced upon my mother in my rooms. The blue haze of a St. Petersburg spring morning blended the heavens and the river, a veil of silver softening any hard edge, when I came in from my morning ride, wearing breeches, high boots, and a simple white blouse, my hair tucked up in a bun beneath a flat Polish triangular hat. She stood by my desk, studying drawings for a new gown.

"Mother, welcome." I kissed her, glancing at the drawing of a stately gown of crimson velvet, stiffly embroidered in gold thread. Besides that, both the stomacher and the skirt were studded with gilt Imperial double-headed eagles, while diamond shoulder clasps held a seemingly endless train of crimson velvet with a rim of ermine fur. "What is this?" I asked, unfastening my riding jacket and my blouse at the throat, feeling hot.

"I need your advice." Mother's eyes gleamed with excitement. "But first I would like you to meet somebody."

"Who is it?" I turned around when I sensed someone move.

Behind us stood the most handsome man I could imagine.

I blushed. Would I feel the same way when I finally came face to face with the King of France? The thought sobered me. I proudly lowered my gaze and took off my riding gloves, ignoring the stranger, who stood at attention. I cast a quick glance around, trying to see my apartment through his eyes. My toiletry set made of tortoiseshell and gold had been laid out neatly on my dressing table. A silk ball gown in a becoming shade of silver, embroidered

with pearls and white crystals, lay draped over an armchair: I was
to wear it later tonight at one of Father's *assemblées* to entertain
up to three hundred guests. Dainty silk slippers were kicked off
next to my monkey's golden cage. A marble game of solitaire on my
desk had been started but not finished, just where Mother stood.
Thank God the maid had closed the doors to my bedroom—what
if this unknown man had seen my plumped-up, starched bed
linen? My cheeks were aflame.

"What shall I wear to my Coronation?" Mother beamed at me,
clearly unaware of the effect the stranger had had on me.

"Your—Coronation?" I stood dumbfounded. No Tsar's wife
had ever been honored in such a way. Ever. It was unthinkable, as
most Tsaritsas had been of lesser boyar families, who should not
be encouraged in their ambitions. Had my astonishing mother,
who had often supported my father more staunchly than any of
his generals, put an end to that custom? Once crowned, she would
reign in Russia as Regent if the Tsar were to leave it on a military
campaign or to travel abroad.

Appointing Anoushka and me as Tsesarevny might have been
only the first step in an era of even greater change.

"Yes. Just imagine! Your father will crown me himself in May,
in the Kremlin Cathedral of the Assumption, where all Tsars have
been anointed," Mother said, turning the drawing of the dress this
way and that. "The whole court has to buy tickets to attend in order
to cover the cost. Such a marvelous idea."

I was unable to tell if there was fear lurking beneath her excitement.

"What about Petrushka?" I asked. Mother's elevation removed
him even further from the throne.

"Oh, Lizenka. I so feel for the poor little boy. Petrushka should
not be held accountable for Alexey's sins. As your father was in
such a good mood, I convinced him that the child needs his own
retinue, however small. Meet Alexander Borisovich Buturlin. He
is to be Petrushka's First Chamberlain."

She smiled up at the tall young man, who bowed deeply. I cast him another glance beneath my lowered lashes. His V-shaped hairline was set high on a tanned forehead, the black hair brushed back. Eyebrows swooped like wings above gleaming gray-green eyes hooded by heavy lids; his high cheekbones as well as his full lips gave away Tatar ancestry. The Preobrazhensky Regiment's dark green ceremonial jacket fitted tightly over his broad chest. Despite his youth, a medal flashed beneath the wolfskin cloak he wore clasped over one shoulder. Long, slim fingers rested on the brass buckle of his belt and the bejeweled hilt of his sword. Buturlin's gaze held me captive as if he read my thoughts. Heat crept up my throat as I accepted his reverence with a polite smile and turned away.

Mother seemed oblivious to my confusion and still admired the sketch. "Once I was a serf girl sold for a piece of silver. Now I shall be the first-ever crowned Tsarina of All the Russias."

"But Mother—" I began.

"Yes?" Rays of pale spring sunshine framed her tall, voluptuous body, making her diamond jewelry sparkle brighter. "What is it, Elizabeth?"

Buturlin's gaze fastened on me.

"But—you are a woman," I said.

Mother gave a small, delighted laugh. "You noticed. And what if I am?"

I felt warm with pride for her courage and attitude. There was no one in the world to beat a mother like mine.

20

Alexander Borisovich Buturlin.

His family were courtiers by blood. They had been *ratshids*—royal equerries—and old Russian aristocrats, *boyary*. They were part of the *voyvody*, the Council of Moscow, and had been close to the ruler's ear ever since the Rurik Tsars, who had preceded my family as rulers of Russia. A Buturlin had shielded my great-grandfather Tsar Mikhail, when he, as the first Romanov, brought Russia peace after the Time of Troubles. Buturlin, who was officially assigned to Petrushka, in truth became the first member of my retinue, together with a French physician, Jean-Armand de Lestocq, whom Mother had called back from banishment in Kazan. Together with my Austrian music and dance teacher, Herr Schwartz, these men formed the trio that was to shape my life.

"Are you going hunting with Buturlin?"

How Petrushka had sneaked into my rooms so early in the morning, crossing the Winter Palace on his own, I did not know. His amber eyes still looked sleepy. I had finished feeding my monkeys and parrots, who were making a racket, rattling their cages and squawking, and now the maid was belting my breeches. As I kissed him, I furtively sniffed his breath. Good, he had not yet drunk alcohol.

"Not only with him. My new physician, the Frenchman Lestocq, and my music teacher Schwartz are coming as well. I was hoping to find you a wolf cub to raise."

"I don't want a smelly wolf cub. I want to go hunting with you. Strictly speaking, Buturlin is my chamberlain." He crossed his arms defiantly.

"Strictly speaking, you ought to be in your study with Ostermann. You will come hunting with me once you've learned where London and Paris are."

"Do *you* know where they are?"

"No. Well, I know where Paris is. Kind of. I ought to. It's next to Versailles, isn't it?"

"Ostermann isn't any fun." Petrushka added, his voice sullen, "You are."

"Tell me something new," I giggled.

"He doesn't like you."

"I don't like him either," I answered and checked my hair—thick blonde plaits were wrapped in a low bun at the nape of my neck as I was to wear my flat Polish hat. I hesitated briefly . . . but I could always remove the hat later, showing off my tresses.

"Can I eat your breakfast?" Petrushka asked.

"Hmm? Yes. Of course." Thinking of the hunt ahead, I had not touched the silver tray laden with chilled caviar, warm *blini*, chopped egg, and fresh *smetana*. Petrushka chewed hungrily while the maid struggled to pull the thigh-high riding boots over my round calves. I had always worn men's clothes to ride, much to Anoushka's horror. I did not mind revealing the shape of my legs and hips. Riding dresses made sitting astride impossible.

"Ostermann thinks you are corrupting me," Petrushka said with his mouth full.

"That's a big word." I turned to the mirror and tucked my shirt tighter, then placed my palms flat on my cheeks, feeling their fire when I thought of the day spent with Buturlin ahead.

"Lizenka?" Petrushka sat, the *blin* in his hand hovering, caviar dripping, waiting for me to answer. I stooped and snapped at the plump little pancake, eating it clean out of his fingers. "Sorry." I chewed and smiled. "I, on the contrary, think that Ostermann is a good influence on you. So grow up quickly, will you? Then you can come hunting with us." I put on my hat. As I left, Petrushka jumped up: "Lizenka, wait . . ."

I blew him some kisses on my way out. "These are for you! Catch them if you can, Petrushka!"

Being accompanied on a hunt by one man only would be scandalous. Taking three along, however, meant I had a respectable bodyguard. I set off with Lestocq, Schwartz, and Buturlin. The clean sky plunged into the Neva, the last floes crashing together in the sea swell. No clouds lingered overhead; it was too windy. Overnight, tiles had blown from the palace's roof, and the courtyard, finished only six months earlier, was already being repaved. The Italian envoy had angered Father by writing that *"St. Petersburg is the only town where ruins are being built to order. It is a city that a man in haste has built in a hurry."* At least the breeze dissipated the stench of the corpses strung up opposite Aunt Pasha's former palace, on a busy crossing in St. Petersburg. A couple of knouted, broken, and decapitated bodies spun there—thieves, tax evaders, slanderers, and Old Believers alike—and a cloud of ravens rose from their feast as I cantered past astride, my hat pulled low over my forehead. We were all in high spirits: hyenas had been sighted in the Karelian Hills.

Buturlin sat as if tied to his saddle. He rode like a Cossack, taut as an iron spring. My new physician, Lestocq, was delighted with his change of fortune on being called back from exile. A Frenchman, he was always hopelessly overdressed. The muddy ride and wild chase would spoil his fine breeches and the carefully tied lace jabot. To prove his worth, he had insisted on bleeding me first thing in the morning, saying: "Your spirits are too high for your own good." I had given in, though the loss of an ounce of blood made me feel dizzy when I tried to master my steed. Finally, the musician Schwartz wobbled along behind us on his sturdy mare, which was also laden with the picnic. At least his enormous Stradivari violoncello traveled ahead with the cook and servants to this night's resting place.

We settled for lunch after a first hunt: Buturlin was a brilliant shot. Already he had added two young wild boars to the tally. While Schwartz snoozed in the cool shade of an oak, his mouth slack and his palms turned up, like a child, Buturlin nimbly stacked the kindling, chipped off sparks with his flint, and gently blew on the first embers, encouraging the flames. I could not take my eyes off his elegant hands stoking the fire, yet I pulled up my knees and hugged my shins, apparently giving all my attention to Lestocq. He did not shoot; instead, he pondered how best to prepare the game.

"If you French aren't eating, you're talking about food, Lestocq," I laughed, reaching for some Isfahan fig confiture that Father's cook had packed, together with three loaves of sourdough bread, a jar of venison pâté spiced with juniper berries, a small vat of pickled onions, and a round of cheese.

"With good reason, Tsarevna. Knowing how to talk about food is essential in Versailles," Lestocq teased. "I am happy to be of service to your Imperial house."

Buturlin had cooled the Rhine wine in a clear and icy brook. Its light freshness made me feel curious and courageous. I saw the chamberlain casting Lestocq an amused glance. "But your services have not always been so appreciated, Lestocq. Why did my father banish you to Kazan? Tell us," I said.

"Oh," Lestocq said vaguely, his smile lopsided, showing a chipped front tooth. His dark copper hair matched his freckles and warm-hued skin. "I had taken a liking to a jester's daughter, but once I got to know her better, she was a bore."

"A jester?" I giggled. "Go on. I want names."

"Very well. It was d'Acosta's girl, with whom I parted ways amicably after a brief flirtation. The Tsar's imp has a beautiful full-grown daughter."

"That is one version, you cad," Buturlin said, lying back in the grass, a straw between his teeth, and lazily gazing at the blue sky. "It wasn't quite so brief a flirtation. The girl fell pregnant. Our friend here refused to marry her. D'Acosta has hated him ever since and beware the imp's anger."

His words were chilling. I tried to shrug off the memory of d'Acosta sitting in the Kolomenskoye kitchen, his dark gaze willing our nurse Illinchaya to cease her indiscreet chatter. She had paid with her life for underestimating the jester.

Lestocq shrugged. "Why serve a life sentence for a week's infatuation? It would have been misery for the two of us. Anyway she lost the baby. But d'Acosta pestered the Tsar to exile me to Kazan, until the Tsaritsa so kindly remembered my art."

I eyed Lestocq over the rim of my silver goblet. "You are quite a gambler."

"What, if not a gamble, is life? We all are given a set of cards. Some receive a stunning hand at birth, being royally lucky—" he bowed to me "—yet lose it all from indolence. Others have but a two of spades and win the game by their cunning. It is more fascinating than any play or performance."

"Well. Not *any* play or performance." Buturlin rose, turning to a little path that led to our resting place.

"What is it, Buturlin?" I felt a bit faint in the hot midday sun. Damn Lestocq and his bleeding.

"A beautiful surprise for an even more beautiful Tsesarevna." He bowed as the jingle of cymbals and tambourines became audible amid the beating of a goatskin drum and the strumming of balalaika chords.

"I know how you adore the old Russian songs and dances, despite the best efforts of our friend Schwartz, who even snores in a three-quarter rhythm," said Buturlin. Lestocq raised his eyebrows: Buturlin had beaten him in a game I was unaware they had been playing.

"Look," I cheered, as young people from the nearby *mir*—a

village with a couple of rickety *izby* along a dusty road, where our horses' hooves had made the sinewy hens scatter in panic—stepped into the clearing. In their old-style Russian dress, which my father had banned, they looked like walking blossoms. The collars of the men's belted, hip-long vests were embroidered in every shade of red—*krazny* in Russian, also meaning beautiful. Their wide trousers billowed around the thighs and then were stuck into knee-high boots with pointed toes. The girls' thick plaits swung with each step; each *sarafan* a swirl of colors, the long, wide skirts ready to fan out and rise in the dance. They belonged to a beautiful world that had passed. One girl in particular caught my eye, her cheeks rosy, her hair as pale as wheat, her smile dimming the sun's luster.

"Will they dance?" I asked, charmed by her beauty, and smiling at her as Buturlin pulled me to my feet. "Not only them, Tsesarevna. Let us see now what snoring old Schwartz has taught you."

His fingers seared my skin; I quickly pulled my arm away. Lestocq's gaze took it all in, silent and alert. The balalaika strummed, and cymbals sounded a tune. The singers' voices rose: the lyrics were funny at first and then became hilarious, telling the story of a fool brewing his beer in a sieve. As I laughed the music gathered pace, urging us along, skipping and dancing in a whirl. I did not resist Buturlin's grip any more when he began to lead me. I danced the woman's part despite my tight breeches, and he spun me away, to let me go and then catch me again, to hold me tight, our breaths mingling. Was this decent? I sensed his fresh sweat and saw earth on his fingers yet did not mind. Perhaps this was what my cousin Anna Ivanovna felt, she who was said to live with her groom? I whirled away from Buturlin and then flew back toward him until my vision blurred.

The beautiful girl popped up again and again, beaming at me, her eyes the brilliant hue of the spring sky, her smile broad, confusing me further. "Buturlin," I breathed as the world closed in. My knees buckled, and I held on to him, feeling the muscles beneath his skin.

"Tsesarevna!" he called. As the chanting died away, I fell, feeling faint, pulling him down with me into the grass. The hot midday sun needled my eyelids, drowning me in the dense blue of a Russian sky thick with curds-and-whey clouds. Buturlin's breath was hot, but I shivered. My eyes closed, and the dancers' voices faded, yet I sensed someone close by. As I squinted into the sun, I expected the beautiful girl to be looking down at me, her fair head surrounded by a halo of light.

Instead I stared into amber eyes, animal fangs flashing. A scrawny neck craned from a silver coat of mottled fur as claws reached straight for my heart, trying to shred my soul. It was the Leshy spirit from the Golosov Ravine. I leaped up, ready to fend it off, screaming and spitting, kicking, and punching, fighting tooth and nail.

21

"How is she, Lestocq?" Buturlin's voice came from afar. Blood throbbed painfully behind my temples. My whole body felt battered. I dared not open my eyes at first. When I did, a golden dusk was filtering through the tent's canvas. We had arrived at tonight's resting place. I forced myself to sit up from the cushions fashioned from Persian silk rugs, despite the reindeer skins weighing me down, my stiff breeches, and cumbersome thigh-high boots. Nobody had dared even to open my belt, to ease my breathing. I longed for a hot bath, a soft woolen housedress, and Anoushka's silver voice reading me a story. Instead the memory of the dance's horrific end flooded me. The Leshy spirit had found me. I cupped my face with my hands. My palms still smelled of cut grass and earth.

Outside the tent Lestocq said, "God knows what happened. She almost scratched the poor girl's eyes out. Perhaps I should bleed the Tsesarevna again?"

"Better not. It will weaken her," said Buturlin.

"Young women tend to hysterics—"

"Young Frenchwomen, yes. Not a Russian Tsesarevna. Why not pour us some cool Tokay instead, Lestocq?" I heard a slap on the doctor's shoulder and was grateful that Buturlin had kept the needles at bay. But as the tent flap was unfastened, I quickly pulled the furs up to my chin. Buturlin peered inside, a lantern in his hand, the worry on his face easing when he saw me sitting up.

"Tsesarevna Elizabeth. How do you feel?"

Like flinging myself at him and confessing all about that god-forsaken afternoon in the Golosov Ravine, my guilt over Illinchaya's death, and the fear of the curse that haunted my family. Instead I touched my temples, attempting a smile. "Much better. God knows what took me. Sunstroke, I suppose. The poor girl. Make sure to send her fifty roubles and a vat of beer as an apology. Good beer, of German make, all cold and frothy."

Buturlin pondered the lighthearted answer but chose to accept my explanation. "I thought it was something of the sort. The girl got off lightly, just a couple of scratches and missing some strands of hair. She did not dare to fend you off." The warmth he radiated was shocking and having him so close to me was almost unbear-able. I scrambled to my knees, careful not to look at him. "Off you go, Buturlin. Let a lady get ready for dinner."

"It's more than dinner. It is a feast. While you slept, I shot a bear, two stags, and three hares." The lantern light made his choc-olate gaze glint; stubble showed on his chin, and his smile caused dimples to appear in his cheeks. He helped me up, and his fingers lightly brushed my inner arm. I held my breath. Surely, he would not dare to do that deliberately. I pulled my arm away and said curtly: "I shall see you outside."

The fire burned high, its flames eating into the near-complete dark-ness of an early-April night. Where their light ended, millions of stars effortlessly took over. I wished for one of Father's English telescopes so that I could see them close up, as he had taught me to do. Instead I settled on the cushions that lay scattered on the dry, crushed leaves. Their spicy balm filled the evening air and blended with the pungent scent of roast game: moisture and mar-inade dripped from the spit. Still studying the endless sky, I heard the music. It was not this afternoon's Russian folk melody with its rambunctious rhythm, but instead it sounded like cascading wa-ter. Schwartz sat with his golden Stradivari violoncello between his legs, holding it as tenderly as the mistress he had probably never had. His masterly use of the bow made the instrument sing of everything between life and death.

"What is that?" I asked.

"It's by a German composer called Bach," Buturlin murmured. "Apparently the Tsar tried to lure him to Russia, but in vain. Schwartz harped on about him the whole afternoon, until I told him to shut up before he scared off my prey."

Which prey? I wondered as Lestocq handed me a chalice of chilled Tokay, and I slapped his wrists when he furtively tried to check my pulse. The heavy, sweet wine lulled my senses. The cook had lathered the stag with *smetana* and mustard, and we mopped up the thick, creamy marinade with warm sourdough bread. For dessert, a thick, layered *medovik* honey tart was served. "I added extra honey, just to see you strong again, Tsesarevna. Russia loves you, always," the cook said, and watched, delighted, as I ate three pieces and afterward licked my fingers, sticky with cream and honey.

"What now?" asked Buturlin as our leftovers were distributed among the servants, who sat shivering in the settling cool of the night, away from our circle close to the fire. He eyed me lazily as I stretched out on the cushions, sipping a hot, sweet mocha. My father's envoy to Persia, Prince Volynsky, had taught us how to prepare it, to seal the stomach and allow for deep slumber: one spoon of coffee, spiced with cardamom and cloves, to one spoon of sugar per cup was brought to the boil three times in a row.

"No more dancing." Lestocq bowed to me. "But luckily enough, my King Louis, the Tsesarevna's future husband, has sent us a special present."

The Tsesarevna's future husband. Lestocq's words were a clear warning.

"What is it?" I sat up, unable to resist a gift.

"Ta-dah!" Lestocq pulled a battered leather etui from his waistcoat.

"A pack of cards? Where's the surprise in that?" I asked. "Deal me my hand. I'll ruin you in a jiffy."

He grinned. "Some other time, gladly. These are not simple cards. It's a set of Tarot."

"Tarot." I tasted the word. "What is that?"

"Tarot knows your fate. Three cards tell you where you are today, how you might continue, and where you will reach," he added. The flames' warmth ceased to reach me. Tarot sounded little different from the evil Leshy spirit's bones and steaming sulfur pools. "Should a scientist like you believe in this? Who wants to know what the future holds anyway?" I asked, feeling goose bumps on my arms.

"I do," Buturlin said. "Tell me the rules, Lestocq."

"Tarot is not a fortune-teller. It unlocks life's mysteries. That's why we call the cards arcana—secrets." He took the pack of cards. "Here are the twenty-two grand arcana. Shall we start with them?"

Buturlin nodded; the flames drew a moody pattern on his face.

Lestocq nimbly shuffled the cards: "There are various ways of dealing. Let us start with a line, which is the easiest. Pick three cards, Buturlin, from wherever you wish."

Buturlin obeyed and laid the cards face down, in a line, rubbing his palms excitedly.

"The first card shows your starting point. The second is where you wish to be. The third is the future. Go for it if you dare," Lestocq said.

Buturlin flipped the first card. It showed a woman taming a lion, both her hair and the animal's mane flaming bright orange.

"Ah. This card means strength, courage, and confidence. Everything you need to succeed in the Preobrazhensky Regiment. No surprise there," said Lestocq.

"What a clever game!" Buturlin mocked, downing a stubby glass of ice-cold vodka, savoring the burn in his throat.

"Carry on, if you're feeling brave enough," Lestocq challenged him.

"Of course." Buturlin flipped the second card.

"The lovers." The French doctor, who reported my every action to Versailles, sighed, eyeing the card that showed a couple locked in a tight embrace. I would not even dare to look at Buturlin. Around us the air crackled as it does in a storm of spring lightning.

"And number three," Lestocq said lightly.

Buturlin flipped the card, smiling and sure of himself, then blanched. It showed a man hanging head over heels from gallows, bleeding from numerous wounds, his hair trailing on the ground.

Lestocq's expression was grave. "Ah. The hanged man—if only the sight were not so hard to evade in Russia. At least it doesn't signify death."

"Are the cards always right?" Buturlin asked.

"Things might happen in one way or another. Force and courage speak for or against you, while love might or might not bring great suffering. Still, the card's message is clear."

"Spell it out."

"You're a fool for love." Lestocq shrugged.

Buturlin rose, clenching his fists in his pockets, his dark gaze settling on me. "A fool for love indeed. Which proper man would not be?" He bowed and strode away to his tent.

Lestocq and I sat in silence, staring into the flames until the fire died down and the stars' shine took over.

22

~~

Upon my return to St. Petersburg I told Anoushka nothing about my horrid vision of the Leshy spirit at the dance, but I could not resist mentioning the Tarot and Buturlin's passionate reaction. "Better watch your step," she warned, then carried on reading. I barely avoided tearing the book from her hands. Wasn't life more exciting than any novel could be?

"Lizenka?" Petrushka waylaid me at the entrance to the Summer Palace; he must have run away from his lessons. He was gasping for breath; Ostermann had been left behind. Good boy.

"What is it?" I pinched his cheek.

"I have a present for you." He raised his closed, cupped hands.

"Have you stolen some sweets from the kitchen?"

"Much better." He lifted one hand, revealing an adorable fluff ball. The chick's beak clamored for food. Its eyes were dark and beady, and the feathers were already changing from dirty gray to tawny gold. "Oh, Petrushka! How wonderful. What kind of bird is it?"

"I knew you would like it. It is a peregrine falcon. When both the chick and I have grown enough, can we all go hunting together?"

"I promise. When the chick has grown, I shall send for you." I embraced him and then carefully held the chick in my cupped hands. It felt like holding the wind and the skies. "Does it have a name yet?"

"No. Naming it will make it yours."

"You are right. Names are magic. I shall call it Molniya."

"Lightning." He smiled. "That's a good name."

"Let us go and dig for worms in the garden," I suggested, as Ostermann appeared at the other end of the graveled pathway, limping determinedly, his cane briskly tapping the stones as if they were my back. So much for digging for worms. "You'd better run, before the German starts laying about him with his cane. They are too good at that," I told my cousin.

Petrushka looked crestfallen, but when they left together, Ostermann's arm lay tenderly over his charge's narrow shoulders, fingers caressing the boy's neck. I stroked the chick's feathers, its minute beak pecking at my fingertips. It would have been impossible for me to imagine then that one day this bird would become the trusted messenger that saved my life.

23

Anoushka and I traveled to Moscow by barge to witness Mother's Coronation. Despite our joy and elation—Mother would be Russia's first-ever crowned Tsaritsa—I felt like a caged animal. The small portholes allowed only a glimpse of the glorious May sky. Being on deck offered no respite either, as the whole court—thirty thousand people—was in transit to witness Mother's unprecedented elevation. Princes, counts, and barons trudged along with their children, servants, tutors, and livestock. The nobles bemoaned their lot; not only did the journey cost them a fortune, but the cellars and larders of their Moscow homes had been plundered to the last grain and bottle. Gaggles of geese and herds of pigs, goats, and cows were driven along to serve as provisions upon arrival. Horses, ponies, and dogs straggled behind in single file, pulling carriages, carts, and wagons. Vast clouds of red dust rose from the wheels, the horses' hooves, the serfs' bare feet.

The stench of the sluggish river under the hot sun was nauseating.

Before our departure I had overheard Count Ostermann warning Father of a third catastrophic summer of drought to come: "We have to make sure the peasants and serfs have access to streams and seeds. Otherwise Russians will cook soup from old belts and make pancakes out of wood chippings again." "Fabulous," Alexander Danilovich Menshikov had cut in, swinging on his chair like a boy, sucking on his pipe and placing his boots on the table. "That means I can double or even triple the price of my grain!" At that piece of self-serving insolence, even Father, who normally forgave his Alekasha any transgression, had trained his *dubina* on him and none too lightly: the knout and Menshikov were old acquaintances.

In the villages we passed, no smoke rose from the *izby*. If children came running, their ribs almost pierced their skin, bellies swollen by worms. Huge eyes in tiny gaunt faces made them look like little old people. Menshikov had by then already forgotten Father's thrashing and threw them bread crusts, laughing himself to tears as the little ones clawed and cuffed each other in their desperation. The sight was unbearable to me. How could Father love this man so much? Yet Menshikov remained untouchable, assured of the Tsar's favor.

I wished for my stallion, a simple tent, my blanket, a goatskin of drink strapped to my saddle, and the freedom I felt on horseback. Instead, I was trapped. We could not even play dominoes or drafts since I had swiped the pieces off the table in a fit of anger upon losing repeatedly to Buturlin. My parrots spread their clipped wings as an indignant lady would her fan, squawking, and my monkey's sharp teeth cracked pistachios before chucking the empty shells all over the barge. If he hit Buturlin, the creature first cackled with pleasure and then ducked for cover when the chamberlain threw the shells right back: "Imp of Satan, I should roast you for dinner!"

Anoushka closed her eyes, as if embroidering in the dull light gave her a headache. Her fine needlework could rival any nun's, while I had not touched Brussels linen or Chinese silken thread for years. "Tell us a story, Buturlin," I demanded, pressing a perfumed, moist lace handkerchief to my nose, breathing in its subtle scent of lavender oil and rosewater.

"What about, Tsesarevna?" He rolled back the sleeves of his crisp white shirt, revealing his taut forearms, and crossed his legs in their tight uniform breeches and thigh-high polished black leather boots. He was perched on a desk, one leg swinging, the other extended, outlining the muscles in his thigh. I averted my gaze as he lit his pipe, his lips curling.

"The last thing I need is tobacco stench," I moaned.

He smiled but did not extinguish his pipe, which irked me. "Let me tell you about my uncle Ivan's wedding. The Tsar made him marry a woman forty years his junior. Both learned only hours before of their betrothal. It was hilarious."

Even Anoushka looked up from her embroidery, frowned, and listened.

"We attended in groups of three, in matching costumes— Friesian peasants, Roman soldiers, Indians, monks and nuns, shepherds and shepherdesses, nymphs and satyrs, and your father's favorite giant dressed as a baby. The invitations were delivered by stammerers, and the runners were fat, gouty men. The groom was dragged to the ceremony in a cart drawn by tame bears, and at the banquet there was nothing to eat, only vats of vodka. Then we danced. The more we stumbled and fell, the more we laughed. Finally the Tsar brought the couple to bed, beating his drum." Buturlin imitated a drumroll by slapping his thighs. "Next door, holes had been drilled in the walls, and we watched the couple—"

I listened, alert. They watched the couple doing *what*? My heart raced with curiosity. It felt as if I were blind, feeling my way over terrain I did not yet know. I thought of my mother placing my father's hand on her lower belly back in Peterhof when we had been made Tsesarevny, their gazes locking, making the air crackle. I opened my mouth and shut it again, blushing: Buturlin was the last person I could ask.

"It sounds horrid. I don't think you should be telling my younger sister these things," Anoushka scolded him, her needle halting.

"I know the saucy stories you order from Italy. Which of us is more honest then?" I challenged her.

"It's an honesty that does not become a future queen," she sniped.

"If we speak about dowdy Sweden, then no. If we talk about

Versailles, you are wrong. D'Acosta says that love is the true ruler of that court."

"Sweden? I have not heard from Karl von Holstein in weeks." She looked hurt. How come she was still thinking about that plain, thin man with his threadbare claim to the Swedish throne? At least young King Louis ruled France for real. It was a point I avoided making. Instead I lunged at her. "Ha! Soon he will be all over you like a rash!" She squealed, wriggling, and pleading for mercy, trying to get away, but I laughed and ordered, "Help me, Buturlin!" He stepped over but tickled me instead. I shrieked, aghast, and delighted to feel him touching me as the scuffle allowed him to do—my waist, my armpits—and sending flashes of lightning through me, a hitherto unknown sensation. Heat rose in my veins as I tried to fend him off; Anoushka and I were in a tangle when Buturlin stumbled over my hem, pulling us with him onto the Persian silk rugs. We laughed, screamed, and tried to get up, only to tumble down again. The air turned treacly. For a heartbeat I lay beneath Buturlin, drinking in his own smell of fresh sweat scented like nutmeg, as well as his perfume combining hints of sandalwood, tobacco, and leather.

"Stop!" I breathed, sliding away, and scrambling to my feet. He stood to attention with burning eyes, hair ruffled, fists clenched, as if ready to lunge. We had both forgotten Anoushka's presence. "Stop. Now."

Stop.

We both knew that no shouted order to push on, to storm and to conquer, would make him go forth with more ardor than this single word.

24

Mother's way from Menshikov's Palace in Moscow's Lefortovo Quarter was decorated with dozens of triumphal gates adorned with garlands of fragrant white blossoms. Father had granted amnesties on tax arrears, which propelled the population into a frenzy of joy. "No wonder," Buturlin had said. "They are all tax-dodging scoundrels." On the day of her Coronation, street vendors hawked pungent meat skewers and crunchy pastries filled with cream, cinnamon, honey, and nuts. Since dawn the fountains had spewed red and white wine. Guards galloped through the streets, tossing six hundred thousand silver coins into the crowd; hundreds of people were squashed in the ensuing turmoil.

Inside the cathedral, stained-glass windows tinted the light pooling on the marble floor, as splendidly dressed people advanced up the aisle's red runner. Suddenly Anoushka sat up straight and hissed: "Look!" Karl von Holstein took a seat opposite us, lithe and fox-like.

"Don't stare at him," I scolded her. "A woman is the only prey that stalks its hunter."

"Look who's talking. What are you playing at with Buturlin?"

"He is Petrushka's chamberlain. I am to marry the King of France," I said, blushing. Had I been so obvious? My blood tingled. Only Anoushka's presence had saved us from turning the horseplay on the barge into something too serious to be mastered. I felt like a flower from a Crimean hothouse, breathing in much more moisture and suffering more heat than nature alone could ever provide.

"Well, yes. But only if your reputation is spotless. De Campredon has you watched. Lestocq reports straight back to Paris. A woman cannot behave like a man, and a Tsesarevna cannot do as other women. Behave, Lizenka," Anoushka whispered.

My mother's ladies-in-waiting floated in, looking like water lilies. Each step made the yards of silk cascading from their tightly laced bodices and stomachers crusted with gemstones and pearls ripple.

"I wish we could do as we pleased—just like men. Why should we not?"

"Ostermann used a brilliant image the other day, when talking to Petrushka, and explaining inheritance and lineage. If you pour water from a single jug into four empty ones, you always know the source. Yet if you pour water from four filled jugs into a single empty one, it is all a muddle."

"What sort of jug is that supposed to be? And who pours what, and where?" I asked, dumbfounded. Yet I sensed that Ostermann's image gave some clue to understanding what would happen with the King of France on my wedding night. "Why do you call that brilliant?"

"Well, I didn't. Menshikov did."

"Menshikov? Ah! I never had him down as a fount of wisdom. Since when is he a reliable judge of anything?" I asked. "And when did you speak to him? Do you remember his face when Father made us Tsesarevny? He seemed upset not to have been consulted."

Karl von Holstein bowed to us. Anoushka gave him her pearly-toothed smile and coyly hid behind her white ostrich-feather fan, while I ignored him. Yet his eyes never left my face: the more I rebuffed him, the more eager he seemed. Then he leaned closer to Ostermann, who whispered in his ear. Being either lowborn or German seemed to be a prerequisite for any advancement at court these days. No wonder the Russian word for the Germans—

Nemetski—by now also stood for "foreigner." It stemmed from *ne moz*, which meant "dumb," referring to those who could not speak a word of our language.

I watched the men whisper. While Petrushka had been left behind in St. Petersburg—once more overlooked by the Tsar—Karl von Holstein's willingness to marry *any* Tsesarevna might fit in with a possible secret plan of Ostermann's. If Anoushka and I were both married off, he could work to advance my nephew's position.

But Father would never sacrifice us as he had done Ekaterina Ivanovna. By crowning Mother today, he showed the world how to reward a true, loving, and faithful partner.

25

"Halt!" Count Peter Andreyevich Tolstoy, the Master of Ceremonies, planted his staff in the middle of the red carpet, blocking the way of both my cousin Ekaterina Ivanovna and her daughter Christine, who had left Izmailov for the festivities.

"What do you mean, halt, Count Tolstoy?" Ekaterina pulled Christine close. "No one blocks my way."

"Certainly not *your* way, Duchess. But these people are not to be here." Tolstoy was not a man to be easily cowed: he had survived not only Father's disgrace for once supporting his usurping half-sister, the Regent Sophia, but also being held prisoner for the better part of a decade in the Ottoman Fortress of the Seven Towers. He frowned and shook his head. Behind Ekaterina loitered a crowd that would have done Aunt Pasha's passion for the stricken proud: a legless cripple, whose trunk was placed on a wooden board on wheels, was pulled along by a hunchback. Two scrawny gypsy girls cowered, arms entwined, eyes scanning the crowd to decide where to pinch a purse or pilfer a silk handkerchief.

"Well, if my sister Anna Ivanovna and her stable boy are welcome, then so are *they*," Ekaterina snapped. "Step aside, Peter Andreyevich, before I push you. You are measuring the same cloth with a different yard, as a cheating tailor would."

Tolstoy raised his thick black eyebrows. "Anna Ivanovna is the ruling Duchess of Courland, her guest her private secretary—not a gaggle of flea-ridden pickpockets."

"Private secretary? Rather Anna's gentleman of the bedchamber," Ekaterina Ivanovna snorted. "She is my *younger* sister and the *widowed* Duchess of Courland. The man is as out of place here as my *pickpockets*. If she brings him, I bring them." She agitated her fan of gray ostrich plumes, sending a cloud of down into the air.

Beads of sweat gathered on Tolstoy's forehead beneath the weight of his heavy, curly gray wig. I rose. The red carpet had become a stage for Ekaterina and him, which was intolerable. Today was meant to be Mother's finest hour. As Tolstoy's men chased Ekaterina's motley crowd of cripples and gypsies from the cathedral, the crowd parted to make way for another arrival.

Tolstoy bowed. "Welcome to Moscow, Duchess Anna Ivanovna."

I turned to look at her, full of curiosity, as I could not remember having ever met my cousin, the second daughter of mad Tsar Ivan. At the time of her ill-fated wedding, I had been an infant. Around us courtiers giggled and whispered: the woman who advanced up the aisle of the Cathedral of the Assumption made even the overweight Tolstoy look small. Like so many brunettes, she had turned gray early and now dyed her hair with an ill-smelling paste made of lead and slaked lime. Her too-black hair was piled up in a way that had not been seen since the turn of the century. When had the cut of that heavy gown, with some crude lace around her ample cleavage, last been in fashion? I wondered—at the time of my birth? Anna's pearl choker looked like paste, while I wore sapphires the size of quail's eggs. The pallor of her face accentuated the broken veins in her cheeks, and her skin was as badly pitted as a Dutch cheese; wrinkles were etched deep into her forehead, between her eyebrows, and ran from her nostrils down to the corners of her mouth. Her sour-cherry eyes, however—inherited from Aunt Pasha—sparkled, revelling in the splendor of these surroundings.

"Stop moping, Ekaterina," Anna Ivanovna scolded her sister.

"You know what it is like. In Russia the wheel of fortune is spinning all the time, either taking you up or smiting you down."

"As your groom is so much on the up, he must be keeping you
down to your satisfaction, Anna." Ekaterina flashed her pointed
ivory teeth, seamlessly picking up the chastening of Anna Ivanovna
where their mother, Aunt Pasha, had left off. She must find it unbearable to see herself as worse off even than her sister, who had
always been their family scapegoat and the butt of many jokes. "I
am surprised that you dare bring this man here. You never did
have any shame."

I could not help but stare: Anna Ivanovna, Duchess of Courland, shielded the man behind her, while his even taller, broad
figure inclined toward her protectively. They both looked to have
been plucked from a tent during a village spring fair, but he tenderly
touched her elbow in a gesture of reassurance. The sight moved
me: when Anna Ivanovna's husband of three days suffocated in the
snow a decade earlier, she had been the age I was now. Who had
been by her side back then? Neither my parents nor her own sister
or mother.

"Cousin Anna Ivanovna. Welcome." I stepped forward, forcing
Ekaterina Ivanovna and Christine into a curtsy. "I am Tsesarevna
Elizabeth Petrovna. When you left for Courland, I was a child."

Anna smiled at me, showing long yellow teeth. "Indeed! You
are the Wolverine." Her companion's quick, bright gaze took me
in before he bowed. "I remember toasting your healthy birth on
the same day the big victory parade for Poltava took place. You
were noisy enough to live up to your nickname. Though today I
should describe you as a white dove, as beautiful as you are," Anna
said courteously. "I am so grateful that the Tsar, my dearest father-
uncle, funded my journey."

"I am delighted to meet you, too." I smiled at her, but my display
of tact and diplomacy was immediately undermined by Ekaterina's
scorn: "After you pestered him with a dozen begging letters!"

I felt my blood quicken with anger and turned to study Anna's companion. He was tanned, and his chin and cheeks were already shadowed with stubble, despite no doubt having summoned the barber just hours ago. It made him look like a robber baron. So this was the infamous groom!

"And I see you come accompanied, dearest Anna?" I smiled welcomingly.

She blushed unbecomingly, looking like a withered apple. "Indeed, Lizenka. Meet Ernst Biren, my closest adviser. He looks after everything for me in Courland, from the throne to the stables."

"I hear he talks to men as if they were horses, and to horses as if they were men," Ekaterina chuckled.

"You snappy old mare, Ekaterina. By God, I would give you a good whipping if I had my crop handy," Anna shot back, keen to protect Biren even though he towered over her.

"At least I have a fine filly to show for my suffering." Ekaterina seized Christine's slender wrist, for once proud of her plain, shy daughter.

"Ekaterina, where are your manners?" I scolded her as tears welled in Anna's eyes. I reached out my right hand for Biren to kiss and his full lips hovered just above my skin in perfect courtesy. "Welcome to Moscow on this fine day, Biren. I like a man who knows his bloodstock. My future fiancé, the King of France, sent me a fine Arab stallion. Perhaps one day we may view it together."

As Biren leaned in, I caught a whiff of cloves and, yes, straw. I bit my lip to suppress a giggle. "I hope to have a moment to discuss its breeding with you," he said. "Your kindness will never be forgotten, Tsesarevna. Those who call you the finest Princess in Christendom do not exaggerate. Your beauty makes the daylight pale." His appreciative gaze made me feel like the only woman present.

"Take your seats. The Tsaritsa approaches!" Tolstoy roared. Cannon shots punctured the morning air. Hooves thundered on the Red Square. Trumpets sounded, and I gave Biren a well-studied gracious smile and slid back to my seat.

Outside, carriage wheels drew to a halt, and guards in their splendid ceremonial uniforms formed a double file towering above us. I spotted Buturlin in the ranks and felt his eyes searching for me. I avoided his gaze. At the altar Feofan Prokopovich stepped forward, his head bowed deep in prayer. The cathedral quieted, and the court held its breath as my mother, the Tsaritsa Catherine Alexeyevna, entered. Her beauty and majesty were steeped in the cathedral's rich light; incense swirled, soothing her fear with the intoxicating blend of frankincense, myrrh, and our audible excitement and admiration. Four thousand ermine pelts lined her cloak and train. A dozen page boys, scions of Russia's oldest and most noble families, carried the train: *arshin* upon *arshin* of crimson velvet. It was so heavy it could have made a dozen men stumble. They steered and supported her with little tugs to left and right, looking like cute mice ushering along a silky-coated cat—a cat who had gotten the cream, I thought, smiling to myself. Mother's crimson velvet gown, which was studded with countless double-headed solid-gold eagles, was literally breathtaking: it weighed a crushing hundred fifty pounds. This morning Anoushka and I had taken turns hanging off her, laughing, pretending we were getting her used to such a weight. She had embraced us, sobbing and laughing at the same time. Its gold-thread embroidery mirrored the thousands of candles burning brightly all around, banishing any shadows to the cathedral's most forlorn corners. She gleamed like a sunburst, setting the aisle on fire.

As my parents left the cathedral after the ceremony, to the accompaniment of the choir's voices rising to the heavens while the rest of us kneeled, our heads deeply bowed, Anna Ivanovna's hand sought Biren's, the telltale movement half hidden by the folds of her heavy, old-fashioned skirt. He engulfed her fingers in his paw: a hand large and strong enough to turn a foal in a mare's belly, to rein in a dozen sullen carriage horses—or perhaps to hoist a quartet of giggling chambermaids on his shoulders, carrying them through a Courland snowstorm, as Ekaterina's vicious tongue suggested.

Anna cast him a loving glance, her gaze as hot and sweet as molten licorice. What better company than that of a former groom could she demand; what else could fate possibly have in store for her? I did not begrudge Anna Ivanovna this thin slice of happiness. It made me think of Buturlin, who guarded the aisle today, and I could not help but look out for him.

26

Three days later, when the city and the court still lay in a stupor after the celebration, there was a slight knock on the door of my rooms in the Kremlin's former *terem*. In the May morning, specks of sunlight made the dust dance before the mullioned mica panes in the antiquated windows. Birds were singing on the Red Square, woken by the ever earlier onset of dawn. It was a rare occurrence. Normally ravens and vultures hovered here, competing for rich pickings of skin and entrails with the scabby, shaggy wild dogs of Moscow. For want of trees, the robins, sparrows, and blackbirds perched on the wooden scaffolds of Moscow's most prominent gallows, which today lay bare in deference to Mother's most glorious moment. Father had decreed generous amnesties to celebrate her Coronation. My maid, who slept on the threshold to the room, rubbed her eyes and rose, but the door was already opening: my cousin Anna Ivanovna slipped into my room. She ducked under the doorframe, which was too low for her height and ample flesh. She turned sideways to fit through the narrow opening. Still, she held herself straight as she crossed the Persian rugs and polar bear skins spread over the flagstones, exuding confidence. For all her poverty and the ridicule she had suffered, she was a Tsarevna still: her poise was inbred.

"Anna Ivanovna, good morning." I sat up, surprised, stroked my hair from my sleepy face and winced. I had forgotten to take off a ring I had worn during last night's celebration; a coin-sized, flawless diamond. Its masterful cut captured the morning light in its icy depths but scratched my cheek. Anna was dressed warmly and comfortably in an embroidered felt cape, a fur cap, and boots: she looked ready to travel. Even in late spring the long, sedentary hours on the road meant it was safest to wear several layers of clothing. Why the haste? I wondered.

"Good morning, Lizenka, my dove. I am coming to say good-bye." Anna summarily pushed my maid out of the door: "Off you go. Eavesdrop elsewhere!" She settled next to me on my bedstead; I had to slide up against the wall to make space for her bottom, and the slats groaned under her weight. She unfastened the toggles of her floor-length cape, which was darned in several places, yet kept on her cap. It was made of tawny, speckled rabbit fur, the cheapest of skins, and still smelled of the hutch when she embraced me. I forced myself not to wrinkle my nose and discreetly swiveled the ring's stone to the inside of my finger.

"Goodbye? But it is so early," I said, suppressing a yawn.

Anna Ivanovna shrugged. "In Courland I always rise early, summer or winter. How else do you get things done?"

"You sound like Father." I pulled my feet aside before Anna should squash them.

"I take that as a compliment. Well, we can all learn from him. My father-uncle is a great man."

"For the way he has changed Russia?" I asked carefully, used to both the admiration that Father's countless reforms caused and the wrath and resistance he encountered at home.

"That, too. I was thinking of how he acknowledged my little aunt sunshine, your mother, the Tsaritsa Catherine. What man, let alone the ruler of the most powerful and wealthy realm, ever does that publicly? Normally any sign of merit is solely theirs for the taking. But he *crowned* her!"

I nodded mutely.

"I would love to stay longer but have to return to Courland.

No one else has treated me—us—with so much kindness here in Moscow, or anywhere else, for as long as I can remember. Certainly no one in our family," she said.

"You exaggerate surely," I quickly replied. "Ekaterina is difficult but not evil."

"She calls me Anna Ivanovna the Terrible."

"I like little Christine."

"That worm who calls Maja a witch who should burn in Hell? They both wanted to turn my mother's most loyal maid out on the streets." Anna crossed herself. "When we were children back in Izmailov, nothing was ever too much trouble for Maja. A devotion such as hers is rare."

"Aunt Pasha, too, was always kindness herself to me," I started.

"Count yourself lucky," Anna said, before hesitating a split second, fiddling with the hem of her cloak. Then she stilled, looking at me; her gaze seemed to pin me to the wall. The air around us quickened. "Why did you save Maja?" Anna asked. "Did she offer you anything in return?"

I raised my eyebrows. "Such as? She is a maid. A servant, if not a serf."

"She has told you nothing then?" Her gaze was as dark as a nighttime forest.

"What could she tell me that might be of interest to any of us?" I shrugged.

"Oh. This, that, and the other. She knew all of Mother's secrets." Anna seemed to relax. Who wanted their dirty family linen washed in public?

"Anyway, I am not only grateful for your protection of Maja, but also for the friendly reception you gave Biren. I beg you will accept this little token to remember me by." She pressed a beautiful icon into my palm. It showed St. Nicholas, the Patron Saint of Russia. Tiny, but flawless, diamonds framed the miniature, and the brushwork was exquisite; the saint gazed at me with large, mournful eyes. Icons such as these were considered a small window into Heaven. Didn't she complain at any given moment that she was penniless? This gift was far too valuable.

"I can't accept it, Anna."

"Please. You must. It once belonged to my father, Tsar Ivan. It shall protect you." She folded my fingers around the icon—her gaze flickered when she saw the huge diamond ring next to the delicate sparkle of the frame. "Life is hard. Everything comes at a price."

I turned the icon this way and that, making the stones in the frame sparkle, before piously kissing the saint. "Thank you. I shall ask Father for a matching necklace."

"I hope he fulfills your wishes faster than he does mine." She tugged at her finger with its double wedding ring, the sign of her widowhood.

"What is it you wish for? Perhaps if you write to him once again," I suggested.

"Three hundred letters are quite enough, I think," Anna said curtly.

"Three hundred?" I was shocked. Finishing just one sheet of handwriting exercises had been torture to me. "What did you ask him for, apart from more money and another husband?"

"That's about it. A home, a husband, a family. What else could a woman hope for? I was a virgin widow."

I frowned. "A *virgin* widow? Is that something like a nun, or a spinster?"

"Kind of. I hope you need never know either state. And how should you, as future Queen of France?" she added.

"Nothing is determined," I said, but could not suppress a proud smile.

"It can be only be a matter of time."

"Yes. Even *more* time."

She shrugged. "Good things take a while, lucky Lizenka. My husband never touched me as a man."

My heartbeat picked up. I thought of Buturlin's fingers brushing my inner arm in the twilight of a tent pitched far away from the palace's prying eyes; of his weight pinning me down for a heartbeat in the barge that had brought us to Moscow. I lowered my voice: "Touched you *how* exactly?" I hoped for further revelations, holding my breath. Anna was a good confidante: closely enough related to enlighten me about the mysteries of men and marriage, yet sufficiently remote in both age and distance from court.

She weighed my question: "It is not my place to tell you. You will lie with the King—as his Queen."

I regretted her refusal but accepted it: "So be it. You, too, Anna, are a queen of sorts. You rule in your own right." I touched St. Nicholas's face. The icon lay open and flat in my palm. "Isn't that extraordinary? No woman has ever ruled Russia."

"And none ever will. I rule but in name," Anna said. "The true master of Courland is Russia. The Tsar will not let me leave there, ever."

I turned over her hands and pretended to read her palms. "Anna Ivanovna, you rule, and you are much loved. I want to be Aunt Sunshine to your countless children."

"We'll see. May God protect you, Elizabeth Petrovna." Anna rose brusquely and retied her cape, looking imperious and forceful.

"Travel safely, cousin Duchess." I pecked her on the cheek and furtively sniffed at her skin. She smelled of crushed camomile and beeswax, a paste that was intended to preserve the pallor of the skin.

"What are you doing?"

"I want to see if you smell of butter," I admitted. "Ekaterina said you lathered yourself in it."

Anna Ivanovna chuckled. "Her husband ought to have beaten Ekaterina even harder. I should take you to Courland with me. You are amusing, Cousin Lizenka."

"How long will it take to reach your country?"

"Give or take a couple of swollen rivers, mud-torn roads, and dozens of drunken ferrymen, anything between two and four weeks."

"Won't you be bored?"

A slight flush crept over her cheeks. "Biren and I have bread and candles to distribute to the poor along the way. They will sing and dance for us in their villages. Also my dwarf and my chambermaid take turns in telling us stories."

"What if they grow tired?"

"I slap them or threaten them with the spinning mills," she said. "I like a good yarn about robbers and highwaymen. How about you?"

"Nothing like hearing a good story." I eyed the icon once more. "St. Nicholas reminds me of Alexey." There: I had spoken his name. Father should never know.

"True," Anna said. "Poor Alexey. One more abominable thing that happened to this family."

This family: *Curse the Romanovs!* I stretched out my bare leg on the bed, my calves shapely and my right foot small, white, and plump. Yet I had kicked the Leshy into submission with it and could do so again.

"Can't you stay a bit longer with us?" I asked.

Anna Ivanovna stood straight with a pride that could not be beaten out of her, whatever Aunt Pasha, her sister Ekaterina, or life had thrown at her. "I prefer to jump instead of being pushed. Biren and I have not been invited to return to St. Petersburg together with the court next week. Moscow will be dead once you all leave—neither dinners, balls, theater pieces, nor *assemblées*. Only merchants' wives stick around, and the lower Muscovite boyars would laugh at us. I have enough of that every day in Courland: my own ladies-in-waiting ridicule me."

I could not help but take her hand, and she kissed my fingers. "Your kindness is a rare quality, Lizenka. I would love to spend more time with you. But I know better than to refuse the Tsar's offer of a travel purse. He might change his mind at any moment. Farewell."

Taking leave is a foretaste of death. Outside, beneath the Kremlin's Red Staircase, I heard horses neigh, a whip crack, men's voices. Soon afterward, the wheels of what must be Anna's hired carriage hit the hard cobblestones. I skipped barefoot to the window, to see four strong ponies strung in single file gathering speed for their dive onto the tight, coiling roads of Russia's former capital. Once they were out of sight, I admired the icon that glittered in my palm still. I kissed the saint's face, the enamel cool beneath my lips. Even though the icon's diamonds were dwarfed by my ring's single stone, it felt like the most valuable of my possessions.

27

～

As autumn's last golden light soaked the October air, Karl von Holstein rowed alongside the Winter Palace. Dozens of swans—his heraldic beast—were harnessed to his gilt barge, fighting the Neva's swell; the barque was decorated with garlands of evergreen. While his musicians aboard emulated the sound of the waves, he called up to the palace: "Tsesarevna! Lizenka!"

Anoushka looked up from the delicate watercolor she was painting, frowning. "What is that he's saying?"

"He's calling, 'Tsesarevna! Anoushka!'" Mother silenced me with a warning look. "He is pining for you."

"Indeed—off you go." I pushed her out onto the balcony, where she stood and smiled, her face rising like a rosebud from the sable collar of her blue velvet cloak. She waved at Karl who, after a brief, surprised pause, was prodded by a Holstein minister standing behind him: he scattered ivy leaves and belladonna berries on the Neva's silver waves, vowing his eternal love and complimenting Anoushka's beauty.

I was delighted for my sister. Also, Versailles's acceptance of Father's offer of my hand felt imminent. Yet that meant leaving Russia: to root my country forever in my heart, I planned to go on a pilgrimage. Who knew how I should be able to honor my faith once I arrived in France?

In summer I had walked from shrine to shrine, from chapel to chapel, until I reached a monastery. Mostly they were built on old

Russian Orthodox earth, surrounding Moscow like a wall of faith. Now, however, a first thick snowfall allowed for a swift advance on the Monastery of St. Sabbas by sled. I was looking forward to the journey through the silent, otherworldly beauty of the countryside.

On the morning of my departure, I went early to the small private Imperial chapel. Only the stables were a hubbub of activity—a string of strong, low ponies, their hooves as big as plates, was being harnessed in readiness to my sled. When I left after my prayers, the far-flung corridors of the Winter Palace were still eerily quiet. The flagstones were covered by a first rime, and my breath clouded the still air.

Karl von Holstein stepped out so suddenly from his hiding place that I was startled.

"Karl! You scared me," I laughed, pressing my hand to my pounding heart.

"That was my intention," he chuckled, his face red.

"What nonsense! I must be on my way." I stepped aside to pass him by, but he blocked my way so that I was forced to retreat. He followed, pushing me against the cold wall. I frowned. Was it counsel on Anoushka he sought? I should tell him all and everything about my sweet, sensitive, learned sister.

"I know. There is nothing so attractive as a pious and principled maiden." He swayed on his feet yet managed a brief bow, his normally harsh Northern German accent slurred. Had he gone to bed at all last night? On his cheeks I saw a blond stubble as fair as his hair, which was normally covered by a wig; his lips, which were as full as a girl's, were moist and his pale blue sled-dog eyes red-rimmed. The lace jabot at his neck was untied and sullied, his jacket crumpled and hastily buttoned—he looked to have been just recently thrown out of a *kabak*.

"What takes you here? Are you thinking of converting to the Russian Orthodox faith?" I asked coolly. "Otherwise, it's a long way for you to be from your quarters."

"My freezing quarters! I have found better, Lizenka. Trust Menshikov to know the best addresses in town. The rascal always chooses something close enough to his palace, though, so he can crash into bed with whomever he fancies."

Menshikov! I remembered the advice he had given Anoushka before Mother's Coronation on how to behave with men, repeating some silly image of Ostermann's about jugs and water being poured. What did my father's favorite crony mean by leading my sister's suitor into debauchery?

Karl bowed exaggeratedly. "I apologize, beautiful Princess. My ministers warned me not to offend the ears of any Tsesarevna, but only to flatter and please them."

"That is sound advice. Especially as Anoushka loves to listen to a good story."

"And what is it you like to listen to, my Elizabeth?" He took a step toward me, trapping me between his arms as he rested his palms flat on the wall. Even though I had thought him slight, so close he stood a head taller than me. I fought the impulse to hold my nose as he reeked of the night before: spilled vodka, stale sweat, and cold tobacco.

"I am not *your* Elizabeth. It is enough for me if you make my sister happy," I said, yet I was aware of how alone I was with him here. The priest who had taken my Confession had certainly slipped back into the vestry and then from the chapel. My maids were busy packing my chest. My heart thumped, and I tried to duck away, but he was faster, seizing my chin in one hand.

"But I like the sound of it. *My* Elizabeth," he repeated, enjoying the words. "I have wanted you from the moment I saw you." His glassy gaze sized me up, and I was grateful to be wearing a dark, double-woven wool cloak, which shrouded me from chin to feet. "You know that, don't you, little vixen? I think you play a game with me. The more you hide, the more I seek you. You are bewitching. Just to see you, is to want to—"

"Stop!" I ordered, disgusted by him, trying in vain to shake off his hand. Instead he grabbed my face harder. "You have asked for Anoushka's hand in marriage. Honor and love her, as I do—"

He snorted. "*Asked* for her? I was given no choice in the matter! I might as well wed and bed a beanpole. I will be covered in bruises after the wedding night after poking her bony little body."

"What?" I asked, not understanding his words.

"It is you I want. Consider my offer. Versailles will never take you. Anoushka and you were both born illegitimate. But I understand what made your father marry your mother: like her, you are as warm and vital as an animal. I am ready to overlook the flaw in your birth, and one day I will make you Queen of Sweden. You will have as much winter darkness and ice and snow in Stockholm as you do here. You'll feel at home there." Before I could react, he grabbed my head between his hands and forced his wet, slobbery mouth onto mine. Suddenly he was everywhere: holding my hands and trying to pin me against the cold, hard stone. His tongue prized open my lips, and I gagged at the sensation. No! I had fought off the Leshy, so why should I suffer him?

When he came up for air, still restraining my wrists, I bit his lip as hard as I could, tearing it and drawing blood. He recoiled with a shout, touching his mouth. I used the opportunity to ready myself to retaliate, not knowing where I should hit him—I just wanted to be free. I kicked him hard between the legs. He howled like a dog, which pleased me, and so I jerked my knee up once more, hitting him right where it had hurt him so much, harder than before. He bent double, coughing and gasping: all the blood seemed to drain from his face. He crossed his hands in front of him and fell to his knees, fighting for breath.

I stepped away from the pillar, running my fingers over my bruised lips; with trembling hands, I rearranged my braids. Red-hot anger seared me: for Anoushka's sake, and for the hurt and anguish Karl had caused me. As he started to lever himself up, I kicked him once more, as hard as I could, in the chest before step-ping away, leaving him sprawling on the ground.

"Shame on you, Karl," I told him. "I shall try to forget this, and even pray for your putrid soul during my pilgrimage. But I warn you: honor my sister! She is worth a dozen of you. Failing that, I shall see that the Devil comes to get you."

He rose at last, pain, anger, and the lust for revenge cross-ing his face. I held up my hand. "Don't you dare come any closer. Never, ever again. Otherwise, I shall let my father know what you did. You shall be thrown from the spire of Saints Peter and Paul at dawn. I will push you myself, your head twisted toward the north-west where Sweden lies, or Holstein . . . or Hell itself for all I care! Then you will never be king."

He stared at me, weighing my words, not sure if he could be-lieve them.

I seized my chance to back away, turn, and leave, willing my steps to remain steady though I shook like a leaf. He did not follow me, but I felt his gaze on my back. Only when I had turned the corner did I allow myself to run, flying back to my rooms, where I urged my maid to hurry up and finish packing.

I wasted my time on that pilgrimage: however hard I tried, my soul would not settle, and my spirit would not be cleansed by prayer as usual. Karl's face intruded into any thoughts, and I felt his loath-some lips on mine. I fasted to purge myself of the memory of his grabbing hands on my body, before eating as much as I could, stuff-ing in food without tasting it, to fill the aching void the encounter had left in me. Finally, I asked a novice to cut a hole in the ice of the monastery lake for me at dawn, taking a freezing plunge while she stood guard. I shook in the morning chill and gasped at the icy shock of the water on my bare skin, hoping in vain to wash away any trace of Karl.

Yet more than his touch, his words had upset me: how could he speak like that about Anoushka? Granted, he had been drunk or hungover; in that state I had observed my father kiss man, woman, dog, and donkey at his feasts, where he also freely insulted friends or even trained his whip and his cudgel on them. Come the next day, all was forgotten. Finally I decided that it was better to let matters rest: any other course and I risked breaking Anoushka's heart.

When I returned to St. Petersburg in time for Yuletide, her betrothal to Karl was announced.

The ice on the river lay an *arshin* thick and was as shiny as a mirror, icicles chiming in the trees along the quayside, when we accompanied Anoushka and Karl to the chapel. Dogs, reindeers, and ponies dragged our sleds, their reins adorned with silver bells, tinkling the sweetest melody. Anoushka outshone the thousands of candles that Father had paid for. When he folded her slight fingers into the Duke of Holstein's hands, I could still remember the feel of those paws on my body. The bite on his lip had healed; he avoided my gaze as thoroughly as I did his. Just thinking of how close he had been to me, and the violence of his advances, gave me goose bumps. Only Anoushka's adoring gaze at her future husband gave me hope.

Karl received her dowry of thirty thousand roubles ahead of the wedding. While sitting in his pew listening to Feofan's blessing of the engagement, Father's broad shoulders heaved, and Mother, too, dabbed her full, rosy cheeks. As we knelt to pray for the couple's health and happiness, I clutched my icon of St. Nicholas, which I wore strung on a short, twisted chain of gold. My eyes were dry. I forced my heart to be calm and trusting. Yet I could not fight off the burning worry I felt for my sister. Even if her body should soon belong to her new bridegroom, I prayed her soul would be forever close to mine—and that Karl would learn to love Anoushka as much as I did.

On the way back to Menshikov's palace, where we fêted the engagement at his expense—which, as always, delighted Father—the

Tsar refused to wear a cap despite the icy wind. When a sudden gale made him lose his wig, too, he roared with laughter and for good measure tore his jacket open while he chased his sled over the ice.

The next day he had contracted a vicious cough and a fever that could not be brought down. Whenever I wanted to see him, a throng of courtiers blocked the entrance to his apartment. Among them I spotted Petrushka's godfather, Alexis Dolgoruky. Of course he had to be here, as opposed to Father's reforms as he was, and rooting for Petrushka. Was he lobbying for supporters? I ignored Dolgoruky but sensed the suspense and fear that thickened the air. A Tsar on his deathbed made even time hold its breath. The country hung in the balance between past loyalties and new allegiances.

Menshikov was heard saying to Mother: "The Tsar made Anoushka and Lizenka Tsesarevny. That does not mean he has designated his heir."

Russia was ignorant as to who was to be its fate.

28

On February 8, 1725, Peter I of All the Russias died in the upper reaches of the Winter Palace. He was not on his own, as no ruler ever is; yet he was lonelier than ever. The church bells had fallen silent, as if gathering strength to give tongue once more when the moment came to carry the word out into the vastness of his realm. In the sickening suspense of those days, I was shocked to see my beloved Father retreat into the shadows, while the Tsar still breathed. The ruler obliterated the man.

The Tsar has died, long live the—

Menshikov was right: Anoushka and I were Tsesarevny, but the Tsar had not designated either of us his heir. On the contrary. *You are not to rule,* he had said in Peterhof.

"The Tsesarevny are to stay in their rooms," Menshikov advised Mother. "Too much is at stake." While Anoushka obeyed and spent those days in Karl's company, I slipped through the corridors of the Winter Palace late in the evening, when the number of courtiers waiting outside the Tsar's death chamber had diminished. With each step I got quicker, sensing time slipping away. I swallowed tears as fear and rage mingled. Who was Menshikov, who was *anyone* to keep me from my father's side? As I was about to open the door to the private apartment, a man called out to me.

"Tsesarevna Elizabeth Petrovna—"

Alexis Dolgoruky rose from a chair and hurried over to me. I hastily wiped my eyes. His presence turned my father into the Tsar again. I sensed his design.

"Has the Tsar designated his heir?" he asked with a cursory bow, forgoing all politeness. His clothes were disheveled, his graying hair tousled, and his eyes bloodshot. No wonder he oozed tension and impatience: his godson Petrushka was the only surviving male Romanov heir. Influencing the young man in Dolgoruky's own antiquated ways would be easy and profitable for him. Who won the Tsar, won Russia.

"No, Prince Dolgoruky," I said curtly, despising his urgency as much as his preference of the former half-Asian Muscovy to Father's semi-European Russia. "I must hurry. As you say—I am the Tsesarevna."

"What about Petrushka?" he quickly asked, but I hurried on. He dared not seize my arm.

In the Tsar's death chamber, the fire burned high. Father abhorred the cold. He had spent too many nights in a freezing tent during the Great Northern War. Candles were lit, and the thick velvet curtains drawn. The air was scented by liniments and camphor, as well as frankincense and myrrh, but I sensed another sickly sweet note. Death was already spreading its shroud. Feofan Prokopovich stood at Father's head: he prayed, seemingly without ever drawing breath, for hours on end, ignoring the jug of vodka placed there for his benefit. His eyes were closed, his parched lips were moving ceaselessly. Three times he took Father's dying Confession and gave the last rites. Both the Tsar's giant body and his unbridled soul were resisting death.

My anger blindsided me: while Anoushka and I were told to keep away, myriad other people hovered at the Tsar's bedside. I fought my way through them to where the three German doctors perched like the crows Father had abhorred. My dark cloak blended with their clothes. Nobody paid me any attention. Mother, Menshikov, and Ostermann stood at the head of the bed, whispering and urging the doctors to further treatment: relieving his bladder, wrapping him in linen drenched in the Neva's icy water, applying another cure of mercury. Hours seemed to pass. Mother and Menshikov took turns sitting by Father's side, alert to his every movement, his every whisper, while Ostermann slipped in and out of the room. Governing Russia allowed him no respite.

"Tsaritsa, take heart. We will end this as we have started it: together," I heard Menshikov say to Mother. He kissed her fingers. We? What was he talking about? Tears blurred my sight. I stood on tiptoe to glance over at the bed. Father looked waxen, his chest rising in short, pained gasps, the interval between each lengthening painfully. If Mother did not rush to dab his parched lips with a moist cloth, she clasped Menshikov's hand, shaking and clinging to him for support.

"I long for rest," she cried. "He suffers so much." Her eyes lay deep in their sockets, her hair was tousled, and she looked pale and drawn.

"You must stay. Nothing has been decided yet," Menshikov countered.

At that moment Father whispered something.

"What does he say?" Mother urged. "Who is it to be?" Menshikov lunged forward, pressing his ear to Father's lips.

"Silence!" Feofan Prokopovich hissed.

We held our breath.

"Anoushka. Bring me my eldest—" Father whispered.

Feofan's prayers picked up again. Menshikov hesitated.

"My love," Mother said, holding Father's hands: "Tell us what you want."

He clasped her fingers. "A scroll," he said. "A quill, ink . . ."

"Get the scroll. Now! Only then will his soul depart in peace," Feofan ordered. I felt like training Father's knout on Menshikov. He took his time to rummage at the Tsar's desk, which as always was in utter disorder. Finally, he returned with a quill dripping with ink and a scroll.

"Here, my love. Be free." Mother helped Father grasp the quill. Ink splattered the soiled sheets as she held the scroll taut. With the last of his strength, Father began to write. He gasped. The quill scratched on the paper. Menshikov turned to us, thundering: "Out, everyone!"

Mother nodded, her eyes serious.

In the corridor I lingered in the shadows, waiting, while the courtiers dispersed.

All was silent inside his room. If rage seared me, my tiredness and grief devoured me. Menshikov could not keep me away one more moment. I was about to lose my father. Ten horses should not keep me away from him. I quickly checked the corridor and slipped back inside his chamber. Mother, Menshikov, and Feofan Prokopovich were nowhere to be seen. Father's bedside was deserted. He lay like a felled tree. My heart pounded: however precious a solitary moment alone with him had been in life, on his deathbed it would be rarer still. The never-again loomed, shrouding my memories of moments spent with him, as father and daughter. His eyes were shut, and his mouth closed; the chin raised as if to face a final challenge. Was he asleep, possibly recovering? My heart pounded.

"Father," I whispered, my breath flying, and reached out with trembling fingers. I recoiled. His hand was icy. No breath stirred his mighty chest. I stared, instantly understanding. I had come too late. Through a veil of tears I spotted the thin strip of gauze that bound his chin. He looked as calm and composed as he had never done in life, suffering from tics and fits. I gave a sob and with unsteady fingers stroked his hair. It felt wispy, like skeins of silk. I cupped my mouth, aghast at my loss. Eternity had made haste, chastising my hesitation and my obedience to Menshikov. The thought suffocated me as I sank to my knees, clutching my father's already unyielding fingers.

"Father," I sobbed, my tears pearling on his skin. Any other word caught in my throat. Yet what else was there to say? I pressed his hand to my lips, the skin waxy and ingrained with tobacco, saddle soap, and ink. The nails were bitten, cuticles torn; its back was veined and mottled. The hard and calloused palms bore witness to his impatient life, from learning how to build ships in the Netherlands to constructing the first cabin in St. Petersburg; from guiding a horse in battle to the *sabrage* of thousands upon thousands of champagne bottles. Already his once gigantic figure shrank, resembling a wax effigy from his Kunstkamera, stiff and bloodless. This was not the quicksilver-like man I had known, and that Russia had feared. I fought for air. Tight chains wrapped around my heart and squeezed all the air from my lungs. Dropping to my knees and curling up next to his deathbed, I let out one long, pained wail, such as peasants' wives and daughters did.

I grasped his shroud, crying uncontrollably, burying my face in it and stuffing it into my mouth to gag my sobs. In vain. I shook until everything ached. My whole being was aflame with grief. I was breathing in lead. As I opened my eyes, I took in the look of his bare hand. The heavy ring bearing the Imperial seal, a huge ruby engraved with the Russian royal double-headed eagle, had disappeared. The sight stabbed me: his fingers had always borne the sign of the Tsar's absolute power. The corpse morphed from my father to the *batjushka* Tsar, the father of the nation. His suffering had made us teeter at the edge of an abyss, staring anxiously into its depth. Now Russia was in free fall.

What, or who, was to follow Peter the Great?

The thought marked an end to everything I had previously known. All my life I had been the Tsar's daughter. Who was I to become now? My thoughts raced and my breath stalled, as I heard voices from next door, behind the leaning door to Father's little library. It was a murmur rising like the Neva's tide, yet those words were ready to erode the foundations of all we had built our existence upon. Russia had a new ruler.

What had Father, with his last, dying breath, decreed?

29

I edged closer to the leaning door, peering through the gap into the cosy chamber, a shrine to father's interests. The fire was burning high, and I saw Mother and the Privy Council—the men whom Father had entrusted with advising him on his rule over Russia: Tolstoy, Menshikov, and Ostermann. I pressed the back of my hand against my trembling lips, tasting salt, eavesdropping on their discussion. Or was I entitled to each word?

"Petrushka is the last male Romanov. He is Alexey's son. Surely he should reign?" Ostermann spoke up for his ward and pupil. "He is twelve years old, almost a man, and in good health. We can declare his majority in three years."

"The Tsar had ample opportunity to name Petrushka as his heir," Menshikov interrupted. "Making him Tsar would betray his will. Did you not see the boy's godfather, Alexis Dolgoruky, lingering? We all know who will really reign if Petrushka comes to power. Dolgoruky is an Old Believer who will reverse the dead Tsar's reforms. Moscow will be the capital once more and St. Petersburg abandoned. The fleet will become firewood. The Baltics will be lost, one by one, in skirmishes against the Swedes, if not by secret deals with France and England."

"Never! Not an inch of the Baltics is to be given up, ever. It is soaked with Russian blood. No higher price could be paid," Mother decided, honoring Father's words. Her determination calmed me, and I felt hot pride surging. If one pillar of my existence had broken, two others remained: Anoushka and my mother, my father's crowned companion. We stood as one.

"True. But above all it is you, Menshikov, who will be undone, if Petrushka comes to power," Tolstoy teased his former crony.

I held my breath. Could it be that the powerful Menshikov was mortal enough to know fear? Who could ever think of toppling him? It was unimaginable.

"How so?" Menshikov duly challenged him. As always, attack was his best defense.

Tolstoy added: "Weren't you the first to sign Alexey's death sentence, albeit with a cross, as illiterate as you are? The Tsarevich died with your knee on his head while the Tsar wielded the sword, urged on by you. You alone fed his fear and hatred. Since forever you have led him deeper into excess, be it in drink or deed."

I cupped my mouth in terror. My throat felt parched. The horrific details of Alexey's death had never been discussed. Would my half-brother possibly still be alive without Menshikov's interference?

"Let the past rest. We are all guilty. You, too, were in Alexey's cell the night of his death." Mother sounded pained when she rebuked Tolstoy. "Nobody touches Menshikov as long as I live. I do not forget a friend, as each of you well knows."

Menshikov bowed, kissed her hand and purred: "Your wisdom allows only one way forward."

"And which way would that be?" Ostermann asked, careful not to betray any emotion. "The Tsar had hinted that the Tsesarevna Anoushka—"

"A hint is not enough on which to inherit Russia. She is to marry a foreign duke. Do you want Karl of Holstein to rule here? Hardly. No!" Menshikov thundered. "Who has forever influenced the Tsar with her mildness? Who is in every way suited to further and fulfill his task?"

I straightened up, listening hard. *We live in times of great change.*

Suddenly I understood. If Anoushka's name was mentioned, yet her claim discarded because of her betrothal, then the next in line would be—me, whose engagement had not yet been confirmed. Me, who had been named Tsesarevna, Crown Princess.

Me.

The world fell silent.

"I doubt that the princes, the boyars, and the Church would condone that move," Tolstoy objected. There! He was right. How would Russia welcome an inexperienced maiden as its ruler and absolute monarch? I clasped my hands, feeling each finger—could they bear the weight of the Imperial seal?

Menshikov snorted: "Any heathen believes speedily enough when facing guards with fixed bayonets. Call the regiments to take the oath. Whoever has the regiments, has Russia."

Trust Menshikov to suggest brute force as the best way forward in order to reign Russia. Russia. I closed my eyes, picturing all my country had to offer. Forests and tundra, brooks and plains, mountains, and endless, changeable skies. Where should ruling it begin, and where would it end? The task had made Father rise before dawn and retire long after midnight. I shivered. Russia was timber, sand, and lime. It was ore, diamonds, and gold. Coal, salt, and copper. Fish, fowl, and furs. Oats, wheat, and barley, feeding its vast populace of aristocrats, landed gentry, merchants, workers, peasants, and serfs—millions and millions of people. Taxes must be raised, fees and fines upon everything stemming from the country's bounty: paints, inks, dyes, oils, gems, perfumes, spices, drugs, jewelry, furniture, books, candles, paper, rope, rugs, tapestries, canvas, hides, leather, horn, feathers, bristles, fabrics, wool, gunpowder. As the vastness of the task dawned on me, I clutched my icon of St. Nicholas, Russia's patron saint, in mute prayer.

There was no further time for me to think. I heard steps and the library door was torn fully open. Tolstoy barged past. I leaned on the doorframe, squinting in the candlelight. Mother turned to me, hair tousled, and face swollen from crying. Behind her, by the fire, cowered d'Acosta, gray-faced from his vigil by my father's bed. Mother reached out to me. She opened her hand, her tender smile reeling me in.

In her open, flat palm, close enough for me to seize, lay the Imperial seal, its ruby flaming.

30

Menshikov was the first to kneel, followed by Ostermann. Mother's smile widened as she first clutched the ring, closing her fist, and then slipped the Imperial seal onto her own finger. It sat tight, stuck at a swollen knuckle. The men took turns to kiss the seal, taking the Oath of Allegiance. As both men rose— Ostermann gasping with gout and Menshikov grinning—they saluted her: "Long live Catherine I! The Tsar is dead. Long live the Tsarina!"

I stood dumbfounded, hiccupping with tears and surprise. Morning had still not broken, but Russia's destiny had been decided.

Me? No. I had not been ready.

"Did Father designate you as his heir?" I asked, swallowing my tears.

"The Tsar died before writing down a name," Menshikov said, showing me the scroll. I read what Father had scrawled: *Give everything to*—before his quill had slipped in a last, deadly fit. "Luckily, we could guess his last bequest."

"Lizenka, come to me!" Mother opened her arms, tears welling anew. I wanted to fly toward her, but first curtsied and took my Oath of Allegiance in turn; the Imperial double-headed eagle veering toward my lips. The ruby's fire was as cool seen from close up as the lions' eyes in Kolomenskoye. Mother pulled me to my feet. I read fear in her face; yet there was a glint in her eyes, like the warmth of a fire that a lone traveler kindles deep in a Siberian forest, determined to survive the night.

"Mother." I kept my voice low, yet Menshikov shamelessly hovered nearby. "How will you cope? Are you not afraid?"

She rubbed her face and then gave a short, almost hysterical cry, which she muffled behind her cupped hands. "Afraid? I am terrified. How can I live without him? How can we all live without him? And Russia that must be ruled." She shivered. "I try and think it might be no harder than when I was a serf and had to sweep a long staircase."

"How does that compare?"

"I never looked to the end of the staircase, only ever at the next step. The corridor that lay beyond would come soon enough." She folded her hands. "Your father is dead. The past is forever still. I need to take care of the living and the future," she said, tenderly stroking back my messy curls.

"But Father said back in Peterhof that a woman cannot rule Russia."

"Russia has changed. We all have changed. Father crowned me since," she said, and I recognized the spirit that had led her from a serf's *izba* to the Winter Palace. Now she would be the first woman ever to rule Russia in her own right: a crowned Tsarina. My pride in her was fierce enough to burn. "All I can do is try to fulfill Father's dreams and finish his work, Lizenka. What does your dance teacher always say?"

"Practice makes perfect." I conceded the point, then asked: "Where is Petrushka? And how will you keep Alexis Dolgoruky at bay?"

"Very alert as ever, Tsesarevna Elizabeth," Menshikov cut in. "The Old Believers are becoming ever more powerful. They cannot wait to destroy your Father's work. I will keep Petrushka safe in Oranienbaum, away from any poison that might be dripped into his tender ear. His chamberlain Buturlin will keep him company there. Oranienbaum is a wonderfully healthy home for a boy."

I weighed his words. Petrushka was to be Menshikov's prisoner, however he presented it. This thought made me profoundly uneasy, as did his standing so close to us, listening to our every word. At least my nephew would have Buturlin for company—which meant that I would not. The thought touched me deeper than I had expected: I had grown accustomed to his dashing ways and daring spirit. Nothing was ever too daunting for him.

Hesitant steps came toward the library: Anoushka appeared on the threshold, clasping her red velvet dressing gown to her, straight dark hair falling in a sheet over her shoulders. "Mother. Elizabeth. What is happening?" she asked. Her gaze was drowsy, yet it darkened with understanding, like a cloud drifting in front of the sun. I had been at Father's deathbed and had already sworn my allegiance to Mother while Anoushka obediently lay asleep. Yet I did not want her to feel excluded for that.

"What is happening? I am the Tsarina's daughter. And so are you," I said, pulling her close and embracing her. We women stood once more in a tight circle, as we had in Kolomenskoye. Before I could help it, the Leshy spirit's words forced themselves into my mind, all the way from the Golosov Ravine to the Winter Palace. Her first prophecy had come to pass.

In your end lies your beginning.

31

Neither Petrushka nor Buturlin attended Father's funeral. I forbade myself any thought of the chamberlain, even though in those weeks I badly missed his daredevil attitude and instant attentiveness to my needs and moods. To know he was missing from his regiment, which was among the fifty thousand soldiers who gathered at dawn on the Neva's icy surface to escort the Tsar on his last journey, was torture to me. If there had at least been word from Versailles, I might have taken some comfort, but de Campredon, the French envoy, steered clear of me: court mourning was not the moment to discuss an engagement. I would wear white for months, while the courtiers dressed in mourner's weeds darker than soot.

On April Fool's Day Mother had all the fire bells rung at dawn. The inhabitants of St. Petersburg dashed out of their houses and palaces, terrified by the thought of another conflagration that would ravage the town. Shivering in the cold, wearing nothing but their nightshirts and caps, they stared at the peaceful morning, where no fire was to be seen, but only their Tsarina, watching them from the balcony of the Winter Palace, roaring with laughter and delighted with her own tomfoolery. To make amends she treated them to free vodka for the day. As the last drunken revelers deserted the streets come nighttime, she still stood by the window, looking out: "It is just not as fun anymore without him," she sighed, and started crying.

* * *

Anoushka continued to prepare her trousseau: bed and table linen, porcelain, silver, dresses, and jewelry. Her household of cooks, scribes, librarians, choirboys, maids, tailors, and two Orthodox priests—she would not convert to the Protestant faith—held themselves in readiness for her wedding and eventual departure for Holstein with Karl. On a day in late April, I found her kneeling in front of a chest. The tip of her tongue protruded between her lips as she counted stacks of heavy, embroidered white linen and lace napkins. She could feed the whole of Holstein at her table. I chased away the memory of how Karl had waylaid me: never since then had there been anything untoward between us, if one discounted his quickly averted glances. I sneaked up to her, hoping to lighten our somber mood for once. I snatched a napkin, twisted it, and placed it on my hair like a Dutch milkmaid's cap; I flapped my hands like a dove and danced about.

"Stop it, Lizenka!" She leaped up to chase me, but I was quicker and chanted in a harsh German accent, "I am a Holstein dove. Or a Swedish seagull. Catch me if you can, darling Karl! Let us eat some *lutefisk* together, the herring you have peed on! Soooo delicious!"

"Just you wait!" She lunged at me, but I ducked free, hiding behind chairs that I toppled to block her way, giggling. She cornered me as I clung to the curtains. My sister was angry. I was only joking—what was her problem? "Cheer up, Anoushka. Waiting a little longer will not harm Karl. He will want you all the more," I said as the doors were flung open. Guards positioned themselves, ladies-in-waiting flocked in, and Mother and Menshikov entered the room.

"Tsesarevny," Menshikov said, bowing and swapping a quick glance with Anoushka. I paid it no heed as d'Acosta was already copying me, folding himself angel's wings from the stack of napkins, skipping about like a portly and aged *putto*.

Mother, too, laughed when she saw the folded napkin on my head. "What is going on here? A play? Why so sour, Anoushka?"

"Long engagements make for unhappy marriages," my sister said reproachfully.

"Well, in that case, I have good news. A date for your wedding has been set," Mother said. "Your father abhorred the dullness of mourning," she continued, dabbing her eyes. D'Acosta, who had come to stand next to her, obediently made sobbing noises. "You are to be wed on the first day of June."

Anoushka's face lit up. "In just a month's time?"

"Yes. Following that, Karl and you will receive a palace on the shores of Lake Ladoga as well as a yearly stipend of a hundred thousand roubles. You have Menshikov to thank for that."

Anoushka gave him a warm smile. Since when was it his privilege to award palaces and stipends? I suppressed a sneer at Mother's estimation of his service to us. A single swallow did not make a summer. I glanced into his dark eyes: owlish and unforgiving. I shivered, sensing how the balance of power had shifted. Who was left to threaten Menshikov with a hiding? With friends like him, one needed no enemies. I straightened, refusing to be cowed by him.

"There is one last condition to be fulfilled," he announced to Anoushka.

"Which is?" she asked, her cheeks flushed.

"You must relinquish any right to the Russian throne for yourself. Your son, if God blesses you with one, may or may not always be named Tsarevich."

Relinquishing the right to the Russian throne? How ridiculous, I wanted to say. I should rather accept that snow could be black.

Anoushka, however, shrugged: "So be it, Alexander Danilovich. That is what Father intended after all."

I was dumbfounded. Since our elevation in Peterhof, the world had changed. Our mother was the first Tsarina of All the Russias. Yet Anoushka could give up her right to the throne as easily as refusing breakfast? What for—marrying Karl of Holstein? I bit my lip as Menshikov's ever-present, enigmatic smile deepened. "I shall have the agreement drafted today."

Anoushka clapped with joy and I took the napkin I had snatched off my head, waving it: "Finally! We will both be queens. Queen of Sweden and Queen of France. How wonderful!"

Anoushka turned to me, eyes as hard as flint. "Oh, no," she said. "You won't be a queen."

"Don't, Anoushka, please," Mother said. I clutched the napkin: nuns had adorned each corner with both the Holstein and the Russian Imperial coat of arms. "What do you mean?" My voice faltered. I was filled with foreboding.

"Oh, Lizenka. Have you not heard?" A small, mean smile spread over my sister's previously sweet face.

"Anoushka, this is not the moment. Relish your own happiness and be charitable," Mother rebuked her, but Menshikov touched her elbow, preventing the reprimand from continuing. He watched us, as pleased as if he had set a successful wager on a bear fight.

Be charitable?

"Heard what?" I asked. Time dripped.

Anoushka placed her words as carefully as her embroidery needle, piercing my heart. "King Louis of France is indeed to marry, Lizenka. But he has not chosen you, who so loves her horseplay with Buturlin. He has just become engaged to Maria Leszczyńska."

"Maria Les—what?" I blanched, struggling with the unknown name, and shook my head. "Who is that?"

"You may be unable to pronounce her name, but she took away your future husband and the throne of France. Her father is the *deposed* King of Poland, yet she is a Catholic and born in wedlock, legitimately a princess. Not like you, *Wolverine,*" Anoushka mocked me. "But I still have the chance to become a queen, the Queen of Sweden, and reign at my husband's side. Karl is mine."

Her words clawed my heart. I clung to the heavy curtains, feeling faint. "Why are you doing this?" I asked, incredulous. I did not recognize her anymore. What had happened to us since our closeness at Kolomenskoye? The Leshy had driven a wedge between us. Then I met Menshikov's implacable gaze. Or had we our good friend here to thank for that, always striving to divide us?

"Why? Did you really think I haven't seen what you were trying to do?"

Mother had paled. "Lizenka, what does Anoushka mean? What were you trying to do?"

"She tried to *steal* Karl from me," Anoushka spat out. "He only had eyes for her, and she encouraged it whenever she could! What did Buturlin call himself when he played Lestocq's silly Tarot cards? *A fool for love.* But not Karl. He has seen your true nature, Lizenka."

"No! That is a lie. He tried to force himself upon me!"

"Slander!" Anoushka threw the word in my face. "You tried to seduce him and steal him from me. You can't abide the sight of other people's happiness."

"Anoushka!" Mother called. "That is not true."

"Everything always has to go your way, doesn't it, Lizenka? At any price! That is why you tempted me into danger. I, too, should know what fate had in store for me. At least, that is what you called it—fate."

I paled. My foolishness in taking her with me to see the Leshy spirit came back to haunt me.

"You get what you deserve: nothing. Karl is to be *my* husband, a reigning duke. Harlot!"

She swept out of the room, leaving a flutter of curtsying ladies-in-waiting and an array of saluting guards in her wake; all of them burning to carry the gossip out into the streets of St. Petersburg.

A pained silence spread like oil on water.

"Is this true, Mother?" I cupped my burning cheeks, feeling overwhelmed with pain and embarrassment. "Have the French humiliated us like this?"

"Oh, Lizenka," Mother said, sounding helpless as Menshikov hovered behind her, watching, listening, hearing it all. His

gaze dwelt on me; the scoundrel had obviously known, and probably for a long time. The Secret Office of Investigation informed
him first of their findings, such as the engagement of the King of
France to an obscure Polish princess. Yet he had not bothered to
soften the blow; he had been too busy dripping poison into my sister's ear, driving a wedge between us. But why?

Mother continued: "It is my fault, Lizenka. Versailles would
never accept the illegitimate daughter of a former washer-maid as
the Queen of France."

"But I am the Tsarina's daughter." My voice was raw with humiliation: I had been publicly rejected. Was this to be my reward
for stifling my feelings for Buturlin? Who was the fool for love now?
"What does de Campredon say?"

Mother shook her head. "He requested his laissez-passer the
day he learned of the Polish engagement. His ship sailed a couple
of days ago." She leaned on Menshikov's arm. "I wish your father
were here. I miss him terribly . . ." She halted herself, tears welling
up. "I feel as if all the marrow has been sucked from my bones.
Reigning over Russia is so hard."

"You have me now," Menshikov soothed her, patting her hand
as if it were a dog. "Let us share my strength."

Wordlessly, I turned to the window and pressed my forehead
against the glass, the cool pane soothing my feverish thoughts. On
the river's choppy surface, the last floes of ice bobbed. The *ottepel*'s force broke them into shards, the sharp planes gleaming like
blades. I already felt stabbed in the heart by Anoushka, the sister I
had loved and trusted.

Mother embraced me, and my knees buckled. I surrendered
myself to her tenderness for a moment, then broke away from
her: with a single furious scream, I tore down the heavy curtains,
ripping the lining and letting the fabric pool all around me. If
Versailles's betrayal hurt, Menshikov's manipulation of Anoushka
was unbearable. He had struck me at my most tender and vulnerable point.

"Don't, Lizenka! I bought those curtains for your father back in Holland." Menshikov looked aghast.

I spun and leaped at him then, my nails unsheathed, going for his face, wanting to draw blood. He seized my wrists as I spat my anger at him: "*You* bought them? And who provided you with the funds? Who would you be without my father? Shut up, Alexander Danilovich. Let me go or I'll have your limbs broken on the wheel!"

Menshikov obeyed and crossed his arms defensively before him, yet his eyes darkened, weighing me up. "Lizenka," Mother scolded, and chased away her retinue with a single "Go!" She kneeled beside me, rocking me like a baby, her warmth seeping into me. If I wept for my broken dreams, I cried most of all for the loss of my sister. After a while Mother let me go, dabbing my face with the silly Holstein napkin. Menshikov still stood close, but I ignored him.

"Not everything is lost," she said, sounding almost cheerful.

"How do you mean?"

"Well, rest for a bit. And then I have someone to present to you."

"Who's that?" I sniffled.

"A cousin of Anoushka's Karl: Prince Augustus of Holstein. Why waste time?"

I stared at her, incredulous. Years of promises, hopes, expectations, and lengthy negotiations were dismissed as if they were nothing. I should happily trade the King of France—the King of France!—for an obscure German princeling, who, quite possibly, had also asked for *any* Tsesarevna's hand? I was like a filly being trotted out of my stable for prospective buyers to assess at a horse market. As I swallowed, my pride tasted salty and sharp, slicing my soul as a sword might an acrobat's throat.

"You are but the Tsarina's second daughter. Better look at Augustus before you stay a spinster forever," Menshikov warned me.

"Surely there is another possibility?" I asked haughtily.

Menshikov's gaze skewered me and he smiled as if I had given him a secret cue. I braced myself as he said: "Oh, there always is."

He turned to Mother, gallantly kissing her fingertips: "My most gracious Tsarina, I request your permission to take Elizabeth Petrovna on a journey."

"A journey? Not abroad, I hope?" Mother seemed glad to leave all further proceedings to him.

"No, no. Just to the Susdal Convent."

The Susdal Convent.

Despite the mild April morning, those words chilled my heart.

32

A nun opened the little window in the cell's door for us to look through before she stepped aside. The stench forced me to keep my breathing shallow. The stale, enclosed air; the reek of sweat and filled, forgotten chamberpots: my mouth filled with a metallic taste, as if I had swallowed blood.

Menshikov stooped and peered inside. A smile flitted over his face, like a swallow darting across a courtyard. He stepped aside, inviting me to take my turn, but stayed nearby. The heavy gold chain that fastened his wolfskin cloak glistened in the dull twilight of the corridor; the fur looked sharp and bristly, almost spiked.

I stood on tiptoe, my heart pounding.

Inside the cell a woman sat hunched on a three-legged stool before a low table. There was neither tablecloth nor cushion, nor rugs, nor curtains. On the floor lay rotten straw, and she bent to scratch her legs, sighing and carelessly lifting the dark cloth of her robe up to her skinny thighs. Bites festered on her shins and calves, among myriad other scratches, bruises, and cuts. She had some tufts of hair on her shorn scalp; scars showed where the barber's blade had slipped. Her bedstead was a sack of straw and a threadbare blanket on a bench of cold stone. The water on the walls probably froze to icicles in the winter.

The woman rose, standing taller than expected, but her robe hung from her meager shoulders like a limp flag from a pole; wrists and ankles were mere bones. "Dunia," she said, turning her head. Most of her teeth were missing, I saw. A faint rustle came from the far corner of the cell, as if a sow were burrowing out of the straw, and a hunchback dwarfess shuffled into view. She was dressed in rags, her hair wild, and face covered in warts. Her wretched mouth opened like a gash in her withered face, with its heavy forehead, beady eyes, and flat nose. She slunk up to the prisoner, babbling and fussing over her, tucking at her dress and attempting with pitiful hops to stroke the woman's bald head, as if coiffing her. I knew why she was forced to babble: slanderers and cheats often had their tongue cut out. Her mistress slapped the creature's hands away, before sobbing and cupping her own face in her hands. Then she stilled and looked up, straight at the gap in the door: she sensed us spying on her. I felt Menshikov's breath on my neck, so close he stood to me. There was no escape.

I turned away, drained by the sight, pressing the back of my hand against my mouth to fight the rising bile. Menshikov watched me, his dark eyes curious and amused. Standing in that gloomy corridor, he seemed to grow taller. I refused to be cowed, yet it took a while before I found my voice again. "Who is this? What has she done to deserve such a fate?"

I pushed myself off the wall and stood before him, spreading my feet to master the trembling in my knees. Before we left Mother had forced a cloak lined with miniver on me, which had seemed too warm in the May sunshine of St. Petersburg. Here it prevented neither the goose bumps on my arms nor the shiver chasing down my spine. I touched my icon of St. Nicholas to steady myself. On Menshikov's sign the nun closed the little window in the door, shutting away the pitiful sight. She lingered, holding an iron ring with a dozen similar keys hanging from it. Twelve more unfortunates were locked away in this hellish place, I realized, buried alive and swallowed from the face of the earth.

"Do you really want to know, Lizenka?" Menshikov towered over me, that little smile that never quite left his lips looking mean now. His eyes were as black and shiny as a pig's that had found a truffle among the shallow hornbeam roots.

"Tsesarevna Elizabeth Petrovna," I corrected him haughtily, yet could not hide the tremor in my voice. "Why else would I ask?" Ever since Father's death, his favorite's ambition soared and advanced like a wisteria plant that outgrew the flower beds Father had introduced from the West, creeping up toward a bulbous cupola or piercing spine, and finally reaching for the sky.

"This is the Tsaritsa Evdokia, daughter to the powerful Lopukhin family," he told me. "She was your father's first wife, mother of your half-brother Alexey. For twenty-five years she has been a guest here. She, too, refused to do what was expected of her. So, yes: there is always another possibility. Wherever, for whomever." His voice was calm, almost luring, as he threatened me, a maiden, with all the experience of a soldier and seasoned statesman.

I recoiled and clutched my St. Nicholas so hard that the diamonds cut into my palm. The saint was savior of the suppressed, protector of the persecuted. Yet was even his power enough to shield me from Menshikov?

Suddenly I understood his haste to marry me off. He already controlled Mother, and Petrushka was his prisoner in all but name. Now Menshikov only had to get rid of Anoushka and me to reach his goal: he wished to rule Russia.

33

Anoushka's wedding day broke after an ashen night as a glorious sunrise set St. Petersburg aflame. The Neva lay still, spread out like a golden sheet. In the early morning hours, I prayed for her happiness and begged that we would find our way to each other again. I did not know any longer what she felt or thought, since she refused to talk to me. The more I had guilelessly turned to her in the past years, sharing my joy in life, the further away I had driven her. Menshikov had read her better than I had. I dressed glumly for the wedding ceremony. Mother had sent a pale pink silk gown and a matching parure of pink and white diamonds to my rooms.

In church Karl von Holstein ignored me, as any jilted admirer would. He knew on which side his bread was buttered. The best tailoring ensured that even his meager shoulders looked broad in the uniform of the St. Petersburg Guards. I was relieved to see him smile tenderly at Anoushka when she floated up the aisle, looking like spun moonlight in her Parisian gown of heavy silver damask. Diamonds and pearls glittered like snowflakes in her dark curled hair, and peonies, the flower of prosperity and happiness, adorned the church, their dewy perfume scenting the air.

"Dinner will be inside but outside," Mother announced as we set off for the Summer Palace. The sails of myriad boats competed with the billowing clouds. In the gardens decorative arches wound with garlands supported a roof of gauze floating above hundreds of tables laid with white linen and gleaming silverware. The kitchens served a few hundred pounds of caviar, oysters, shellfish, eels, and anchovies before we moved on to tender marinated venison, whole suckling pig adorned with apples, as well as swans stuffed with chicken, pigeon, and sparrows. The wedding cake was decorated to look like the Winter Palace. As I stooped to admire it, I caught my breath. I seemed to see myself, entrapped in that sugar icing. An Ice Princess, frozen in her loneliness and despair, held captive behind the shiny, sweet windows. The guests were oblivious to my misery: they ate, drank, and laughed, faces glistening as they stuffed themselves like pigs ready for the slaughter. They chewed me up and washed me down with vodka. Finally they were so drunk that they pelted each other with pieces of the cake, making a mess on the dance floor, screaming with laughter and rolling in the debris.

Menshikov had placed himself in the position of honor next to Mother, the Tsarina, his haughtiness keeping pace with his thirst for power. Where would he stop—if he could be stopped at all? The thought that he kept Petrushka "safe" in Oranienbaum made me ever more uneasy. To what end? So far Mother had not designated me as her heir, though I still bore the title Tsesarevna. At least Buturlin was by my nephew's side. I envied Petrushka the fun and warmth of his company—and more, I thought, as I watched Anoushka gaze lovingly at Karl. She finally had what she wanted: a husband's hands given license to touch her, every night of her life, as his wife. Though I did not envy her for having Karl himself, the thought of marrying filled my stomach with butterflies. I had saved myself from temptation with the prospect of one day being Queen of France, resisting my attraction to Buturlin. But that hope had vanished like a phantom.

What now for me?

34

"I think Prince Augustus would like to see Peterhof, don't you? Right now," I said when the Holstein princeling was barely out of his coach after his arrival in St. Petersburg. His coat and shirt were sweaty, boots covered in Baltic muck. He bore no similarity to Karl: the red dust of the Russian roads blended with his thick auburn locks, which fell in an unruly tangle to his broad shoulders, curling around a strong neck and echoing the russet freckles on his nose and high forehead. Exhausted shadows lay under his thoughtful gray eyes. He had dimples. It looked as if he liked laughing. Soon he would be begging to leave.

"I will stay in Mon Plaisir. Augustus can be in the Marly Pavilion at the opposite end of the park. I will show him the grotto," I said, smiling sweetly.

"You'll show him the grotto?" Mother sounded alarmed, but Menshikov shrugged—the quicker he got rid of Anoushka and me, the better. A month had passed since my sister's wedding. I was overstaying my welcome. Mother's cheeks looked swollen, and her fingers so puffy that the Imperial seal ring had been hammered to a wafer-thin strip of gold. She was constantly out of breath and leaned heavily on Menshikov's arm.

"I'll show Augustus the grotto," I said.

The twenty *versty* out to Peterhof was one of the most beautiful rides in Russia. As at Kolomenskoye, the rooflines, windows, and balconies of the *dachy* reflected styles of building from all over the realm. Their façades were painted in delicious pastel shades of pistachio, vanilla, duck-egg blue, and even mauve, looking like a frosted row of timber birthday cakes.

We should see if this guy could ride at all, I thought, swinging myself into the saddle of the stallion Versailles had sent me. I felt heavier than usual, though: wherever I was, my inner Ice Princess came along, weighing me down from deep inside.

"Let us go!" I spurred my horse, not even turning to look at Prince Augustus.

He could eat my dust as far as I was concerned.

How long before me Augustus had arrived in Peterhof, I could not tell. He awaited me, wearing clean, pressed clothes and with his face looking fresh and flushed, as after a visit to the *banja,* when I cantered into the courtyard before the stables, breath flying and hair tumbling. The sparkle in his eyes was infuriating, and I allowed him only the merest of nods when he said: "Let me know when you are ready to show me that grotto."

As soon as I had settled in Mon Plaisir, there was a knock on the door: Augustus's chamberlain, whose long torso and short legs made him look like a dachshund, was almost concealed behind an enormous bouquet of two dozen lilies. The flowers were artfully arranged and beautifully held together by a silk ribbon. The man also offered me an exquisite tray of sweets, stammering some carefully devised words supposedly given to him by Augustus. They must have taken up a collection for these gifts in Holstein; the state was notoriously hard up. Wooing a Russian Tsesarevna was presumably seen as a good enough reason to loosen the purse strings.

"What is this?" The delicate shapes were adorned with dried berries and chopped nuts. They looked mouthwatering. Augustus must have been informed of my sweet tooth.

"It is marzipan, a speciality of Northern Germany, made of rose water and almonds," the chamberlain boasted. I sniffed at one of the sweets. It smelled heavenly. The chamberlain's eyes lit up, as he hoped to tell Augustus of my delight.

"Yuk! It smells like cow's pee," I said, opening my monkey's cage. The first sweet I gave the animal to nibble at, the rest I tipped onto the soiled floor, shoving them to the center. The wet straw stuck to the delicate paste morsels, spoiling them. The monkey screeched with delight, stuffing its greedy mouth. "My monkey doesn't seem to mind them. It might, or might not, write a thank-you note to Prince Augustus. We'll see," I laughed. "I shall meet your master in two hours' time in the garden, by the ponds."

I had hoped to wander about in Mon Plaisir, visiting the Chinese cabinet or seeking out the pantry where we had spent happy times as a family. But those days now seemed like a dream. The memories of our past happiness were too painful. I longed for Anoushka more than I could say. The feeling surpassed even my anger and humiliation at being hawked around to minor German princelings. I stayed in my room, asking my maid to draw me a bath, but even the steaming-hot water could not keep the Ice Princess at bay. There was no evading her. She slyly slipped into the tub with me, her smile sickly, her stare frosty, and her fingers like icicles, picking at my soul. I lay in the water, weeping, until it had cooled, and the lavender-scented soap left a slimy rim on the copper tub.

"Father had the gardens designed by Alexandre Le Blond, who worked on Versailles," I explained to Augustus as we circled the pond, hidden from the view of onlookers by high hedges. The Prince's retinue waited gamely on the vast terrace, gawping in awe at the park's many pleasure houses, cascades, and fountains. "He was inspired by the beautiful French palace."

"Are you sad?" Augustus asked, his gray eyes fixed on me.

"About what?" I looked up at him in surprise.

"About not going to Versailles as the future Queen of France?"

I halted and shielded my eyes against the rays of the afternoon sun. In all those months since de Campredon had fled St. Petersburg and my fight with Anoushka, nobody had inquired about my feelings. Augustus waited for my answer, his dancing freckles belying his serious eyes.

"It is hard to wait for something so long only to be denied it," I admitted.

"I can imagine. And what will happen if Karl is not made heir to the Swedish Crown?"

I had not thought of that before: Anoushka's disappointment would be crushing. But I would be by her side and do anything to help if she would allow it.

"I hope, though, that they are friends enough to weather that storm should it arise," Augustus continued.

Friends? What a strange notion of marriage.

"Now what is it about this pond that you particularly wanted to show me?" he asked, leaving me no time to consider the idea further.

"Look," I said, and moved a lever hidden in the hedge. With a brief humming sound, three copper ducks emerged from the water, amid gushing white foam, making quacking sounds.

"Splendid!" Augustus laughed.

"Just wait." I moved a second lever. A metal dog leaped from the waves, chasing the ducks in circles. "I have never seen the like," Augustus marveled. As he reached out, as if to touch the metal animals, I spotted a faint star-shaped tattoo on his wrist.

"What is this?" I asked, but he quickly covered the inky shape with his shirtsleeve, embarrassed. "Oh, that. A little liberty I took some years ago. I wanted to be a sailor, but my father belted me too severely for me ever to make it to Kiel harbor. Now I am a sailor in the Holstein Navy. In name, at least. I still love ships, though, just as your father did."

What a paltry attempt to bond. Time to get serious. "If you liked this pond, you should see the grotto," I tempted him.

"Gladly. Is it down by the sea?" He turned to the Bay of Finland, whose steely water matched his gunmetal eyes. The salty air had parched our lips; I smeared a paste of beeswax and honey on mine, pouting and smacking them, but I did not offer Augustus any.

"As you wish," I said coyly, and walked ahead, swishing my pale green damask skirt. White gravel crunched underfoot as we followed the paths down to the shore. Waves lapped at the dark sand. The seagulls refused to settle on the shore that day; they bobbed up and down farther out to sea. The grotto's mouth lay among piled-up rocks and boulders, artfully overgrown with creepers and guarded on either side by an enormous bronze statue. Augustus rapped on these admiringly, and they gave a hollow metallic sound. "Those are trusty warriors," he joked. "I shall fear their wrath."

I smiled deeply. "Indeed. Step inside, it is quite wondrous."

He stood in the cavern, tilting his head, admiring the mosaic of tiles, precious stones, and shells that covered both walls and ceiling. I slipped along beside the wall, reaching into a hidden niche. I found the secret button, concealed between two large conch shells—and pressed it.

"Marvelous," Augustus said, as a slight movement from the entrance caught his attention. "But . . . I must be going crazy. Haven't the guards just spun around?" he asked. "And did they have their guns raised before?"

"I really don't know," I chirped—and hit the lever beneath the button.

"What the—?" he started to say, but the statues were already spouting seawater at him, full force, making him stagger. His knees buckled, and he gulped for air while the jets pelted him mercilessly. As he shielded his face, gasping, he struggled to rise, trying to evade the force of the onslaught, but now the water also rose from myriad pipes and nozzles in the floor. It foamed underneath his feet, making him slide. The more he tried to escape, the more he slipped, stumbled, and fell—it was hilarious to watch.

"Amazing, isn't it?" I shouted, tears of laughter in my eyes. Water bombarded him from all over the grotto, drenching him to the skin. I was helpless with mirth, holding my sides and cupping my face, until, very slowly, the streams abated. The metallic guards slotted back into position, facing the sea. All was silent. Augustus stood before me, trembling and soaked: his hair stuck to his head, and water dripped from his eyelashes, nose, and ears. His fine breeches, waistcoat, and jacket were destroyed, clinging to his, I had to admit, tall and lean body. Menshikov must settle the bill for a new wardrobe for him before Augustus's return to Holstein.

"Sorry, I had no idea that could happen," I cackled, wiping my eyes. "But how funny! Don't nice German maidens like a bit of a joke?" I gathered my skirts in my hands before I stepped over the wet floor: our gentle little walk was as finished as our acquaintance. All I longed for was the silence and peace of Mon Plaisir. I tried to slip past Augustus and back into the garden.

"Not so fast!" He seized my wrist and reeled me in. I gasped—nobody, except for his awful cousin Karl, had ever dared touch me like that. Was this a Holstein thing? He was holding me almost painfully tight, his eyes dark with anger. "Nice German maidens do not drench their suitors," he said, his jaw set.

"Stick around, and there will be more where that came from," I snapped. "Now let me go." I wriggled to free myself, but in vain.

"I shall let you go, Tsesarevna," he said, "but not quite now."

I was breathless with shock as he lifted me up and swung me over his shoulder, like a sack of barley. I drummed his back with my fists and kicked the air with my feet, screaming for help, but Augustus sprinted down the path from the grotto and onto the pontoon. Ahead of us lay open water.

"No!" I shouted, but it was too late. He gathered speed, laughing.

"Yes! Now it is your turn to be soaked. Enjoy!" He leaped ahead into the sea. I screamed as we were both submerged in an almighty splash. Salt water swirled all around me, filling my mouth and nose, dissolving my hairdo, and soaking my new silk dress. I gasped as I came up, thrashing and ranting, then felt gravel and mud beneath my embroidered slippers. We were not far from the pontoon: the water barely reached my waist. Augustus stood close by, stroking back his wet hair from his forehead, water drops running over the star tattoo on his wrist.

"You look splendid, Elizabeth," he laughed. "Like a wet cat. I wish I could have you painted like this, to keep the memory forever."

"The memory you may keep. I myself am not to be had." I leaped at him, ready to scratch and maim. He seized my wrists and smiled: "I am not so sure about that." He bent my arms behind my back, forcing my body closer to his. My breath caught in shock: one more tug, one breath closer . . .

"Don't you dare!" I struggled against his grip, but it was useless. The world beyond seemed to disappear. I felt his chest against mine and Augustus's strong heartbeat. My breath flew from me, shallow and hot. His mouth was close to mine, smiling to reveal white, straight teeth in the face of my spitting, clawing anger. I fell silent, stunned, held hostage in his grip. He murmured, "I wanted to do this before, when I saw you at the Winter Palace."

"What . . ." I started to say. He kissed me. First I wriggled, but then I held still as a slow warmth spread through my veins. His lips were careful yet confident, tasting me, searching for my reaction. Though I tried to break free once more, by some strange natural law I slid closer to him. Even as he eased his hold on my wrists, I clung to him, which made his kisses deeper, hungrier. I felt so awkward and naïve—what was I supposed to do? Open my mouth? Close it? And then any thoughts dissolved in a maelstrom of feelings, as his mouth held me captive more surely than his grip did. I heard a sigh—was that me?—as I softened, losing my footing and melting against him. Standing in the cold autumn waters of the Bay of Finland, I felt miraculously warm.

"I could have drowned," I gasped.

"No. I know how to swim. A sailor saves his girl. Always," he whispered.

"His girl?" I hesitated for a heartbeat before I went on tiptoe and cupped his face in my hands. Now it was I who kissed him. His mouth tasted different with each kiss: strawberry, *smetana*, *medovik* honey tart—all my favorites. The waves came and went, washing me closer to him. I clung to his neck, dissolving with sudden desire. Hesitantly I spread my hands on his chest, not even taking the time to breathe, dizzy with fear of the unknown, feeling his smooth skin and the strong body beneath. I shivered. He gently kissed my fingers before he smiled at me. "I admit defeat. You have spirit enough for ten. Come."

We waded back to the pontoon where he heaved me onto the planks. He stroked my soggy hair from my face, his star tattoo visible once more. He remained waist-deep in the cloudy water, eyes sparkling as he smiled—that funny, warm smile of his—and said: "Marry me, Lizenka."

Marry me. I caught my breath. Was it that easy? A firework went off in my mind, showering me with happiness, as well as doubt. Everything came flooding in: my parents' blessed marriage; Ekaterina's battered face; Anna Ivanovna's miserable, penurious widowhood; my confused, barely restrained desire for Buturlin that was not to be; Karl's assault; Anoushka turning her back on me; and finally Augustus's lips, which laughed, kissed, and spoke the words that offered me freedom.

It took me but a breath to decide.

"I will." My words were as simple as his. Up close I could see the blue Peterhof sky reflected in his steady gray gaze. I thought about counting his freckles, but in vain—I would leave that for another moment. We were to be married. There was plenty of time. He kissed my hand once more, his gaze shiny with delight. Behind us we could hear footsteps and shouting. Our servants came running along the sea channel, calling out and jostling each other, falling over their own feet.

"Come up here," I said to Augustus. "Otherwise you'll catch a cold."

He heaved himself up on the planks, and we took hold of each other's hand, turning to face the world together. By now the sun's rays had cooled, and our teeth chattered. We were quickly wrapped in woolen blankets and offered glasses of vodka, which we tossed down. While the spirit gently warmed me, I looked out over the sea once more. Clouds billowed, their darker linings promising evening rain. Mist rose from the water, veiling the hazy horizon.

I squinted: it looked as if something moved in the water, struggling to stay afloat. It was everything that had weighed me down—my inner Ice Princess. Augustus's embrace and proposal had washed her straight out of my soul. I relished her futile struggle against the current, which dragged her out to sea. Good riddance to her!

35

The following weeks in Peterhof forever belong to Augustus, though surely Mother and Menshikov were kept informed by daily dispatches. This was what they had hoped for, after all. Augustus joined me every morning in the pantry at Mon Plaisir: I wore my hair in a loose plait and dressed in a simple, unlaced housedress and a felt jacket with fur collar and leather toggles, while I stirred our kasha. He licked his porridge, which was sweetened with *smetana* and honey, off my fingertips, before bringing the samovar to the boil, adding a good shot of vodka to the *chai* to start the day. We talked, and we listened to each other, and best of all, we fell silent together.

Augustus was good at asking questions—about my lonely childhood, the making of St. Petersburg, and my father, whom he called "The Great Tsar." Together we marveled at Menshikov's arrogance, pitied Ekaterina for her brute of a husband and Anna Ivanovna for her poverty-stricken life in Courland. I laughed myself to tears when he copied stiff, gouty Ostermann, and Augustus held me tight when I cried about my rift with Anoushka. When I was with him, my heart ached less for the past, and I looked forward to our joint future. Since that first kiss we had quickly grown more daring. It seemed that my thoughts about Buturlin had laid a fire that Augustus could set aflame. He served me at the table, holding my hand while I ate, kissing my fingers, then pulling me over and on top of him, his mouth making a single demand and I giving in to it. I felt him, sitting astride, and he undid the toggles of my hussar's jacket, his hands cupping my breasts through the fabric of my shift. "The perfect aristocratic handful," he said.

"That is because you have big hands," I teased, and kissed him. "Much bigger than a prince should."

He kissed me back but would go no further. "I told you, I am a sailor at heart. But I want you as my wife," he said, pulling away.

Yet we pushed the boundaries of our desire further and further. We rode out hunting—he was an even better shot than Buturlin, whose image paled in my memory—and found a clearing where the moles' little pink hands had not pushed up too many hills. Mushrooms sprouted all over the musty, red-and-gold speckled leaves, but it was more their scent than the sight of them that gave them away: ceps, chanterelles, portobellos, and curly baby, which was delicious in scrambled egg.

We tethered our horses; they grazed and nuzzled at each other. Augustus skinned the hare he had shot before making a fire, deftly stacking the dry kindling in a cone, stuffing arid moss in between the sticks, and lighting them with a single strike of his flint. The game he set to roast while I gazed up at the dense blue sky, wearing my fur hat at a rakish angle, my shirt daringly unbuttoned, sitting in my tight breeches and thigh-high boots on his cloak, which he had spread out for me on the moss. Sips of heavy red burgundy set our kisses alight. He came closer, and I slipped backward, his body deliciously heavy on mine. I arched my spine with pleasure as his lips slowly traveled from my mouth down my throat. He pushed back my shirt, kissing the delicate skin of my shoulders and inch by inch moving the neckline lower, opening toggle after toggle, tasting my skin. The cool air grazed my nipples as he caressed me.

"I so want you. I shall love you every day of our lives, every morning and every evening. For starters, for main, and for dessert at lunch, believe me. We shall have dozens of little Holstein princes and princesses because I will not ever tire of you. But I want you as my wife, and I shall not dishonor you before that," said Augustus, sitting up with a sigh, his silvery gaze fixed on me. "I love you, Lizenka," he said, and the simplicity of his words overwhelmed me. Who would have thought our love could be so beautiful, so easy? The evening descended, and its cool made us shiver; the hare on the spit had turned into a charred lump. "That's a small sacrifice to the god of love," Augustus chuckled, flinging it into the thicket for the wild animals to feast on. "As long as I have you, my hunger is sated."

We played hide-and-seek in the Peterhof maze: he found me hunched behind Venus and lifted the small statue off its pedestal, to place me there instead. "This is where you belong," he said, taking off my slippers. He kneeled and kissed the soles of my feet and their soft insides through the sheer silk of my stockings. I leaned into the hedge's deep sheltering green as he lifted my wide, heavy skirt up to my hips. "Augustus!" I gasped, but he went on caressing the skin of my calves, the backs of my knees, and my inner thighs, making the silk crackle beneath his tongue. I melted with lust as he touched me, bit my thumb so as to not give us away at the shock of his tongue sliding into me. I froze—what was he doing? "Don't!" I gasped, and he stopped for a moment.

"No?" he asked. "You don't like it?"

"No! Well—yes! I mean—do," I begged, and fell silent, incredulous, as he licked me, slowly and tenderly, as if I were a delicate little cream cake. How much must he love me to do this? His tongue settled on one spot. I held my breath, not knowing what to expect. Golden lights danced senselessly behind my closed eyelids as his tongue circled tenderly. I writhed, my fingers laced in his thick auburn curls, as an unknown, utter abandon built up in me: I gripped the sides of the pedestal, almost passing out with pleasure. "My Venus," he whispered, holding me close. "I cannot wait until you are mine," he said, his eyes dark with desire. "But we mustn't do any more for now."

I felt mad with frustration. "What else must happen to make me yours?"

"We will be married, never fear."

"But what if the moment never comes?"

"It will." He grinned. "If by then you have not tired of me."

"Never," I said fervently. "Neither my mind nor my body shall ever tire of you."

"I have never met anyone so full of opposites as you, Lizenka." He looked at me tenderly. "I love how you force me to think about you."

"What do you mean?"

"You grew up as wild and free as a peasant's daughter in the Russian countryside but were set to become queen of Europe's most sophisticated court. You are so pious that you would go on pilgrimage sliding along on your knees, yet you hide in the bushes, here with me. You ride sitting astride, dressed as a man, but also own an untold number of splendid gowns. You live in a palace but prefer sleeping in a tent and cooking on an open fire. After your initial disdain, you now love me fervently. You will not suffer that your family is done any harm, but accept that your brother, the Tsarevich, had to die—"

"Silence," I warned him, and pressed my finger to his lips.

He nodded, understanding my anguish, but kissed my fingertips, saying: "You are truly my Russian girl."

There was a heartbeat of silence. Finding that we could share everything together was a revelation to me. I delighted in seeing him try to understand me and who I truly was.

"A Russian girl? I am indeed," I said.

We left Peterhof when the Karelian Plains were drowning in heavy autumn rains; as the carriage passed the entrance to Oranienbaum, I looked out of the window. Of course neither Petrushka nor Buturlin was to be seen. Back in St. Petersburg, winter soon came with its dry, crackling cold. *Ded Moroz*, Father Frost, covered every twig with his crystalline breath. The court launched into a Yuletide more pompous than ever before. Menshikov succeeded in keeping our family apart. Anoushka and Karl had moved to Ekaterinenhof Palace; I was delighted to hear of their contentment. Seeing Mother on her own was next to impossible. The more Menshikov had, the more he wanted—such was his nature. His greed and his ambition were boundless—like my happiness. Augustus's love had fended off the Ice Princess, weighing her down to the bottom of the Baltic: our engagement was to be announced the day after Epiphany and the sacred blessing of the waters.

Everything would change for me then.

36

"The Count Peter Andreyevich Tolstoy," my lady-in-waiting announced. "And your Imperial sister, the Duchess of Holstein."

I turned in surprise. Tolstoy was so old now that he hardly ever left his dacha, where he loved to watch birds. Also I had not expected Anoushka to visit from Ekaterinenhof: Karl had taken the best revenge he knew by deepening the rift between my sister and me. Thick snow had been falling since the previous afternoon, making the city's roads impassable. Outside I spotted Tolstoy's coachman chatting with the guard at the palace gate, both of them warming their hands at the sentry-post brazier. I was still in my velvet dressing gown, teaching my parrot some fine, juicy words. Later I was to meet Augustus for a game of chess. "See them in," I said, placing the squawking bird—which hurled the funniest cacophony of slander at me—back in its cage.

My heartbeat quickened when I curtsied to Anoushka, who lingered behind Tolstoy on the threshold. How gladly I would share my joy in Augustus with her and thereby double it. "Sit," I said, "and have some spiced *chai.*"

"We have no time, Tsesarevna," Tolstoy wheezed. "We have to go and see the Tsarina."

"See Mother? Why? What has happened?" Already I was looking for boots to wear, slipping out of my soft leather *pantoffels.*

"Menshikov is to announce the engagement of his eldest daughter, Maria, to Petrushka," Tolstoy said.

I was dumbfounded. "That is impossible. Maria Menshikova is almost thirty years old, and Petrushka barely thirteen!"

"To Menshikov nothing is ever impossible. Petrushka's godfather Dolgoruky came to see me this morning, all wheezing and upset. He was at the Winter Palace, but neither the Tsarina nor Menshikov would receive him."

"No wonder—he's a disgusting Old Believer. He must be beside himself with fear. This engagement will make him lose any hold over Petrushka," I said, satisfied by that thought at least.

"Not only him. Our existence is threatened, too," Tolstoy warned.

"Menshikov wants the throne. We have to stop him." Anoushka's voice was clipped, and she made it plain there was to be no further conversation between us, turning away from me and sighing at my slowness. I hurried after them, pulling on a fur-lined cloak while I was walking. What would happen to Russia if Menshikov succeeded in placing his daughter on its throne? Petrushka was to be his puppet and Russia his personal purse, funded by the endless sources of the realm's bounty and its millions of men, toiling endlessly like armies of ants.

"I cannot go back on my word," Mother wept, struggling for breath. "I have agreed to Menshikov's proposal."

"Allowing this marriage will endanger not only Russia, but also your daughters' lives," Tolstoy said, kneeling before her, palms pleadingly upturned. "They pass on the right to occupy the throne, if not to inherit it themselves," he added, looking at me.

Mother panted, one chubby hand placed on her heart. In the almost two years of her reign, she had undergone a shocking change, gaining weight and losing all interest in life. When Father died, he had taken her spirit with him to the grave: they were always one being.

A faint rustling came from behind a folding screen next to her desk. I turned to look. Someone was hiding there and listening. "There will be a double engagement—Lizenka's betrothal to Augustus and Petrushka's to Maria Menshikova. Do you not wish for his happiness?"

"If you did, you would never contemplate such a match," Anoushka said.

"Menshikov wants to drive us apart," I added. "Petrushka will be at his beck and call. He wants to rule Russia! Do you know what that means for me? Your decision places me in mortal danger, for I have not yet renounced my right to the throne, as Anoushka did."

"You exaggerate, Lizenka," Mother said, but sounded hesitant.

"Enough!" At that moment Menshikov stepped out from behind the screen, unashamed about his eavesdropping. His face, set with anger, looked more than ever like that of a roughly hewn puppet at a country fair. "You will pay for this, Tolstoy," he snarled.

The Count rose to his feet, looking despondent. "You are the traitor here, Menshikov. The She-bear Russia will have your bones. Just give her time."

"Then she will crunch you up for starters." Menshikov stepped closer to Mother, glaring at Anoushka and me. "Once your engagement has been announced, Lizenka, both of you girls are off to Germany. Spring is as good a time as any to travel there."

"I feel faint," Mother murmured, sniffing at a silk handkerchief, which was stained with blood. She wiped her face; thick red clots stuck to her pasty white makeup.

"Mother . . ." I started to say. The sight had scared me witless. Did she suffer from consumption? A move to the clean, salty air of Peterhof would be the best thing for her.

"Come, Catherine Alexeyevna, you need rest," Menshikov soothed her, and Mother looked at us, pleading for our forgiveness while unable to resist him. He led her into her bedroom, kicking the door shut. From behind the closed door came hushed talk and muffled sobs. I could sense him holding her, loosening her grip of the reins of power.

For a moment silence reigned. "By my soul, I have tried to prevent this," Tolstoy sighed.

"Karl and I wanted to leave for Germany in any case," Anoushka said, looking shaken.

"Having to leave is different from wanting to leave, Anoushka," I said. "Russia is our inheritance. What if you have a son? Once Menshikov has Petrushka wed to his daughter, nothing prevents him from taking aim at the Russian throne."

In the icy corridor Prince Alexis Dolgoruky waited for us, leaping up from a stool. "There you are!" He clawed at Tolstoy's lapels, sounding terrified. The thought of losing all influence over Petrushka through a wedding to Menshikov's daughter ended all his hopes and ambitions. "This must not be! We cannot abandon Russia to a scoundrel and an upstart like Menshikov." Even if he was hostile to my father's reforms and sounded pompous—the Dolgorukys themselves had founded Moscow in the twelfth century and had laid the Kremlin's foundation—I nevertheless had to agree with him.

"We have no choice. Russia listens to the Tsarina. The Tsarina listens to Menshikov. He will have his way," Tolstoy said. "But the Tsarina has yet to designate her heir." His words hung ominously in the air. I lowered my eyes to protect my thoughts from showing. Petrushka was not Tsarevich yet. Should I, too, be asked to give up my right of inheritance upon marrying Augustus? Me? This thought made me as irritable as a Siberian tigress starved after the long winter.

Just weeks later, Mother looked magnificent at the traditional blessing of the waters at Epiphany, wearing a riding habit of silver cloth and a wide-brimmed triangular hat, white plumes swishing from it. The parade on the ice lasted for four hours; in the late afternoon she coughed blood and fainted.

Menshikov delayed the formal announcement of both my and Petrushka's engagement and camped by my mother's bedside. No private word with her was possible, though I spent every waking moment with her, bursting with last questions to which I sought answers, last words of love for her. Her end was near and I longed for a moment on our own, but Menshikov stuck to me like a second shadow, or worse, like muck to my heels. I had never doubted Mother's devotion to us, even though loneliness had been our playmate while we were young. All I wanted was to hold her; to whisper last words of gratitude. Oh, to fold my fingers around hers and pray together for her soul's peaceful passage into the afterlife, where Father awaited her. If only she could tell him of what was happening, if only he could strike Menshikov from beyond. There was no such thing as privacy for an empress dying. Her status obliterated the mother in her, as had already been the case for Father. Even Anoushka joining me did not change that. Anoushka's face was stern and drawn when I curtsied to her and kissed her hand. While Augustus leaned at the wall, his mere presence supporting me, Karl kept close by, preventing me from sharing my feelings. Yet did she not share my fear? We were to become orphans in the span of just two years, outcasts, and on our own now—a terrifying thought in the face of Menshikov's determination.

Courtiers, military commanders, and high officials jostled for space in the death chamber, a tussle barely kept in check by Mother's ladies-in-waiting. Outside the door Alexis Dolgoruky headed a swarm of courtiers who all waited, undecided whom they must flatter and fear, ignorant of who next would decree their fate. I heard them whisper: "Has the Tsarina designated her heir?"

"Is it Menshikov?"

"A pie-maker's son? He is no better than a heyduck. No, it has to be Tsesarevna Anoushka."

"Hardly. She is to marry a foreign Duke while Petrushka is the grandson of Peter the Great, the last living male Romanov. He can be the only true heir!" Trust Alexis Dolgoruky to point that out, forgetting the power Menshikov had over his young godson.

Inside Mother's bedchamber swathes of frankincense and myrrh rendered breathing painful; a fire blazed, its smoke choking us. The windows were closed, curtains drawn. The room was as hot as a *banja* when Menshikov bowed down, listening with a frown to Mother's whispers, her last wishes. Her hand sought his fingers, clasping them, before he rose to announce: "The Tsarina's will be done! Petrushka Alexeyevich Romanov is to be Tsarevich and heir to the throne. He will marry Princess Maria Menshikova and come of age at sixteen. Until then a State Council is to reign: the Duke and the Duchess of Holstein, the Tsarevna Elizabeth, Vice Chancellor Ostermann—and me."

Tsarevna Elizabeth. I clenched my fists: I was not to be Tsesarevna, Crown Princess, anymore, but simply the Tsarina's daughter. So be it. My mother gasped in pain. I knelt by her bedside, touching her cheeks and forehead, which felt waxen. The silence between each gasp lengthened, while Menshikov continued: "The Duchess of Holstein and the Tsarevna are to receive one million roubles each for relinquishing their right to the throne to Tsarevich Petrushka and his possible descendants."

Anoushka was dissolved in tears, but glanced at Karl, who gave a curt, content nod. His gambling was the talk of town; still, they presented a united front, a wall so finely rendered that no crack was visible in it. "The Tsarina's personal possessions—her dresses, silver plate, china, and jewelry—are to be divided between her daughters," Menshikov added. My sister buried her face in her hands but ignored my pleading look: let us make peace, here, at our mother's deathbed. Who else but us two is there left?

"The Tsarevich!" I heard a voice call as the door opened, and Petrushka entered, followed by Buturlin. Before anyone could prevent him, Dolgoruky slipped in behind them. Petrushka squinted in the candlelight, still wearing his nightgown, clearly bewildered after the chase from the countryside to the city in the middle of the night. He had grown almost as tall as Father. Menshikov glowered at Dolgoruky, his gaze a clear warning, as one great beast might challenge another: the Tsarevich was his prey!

All I cared for was my mother. She sighed in pain, and I slid on my knees to her head, where I squeezed between the praying Feofan and her bedstead. I saw the blessing in his eyes as I cradled and kissed her, my breath hot on her icy forehead as the darkness drew close, cloaking her. She had settled all that was to settle and had taken leave. It was time. Despite my sobs and Feofan's prayers, the silence around her widened, a silver lake on which she would soon embark upon her last journey. As she took her very last breath, a short and painful-sounding gasp, her gaze plunged into mine, her fingers grasping my hand, before her eyes paled and stilled. A heartbeat later, her thumb ceased to caress my palm, and her raised chest stalled, caught in its last gasp as if by one of the many surprises her life had offered. Menshikov and Dolgoruky lunged forward. Both wanted to wrestle the Imperial seal from her finger. "Stay!" I snarled, and folded her hands inside mine, hiding them away, protecting her and Russia from the vultures and the usurpers if I could. Petrushka watched us in silence, frowning. The sight of him reprimanded me. What was I doing? The ring was his by any law in this world—and from all my heart. "Forgive me, my nephew," I said, and twisted the Imperial seal off. As I handed it over to Ostermann, my fingers trembled. The Vice Chancellor marveled at it for a second or two before bowing on his aching, swollen knee to Petrushka, his former pupil, who shook his head, saying: "No, don't." But Feofan Prokopovich had already blessed the young Tsar, and Ostermann slipped the ruby ring onto my nephew's long, slender finger, where it hung slack, before pressing his lips to the crimson stone.

He struggled to contain his emotion as he rose and shouted: "The Tsarina is dead. Long live the Tsar! Long live Peter II." Then he cried uncontrollably, clutching both Petrushka's hands, kissing his fingers again and again. As I, too, fought tears, I met Buturlin's eyes. He stood tall, guarding his young Tsar. Even though Augustus had stepped up behind me, and his hands lay on my shoulders in a gesture of comfort, my eyes meeting Buturlin's made the air between us crackle like a lightning strike. I felt his restless, pent-up energy from endless, sedate months spent with Petrushka in Oranienbaum. While I had never told Augustus about my forbidden, foolish feelings for Buturlin, his searing gaze singled me out, and his longing for the unattainable was palpable. No! Life had moved on for me, and the childish past must be relinquished. My way forward was a future with Augustus. Then it was my turn to curtsy to Petrushka and swear my Oath of Allegiance to the young Tsar. Yet as he raised me to my feet—standing two heads taller than me—his hands would not let go of mine. Surprised, I looked up: his eyes were no longer a boy's, but a man's.

My skin prickled. I felt as if I were surrounded by a pack of wolves—wild, ferocious beasts that the plains of Holstein at least no longer harbored. I thought with relief of my imminent escape to safety there.

37

Menshikov lost no time. As Mother's lying-in-state was being prepared, he banished Count Peter Tolstoy, who was in the eighty-second year of his life, to Solovetsky Monastery on the White Sea. There were no birds to watch. No one ever returned from there, nor did Tolstoy. Anoushka slid in and out of the death chamber, an ever slimmer dark shadow, accompanied by Karl, who greeted Augustus cordially and gave me only the curtest of nods. How would things be when we were all in Holstein? I chased away my misgivings.

We took turns sitting and praying by Mother's coffin until the interminable queue of courtiers, officials, and wealthy people from all over Russia, who wanted to see their dead *Matushka,* had finally dwindled. A priest stood at her head, chanting an interminable liturgy of prayers, supported by a miraculously refilling jug of vodka. The sight of Mother illuminated by banks of candles was unreal. Surely at any moment she would turn her head; we would see her dark unruly curls slipping from beneath the tiara, those green, slanted eyes shining with mischief. But no: she lay still, the back seams of her velvet Coronation gown sliced open to accommodate her ample flesh. I stepped closer, squinting in disbelief: some of the studded gold double-headed eagles were missing from the dress already, plucked off by fingers seemingly folded in prayer. I checked further. In the first days of lying-in-state, her body had been decked with jewelry, barely an inch of flesh showing. Now bracelets were missing, and she wore only one earring. Her tiara had shifted. Was that Menshikov's doing, too?

Already he had taken the Imperial seal from Petrushka, for, as he put it, "safekeeping." I could not turn to Anoushka. Also, Alexis Dolgoruky had convinced the young Tsar to place Feofan Proko-povich, the last friend I had ever since my childhood days, under house arrest. What was the next step for my father's trusted, cunning advisor? I feared the worst.

It was winter, and *Ded Moroz*—Father Frost—had touched my soul. Augustus stroked the hair gently from my forehead as I cried on his shoulder, both of us numb with grief and terrified by Tolstoy's and Feofan's incarceration. "I will keep you safe. We will be formally engaged as soon as the mourning period ends. Come," said my fiancé, leading me to the bed. We lay together between the starched linen and the heavy furs. Feeling his strength next to me was the best consolation I could imagine. He whispered endearments to me as well as promises of eternal love.

The moment for me to leave for Holstein and marry Augustus there drew closer. To arrange to receive my dowry, my inheritance from Mother, and all the smaller sums and gifts that had been promised to me on marriage, I asked for an audience with Menshikov. The young Tsar was once more in Oranienbaum, supposedly because the Baltic air was good for his lungs.

Menshikov made me wait for long weeks. The hour finally came early on a late spring morning, just days away from my formal engagement to Augustus. Mother's death had delayed the ceremony, but it would still coincide with the public announcement of Petrushka's engagement to Maria Menshikova. A fresh wind chased away the last of the winter chill, helping along the first buds on the fruit trees planted on the quays; on the Neva the last ice broke, the glare of it flashing among the steely waves. I still wore white, mourning my mother, when Menshikov invited me into my father's former study.

"Come in, Lizenka," he said, withholding my proper title, his familiarity a calculated slight. Yet I should not play into his hands by reacting angrily. Worse than his insults was the sight of him sitting at my father's desk, legs stretched out and feet comfortably crossed. His fingers twirled the great Tsar's quill—what for? He could not even read or write! The man he was today had obliterated any memory of the loyal, low-born friend he had pretended to be, who had been raised literally from the Russian dust.

"What a delight to see you." Menshikov shifted one buttock half-heartedly but stayed seated in my presence on a chair my father had made. The great Tsar had lathed the night hours away to chase his demons or hatch new ideas.

"I see you are busy," I said, trying not to let discomfiture color my tone. "But where is the rest of the State Council? I thought this was a formal meeting."

"Too many cooks spoil the broth." He crossed his arms behind his head and leaned back in the chair, balancing it on two legs like a schoolboy. "How can I help?"

"I come for my mother's bequest to me. My dowry, as well as recompense for relinquishing my right to the throne to Petrushka's possible heirs. It can all be sent to a Hamburg bank. Mother's plate, silver, and jewels I shall take with me in person. I trust no one here," I added, smiling sweetly, looking him straight in the eye.

"Bequest? What bequest?" Menshikov shuffled some papers on the desk, as if to find the answer there. He frowned and shook his head. "I am at a loss, Lizenka. Nothing is owed to you, and the Tsar has generously given all your late mother's belongings to his beloved fiancée, my daughter Maria." He gave a short, wolfish grin.

"I was promised one million roubles in recompense for relinquishing to Petrushka and his heirs my right to the throne—" I started, unable to contain my anger.

"The wisdom of your decision will be remembered. Tsar Peter is delighted."

"I imagine. My mother's will . . ."

". . . of which I am the careful executor, remember."

"Careful indeed," I interrupted him, my voice brittle, remembering my mother's lying-in-state: had Menshikov himself plucked the rings off her fingers, carelessly breaking a bone or two in the process? Had he untangled the tiara from her tresses, or had he simply torn it off, and clumps of hair with it? I hated him so much then that my voice failed me. I had to clench my fists so as not to claw him. "What shall I live on?" I asked, fighting back tears. "Augustus is a minor prince of the House of Holstein."

"You made your bed, you must lie in it. Surely young Augustus has a stipend or possibly wages as a sailor in the Holstein Navy?"

"Not that I know of." A sailor's wages would not pay for a single ribbon on one of my dresses. From the impoverished existences of my cousins Ekaterina Ivanovna and Anna Ivanovna, I knew what kind of life I was facing. Augustus and I were to reside in a far-flung, freezing corner of an inhospitable castle in Gottorf, more suffered than welcome there, running our meager household and touchy retinue on a shoestring. Each log on the fire would be counted, and only rind should enrich the pea soup, never proper bacon. During big family dinners, once or twice a year, we would be served last with the scraps from the platters, the servants already hovering, impatient to get away. At Easter my painted egg would be cracked; for Yuletide an unwanted gift from the past year's celebration would be offered. My children stood to inherit nothing. For as long as Karl reigned as Duke in Holstein, we would walk two, if not three, steps behind him and my sister. How had life turned the tables so swiftly on me? Well, I could do it, I decided: I could live with the fall in status because I loved Augustus.

Menshikov watched me, alert. "There is no room for further negotiation. All your mother's belongings are already with Maria," he said. "Including her furs. My daughter, the future Tsarina, does love a good sable coat. Petrushka will offer her your mother's crown. My grandchildren will rule over All the Russias. Better give in, Lizenka. We are a family now. One large, loving family."

Give in? Never! He was basted in self-regard. I fought back the tears for good. I was not a little girl but a Tsarevna of All the Russias, claiming her rightful inheritance. Any show of weakness would be fatal. "You owe everything you are to my father. My mother, the Tsarina, left her daughters a fortune."

Menshikov slithered out from behind the desk toward me, teeth bared, all vice and venom. "Believe me, I am intent on repaying all debts. Without me, Petrushka would not become Tsar. There is always someone else, Lizenka—someone such as you."

Me?

His eyes pinned me to the spot. "As you so helpfully recently pointed out, you have not yet renounced the throne. You would make a spirited Tsarina, wouldn't you? Possibly the regiments would support you, for some . . . consideration?" It took all my self-control not to slap him for that insult. "Whoever is favored by the Russian regiments, is favored by fate. But there can only be one ruler, my dear girl."

My dear girl. I saw every broken blood vessel in his cheeks and could smell his perfume of sandalwood and jasmine, too sweet for a man, as well as his sour breath—his steady chewing of cumin was in vain; his teeth had reached the point of no return. The threat was clear: if I did not leave for Holstein, he would stalk and slay me here. Better not to test his ingenuity in dreaming up a justification for it. Menshikov smiled as if reading my thoughts. He laid one hand casually on the nape of my neck. I froze at his touch, our gazes locking. For an incredible moment it seemed he might actually force a kiss on me. I stared at him, and he hovered, undecided, not moving any closer. Finally, he said: "So in memory of all the generosity your father showed me, I am letting you live. More so,

I am letting you *leave*. How long would you survive a damp, freezing nunnery, lovely Lizenka? There is not a shred of sanctity about you. I know what Augustus and you did in Peterhof."

I blushed deeply.

"But what might His Majesty think of that, who loves you as an aunt and wishes to respect you as a Tsarevna of his house?"

I freed myself from Menshikov's grip, my eyes blazing. "I am engaged to marry Augustus," I said, gathering my last shreds of dignity.

"Yes, he is only your husband-to-be," Menshikov chuckled. "That which made your father virile, makes you a harlot. Such behavior in a woman warrants a heavy punishment."

"What do you mean?"

"*Death,*" he mouthed, as ruthless as a gun dog. "The choice is yours. Cease your demands, and your carriage to Germany is ready to depart at any time you choose. Persist in them, and you will be shamed and punished severely. Now is there anything else? I have a country to rule. But I am not ungrateful." Once more he sifted through the papers that were waiting to be sealed and signed. "I might or might not forget the words you spoke to me today."

Anger and pride won over fear. If I had to leave the only country I should ever love, I refused to do so like a stray dog, my tail between my legs. With a single movement, I swiped the desk clear of all the papers. They billowed and flew up in the air before scattering all over the beautiful rugs and parquet, like doves spreading their wings. Now it was I who leaned in, placing my knuckles on the Tsar's desk. Menshikov shrank back, taken by surprise. Time flowed slowly, like fresh sap bleeding from a tree. It was true, the choice was mine.

Menshikov startled when I spat: "Rule the country? You might as well pee against the wind, callous coward that you are. A man like you cannot even begin to rule Russia. You are dust!"

The last vestiges of civility between us had disappeared. Menshikov's eyes became hard and unforgiving, that nasty smile lurking at the corners of his mouth. I should not be fooled by it ever again, but would hide my feelings. Otherwise the hunter in him would feast on them, devouring his prey's most tender part with relish: the heart.

"And you? No wonder France rejected you! What a joke it was to the Bourbons: the illegitimately born daughter of a serf, a washer-maid, wanting to reign in Versailles! And France knew only half the story. I plucked your mother from a heap of prisoners of war because she was as irresistible as a beautiful animal. She had me to thank for everything—and she did, believe me, many times over. You have forgotten where you come from, Lizenka."

Menshikov was not wrong.

He did not know how grateful I was for the reminder.

38

"You don't need money," Augustus consoled me as I paced my rooms, raging and wringing my hands, stamping my feet, and kicking furniture about. If only that toppled chair or skidding footstool were Menshikov! Evening fell. Outside, the Neva's banks took on a silver hue, allowing the glossy day to blend into a White Night. I felt immune from the beauty of the scene, a thought that only increased my pain. I should take it all in before I was forced to leave it forever.

"No? Do you have any money then?" I asked, hands on hips.

"No," he admitted, looking tired. "To be honest, I was rather looking forward to acquiring your dowry before I met you. Now I would take you without a shred of clothing on your body. Actually I'd especially take you without a shred of clothing on your body."

I had to laugh. Augustus would happily have lived as a sailor, free and poor. Life with him would be good—he was always able to soothe my worries, a priceless gift. He kissed my fingertips, his eyes shiny and cheeks flushed. As I caressed his thick, dark auburn hair, his forehead felt clammy. No wonder: he was as excited as I was. In a couple of days' time our engagement was to be announced formally, together with Petrushka's. Menshikov had presented this as a mark of Imperial favor: my parents' deaths and my nephew's accession had reduced me in importance and rank. It seemed I should be grateful to be included in the pomp and splendor of other people's celebrations. A reception, banquet, and ball were planned, and the palace was already buzzing with excitement.

"Soon we shall be engaged. On that day my new life begins," I said, forcing back tears. "Nothing else counts. I shall not allow Menshikov to spoil this moment. We will be happy together."

"It is the day I was born for," Augustus said.

I pushed back the two leather strips he wore around his wrist—beneath, all around the hidden star tattoo, the skin looked red and angry, as if a slight rash were breaking out. I tenderly kissed the tattoo. "What is this?" I asked then, touching the slight bumps and pimples on his skin.

"Just a bit of an irritation," he said, pulling his sleeve back down. "Listen. I have learned a Russian love song, just for you." I listened while he began: "Shine, shine my star." He sang out of tune, butchering the famously romantic lyrics, but that made me smile once more. When he stopped, he shivered and tightened his silk jabot around his throat, saying: "I think I might be getting a sore throat."

I kissed him. "As long as you can speak your vows."

I had last worn my pink and silver dress and the matching diamond parure at Anoushka's wedding, I remembered as I sat and waited for Augustus two days later: somehow, they had escaped Menshikov's purge of my belongings. Soon Augustus and I would step into the Winter Palace's Great Hall for the festivities to begin and our engagement to be announced. This might be the last time I should appear at court as a Tsarevna; for his sake I wanted to be the most beautiful woman present. My hair was twisted in a braided crown on my head. Once engaged, I must not wear it loose, as it might entice other men.

While waiting I thought of everything that had led to this moment. In hindsight the last two years had been like being pulled along by a raging river, struggling to stay afloat and not to sink and drown. I did not notice the time pass. Suddenly, though, morning had turned to noon: clouds skimmed through the sky, and swallows darted about. The sounds of St. Petersburg reached my ears: the guard changing, cartwheels on cobblestones, pie-sellers touting their wares, wind catching in sails and making the canvas crack like a whiplash, seagulls crying, horses neighing, children calling.

Augustus was late.

I did not wish to embarrass myself by sending for him, so I sat and waited a bit longer. My monkeys and parrots shrieked and squawked as my ladies-in-waiting shuffled and whispered in agitation. Had I, the Tsarevna Elizabeth, been rejected by my fiancé? Their eyes sought me out, gazes quickly averted when I looked up.

I could read their thoughts.

Enough. I got to my feet at a knock on the door.

A lady-in-waiting opened it and stepped back. "Tsarevna," she started to say, sounding unsure.

On the threshold stood a Holstein soldier, looking flushed from his run across the palace. "Prince Augustus's chamberlain has sent me. Come immediately, Tsarevna, please!"

I left my rooms calmly, head held high. Once the door had closed behind me, however, I kicked off my shoes to run, gathering my skirts, flying down the almost empty corridors of the Winter Palace, my hair coming undone. Silence reigned. Why had the soldier vanished and not escorted me back? Few courtiers were out; only a handful of guards manned the many doors and staircases: after the long years of relentless service under my father's watchful eye, indolence ruled.

Even at Augustus's door, his Holstein guard was nowhere to be seen. I hesitated: in the antechamber, the curtains were drawn, and a man sat slumped on a low armchair. At the sight of me, he fell to his knees: it was Augustus's chamberlain, the dachshund. "Thank God you came, Tsarevna!" he gasped. "I dare not stay." He pushed past me and out of the door. As he fled, the tails of his coat flying, his metal-capped shoes struck the marble floor, sounding like shots.

I turned back toward the inner room. A rasping sound came from the bedchamber that lay beyond, like the pained breathing of a suffering animal. "Augustus?" I asked, my voice unsteady. No answer but a low moan from next door. My heart pounding, I stepped into the small corridor linking the rooms. An unbearable stench hit me, worse than anything I could imagine. With every step I took, the air thickened. I covered my mouth and nose with my lower arm, sucking in my gown's rosewater scent. Another low, pained moan repelled me as much as it forced me onward: Augustus needed me, whatever had happened here.

I halted on the threshold. The bedroom was dark, curtains drawn. Yet I saw that the walls, rugs, and bed linen were horribly stained. Augustus lay slumped like a rag doll on his bed. At the sound of me, he turned his head, grimacing in pain, but his ashen face lit up. He was too weak to rise; as his cracked lips tried to smile, his eyes stayed dull. Their whites were sickeningly yellow.

"Shhh. Don't move." I rushed forward, placing my fingertips on his mouth. His breath scalded me as he whispered, "I feel so hot, Lizenka." I hurried to pull the curtains back and opened the windows to let in the May breeze. The Neva below glittered in the bright light, and the trees on the embankment burst with blossom. Such beauty felt like an insult.

"Help me, I want to see." He tried to rise, but his arms buckled. I hastened to catch him, stumbling under his weight. He rolled off the bed, and together we tumbled to the floor. He gasped with pain. His nightshirt slipped, and I suppressed a scream: his whole body was now covered in a deadly rash, angry red spots that combined here and there in raised, knotted pustules. It was monstrous.

"Don't look at me," Augustus sobbed. "And do not *touch* me, Lizenka. We both know what this is." He clawed at his sheets, struggling in vain to get back to bed. I stayed on the floor, all the strength seeping out of me, and then he, too, collapsed next to me, leaning against his bed, his head lolling and his legs long and bare.

"Not touch you—never!" I tore down the soiled sheets to cover him. "You mustn't be cold," I sobbed, choking and blind with tears, trying not to think of what lay ahead as I rested my head on his terribly bony shoulder. His illness had sucked him dry, leaving him brittle and parched. "I feel so dizzy. Today you are to be mine. Today we are to be engaged." He sighed, exhausted.

"Yes, my love," I wept. "We will be." I kissed his burning forehead, and he gave a shadow of the smile that had won my heart just months ago, while we stood waist-deep in the Baltic Sea. Yet his eyes reflected bottomless sorrow, and his bloodless lips were pale compared to the rash spreading over his face. He coughed, cramping up, before violently vomiting yellow bile all over my finery. I shrank back while he doubled over, made breathless by stabbing pains to his back and abdomen. I held his head steady until he could breathe again. Together we wrestled him back into bed. "Close the window. I am so cold!" he pleaded, shivering with fever and shielding his eyes against the spring sunshine. "I can't bear the light. The rays stab me."

"Let me get Lestocq. He will treat you." I choked back tears and reached out to caress the sweaty curls that stuck to his temples.

Augustus recoiled. His eyes were wild. "You mustn't catch this."

I sobbed and hurried out to summon Lestocq, leaving Augustus to the twilight of his room.

The chamberlain had returned but cowered in the antechamber. He would be flogged later for his cowardice, but now I needed him. "Get me fresh linen, well starched and scented. Send for hot water. Have camphor burned to clean the air, or I'll have your skin for a rug!"

He returned, arms laden with all I had ordered, his face twisted by fear and disgust. "Leave. I'll do it," I said, setting alight the dried bundle of herbs in the warming pans, their smoldering scent cleansing the air. As I struggled to change the linen, Lestocq arrived. He pulled me away as soon as he saw Augustus. "God in Heaven! Move away, Tsarevna. It's the smallpox."

We both know what this is. The smallpox: merry at dawn, buried by dusk.

I shook my head like a child, wiping away snot and tears with my sleeve. "No. I will not leave him alone."

"Let me do what I can," Lestocq offered, and bled Augustus by puncturing his forearms and neck. The wounds looked like snakebites; blood seeped slowly out of his tortured body, dark and thick. Augustus shrank like a goatskin flask emptying and flattening. How could "red" and "beautiful" share a single word in our language: *krazny*? The rash gained force all over his body. "Don't scratch," I pleaded, but he was crazed by the urge, clawing the pustules open, their poisonous mix of blood and pus staining everything, including me.

"It will not be long," Lestocq admitted defeatedly.

Could I contemplate a lifetime spent without Augustus? "You go," I said, blinded by tears. "I stay until the end."

"I will call a priest," Lestocq offered and left.

The priest came and went, taking the patient's delirious whispers for Confession. As Augustus's fingers slackened in mine, I murmured to him, reminding him of our sun-filled, happy days in Peterhof. When all that was left was to pray, I folded my hands over his, caressing the small tattoo on his wrist. "Shine, shine, my star," I tried to hum—*"Gori, gori, moya Zvezda"*—yet I choked on the lyrics. The White Night drained the color from the day. The city did not sleep, merely changed pace; a night without darkness signified the madness my life had become. Augustus lay still, his breathing labored. I cooled his forehead with a moist cloth. Then I, too, fell asleep, exhausted.

When I woke, my neck was stiff, and my tongue rasped in my dry mouth. The room was blue with a cool dawn light. Augustus's fingers lay slack in mine. As I shifted the leather strings on his bony wrist to kiss the star tattoo one last time, his skin was frosty beneath my lips. The very day after the one intended to mark our engagement, my warm, funny, lively, principled, and handsome Augustus was dead. The silence made my ears ring. I crawled to the window and opened it as the sun set the morning alight. On the square outside the Winter Palace, a breeze blew clean the dandelion clocks that sprouted between the cobblestones. Their stalks stood lonely and bare.

I dropped to the floor, and the world closed in on me, dark and silent.

39

While Menshikov went ahead with celebrating the engagement of Petrushka to his daughter Maria, I had Augustus's rooms aired and cleaned. The soiled sheets I myself burned on a pyre behind the palace, taking in the poisonous and vile stench through flared nostrils, my eyes watering from smoke and tears. His belongings I packed for their return to Holstein. He had not brought much with him to woo a Russian Tsarevna. A man like Augustus needed only himself. When I found his diary, which was bound by leather strings like the ones worn around his wrist, I weighed the book in my hand, burning with curiosity. No. Onto the pyre with it!

Voices, singing, laughter, and music filled the palace; Menshikov had the Great Hall adorned with a whole orange grove in bloom. Champagne corks popped long into the pale hours, and dancers spilled out onto the courtyard, frolicking among the pillars and beneath the wide windowsills. Maria Menshikova was decked out in my mother's jewels. Petrushka's cousin, Crown Princess Maria Theresa of Austria, sent preserved lemons from Italy and a suite of black pearls. King Louis of France, my former possible fiancé, offered an exquisite Limoges jug with five dozen matching glasses. From England the new King George II, another cousin of Petrushka's, sent a pack of hounds. This wedding was to be the fulfillment of Menshikov's wildest ambitions. Soon he would be Regent. Nobody could stop him, it seemed.

If Anoushka, too, celebrated with them while my world had crumbled, I did not know. I had no word from her. Instead, two days later, Menshikov sent me a messenger bearing a ceremoniously rolled-up and beribboned scroll. It was no letter of condolence but a list of possible matches for me: the names of princes in realms ranging from Persia to Portugal. I could only learn from him. He knew how to strike where it hurt most.

After a week I finally heard from Anoushka, who wrote to me from Ekaterinenhof Palace: *"Dearest sister, we share your grief and distress and invite you to come and live with us."* The words seemed stilted, the invitation half-hearted and too late after the long months of painful silence and my days of solitary mourning. Anoushka's words fell into my soul like a stone into a deep, empty well, not causing a ripple. While I longed for company, the thought of being at Karl's mercy, or of them both flaunting their happiness all day long, made me the more determined to survive despite my solitude.

When Augustus's coffin was about to be closed, I slipped the leather strips from his wrist and strung the icon of St. Nicholas on them, wrapping them twice around my neck: these two things I valued most in the world. I had had the pink and silver engagement dress cleaned and sold to pay for the frigate back to Holstein. The ship was rigged in black sails: it slipped out of St. Petersburg like a nightmare, spoiling the dreamlike beauty of summer's White Nights.

Curiously enough, the days to come made me think of my cousin Anna Ivanovna, the Duchess of Courland, who had suffered fate's twists and turns herself. She must know what was happening to me, and to Russia, as Menshikov was trying to get himself elected Duke of Courland in her place. In vain, fortunately for her. Even though his thugs first beat up the Duchy Council, and then he threatened to shoot the burghers, they ridiculed him whenever possible, even naming a greasy sausage after him.

Laughing at Menshikov seemed to be the only recourse against his rise to power. Yet my laughter made me choke; he had me in his grip, like a puppet whose strings he could snip at any moment, before casting me out to live in a dark, damp nunnery.

Following Petrushka's engagement, Menshikov had me shunned at court. At least he was still concerned enough about appearances to ensure I was granted an apartment in the Summer Palace. Both Lestocq and Herr Schwartz, the dance and music teacher, moved in with me. The snug rooms, with their long windows and high stucco ceilings decorated with murals of birds and flowers, at least offered me the solace of a home, even if it was away from the young Tsar. He was the last family member I had left, apart from my sister. Who was by Petrushka's side, I wondered, guarding him against Menshikov, if not loving him? I had seen what the man could do. At least Ostermann was devoted to Petrushka, and Buturlin still served the young Tsar as his chamberlain. What did he make of the frightening turn my life had taken? I forbade myself any thought of his uplifting company. I was in mourning.

There was no mention of any official funds to be granted to me. I had to face up to my fears for the future. What did one need to live on, how many roubles exactly, and how should I procure that sum? I had no idea, remembering suddenly how Anoushka had patted her pockets in the Golosov Ravine and the Leshy spirit's evil snarl: "Ah! The fine young Tsarevny. Never carry roubles, eh?" My sister had received her dowry, and Karl was awarded one hundred thousand roubles a year as an officer's stipend. I had neither a fiancé to support me, nor estates to pay me revenue, nor a remunerated position at court. Every day I lived free, I was a threat to Menshikov's plans. If I had agreed to relinquish my right to the throne to Petrushka's possible descendants, I had maintained my right of succession to the young Tsar himself, should anything befall him before he had children. Starving me out was part of Menshikov's strategy: either I picked one of the suitors from his abominable list, or I must voluntarily retreat into a convent.

Finally, after the third week of eating sauerkraut and fatty meat, I'd had enough. "You need a budget," Lestocq said, after checking an interminable list of items and numbers, which meant nothing to me. A frown had taken up permanent residence on his forehead these days.

"Does that mean something good to eat for a change?" I asked, caressing my Persian cat, which had settled in my lap.

"No. It means that you have to learn to get by."

"And what does that signify?" He might as well have spoken Chinese.

"You have to tell me what we really need—from the market and the *gostiny dvor*."

I shrugged. "I have never been to a market. And the *gostiny dvor* sent all bills to the palace always, whatever I bought—stockings, fans, cloaks, or gowns."

He sighed. "I see. Well, let me try to sort this out. I should be good at it by now, having once been poor and exiled. In the meantime you should do what you are good at."

My hands stilled on the purring cat's slate-colored fur. "And what would that be?"

Lestocq's eyes met mine. There was a moment of silence.

"Time will tell," he said, devoting himself to his "budget" again. Already I did not like the sound of that word at all.

Time will tell—but how? Both Lestocq and Schwartz, on behalf of Versailles and Vienna, helped me where they could. I was not proud of having to be bankrolled by foreign powers, but this is how it was. When ends still would not meet, I suffered the shame of accumulating debts: being the Tsarina's daughter still opened many doors. It was abominable having to humble myself, though. While everything had always been offered to me, now I had to ask for it, my heart burning and the words turning sour in my mouth.

Finally I sold the last of my dresses—I had had literally hundreds of gowns—and remaining jewelry. My best customer was the Princess Cherkassky, who owned countless "souls" and as many *versty* of the Russian Empire, and whose family had served mine since the first Romanov Tsar. She often paid double what I would have settled for and passed on the dresses to her ladies-in-waiting. For her to wear my very recognizable, splendid wardrobe in public would have meant defying Menshikov. For every Russian, however highborn, there was always a seat available on the next sled heading to Siberia. I from those days on dressed simply, in a white taffeta top over an underrobe of black silk or velvet, tying a colorful sash of silk around my waist. Living like a Tsarevna on a peasant's purse was hard work.

"What will you do with that money?" Lestocq asked, as he caught me counting out roubles after the Princess Cherkassky had been by.

"Psst," I said, frowning in despair at my lack of skill in counting. Why had I not paid more attention in the classroom? "Now I've made a mistake and have to start again."

He could not help but grin. "It will never be enough, however often you count it."

"How do you know?" I sulked, letting the money be.

"Because I know you."

"I shall buy weapons to arm my servants here. Have you heard about the latest burglaries? I am terrified of robbers. I also must repay Schwartz and you. Music and my health are important."

"Don't worry about paying us."

"You have to eat," I teased. "Any Frenchman needs that, no?"

"None of us will starve," he said, his face mysterious.

I hesitated, not pressing him for an explanation. "Fabulous. Then I even have some money left."

"That is what you think! Menshikov is willing to let you buy back some of your mother's furniture," Lestocq said.

"Is he now? Of course. I will have to; there's no real choice. So much for my visit to the *gostiny dvor* this afternoon. I wanted to get that adorable golden monkey I saw there last time."

"You should get a phoenix as a pet instead. That would suit you."

"What is that?"

"A mythical bird that rises from its own ashes," he said.

"Mythical—I have not heard of that country before. Is there a prince that Menshikov might suggest I should marry?" I kept my face straight.

"Tsarevna, your situation is bad," Lestocq rebuked me for joking.

He spoke the truth. Yet if I did not try to keep my spirits up, the inner Ice Princess would conquer my soul once more, freezing me to the core. That would be infinitely worse than poverty. "All right then," I sighed. "Find the shop in the *gostiny dvor* that sells phoenixes. Put an order in. I shall have two of them at least."

Like that, I learned to get by.

The summer melted away. My lonely days dragged by with little or no difference between them, like identical twins. Lestocq and Schwartz kept me company, reading to me and playing music. Menshikov's list of suitors remained unacted upon. As the White Nights shortened, I relished the return of dawn and dusk. The tawny hues of the autumn leaves filled the city with their golden glow; there was a scent of freshly picked apples and pears in the air. The season bridging Russia's unbridled joy in life and its long months of darkness was the background to my mourning for Augustus. Any merriment meant nothing to me; the Winter Palace was just a *verst* and yet a world away. He was closest to me when my thoughts joined him at night, in the darkness that held him to its heart. When I drew the curtains, the stillness brought Augustus back to me. I so missed everything about him—his talk and, oh, his touch; both had kindled a fire in my veins that would burn for life.

* * *

As the first leaves fell, Menshikov stopped sending his lists. His patience was running out. Sometime soon, I would be shorn and sent to a convent. For how long would the memory of summer days spent with Augustus illuminate that darkness? I feared the answer.

I had neither family nor a true friend left. If the memory of Buturlin came into my mind, I pushed it straight back out.

It was late September when Schwartz arrived back from the Winter Palace, where he gave Maria Menshikova singing lessons—he playing his divine melodies and she cawing away. The big man carefully put down his cello case—it was big enough for me to hide inside!—and opened it, untying one of the many small pockets and compartments within.

"I have a gift for you," he said with an almost tender smile.

"A gift? From whom?" I rose from a seat by the window and replaced my silky-furred black-and-white colobus monkey in his cage, as he liked to grab anything within reach and tear it up. He retreated to his swinging bar, sucking his teeth like an indignant old woman.

In a convent watching the icicles freeze on the wall was all the entertainment I should have.

"Buturlin," Schwartz said, lowering his voice even though we were alone. I could not help but rush up to my music teacher. Not everybody had forgotten about me then!

"What is it?" I could not help feeling excited. "A letter?"

"I do not have Buturlin down as a poet and a writer. Do you?" Schwartz grinned. "No. He was out riding this morning, he said." Schwartz handed me a squashed little bouquet of flowers, holding it almost tenderly in hands that could easily bend a horseshoe.

"Oh," I sighed. Buturlin had picked for me a bunch of the last late summer and autumn flowers blooming on the Karelian Plains—September jasmine and autumn asters. The thought of the meadows went straight to my heart, even though the carefree people we had once been were long gone. I had not yet turned twenty, but felt weighed down by all I had lived through. What utter nonsense Lestocq's Tarot cards had been, predicting suffering and even the hangman for Buturlin. His career had prospered since he had become Petrushka's most cherished chamberlain; he was considered irresistibly handsome and adored by all at court—or so I heard. A man like him was probably a fool for love for another woman by now, though could he perhaps be a friend to me? Hope is a treacherous ally, unreliable as quicksand, fickle as dust. I chose a dainty vase of Venetian crystal for the flowers and, once they wilted, pressed them to dry and flatten in one of Father's encyclopedias, to be framed and remembered.

I should thank Buturlin for them in due course.

Herr Schwartz, who despite his size and weight slipped so easily between worlds with his celestial playing, had more surprises to spring. On one of the last days of September, he arrived early for my music and dance lesson, in which I rehearsed steps on my own, dancing with invisible gentlemen, laughing at imagined pleasantries, while he played his beautiful Stradivari. That day he lingered in the doorway, blocking my view into the corridor, and said: "Your sister the Duchess of Holstein is here to see you."

I tugged at the icon of St. Nicholas so that the leather strings cut into my neck.

"Ask her in." I braced myself.

Anoushka stood by the window of my apartment's small, cozy living room, head held high, shoulders covered in the shimmering yellow satin of a splendid mink-trimmed cloak; her dark braids were twisted onto her crown and adorned with pearls, shimmering softly like dew. She looked over to the opposite shoreline, where sunshine lit a pale fire on the palace's flat façades. The Neva's intense almond-green light flooded the room; Father had had the paneling painted in the same shade, to enhance the effect. I halted on the threshold, taking in the sight of her: she was a Duchess, happily married to the possible heir to the Swedish throne. As she turned, I caught my breath. She wore her gown unlaced and a neat bump had appeared at her hitherto slender waistline.

Her happiness was to be complete.

40

"Duchess." I curtsied to her, steadying myself and expecting a cool and measured reply. Instead, she flew to me, arms outstretched. Her embrace was so fierce that I warned her, "Careful! What about the child?" As I held her, we both started to cry, and our tears washed away the humiliation she had made me suffer. Since meeting Augustus, I understood how she must have felt when Menshikov had told her about Karl, her longed-for suitor, seemingly favoring me. Since then, I had tried to forget her husband's transgression; he had been drunk and tired. Anoushka and he were happy; he honored her as a good husband should.

"Don't cry, Anoushka. What is it?"

I gently folded one arm around her, leading her to a yellow-and-gray-striped silk sofa. The samovar murmured, low and comforting, and I poured us both some hot *chai*. Little in life cannot be cured by a good strong cup of it, preferably laced with a shot of vodka. Anoushka settled, spreading her exquisitely embroidered skirt, one hand resting on her bump as she blew on her *chai* with her gaze lowered. Her long, dark lashes cast shadows on her pale cheeks. Her tears did not surprise me: women in these circumstances could be a bit tetchy. I had no direct knowledge of pregnancy, but she was possibly four or five months gone. God knows how Maria Menshikova would behave once Petrushka made her with child—what an unpleasant thought! Anoushka placed her cup of blue-and-white Meissen porcelain in its saucer. "It is so good to see you, Lizenka," she said stiffly, as if needing to recover from our embrace.

"It is. I think of you every day," I said truthfully.

"That is *so* like you. Quick-tempered, though always ready to forgive. You are just like Father." She tried to smile, but her lips trembled. "I so wish he still lived and that he could witness this."

"Yes! He'd be delighted. Just imagine—his grandchild!" I squeezed her hand, beaming. "Congratulations. I shall offer the boy my finest stallion and all my riches—well, not that I have any."

"Yes, a grandchild, of course. That too," she mumbled, her white, slender hand once more brushing her belly. She wore a dark, long-sleeved gown; her wedding ring was her only jewelry. "I was thinking of Menshikov. I wish Father were here to deal with him."

Clearly this talk needed more than just *chai* to fuel it. "Vodka?" I said, fishing the bottle from its secret hiding place behind the settee. She smiled, knowing all about thieving, drunkard servants, and raised her cup. "Yes, please. A good shot."

"What is Menshikov up to to anger you so? I thought Karl—you and he—were good companions," I said carefully, after checking that all the doors were closed. I had no doubt that the servants in my household were on Menshikov's payroll. He was just waiting to strike.

Anoushka snorted. "Companions? I regret every day what he made me do to you—fool that I was! Can you forgive me?"

I nodded, and she continued speaking. "What is Menshikov *not* up to? He has pilfered our inheritance and even requisitioned Mother's carriages and horses, which should have taken us to Holstein." She fingered one bare earlobe regretfully. "Our birthdays have been excluded from the court calendar, Lizenka. No official prayer still includes our names. Karl has lost his office as head of the Guards in St. Petersburg. My dowry is spent. I have sold my dresses and my diamonds. Meanwhile Menshikov's daughter is to be the Tsar's wife. What next? I dare not wait and see. If I carry a son, he will be in mortal danger from the day of his birth." She cradled the bump. "I feel my child quickening, Lizenka. It will be a strong and healthy son for Russia."

Her sudden openness, after all this time spent shunning me, was surprising. But what does family mean, if not forgiveness and forgetting? Still, I was on my guard. "I suffer the same slights and penury, Anoushka. Who knows how long Lestocq and Schwartz will stay by my side? I shall be a spinster, for who will marry me now? I am a nobody, and a penniless one at that. Though just one day after Augustus's death, Menshikov drew up a list of new suitors for me."

"The swine! He shall pay for it."

"Yes, but how and when? Who is to protect me if he sends me to a nunnery, shorn and clad in a hair shirt? At least you have Karl. He must be so proud that you will have his son."

"Proud?" she asked. "Let me show you something."

The air in the small living room grew stifling, be it from the rays of the last September sunshine reflected from the golden parquet, or else the strange glow in Anoushka's eyes as she unbuttoned her sleeve, her pale fingers wrestling with the buttons. One by one, they revealed red and blue patches beneath—traces of violent pinching—and even purple flaming bruises on her ivory skin. The worst mark was a round dark spot, at her wrist, just where the veins showed blue. I had seen similar spots on tablecloths and napkins many times over, bearing witness to my parents' heavy feasting. It was the burn mark of a cigar.

"Please don't say it was Karl who—" I started and held on to the icon of St. Nicholas, the way a drowning sailor might to a piece of driftwood. I choked with silent rage as I remembered Karl's greedy, careless lips grinding against my mouth. No. Not Anoushka. Not my sister!

Anoushka swallowed hard, struggling with her pride, yet her eyes begged for my understanding as she nodded. I knew what it cost her to be here. She must be at her wit's end. She cried again, sobs strangling her. Her bruised wrist dropped into her lap.

God, I hated Karl then, the thin German with his coarse, clammy hands—the hands he'd hurt me with, the hands he'd dared raise against my sister!—*hated* him with such a passion that it took my breath away. For Anoushka's sake I had given him the benefit of the doubt. "Remember what he was like at first—so polite, gallant, and romantic? His musicians played beneath your window. His barge was drawn by swans harnessed in silver. He scattered ivy and belladonna on the waves of the Neva," I said, still in disbelief.

"That was what he wanted us to see. As soon as he had me, he changed tack. When he is drunk—which is all the time—he is abominable. Even this child. If you knew how it came to be!" She curled over in shame.

"Anoushka!" I leaped up to embrace her. The thought was unbearable. A Tsarevna, mistreated like a housemaid? She gave in to my tenderness, her heaving body as brittle as a branch after a long hot summer, ready to snap.

"Is there nothing that can be done?" I asked. Breathing in hurt me, such was my shock: would Augustus, too, have become a wife-beater and a rapist, after wooing me with his ease and charm? If I believed that, my memories of him would be tainted. I could not allow it to happen.

"No. Karl and his Holstein friends drink and gamble every evening into the early morning hours. Failing that, they roam the St. Petersburg brothels," she said. "Whom could I tell if not you?"

"We will always have each other. Ekaterinenhof is not far away. I shall visit whenever possible or perhaps move in with you after all?"

Anoushka sat up straight, folding her hands. "That is another reason why I came to see you. We are to leave Russia. The child is to be born in Holstein. Our departure is planned for the end of the month before I am too heavily pregnant."

"Can't you stay?" I begged.

"Why? For Menshikov to kill my son? Look at Ekaterina Ivanovna, who is merely suffered, and who does not belong anywhere, ever again. I have no choice. I am married and pregnant
with an heir to the Russian throne. I must follow my husband and
protect my son. We sail in two weeks, Lizenka."

I watched Anoushka depart to her waiting carriage. She walked
heavily, weighed down more by sorrow than by pregnancy. Her duty
was to give birth to the child of an already estranged husband in a
faraway land. We both faced loneliness, which any Russian fears
as the Devil shuns Holy Water. We are a communally minded
people, perpetually divided between mistrust and dependency. As
the carriage door was closed, the Holstein coat of arms flashed
in the low autumn light: stark red, yellow, and blue, depicting
lions and a swan. Her coachman cursed, chasing away beggars and
children, chucking gravel at them for good measure. She leaned
out to look at me; when her slim, pale hand waved goodbye, the
cuff of her dress was tightly buttoned again, long sleeve guarding
the terrible secret beneath. The horses pulled away, their hooves
trampling my heart. Autumn closed in. The Neva's surface rippled
as a gust of wind chased the leaves lying ankle-deep on the quays.
In the mottled sky leaden clouds hung low.

I sank to the floor, weeping. In the short space of six months,
I had lost both my mother and my fiancé; now my sister was to depart at the very moment we had found each other again. I lay there
until I had emptied myself of tears. Finally I sat up, wiping away all
traces of them. Crying would not help me.

41

While Karl von Holstein had boarded the ship before I was forced to take leave of him politely, Anoushka clung to me, her body heaving. "Pray for me and for my child," she begged, before two maids helped her up the plank, keeping her balanced. Her husband could not be bothered to help. I stood on the quay, watching how the anchor was lifted and the sails were rigged, the canvas beating in the wind with the sound of gunshots. Slowly the ship turned up the Neva estuary. Anoushka was a dark, ever smaller figure on deck, raising her arm in a last goodbye. I was furious at my helplessness and blinded by tears when the frigate disappeared over the horizon, its sails blending with the billowing clouds. Flocks of seagulls accompanied it, filling the sky with their cries. A Russian sailor, Semyon Mordvinov, had agreed to carry our letters between St. Petersburg and Holstein.

I asked Lestocq for more money, and he was wise enough to give it without inquiring after its purpose, trusting my decisions. In the *gostiny dvor* on the Nevsky Prospect, I had a small scarlet leather cap made: Molniya, the beautiful peregrine falcon Petrushka had given me when he was a lonely little boy, had grown into my finest hunting companion. She killed swiftly and silently. No prey—be it hare, fox, or ermine—ever heard her approach or escaped her claws' frightening precision. Would she strike larger game as well? I wondered, smiling to myself. Menshikov jealously guarded his power and position as any ambitious man would, wary of soldiers' swords and swagger. Yet he was blind to a woman's wiles.

When the cap was ready, I caressed Molniya's tawny feathers and fastened a silver bell around one delicate ankle. I called for Herr Schwartz, the dance teacher, to assist me in the next stage of my plan. It felt like sending a child out into the world.

He came huffing and puffing up the narrow, steep staircase. A footman carried his Stradivari violoncello. "Herr Schwartz, good morning. When you go to the Winter Palace today, will you take Molniya here with you? She is a gift for the Tsar. Please ask Alexander Borisovich Buturlin to pass her on to His Majesty," I said.

"But—" Schwartz broke into even more of a sweat as I pushed the thick leather glove over his chubby fingers; God knew how he played such magical music with those paws! The bird was perched on his wrist, and he kept it at a safe distance, gingerly, arm outstretched like a scarecrow's. Molniya sensed his lack of confidence, flexing her talons and cocking her head.

"Don't be afraid!" I said. "You are too big for her to bring down."

"What about my fingers?" he moaned.

"They *do* look very appetizing," I teased. "Just keep them out of sight."

"How can I carry my violoncello if I have the bird with me?"

"That might be one of the many reasons why God has given you two arms."

On his wrist Molniya spread her wings as if ready to fly. "Hush, my beauty." I tenderly stroked her bony head beneath the leather hood, which was as vermilion as the Imperial seal. Tears stung my eyes. "We shall see each other again soon, I promise."

"Any other message for Buturlin?" Schwartz sighed. "Or the Tsar himself when he receives the bird?"

"No."

When Schwartz had left with Molniya, I knelt down in front

of the little altar in my room: more than ever before, I needed God on my side.

"When? Just say when, beautiful Lizenka!" Petrushka exclaimed, his broken voice deep as a man's now. He barged into the library a couple of days later, holding Molniya on his wrist, just as I was checking on Buturlin's flowers. They were not quite ready to be mounted on cardboard and framed. Was the gift of my bird all it had taken to make him disobey Menshikov and come to see me? I had lacked the strength to act earlier.

Petrushka's arrival was a joyous, invigorating whirl of overlong legs and gangly arms. There were pimples on his face among the first hairs sprouting there, but he'd grown into a handsome young man, bearing Alexey's fine features and tawny coloring. His pack of baying hounds bounded around outside in the fresh autumn air, and his large entourage was dressed in gloriously colored hunting clothes of velvet and leather.

His guards positioned themselves at the door; Prince Alexis Dolgoruky politely kept his distance. He looked smug, I noticed: his growing influence with the Tsar heralded the rise of the Old Believers. I only hoped that Petrushka saw the wisdom in Father's reforms, despite all the hurt and humiliation he personally had suffered. At least none of Menshikov's household was to be seen, though I spotted a stunningly beautiful young woman lingering behind Dolgoruky. Just then the dwarf d'Acosta somersaulted into view; the silver bells attached to the jester's ankles and wrists jingled merrily. Petrushka had inherited him from my parents. Time wilted any average person, but age suited the little people, their faces becoming gnarled like wise old trees. D'Acosta circled the room, flapping his arms like wings and calling hoarsely like a bird of prey, eyes beady when he looked at me. Was he, who had survived two Tsars already and now served a third, my friend or foe?

"Petrushka." I rose to my feet, smiling at him: he was like the little brother I had never had, wearing his finery and new office with ease. Luckily I had chosen my best silk scarf to accentuate my waist, and riding had tanned and shaped my arms. As Petrushka stooped to embrace me, I smelled vodka and tobacco on his breath. I wanted to back away and curtsy to him as I should, but he held me there, cupped my face in his hands and kissed me on the lips. I first froze at the intimacy of the gesture, then made light of the situation. "I ought not to call you Petrushka any more. Welcome to your Summer Palace, Your Majesty."

"Don't you dare, Lizenka. The day you stop calling me Petrushka, I'll die!" His smile blazed in his face. His cheeks had filled out—no one dared refuse him food any more. "Now I am truly the captain of a boat."

"And what a boat it is! The proudest frigate one could imagine, if not a whole Imperial fleet." I mimicked a sailor standing to attention on the deck of a ship, my fingers held to my temple. "Welcome aboard, Captain Petrushka!"

He was flattered. "It is so good to see you. The business of state has kept me away for too long. Awful what happened with Augustus, though God's ways are unfathomable. Also, your loss is Russia's gain—and mine." He handed Molniya to d'Acosta. The dwarf held her at a safe distance—if she opened her wings, she could topple him. "Isn't she just the finest bird? Are you sure you can part with her?" Petrushka asked.

"If she is the finest bird, then she is just about good enough for my Tsar."

The answer pleased him. "Let us share her then. I want to share everything with you. It has been far too long since we met. How about a hunt tomorrow? It is the best season. Pick your horse. I will have everything prepared. Do you like chilled caviar and cool Sauternes for a picnic? Who else should come? Nobody boring, please." He bubbled over with pleasure in his new freedom, making up for all the years spent lingering in the shadows, longing for light and love. It had indeed been far too long since we had seen each other, and I was glad that I had made the approach to him.

Petrushka's cheeks were flushed when he turned to speak to his godfather. "Dolgoruky, you hang in the saddle worse than a wet sack of stones—and more unbearable than anything, you constantly rattle on about methods of ruling Russia. So boring. Stay behind. But do send your daughter Katja in your place." He smiled at the beautiful girl standing on the threshold, who curtsied to him. Her large blue eyes contrasted with her raven hair and milky skin. She reminded me of Anoushka. I could not help but notice her rich gown and the strings of pearls in her thick braids. Betting on Petrushka had paid off for the Dolgorukys. Her father bowed smugly, happy to see his child so close to the young Tsar, who said, "Katja, do ride with us before you leave for Vienna with your handsome husband-to-be." Petrushka rolled his eyes. "Katja is actually *in love* with her betrothed. How indecent is that? Count Melissimo is said to be the most handsome man who ever walked the earth. May I be godfather to your children?"

Katja blushed. Lucky thing! How did that ugly crook Alexis Dolgoruky father such a stunning beauty? Better not ask. She would be a welcome addition to any court.

"Of course," I said. "Let us have a real Russian hunt for Katja, something to take with her in her heart when she leaves us. When is the wedding to be?"

"Sometime early next year, after His Majesty's Coronation in January," she gushed, and then said to me: "My fiancé is a diplomat in the service of the Emperor of Austria, our Tsar's uncle. I shall follow wherever his duty takes him."

"Who else should we ask to join the hunt?" Petrushka asked.

"How about Maria?" My voice was innocent.

Petrushka looked at a loss. "Maria? Which Maria?"

I feigned surprise. "Your fiancée. Maria Menshikova."

"Oh, her." There was a moment of silence before he cupped his mouth like a naughty boy, his eyes twinkling, and shrugged.

We both giggled helplessly, the Dolgorukys quickly joining in our mirth. D'Acosta wobbled around the room, copying Maria Menshikova's heavy gait, still holding Molniya at a distance. "Stop," I begged, doubled over with laughter. Petrushka, too, had a coughing fit and gasped between giggles: "Enough! Maria Menshikova is coming nowhere near me if I can help it. Why take that old crow when I prefer the world's sweetest nightingale?" He gallantly kissed my fingers, but then wondered: "Can I do that? I mean, leave her behind?"

"The Tsar can do whatever he wishes," I said. "If only your father were here to see you, Petrushka—strong and in command. Alexey would be so proud."

How strange it felt to be able to say my half-brother's name without fear of reprisal!

Petrushka turned somber. "Yes, if only. Thank you for your kind words," he said, kissing my fingers. "Oh, and of course Buturlin has to join the hunt."

Buturlin! My heart leaped when I heard his name. His daredevil approach to things, wicked sense of humor, and dark good looks were suddenly all too present. My cheeks burned: I still mourned Augustus and remembered with regret his lost tenderness as much as our passion, which had just begun to blossom.

"Buturlin!" Petrushka called. "Where is the rascal? Never mind. I'll surely find him in your kitchens, seducing maids." He still held my hand. "After all, I owe him, don't I? Who but he would have dared to bring me Molniya?" He winked at me. "Our beautiful bird gave me the perfect excuse to come and see you. Long may she fly. The Tsar has to thank his aunt for her generosity."

"Indeed, you do," I said coyly.

As Petrushka and his retinue were leaving, d'Acosta hopped onto the back of one of the hounds, but it snapped at him. The dwarf flick-flacked away, halting his somersaults while bent backward in the doorway. Upside down, he gave me a grave, knowing look.

"What is it, d'Acosta?" I crossed my arms defiantly as his funny face twisted into a warm smile, and he straightened himself before bowing deeply to me.

I stood alone. The light in the library turned mustard-colored; the air thickened like the first Peterhof honey after the bees had gorged themselves on roses and lavender. Dusk seeped into my veins, and I felt incredibly tired.

A good sleep would prepare me for a strenuous day in the saddle tomorrow.

42

Winter was close: the sun turned into a dull copper coin in the heavy sky. St. Petersburg gleamed in shades of mother-of-pearl. As promised, Lieutenant Semyon Mordvinov brought and took bundles of letters between Gottorf Castle and St. Petersburg. Lestocq read Anoushka's words to me, but even his funny French accent was unable to disguise the despair that tinged her words. Her pregnancy was advancing, she wrote, but the castle was cold and drafty. She feared the gray winter of the Northern German flatlands as well as the low skies, which promised buckets of rain. The castle's cellars were filled with barrels of sauerkraut, and she had to eat potatoes every day, without a sprinkle of salt or *smetana,* as money was so tight; Karl had gambled away her dowry, and the funds from Russia had ceased. Her German was heavily accented; the courtiers laughed at her clothes and manners. She signed off with, "*Not a day passes without my weeping for you, my dear sister!*"

Lestocq barely prevented me from sending a ship to fetch her home there and then. "You cannot do this, Tsarevna. She is married and with child. Her path is chosen. She will have to walk it to the end."

When he'd left, I felt lonelier than ever.

I climbed the stairs. This evening the house seemed curiously quiet. The servants seemed to have vanished, and the door to my room stood ajar. I hesitated. Light trickled through onto the dark landing.

A footman must have been in. Flames crackled in the fireplace: a welcome surprise on a cool evening.

I pushed the door open but halted on the threshold, my fingers searching for the high European handle. A man sat in one of the low armchairs by the fire, his hands folded, as if waiting patiently. His casually rolled-up white shirtsleeves showed tanned, strong arms, and his muscular legs were extended to display his soft beige kidskin breeches and shiny boots. The flames' flickering light chiseled his cheekbones and glinted in his dark eyes. He wore a slight smile, and the black hair ruffled around his high forehead made him look devilish—or devilishly handsome. "Buturlin," I said, trying to sound aloof. I slowly closed the door, leaning against it and folding my arms behind my back as he came toward me: a hunter closing in on the prey he had stalked for a long time.

If Petrushka owed him, Buturlin knew all too well how to collect any other outstanding debts: his lips searched mine. His kiss was deliciously tender. I made no move, though every bit of me veered toward him. He was a soldier—it should not be made too easy for him. His kisses grew deeper, moving down my throat, sending jolts of pleasure through my body. I melted into him and drank in the scent of his skin, his hair, his clothes: a hint of autumn fire, leather, sandalwood, and heavy musk. He cupped my bosom, weighing it hungrily. "I knew it. Tits like a milkmaid!" I wanted him so much— him and to regain that feeling of life and lust to which Augustus had introduced me. What good had it done the two of us to wait?

I tore at Buturlin's shirt, unlacing it at the collar, raking the dark curly hair on his broad chest with my fingers. His hands moved down, lifting my skirts in a soft, silky rustle. He brushed his hand over my stockings before his fingertips slipped into my moisture, brief and brazen. I arched with pleasure then gasped: "No. I mean—I have never—"

He hesitated, amazed. "Did you and your little German prince not make love?"

I shook my head, my cheeks burning.

"What a fool that poor man was." He smiled and held his fingers up to the candlelight: they glistened with my lust.

"Look." He slowly licked the tip of one, a gesture as plain as it was arousing. "I came to take you as I would a chambermaid. But now I would rather make love to my beautiful virgin princess. Come. You are shivering." He lifted me up and carried me over to the fireplace where he kneeled down on a bearskin as white and soft as powdery snow. "Open your legs wide," he whispered, and I obeyed. Slowly, carefully, he eased me onto him, kissing and caressing me as I slid astride his hips. I gasped at the sudden, sharp pain when he made his way into me, gentle but determined. "Shhh!" He covered my mouth with his, kissing me and nibbling my lips as he pulled me deeper until we held still, our hearts racing, our eyes locking—it was like nothing I had felt before.

"Move," he whispered.

"I can't," I gasped.

"Let me help you." His hands cupped my buttocks, lifting me, and slowly I started to move. He laughed, breaking the tension. "See, you can, sweet Lizenka. Your face is like an angel's and your ass like a cream-fed courtesan's. Move slowly. Take your time. Enjoy it!" His heavy-lidded eyes glinted as I obeyed once more. His hands first cupped my breasts, then opened my thighs wider still. "The more you move, the better it is for you. But there is no hurry," he said, his mouth hot on mine while he pressed my wet openness to his root, caressing my secret spot while I felt him deep inside me. "Slowly," he whispered. "I am here for you."

I sobbed helplessly, lust building in me like a river rising against its dam while he slowed my movements, almost unbearably so, and then made me stop.

"Feel me," he whispered.

"Please," I begged, but Buturlin slipped his moist fingertip over me, as soft as a butterfly's wing. Lightning flashed in my head. I shouted out as molten gold rushed through my veins, dousing my soul in a fiery shower. I arched my spine just as he let me slide backward and lay on top of me, moving deeply and slowly, until we clung to each other, our hot breath mingling, and our bodies melded. As I came back to earth, I slackened beneath him; his head rested on my shoulder. We clung to each other. My skin stuck to his; we were one, in spirit and soul, after riding a storm through the skies. After a moment he forced me to look at him. It embarrassed me after what had just happened.

"Why did Augustus and you not make love?"

"We waited," I said, my voice strangled by emotion.

"What for?" He looked stunned.

"The right time. When we were married."

He stroked my thick curls from my moist forehead, cupping my face. "Lizenka. This is Russia. The right time may never come. You, above all, should know this." As tears welled in my eyes, he rocked me as he would a child. "Shhh. Cry, little bird. Cry, Lizenka. I am here for you. Do not worry. I am indeed a fool for love, as Lestocq's silly Tarot cards said. I love you, I always have, and I will speak on your behalf as long as I live."

His words made me cry even more; I cried for everything that had happened: my parents' deaths, Menshikov's betrayal, Augustus's passing, Anoushka's departure, and the lack of love in her life for every day to come. And especially for what I had just experienced in Buturlin's arms.

43

I existed only for the evenings when my lover flew up the stairs to my rooms, taking two steps at a time, already slipping out of his jacket, and loosening his jabot. Once, when he arrived unannounced, I was having a snack. The *chai* was laced with sugar, vodka, and nutmeg; the maid had prepared a plate of fresh *blintshiki,* chilled caviar served in a bowl of mother-of-pearl, with accompaniments of chopped sweet red onions and boiled eggs, as well as *smetana.* I did not rise as one of my cats lay purring on my lap but sleepily tilted back my head, eyeing my visitor from beneath heavy-lidded eyes. "You fall short on the promises you give, Buturlin. You might not mean to but . . ."

"But?" he asked, rolling up his shirtsleeves.

". . . you promised to take me as if I were a chambermaid."

My heart pounded. What would he think of me for using these words? His face was blank and his gaze inscrutable. I held my breath as he came toward me; my insides dissolved when he kneeled before me, his eyes dark and mysterious in the twilight. He slowly lifted my skirts, his fingers making the silk of my stockings crackle. I briefly felt his nails on my thighs and suppressed a moan when he parted my legs without further ado. I panted and reeled at my own brazenness.

He smiled, making me wait and long for his next move. "First, I want some caviar," he said. "And I will show you how I like to eat it." He pulled me forward, placing my calves on the arms of my delicate chair, licking my silk stockings, and then kissing the soft, sensitive inside of my thighs, making me shiver with lust. Then, without warning, he licked me, once, twice, his tongue rasping like a cat's. It made me arch my back, gasping. "Nice and salty," he murmured, "just like the sea this came from."

He reached for the caviar, a boyish grin spreading over his face.

"You won't," I gasped, biting my lips in suspense.

"I will—"

Petrushka set up countless hunts and excursions for us—the fact that Menshikov was unable to hide his anger about us keeping company heightened the young Tsar's and my joy. We chased over vast fields of stubble as a chilly wind announced the first frost. Very soon it was time to surrender to the unyielding winter months, and our horses cantered through an *arshin* of snow. Each hunt was punctuated by stops to ice-skate or toboggan before we arrived at the designated meeting place, where fires were burning high and velvet cushions and fur blankets piled up invitingly. I remember the onset of one night in particular, the smooth darkness spread above us like a velvet blanket, embroidered with golden stars. Peasants had joined us to greet their *batjushka* Tsar. Their simplicity and sincerity delighted us; they willingly shared the little they had. When I wanted to refuse a toothless old serf woman's offer of a cold piece of set kasha, she scolded me, "Take it, Tsarevna. The more you give, the more shall be given to you. That is the rule we Russians live by." I ate the lumpy millet cake, chewing and almost choking, as she watched me, smiling and nodding, going hungry herself.

These excursions made me forget all about the precariousness of my life. D'Acosta followed us on our hunts, riding a donkey out of the palace gates, and we endlessly teased beautiful Katja Dolgoruky for being so in love with her handsome fiancé, Count Melissimo, who was in Vienna, awaiting his new deployment. He would join Katja in Moscow for Petrushka's Coronation in late January. Buturlin, who kept a respectful distance by day, was my master at night. While I was under his caresses, reality faded and dreams lit up the somber hours afterward. Just to meet his eyes when I mounted the saddle made me long for him again. His fingers brushed my ankle while adjusting the stirrups, the touch setting me aflame. When he tugged the glove over my hand, I yearned to be in his arms, impatient to discover what he would do to me, or what he would make me do.

His imagination knew no bounds.

Darkness drew in earlier every day. When I lay in his arms after making love, he whispered as if even the shadows were spying on us: "We ought to be careful."

"Careful of what?" I drowsily asked, snuggling up to him.

"Menshikov. And the Tsar. In this city, the walls have eyes and ears." My eyes fell shut before I could take in his warning, thought slipping from my mind like a thief in the night.

We ought to be careful. But everything was as I had hoped: Petrushka ignored Menshikov's wrath and avoided Ostermann's lessons. He followed me around, appreciating my every joke, complimenting my wit and beauty; reaching out to help me from the saddle, his hands lingering longer than necessary on my waist; holding my hands and kissing my fingertips; begging me to return to court fully. I would not dare do that as long as Menshikov was powerful enough to strike me down. Instead I bided my time and playfully pushed Petrushka away, as if he were still a puppy-like boy. I had forgotten that puppies grow into big dangerous dogs, develop teeth that bite ferociously.

If the next day never came, at least I had lived until this moment.

Buturlin not only gave me my life back, but also the strength to face it.

44

S hortly before Yuletide, as the planning for his Coronation was in full swing, Petrushka fell ill with a choking cough and high fever. We were warned that he needed weeks to recover. Yet soon enough his condition worsened: he was wracked by spasms and breathed wheezily; his ribs showed underneath his skin. More than once, and then more and more often, he brought up blood in his phlegm. The sight scared me witless: I remembered the crimson-stained handkerchiefs that Mother pressed against her mouth in the last months of her life. Was my family diminishing further, carelessly plucked from life, like petals in a young girl's game?

"You and your incessant quest for amusement have brought this upon him," Ostermann accused me, when I met him with Menshikov in the corridor leading to the Tsar's apartments. I sensed their puzzlement: how come, despite their best efforts, I was back at court, and so close to the Tsar?

"What nonsense! If anything, exercise in the fresh air is good for anybody," I countered, ignoring Menshikov's dark looks.

When neither of them was paying attention, I forced the Imperial quacks aside and asked Lestocq to give me his opinion on the Tsar's health.

"His lungs are impaired. We will have to keep him safe and warm."

"Of course we will," I said, determined to guard Petrushka with my life.

* * *

As always, travel was easiest before the onset of the *ottepel*. In the bleakest and coldest days of early January, the court left St. Petersburg for Moscow. Once more thirty thousand people were on the road for a Coronation, this time Petrushka's. Katja Dolgoruky, Buturlin, Petrushka, and I shared a sled, while Maria Menshikova traveled with her family, so as not to cause any scandal before she was married to the Tsar. Also Menshikov, who himself was as strong as a horse—had I ever seen him so much as sneeze?—abhorred illness or any show of weakness. Petrushka lay slumped in Buturlin's arms to be carried to the large Imperial sled. My nephew looked like a man of glass, all thin limbs and translucent skin, against my lover's tanned face, broad chest, and strong arms. Inside the sled I covered Petrushka with bearskins and velvet blankets, stuffing a cushion under his head and placing a closed copper pan filled with hot coals at his feet. Finally I kissed his clammy forehead, smiling and saying: "You have to get healthy, darling Petrushka."

By the time we reached Tver, Petrushka was steadily coughing up blood. Even though Menshikov refused my demand for a break, I took the advice of both Lestocq and the Imperial physicians and halted our train of carriages and wagons.

"You might be held responsible for this," Lestocq warned me.

"I hope," I answered, "this is about saving the Tsar's life."

Instead of staying at a filthy inn, I requisitioned a dacha, which sat snugly in its own grounds and was shrouded in snow. Its low roof, the smoke rising from the chimney, and the large terraces where birds came to feed made it look like a house from a fairytale. However the dacha was not intended for winter living: no second set of windows could be placed inside the frames, the well was frozen solid, and the tiled ovens battled against the steady drafts. The floorboards had finger-thick gaps between them. Wet green firewood smoked up the rooms, worsening Petrushka's condition. I had camphor burned in warming pans in the Tsar's room and added dried mint to bowls of steaming water, watching the leaves unfurl before placing them next to his bed, as well as below it. The scented steam should ease his breathing.

While the Imperial bride Maria Menshikova stayed away, terrified of falling ill herself, Menshikov, having already reached Moscow, turned back when he heard of our pause.

"Who has defied my order, and what are you doing dithering here?" Menshikov barked, barging uninvited into Petrushka's sickroom. His face was crimson from the hard frost, his cloak of velvet and wolfskin still steaming, and his muddy boots sullying the white floorboards and colorful rugs. His burly frame filled the room, and I was glad of the other men's presence: Buturlin leaned on the windowsill; d'Acosta squatted before the oven, poking at the embers; and Lestocq, overseeing the Tsar's treatment, sat with me by Petrushka's bedside.

"You will travel straight to Moscow. Now!" Menshikov ordered. "The Coronation is proceeding as planned." He cared only for his own ambition. If Petrushka died, his daughter's wedding would never happen, yet this would only make him more dangerous; then Menshikov himself would go for the throne.

"Good day to you, too, Alexander Danilovich Menshikov. It was I, Tsarevna Elizabeth Petrovna, the Tsar's aunt, who ordered this halt so that he might rest and recover," I said, keeping my seat and steeling myself to meet his gaze. This was the man who was truly to blame for my half-brother Alexey's death. I knew how ruthless he was. Menshikov stepped closer. Petrushka lay between us, his thin body barely showing beneath the many layers of blankets piled on him. His glassy eyes were half-closed, and his breathing labored.

At the sight of the Tsar, Menshikov swallowed a rebuke before kneeling to kiss the Imperial vermilion seal, which hung slackly on Petrushka's finger. His hands were skeletal; he kept down no food, except for a couple of sips of the thick soup, prepared according to a secret recipe, that had strengthened Mother after each time she had been brought to bed.

Menshikov turned to Lestocq. "Is it so bad?"

"Worse," he said. "The next few days will decide if he lives or dies. If all goes well, I suggest a summer stay at Peterhof following the Coronation. The salty air of the Baltic seaside will do wonders for his lungs."

"His Majesty is welcome to Oranienbaum, my summer house next to Peterhof," Menshikov decided. "It's the same salty Baltic air there, surely?"

Lestocq bowed. "The Tsar's health clearly benefits from the Tsarevna Elizabeth's care. And she is in Peterhof."

"As your French Court of frog-eaters clearly hopes to benefit from *your* attention to *her* care," Menshikov growled. "I know who pays for the Tsarevna's household. Foreigners!"

"Since she is deserted by her own people." Lestocq smiled thinly. "We eat frog's legs, you like fish eggs. There is no major difference, is there?" He gathered his black calfskin doctor's bag and, in a silent warning, placed a fingertip to his lips: Petrushka had finally slipped into a restless slumber. Sweat glistened on the Tsar's forehead, and his parched lips opened and closed soundlessly.

Menshikov slipped his gloves back on and turned to me. "You might be sitting by his bedside now, but do not get your hopes too high. Both Count Ostermann and I will see that there is no marriage between the young Tsar and his wily aunt."

"My regards to Count Ostermann. What nonsense are you alluding to? All I am doing is serving my sovereign."

Menshikov grabbed my wrist, pulling me to my feet and speaking through gritted teeth. "I know what you do. You are a disgrace to your house." He shot a look of knowing contempt at Buturlin, which chilled my soul. Yet I said: "Let me go. Now. And never dare touch me again."

Menshikov left behind him an impression of callousness and hatred. Ever since he had assumed power, I had only seen him raging and haunted. If legitimacy cloaked a ruler, then Menshikov stood as bare as a sinner on Epiphany, ready to plunge into the icy waters pleading for absolution. There was no such hope for him. He had betrayed my family too many times. I swapped glances with Buturlin: Menshikov, whose ambition, power, and greed were constant threats to my life, knew about us. If only I could speak to Anoushka. But not even my private letters to her were safe from prying eyes.

"Tsarevna, may I have a word?" Lestocq asked, as I fought to hide my concern. He clutched his doctor's bag to his chest.

"Buturlin, d'Acosta, you guard the Tsar," I ordered. The dwarf rose from the oven-top where he lay curled up like a dog. He wriggled his stubby fingers, making all the bones crack, before he leaped to the floor and shuffled up to Petrushka's bedside, his withered face looking worried. I felt an odd tenderness for the funny little creature who had been around all my life: he had loyally and unquestioningly served my family, for better and for worse. When I turned back on the threshold, the dwarf was shyly stroking the Tsar's slack hand, his own skin ruddy with health compared to Petrushka's glassy pallor.

45

In the corridor Lestocq stuffed tobacco into his thin, long ivory pipe, his expression pensive. Behind him Schwartz's burly frame filled the narrow space. Buturlin slipped out of Petrushka's sick chamber—against my orders!—closing the door firmly behind him. I drew my embroidered Persian shawl tighter, relishing its light softness: it was drafty in the passage, and icy patterns of otherworldly beauty clung to the windowpanes, through which milky blue light seeped into the corridor.

"Schwartz, what are you doing here? I thought you were in Moscow already. Though a merry tune might help the Tsar. And you, Buturlin, were told to stay inside," I said, already understanding: these men formed a Council of sorts, which was not meeting for the first time.

"Extraordinary circumstances call for extraordinary measures, Tsarevna. Schwartz is waiting. I am waiting. We all are waiting," Lestocq said, looking me straight in the eye.

"Waiting? We shall reach Moscow soon. The faster Petrushka is crowned, the better it will be. Summer in Peterhof will benefit the Tsar," I said. "I will do whatever it takes to restore him to health."

"I am speaking neither about traveling farther nor about His Majesty's convalescence," Lestocq said bluntly.

"Why? Is there no hope for him?" I remembered my doctor's blunt but accurate judgment when Augustus lay dying.

"There might well be. We are waiting for *you*." Buturlin's gaze was lit by pride and belief in me, warming my heart.

"What I am to do?"

"I would like to bleed the Tsar," Lestocq said.

"Bleed him?" I peered at the door behind which Petrushka lay as pale as the linen that covered his gangly limbs, too weak to move, eat, or drink. Bleeding him would make the life drip from his veins. The thought stirred me deeply, remembering Augustus's final hours. I shook my head. "No. Never. That would kill him."

Lestocq's gaze held mine; Schwartz shuffled nearer, standing closer to my physician than France and Austria ever were. Buturlin leaned against the wall, crossing his arms, his face somber. "Yes. It would," he said slowly. Lestocq squinted at the smoke that rose from his pipe. It thickened the dacha's soupy air further, making it unbreathable. "Must we spell it out?" he asked, his voice hushed.

I pressed my hands to my throat, feeling the St. Nicholas icon. My half-brother Alexey had died at our father's hand, bringing years of suffering to our family. In reparation I would shield Petrushka from all evil. This I had sworn to myself, and I would not go back on my word, determined that no further drop of Romanov blood would be spilled. "How *dare* you suggest this to me?" I protested. "My nephew is Tsar of All the Russias. To lay your hand on him is to flout the Divine will."

"The Tsar is neither crowned yet nor anointed with the sacred oil," Buturlin countered.

"You have sworn allegiance to him!" I hissed, raising my fists. "Shame on you, soldier."

Lestocq checked over his shoulder and spoke on, low and urgent. "The Tsar is terribly ill. Great things are at stake here. If God decided to call young Petrushka to him, who would inherit the throne? Menshikov? You cannot possibly want that. You are next in line. Give Russia the stability it yearns for. Your father's work is far from finished. Make his dreams come true. Set his legacy in stone. If the Tsar lingers on like this, Menshikov will seize power, and then God have mercy upon your country—and you."

I closed my eyes, put my hands over my ears and shook my

head. "I can't. It's against everything I was raised to believe in." I had stepped into a circle of traitors and regicides! Schwartz, no longer the harmless musician he'd seemed to be, urged me, "Tsarevna Elizabeth, do you even know the state this country is in? The coffers are empty. No ruling is done. Everybody in any sort of authority fills their own pockets. Of a hundred roubles in tax, only twenty reach the Imperial administration. Alexis Dolgoruky will move all offices, privileges, and duties back to Moscow. Russia will once more become everything your father feared and fought—closed to the world, small-minded, and centered on Moscow."

Despite the corridor's chill, I felt sweat gathering in my armpits. *You are next in line.* I had always been a second daughter, loved and spoiled but of no real importance—other than as marriage material. Then Mother had worn the Imperial tiara, slipping the almighty seal onto her own finger. So, yes: what if Petrushka perished, here and now? I fought the prospect with all my might: it was the Devil tempting me.

"You can't be serious, Lestocq. Is this what Versailles rewards you so royally for?" I needed to buy time. "France can't wish me to rule. It didn't even want me as its Queen, preferring the dour daughter of the deposed King of Poland," I reminded him. The old wound still festered.

"You will be better as reigning Tsarina of Russia than as a subdued, breeding Queen of France. Versailles knows that. De Campredon was no fool."

"So does Vienna," Schwartz cut in. "Let us not forget that Austria signed the Pragmatic Sanction, making Maria Theresa the Habsburg Crown Princess. She will rule. As might you."

"The Tsar and Maria Theresa are cousins," I said.

He bowed in a preemptive gesture of mourning and respect. "Vienna would deeply regret the young Tsar's passing. But you are so young and so beautiful that many an archduke is ready to learn Russian and even convert to the Russian Orthodox faith. Believe me."

Lestocq frowned, but his hands were tied. King Louis XV had had his chance. Instead, my physician beat his pipe against the raised sole of his boot. Burned tobacco fell in dark clumps on the whitewashed floor, thick as curdled blood. "What if Russia *wants* you?" he asked.

"Who is to know what Russia *wants*?"

"You do," Buturlin said simply. He pushed off the wall and kneeled in front of me, seizing both my hands. His expression was adoring, his fingers warm, their gentleness known to me. I almost yielded; the intensity of his gaze was hard to bear. "You *are* Russia. Your father was the Tsar anointed by Heaven, your mother the Tsarina, a daughter of the Russian soil. Legend and lore, law and logic, are combined in you. The Russian people worship you. For any soldier you are the Tsar's daughter. But more so, you are the Tsarina's daughter! Your mother has reigned. Why shouldn't you?" He kissed my fingers, then placed his hand on his heart. "The regiments are with us, I promise."

"*Whoever is favored by the Russian regiments, is favored by fate,*" Menshikov had said. The air thickened with tension. A mere nod of my head given in the frosty corridor of a far-flung dacha, somewhere between St. Petersburg and Moscow, would suffice for Tsar Peter II of All the Russias to be bled to death. Yet I needed to think further. We were in the middle of nowhere, and Menshikov was on his way back to Moscow, where thousands of soldiers manned the barracks. He could beat me to claiming control in the event of Petrushka's sudden death. That would mean the end of the Romanov Dynasty. I weighed the thought, barely able to breathe.

What should I decide?

Petrushka the lonely boy, had become the even lonelier man, lying desperately ill on his sickbed: if he had ever loved and trusted someone, it was me. I had been all the family he had known. All around us the dacha creaked. It felt like my nephew himself: frail and brittle, not made to withstand a winter, but in need of summer sun and gentle winds. Lestocq, Buturlin, and Schwartz were serious. If I took Petrushka's death on my conscience, I should be no better than Menshikov the day he had pushed my father to kill Alexey. My uncertainty gave way to anger.

"Get up, Buturlin! On your feet, soldier. Your limbs should be broken on the wheel for your treacherous thoughts, your entrails fed to the crows. What you think . . . worse, what you say . . . is punishable by death. I shall not betray my own blood, ever."

Buturlin stumbled to his feet, shocked by my outburst. Lestocq's fox-like face frowned. I clasped my thick *shatosh* to me, pulling it tighter around my shoulders. "You have served Russia well, gentlemen. I put your words today down to worry and shall forget and forgive. The Tsar is not to be bled."

I turned back to Petrushka's sick chamber. Buturlin opened the door, slipping into the room after me. "Lizenka!" he whispered, but I raised my hand, stopping him, fighting tears. He looked at me mutely, bowed, and went to lean on the windowsill, once more standing there with a sentry's patience, his gaze fixed on me. I longed for his embrace but settled at Petrushka's bedside instead.

D'Acosta shifted his tiny backside, making space for me, still holding his ruler's hands and humming songs, as if the Tsar were a sick child. Petrushka's face was as waxen as the candle next to his bed, its light slicing the cool blue air. I patted the dwarf's salt-and-pepper curls. "Go to the kitchen, d'Acosta. The hunters have brought back some hares and a wild boar. See if you can get yourself some of the grilled offal."

"Yes, go and stuff your greedy little dwarf face, creature!" Buturlin snapped jealously.

D'Acosta put out his tongue at him and slid out into the corridor: Schwartz had disappeared, and Lestocq retreated. The slight of him impregnating d'Acosta's daughter and not marrying her surely had not been forgotten, knowing the dwarf. Once the door had closed and all the footsteps had faded, I clasped Petrushka's hands, ready to pray for his life. Instead, I felt a slight pressure against my fingers and met my nephew's amber gaze: it was the first time he had woken fully in days. His freckles looked like dark poppy seeds on yeast dough. "Lizenka. Thank you," he whispered. "Was that Menshikov shouting at you earlier? He must not, ever. Did he make you sad? Tell me."

I kissed Petrushka's hands, my tears falling on his parched skin. "He harasses me to no avail," I said stoutly, though the fear I felt was monstrous. With Petrushka's life hanging by a silken thread, one snap of Menshikov's fingers would suffice to get rid of me. "But I will not give in. Nothing but your health counts for me. We will spend the summer together in Peterhof."

His face lit up. "Will we? Just the two of us? Together in Peterhof? I promise to get healthy. If I can only be with you."

"Don't you dare forget that promise!" I replied, fighting the memory of Lestocq's words that still dripped their poison into my soul. If Petrushka had no heir, Anoushka's child and I were next in line to the throne. Menshikov would do everything he could to tear all of us, and Russia, apart.

My mind was made up.

46

A couple of weeks later, when Petrushka had gathered strength, Maria Menshikova sat by his side at his Coronation, swathed in a heavy silver gown, her stomacher encrusted with diamonds, her flat chest adorned with the vermilion sash of the Order of St. Catherine. Her face had already started to show lines, and her scrawny neck twitched chicken-like beneath the weight of her pearl and diamond choker, each gem the size of a hazelnut. One of Mother's tiaras sparkled on her mousy hair, and droplets of snot hung from her flared nostrils as she struggled with a cold, dabbing her face with a handkerchief of Lyons lace and anxiously seeking her father's eyes. His gaze was steering her with cold precision.

During the ceremony in the Kremlin's freezing Cathedral of the Dormition, fits of coughing tormented Petrushka. To my surprise it was not Feofan Prokopovich who conducted the service—was my Father's trusted adviser, who had been a wise friend to me throughout my life, still under house arrest?—but a priest I had never seen before. At his sign Petrushka's heavy coat of crimson velvet and ermine was folded back and the bright blue sash of the Order of St. Andrew lifted off. As Buturlin undid the gold buttons of Petrushka's dark green Preobrazhensky Regiment jacket, the Tsar's wheezing breath was the only sound beneath the gilt-vaulted ceiling. The strong scent of his liniments—camphor and mint—blended with the censers' frankincense and myrrh. I folded my hands, gathering my thoughts, begging for strength. The priest's words reached me through a veil of fear.

As I let my gaze sweep over my surroundings, it met the eyes of a woman who sat in a loge, elevated above the courtiers. I would have recognized her dark eyes above a thousand others, even though my visit to Susdal Convent was a while ago. Back then she had been a miserable wretch lingering in a dank cell, a maimed dwarf her sole companion, counting the endless days. But the wheel of fate had spun more surprisingly than ever. Evdokia, my father's first wife, witnessed the Coronation of her grandson as the widow of an Emperor, as if my mother had never breathed; the choir's chant rising to the realm of Heaven while the court of Petrushka's earthly Empire bowed to her.

I lived day by day, trying to sound the depths of the court's deadly undercurrents, feeling them tearing at me without leaving so much as a ripple on the water's glittering surface. I knew that Vice Chancellor Count Ostermann minded my gaiety more than anything: the wiry German kept close to my sour-faced cousin Ekaterina Ivanovna instead. Under her steady stream of abuse, her daughter Christine had grown into a glum girl, who cowered next to her mother like a beaten dog. During the general rehearsal for the Coronation, I had tried to make amends. "Count Ostermann. My Ivanovna cousins are close to you, I know, perhaps because of their German alliances. Is there word of my cousin Anna Ivanovna, Duchess of Courland? Will she attend the Tsar's Coronation? As I do not like writing and reading, I have to rely on others to bring me news."

"My once having been German does not mean my interest lies there, Tsarevna," he said. "Only Russia counts for me. The Duchess of Courland has indeed asked His Majesty for funds to attend his Coronation."

"As is her right as Imperial Princess," I replied, angered by his impoliteness.

"Her being here, or not, makes not the slightest difference. Even less desirable is the presence of her, um . . . what shall I say? . . . private secretary, Herr Biren. But the Tsar wrote and answered her kindly enough." He rummaged in his folder of state papers for the crumpled draft of the letter and read aloud, "*Most Kind Sovereign Tsarevna and Duchess! I wish from the bottom of my heart to see you in Moscow in person to share this day of joy and glory with Us, however . . .'*"

"I am unable to include a bag of gold, which would give these kind words any substance," I interrupted him.

"True. But one need not say it so clearly. A valuable lesson to the young Tsar not to be as outspoken and temperamental as— others." He smiled meanly at me. "And, certainly, a more valuable lesson than the mindless pursuit of happiness he also learns from—others."

"Others who happen to love him. Petrushka needs warmth and affection," I flared up.

"Spoil him, and you destroy him," Ostermann returned with unusual emotion. "The Tsar doesn't need love. He is totally engrossed in seeking amusement—and you. His Majesty has a swift mind and a good heart. But only proper examples will enable him to rule Russia. Nothing is more important than that. Nothing."

He bowed briskly, insultingly so, and left. My eyes followed him until the gaily dressed crowd swallowed up his limping figure, which was as always clad in shades of navy and gray: only his loyalty to Russia drove him on. Whatever else I thought of him, the example he set Petrushka was impeccable.

That was what love meant to Count Ostermann.

Cousin Anna Ivanovna and Herr Biren were in Courland when the Imperial crown was lowered onto Petrushka's head. He squeezed his eyes shut and bent his neck forward to bear the sudden weight. His pallid face and slim shoulders, as well as his hollow chest, glistened with the chrism, honey-colored oil, with which he had been anointed. Still, Anna Ivanovna sent her nephew a valuable gift: a pack of six hounds, marvelous creatures with sleek sides and gleaming fangs. Three of them were trained to hunt big game such as bears, stags, and wild boar; the three others to pursue foxes, deer, and hares. They were fine beasts; she must have run up a debt to pay for them and their training. In another, private letter to Ekaterina Ivanovna, she wrote, "*I beg you, my sister, send me a new almanac for the year thirty as a diversion. Please do think of me, just for once.*"

"Think of her for once? Why should I?" Ekaterina Ivanovna had mocked her younger sister Anna by reading the words aloud to us. "Moaning, that is all Anna ever does. Her randy stable-boy Biren should be entertainment enough for her. She is a cause of shame to us all; always has been and will never be more than that." She tossed the crumpled letter away, sending the hounds into a frenzy: they leaped at the paper, tearing it to pieces.

"Don't, Mother, please," Christine started, but Ekaterina cuffed her daughter in full view of the court before leaving to pay homage to Tsar Peter II and his fiancée, Maria Menshikova. Anna Ivanovna in her faraway duchy was less than nothing to her sister, as well as to everyone else at the Tsar's court.

Anoushka gave birth to a healthy boy in Gottorf Castle, naming him Karl Peter and proclaiming him heir to Holstein and Sweden, wisely avoiding any mention of his right to the throne of Russia. Still, Menshikov forbade any celebration of the birth: neither church bells pealing jubilantly all over the vast realm, nor a three-hundred-cannon salute puncturing the frosty February air. I was overjoyed and dictated long letters to Anoushka as my thoughts somersaulted. The many times our mother had been brought to bed she had followed firm rituals: was Anoushka herself staying warm and keeping the air in her chamber fresh? Who was boiling her chicken broth, and was it properly laced with soaked dried fruit and red wine? Surely only a Russian wet nurse would do; I was planning to start inquiries now. Before the early summer, when Petrushka was planning to join me in Peterhof, I wanted to visit

Holstein, just to kiss my nephew's little feet. They would be as ticklish as ours had been. We would raise the boy to be a good Russian: it was as holy a promise as any pilgrimage I had ever made.

"Let us arrange a twin ball to celebrate little Karl Peter's birth," I suggested to Petrushka, simply to defy Menshikov. "With the best food available and the most beautiful music. And we need fireworks as well! Shall we celebrate at the same hour in Gottorf Castle and in Moscow? That way, we are as good as feasting together."

"Whatever you wish, Lizenka." He smiled indulgently. "A twin ball it is. But the first dance with you is mine. Or better still, block out your whole dance card for me. That is an Imperial order."

I danced that April night away, and while I whirled around in Petrushka's arms, with only a moment to breathe when Menshikov forced him into a polka with his fiancée, I imagined how happy my idea must have made Anoushka, so far away from home. How good it would be for her to dance and be merry.

Oh, yes, so good.

It had been my idea alone.

No one else was to blame.

47

"Mmm, breakfast, how wonderful!" Katja Dolgoruky sighed as she slipped into my Kremlin rooms. Petrushka had assigned me my mother's lavish yet homey apartment in the fortress's former *terem*. The court remained in Moscow, enjoying the first warmer days as well as the ease of living here compared to St. Petersburg. In the old capital, everything was procured more easily and cheaply. Katja's riding habit with its tightly laced stomacher and a sweeping skirt showed off her slim body, her cheeks were rosy, and strands of her ebony hair had come loose from her coiffed plaits during her morning ride. I still wore my Brussels lace dressing gown, my thick honey-blonde curls tumbling down to my plump waist. Buturlin had slipped from my room just minutes earlier, and I still glowed from our love.

"Come, sit with me," I invited her. Katja kicked off her riding boots and hopped onto my bed, beadily eyeing my breakfast tray: "soldiers" to be dipped in soft-boiled egg halves, served with caviar piled in a mother-of-pearl bowl standing on crushed ice. A stubby vodka glass stood next to a silver jug filled to the brim with steaming hot chocolate.

"Stop it or you won't fit in your wedding dress," I teased as she chewed and licked the runny yolk off her fingers. My maid loaded gowns from the open chests onto my bed, so I could choose my wardrobe for the festivities in the days to come. Petrushka had opened his purse strings. I had recklessly spent all the money at the *gostiny dvor*, that most glorious of Moscow places: two stories built in red brick and devoted to shopping. Before I knew it, I had amassed two thousand gowns, cloaks, furs, housedresses, underwear, and woolen, cashmere, and lace scarves, as well, of course, as a dozen riding habits tailored in the male style for the season ahead. If I liked something, such as a headdress or a fan, I ordered at least a dozen of them. My chests were as full as my heart with this change in my circumstances: the maid who lifted out the gowns as good as disappeared behind the yards of silk, taffeta, velvet, damask, and lace, making my bed look like a blooming spring meadow. Katja chewed on her third soldier, hungrily eyeing a fourth, while I pondered: the low-cut bodice of blue damask matched my eyes, while the demure pale pink taffeta, with its softly billowing sleeves, enhanced my blush. Or better settle on the dove-gray silk, pretending to possess a tame, pliant nature—men were so gullible, believing what suited them. At least I did not try to fool myself. That ship had long sailed. I held the dresses up to my face, one by one, turning to the mirror, losing myself in a couple of dance steps before dropping a gown carelessly on the floor and picking up the next.

"Look who's talking! I might not be the only one who needs to fit into a wedding dress?" Katja cheekily licked her fingers, eyeing my waistline.

"No wedding dress for me ever, Katja."

"Don't say that." She leaped off the bed and embraced me. "Augustus's death was unfair."

"Life is not fair," I said, with tears in my eyes.

"I apologize, Tsarevna," she said. "Anyone would want to wed you, surely? Our young Tsar adores you."

"Shhh," I warned. "You speak high treason. Menshikov will have your tongue if he hears, and Ostermann will banish your family to Beresov. I love the Tsar as my nephew and am delighted that he weds Maria Menshikova."

She grimaced, then smiled. "What did you think of him?"

"Of whom?" I teased, knowing full well she was speaking about her fiancé, Count Melissimo. At least one woman in the world could follow her heart. That must be solace enough for the whole sister-hood.

"You know who." She blushed.

"He is very handsome and dashing. When is the wedding planned for?"

"Still no date set," she sighed. "But soon, I hope. If ever I have a child—" she blushed even deeper, looking impossibly beautiful "—may I ask you to be godmother?"

"With pleasure."

Katja settled back onto the bed, dipping a fifth and last soldier into the caviar, mopping it all up, when there was a knock on the door. She stopped chewing, her hand hovering midair. I froze with fear. Menshikov arrested his enemies at dawn, dragging them to the deepest dungeons before the Kremlin woke. "Who might that be at this early hour, Tsarevna Elizabeth? Do you have a lover?" she whispered, her anxious gaze belying her jocular words.

My heart raced as I raised my hand in a mute warning. At least I was not alone! Though two women were all too easily overcome. I stepped to the door. "Who is it?"

"It is me, Lestocq," the Frenchman said, his voice sounding muffled. I opened the door, peering into the dark corridor. Ever since Tver, doubts about Lestocq's loyalty and reasons for staying in my retinue had tormented me. Was his allegiance to me genu-ine, or was it for sale to the highest bidder?

"Tsarevna," he said, and stepped aside.

I delightedly clapped my hands. "Oh, you bring Semyon Mord-vinov. All the way to Moscow. Sailor, what news from Gottorf Castle and my sister? Is it urgent? Do you bring me a first portrait of my little nephew?" I asked, but neither Anoushka's messenger nor Lestocq joined in my gaiety, their expressions grave. Semyon fell to his knees, his boots caked with mud and shoulders slumped under the weight of his news.

"Katja." I reached out to her. She came to my side as Semyon looked up, shaking his head, his eyes moist. "Do tell me how my sister loved my idea of the Twin Ball . . ." My voice faded. I felt short of breath, though I was not laced.

Semyon placed his hand on his heart. "The Duchess of Holstein adored the Twin Ball and the spectacular fireworks, which she did not want to miss—"

"And?" In silent prayer I held on to the icon of St. Nicholas.

"The Duchess of Holstein stood at the open window to admire the display. Afterward, she went on reading, I hear, never having closed the window."

"Say it, Semyon," I whispered while Katja stifled a sob. Tears rose, blinding me.

"Your Imperial sister, the Tsarevna Anoushka, died from pneumonia on the fourth of May. Her coffin awaits its return to Russia as soon as a ship is sent. She wished to be buried in Saints Peter and Paul Cathedral, by her parents' side. Awaiting you, one day. Those were her last words."

I was winded by sudden pain. The very night during which we had celebrated life had brought about Anoushka's death.

The Twin Ball festivities had been all my idea. I had killed Anoushka, failing to protect her just as I had Illinchaya back in Kolomenskoye. Sobs suffocated me; my knees buckled. Those wretched romances my sister had read, and my heedlessness, had led to her death, rendering her son motherless in a foreign land. The way ahead for him was bound to be dangerous.

Katja tried to embrace me, but I shrank back in horror: before my eyes, her raven tresses turned silver, mottled fur covered her smooth skin, and her pearly teeth gleamed like fangs. "Go away!" I screamed, lunging at the evil Leshy spirit. My fists rained down on the demon, my nails clawing her throat and face, tearing her skin. It was Lestocq who restrained me, holding me so tightly that I could neither move nor breathe, and then I fainted.

"*Will I give life?*" Anoushka had asked the evil spirit, who casually, callously, gave her response a lethal spin: "*A life you will give indeed.*" Once more a prophecy had come to pass.

48

The summer in Peterhof healed both Petrushka and me. Once again I found respite in the Russian countryside's simplicity, beauty, and calm, far from the court's prying eyes. It was truly the sweet season. Buttercups and poppies were blossoming, while the air was abuzz with bees and tumbling butterflies. Lestocq attended the Tsar daily, and I watched, hawkeyed, as he sounded Petrushka's sunken chest with his knuckles, attentively listened to his breathing, and checked the ever smaller amounts of phlegm the Tsar brought up, squinting and moving the little silver bowl this way and that. Then, one day, Petrushka's handkerchief stayed miraculously clean, showing no further trace of blood.

"The Tsar's lungs have cleared. It is quite miraculous: I can only put that down to your constant good care of him, Tsarevna," Lestocq declared, not meeting my eyes.

Petrushka looked at me and sought for my hand, his fingers warm and clasp firm. He lay on the terrace overlooking the garden, his freckled skin lightly tanned. He had even tasted some of the delicacies I had ordered for him from the kitchen: elderflower cordial, stirred with crushed ice and water, and a moist strawberry cake, gooey with custard and splattered with the black seeds of Persian vanilla pods.

"I have so much to thank you for, Lizenka," he said.

"Indeed," said Lestocq. As Buturlin handed him a filled purse, the two men exchanged furtive glances and walked away in silence, their shoulders almost touching.

* * *

Petrushka slept in the Great Palace. I preferred Mon Plaisir. Barefoot I roamed the pavilion's small cozy rooms, the gallery, and entrance hall. I wore my hair twisted in thick braids and my cotton summer dress unlaced. I found peace here, yet it was haunted by the happy hours of my childhood, especially the pantry, where we had breakfasted as a family. The pump's brass handle, on which I still seemed to see Anoushka's slim white hand, creaked as if it had been moved, sending the cobwebs across its spout quivering. The Delft tiles on the walls were dark with grease or else cracked. China and copper had been plundered from the shelves and walls. In my secret distress I walked the gardens, vainly seeking the happiness and sense of destiny I had shared here with both Anoushka and Augustus. I found neither. There is never a way back: I must start anew and forge a new future for myself.

Neither the days filled with hunts and games with Petrushka nor the stolen nights of pleasure with Buturlin lightened the burden of guilt I felt for causing Anoushka's death. The Bay of Finland's gray waters would carry her coffin home. Their lapping on the shore was like a low murmur of disapproval. I squinted out to sea, brushing my loose curls from my face: were those faraway sails billowing in the breeze her last passage to St. Petersburg? I shielded my eyes against the light, which in those weeks did not darken but only blanched into a hazy hue of silver: clouds raked the dense blue sky, their shadows flitting over the pale sea and dissolving, like Anoushka's soul slipping into another world.

I spoke to her before finally shouting and raging, hurling questions at the wind to carry away to sea, forever unanswered. I recalled the good times we had wasted in fighting, not knowing our days together were to be cut short. Father had been so right! Just as death could not be reversed, lost time could never be retrieved. I hunched over in the coarse gray sand, cupping my hands and scooping up the clear salt water that drenched the hem of my dress. I splashed myself with it, washing away the tears, then smeared sand all over my face, kneading the mud until my skin was sore. Yet even that physical pain could not end the torment in my soul as the absoluteness of Anoushka's passing dawned on me: I wished my grief would dissolve like the laudanum in Lestocq's potions, but it never did. I rose and stepped into the leaden water; my heavy mourning dress was soaked up to my thighs. It would weigh me down and make me sink like a stone if I allowed myself to fall. Yet if Anoushka had let go of my hand and was slipping into darkness, I was not quite ready to follow her. Until then, I vowed, I should think of her every day.

Every single day, I promise, my sister.

Meanwhile I had Russia to live for.

Whenever Menshikov, who had taken up residence in the neighboring Oranienbaum Palace, called on the Tsar, I made sure that Petrushka and I were out on treasure hunts, picnics, or boating, sometimes staying away for days on end. I received reports of him prancing about like an outraged peacock, shouting and laying about him angrily with his diamond-encrusted walking stick. They raised my spirits no end. That season, I shot nine stags, seventy-five hares, sixteen roe deer, sixty-eight ducks, four boars, and a wolf; from its skin I had a fine cloak made for Petrushka. The bristly gray hide was lined with crimson velvet and worn over one shoulder only, where it was fastened with a chain of solid gold fashioned in the shape of Imperial eagles. Petrushka and I shared Molniya, the peregrine falcon, and if she was not with me, my crossbow was almost as keen and accurate: a good huntress strikes but once.

One morning when the sky was red-veined, conjuring a day of still, late-summer heat, I was out on my own with the pack of hounds that Anna Ivanovna had given Petrushka. Molniya floated high in the sky, lifted by a breeze and calling upon the clouds, the sun's glare blackening her silhouette. I carried no other weapon, as was the custom when hunting with birds. The hounds rushed ahead, and I followed, urging them on, imitating their baying, my boots noisily breaking branches and my hands snatching at bushes, to let them snap back as I walked deeper into the thicket.

The she-bear and her cub rose suddenly and as if from nowhere: they were a perfectly camouflaged part of this forest, their coats as tawny as early autumn leaves. I froze in my tracks and exhaled slowly. A beast like this could tear me apart with a single swipe of its paw. I silently prayed to both God and all the spirits of the forest to help me. My teeth chattered. I bit my lip to still them as the beast rose on her hind legs, standing twice my height. Her fury filled the air between us like a veil that separated my life from my death. I sucked in air, making a small, helpless hiccupping sound. She was an overwhelming, invincible foe; larger than anything I had ever seen before. Still, I would not retreat, either because I dared not or could not.

I watched in horror as her solid mass came rolling toward me, ready either to kill or to lay down her own life for her cub. She bared her fangs as if testing them; the heat of her anger was searing. Any step I took, in any direction, would be my last, I knew. I let go of the icon and raised my hands in the air: here, look, I come unarmed. A single deep growl chilled my blood, but it was from one of the hounds. It launched itself at her like a bullet, its flanks sleek and fangs gleaming. The hound bayed with foolish delight finally to encounter the enemy it had been bred to fight. The bear stopped it short, slamming it with a single strike of her paw, swatting it away. There was a harrowing crunch, as of cartwheels stuck in hard, thick snow. The hound spurted blood and convulsed as the bear clamped it by its neck, shaking it once, as a child would a rattle, snapping its spine like a twig.

She eyed me, her soul searching the depths of mine. I cupped my mouth in horror, mourning the brave four-legged companion as much as fearing her next move. In her jaws the hound went limp, its lungs rattling in a last pained breath. I heard a bird call from far above and peered up: Molniya circled over us, her wings spread and floating, the only dark spot in a clear sky. The air stilled. With a grunt the she-bear slung the hound's body into a ditch, without so much as tasting it: she had proved her point, and such was her contempt that she left the cadaver for the crows, hyenas, and vultures. As silent tears streaked my cheeks, and I stood trembling, she picked up her cub, which hung slack and shiny from her mighty jaws.

Together, with last disdainful glances back at me, they disappeared into the darkest thicket of the Russian forest, where no one should ever dare to follow.

I stood frozen, my blood still rushing, counting first to three hundred and then another hundred more, for good measure, until my pounding heartbeat abated. My mouth was dry with terror. It took a long while before my hand was steady enough for me to raise it for Molniya to settle. Feeling her weight on my wrist calmed me. Shivering, I stepped over to the twisted, bloody cadaver of the faithful creature that had so bravely laid down its life for my sake. I wiped the tears from my face, yet they weighed me down like drops of molten lead. Molniya cocked her fine head, her beady eyes confirming what I had already realized: Russia herself had taught me a lesson about how to deal with enemies.

Menshikov would never know what hit him.

49

Summer faded away. September brought the earlier onset of dusk—a brief blue hour dissolving into the inky night—and darkness blotted out the White Nights once more. Back in St. Petersburg, Petrushka and I would not be close anymore. Soon he was to marry Maria Menshikova. When the Menshikovs finally managed to see us, Maria wore my mother's altered gowns as well as her jewelry, just to spite me: the women of Menshikov's family had riches enough to buy a thousand new wardrobes for every season of the year. Petrushka greeted her curtly, his gaze skimming over her flat chest and sallow skin before he was all too glad to give an excuse and follow me out. Upon leaving the room, I caught the quick glance that father and daughter exchanged: I had only days left in which to relish the freedom of Peterhof. In Susdal, or any other convent, there would be only a lifetime of loneliness behind unbreachable walls.

As we walked among fields high with wheat, the serfs' backs bent in hard labor until nightfall, I sighed. "This estate should really belong to the Crown. It is so splendidly fertile. Alas, Menshikov requisitioned it last summer as his private property."

When Petrushka became fretful, breaking a sullen silence by prodding me and asking, "Are you running out of stories, Lizenka?" I was careful to steer my reply in the same direction.

"Possibly. I should love to invite Katja Dolgoruky to join us. She is so amusing and full of ideas. Unfortunately Menshikov has banned her from seeing us. I wonder why? Might Maria Menshi-kova be jealous of her light heart and her great beauty?"

The gardens were still resounding with birdsong, the feathered creatures calling belatedly for mates. We noticed work had ground to a halt at the grotto where I had once drenched Augustus. The winches rested idle and buckets hung empty, as supplies of sand and stones had been siphoned off.

Petrushka frowned: "Why has this work been stopped? The repairs were urgent."

"Oh, Menshikov has ordered the workers over to his palace. The public purse is being diverted to the work on Oranienbaum instead."

For the rest of the walk, Petrushka brooded, kicking up gravel, breaking off a branch and whipping the hedges with it, like a boy beheading thistle. I was careful not to disturb his thoughts. In this way not a day passed by without my bringing up the subject of Menshikov, just as steadily dripping water gradually hollows a rock.

Yet everything comes at a price, as my cousin Anna Ivanovna had once warned me before she returned to her barren Duchy of Courland.

As the seasons changed, and the serfs worked frantically in the fields to beat the autumn rains, I felt the time was ripe for me to gather my very own harvest.

"Grant me the favor of a final dinner together," Petrushka pleaded on our last morning in Peterhof, not letting go of my hand when we took leave of each other for a couple of hours' rest. "Meet me in the Central Hall of the Grand Palace."

Schwartz sat close to one door, playing the harpsichord, pouring his soul into the music, the notes pearling like water. Buturlin shadowed Petrushka, as was his duty as chamberlain. I felt him lingering in the background, his presence reassuring and as warm as his caresses, but I forced myself to ignore him, which was hard to do. He emanated more heat than a fire on a cold night.

Beneath the vaulted ceiling with its floating fresco of the four seasons, servants had laid a table with crisp linen, gilt underplates, and blue-and-white patterned Meissen porcelain. Garlands of wild roses wound between the cutlery and the crystal, their petals redolent of summer, the dewy scent bewitching. Murano goblets gleamed, breaking the light into countless facets: no wonder that any apprentice seeking to leave the Venetian island and disclose the secret process of their manufacture was executed. The lights of the candles flickering in the silver candelabra were reflected in dozens of mirrors and bathed the stucco walls in their glow.

The caviar was perfect: each pearl was firm, yet burst with a fresh, salty flavor on my tongue, spreading a taste like dark star-light. Juicy wild pigeons were stuffed with the first mushrooms and chestnuts of the year, blending pungency and sweetness, before we enjoyed fresh forest berries on fluffy peaks of *smetana* and crisply baked meringue. As I licked some cream from my fingertips, I la-zily eyed Petrushka, sitting close by. "I want this moment to last forever," I sighed. "I wonder how often we will meet once we're back in St. Petersburg."

"Oh, so do I," he sighed, his face flushed with wine. "We shall meet all the time. Let us have lots of dinners like this, shall we?"

"Yes. Let us try to be simple." I brushed my St. Nicholas icon, silently pleading for his support. "Though I am sorry that I cannot adorn myself for you, my Tsar. Menshikov has robbed me of my mother's jewels."

"The wilder you look, the more beautiful you are," he said, then frowned. "How come he took the Tsarina's gems? I honor her mem-ory. She treated me with kindness whenever possible. What did he do with the gems?"

I shrugged my naked shoulders, which my maid had scrubbed with pumice. I knew my skin shone like alabaster. "Your guess is as good as mine. He cannot have sold them, no? Otherwise, surely some funds would have been sent to Gottorf Castle to guarantee the upbringing of Anoushka's son." I blinked away tears but was careful not to smudge the thin line of kohl I had applied. They made my blue eyes sparkle more than ever. "It's shameful. The little boy is an heir to the Russian throne. The two of you share a grandfather—and not just any grandfather: the great Tsar who loved us all, in his way."

"Well, it was a very curious way as far as I was concerned. Nobody has ever hidden their love for me as well as Grandfather did," Petrushka said bitterly.

I took his hand, squeezing his fingers and looking at him sympathetically, tears welling up.

"God, I know," I whispered, choking on the bitter memories. "But you *are* family. Whatever Menshikov says!"

"Why, what does he say?" Petrushka asked, his voice sharp.

I bent forward, afraid of eavesdroppers, and saw Petrushka's gaze change direction to the low neckline of my gown. I had pressed my ample flesh forward with my arms and now quickly sat up straight again, giving him a coy smile. He must listen to this as my nephew and as Tsar. "Menshikov didn't even grant the boy a salute at his birth. Little Karl Peter has no stipend, and his birthday is not included in the court calendar. Could there be anything more disrespectful? Who, I wonder, is next on his list? Nothing would surprise me, after what he has done to me."

It was not difficult to look tearful as Petrushka downed another glass of the clear, chilled vodka that finished our meal. He rolled the stubby glass between his palms, looking thoughtful. "We have to stick together, Lizenka. After all, how many of us are left? The Romanovs seem cursed." He rose abruptly, sending his chair toppling, and seized my hand. "My beautiful, warm, and adorable Lizenka. Together we can face the world. Say goodnight to me . . . but do it properly for once."

He stepped around the little table, pulling me to my feet. His eyes were glassy from drink, and his lips moist when he placed them, fervently, everywhere: on my palms, my wrists, my bare inner arms. "I so wish you'd dream of me tonight," he murmured, drawing me closer. The acoustics in the rotunda meant his voice carried further than he had intended it to. I tried to hide my shock at the passion he was showing, conscious all the time of Buturlin watchful in his attendant's niche.

"I shall, my Tsar," I whispered. Petrushka held me tight, forcing me against him, hands pressing my lower back and neck. There was no way out. His breath was laced with champagne, burgundy, vodka, and schnapps.

"I wish . . ." His lips hovered over mine.

"You wish, Your Majesty?" He held me too tightly. My heart raced with fear. Had I overplayed my hand? He cupped my face and gazed at me adoringly. His face drew closer, and he kissed me, not as my nephew and not as a friend, but as a clumsy lover: passionate and greedy. I tried to wriggle free, but suddenly his hands were everywhere, groping me and tearing at my gown. His tongue prized my lips open, forceful and crude, and he pushed me backward onto the table, spreading my thighs. This was going much too fast: we had not yet arrived at the conclusion I desired.

"Don't," I gasped, as he hungrily bit my mouth once more, sucking my lips, pressing himself onto me. I felt his desire and his excitement. This newfound strength after the long months of illness was surprising and shocking; Schwartz's playing stumbled once, but then the melody danced on. Nobody would move, even if Petrushka forced himself on me here, right in front of their eyes.

"I want you," he groaned, hauling up my skirts and groping between my legs, his fingers probing, seeking their way in past my silk stockings and tender skin. It hurt. "Here, now!"

With all my strength, I shoved him away and rose, smoothing my skirts, my face on fire. I touched my bruised lips. "No! We must not! If Menshikov finds out, he will kill me," I gasped, but Petrushka came forward again and clasped my face, his hands almost crushing my skull. "I have always loved you, Lizenka. I do not fear Menshikov's wrath any longer. I want to be free, and I want to live with you. Be mine."

"I can't. Not like this." I tore myself from him. The garden offered sanctuary. I backed away, and Buturlin quickly stepped forward, bowing to his Tsar, ready to accompany me back to Mon Plaisir. "If you do not fear Menshikov, I do. I know what he is capable of."

But Petrushka called, "Lizenka, my love. Wait!" He stood trembling before us, clenching his fists. "If it is Menshikov you fear, what can he be charged with?"

I took a deep breath. The moment had finally come to clear my family of original sin. The blame should be put where it rightfully belonged: on Menshikov's shoulders. I knew who had urged on my father to take the measures he had against Alexey; who had assisted him at the height of his rage.

"You name it, he has done it. Even murdering a Tsarevich."

"Murdering a Tsarevich?" Petrushka staggered against the table, looking crushed. "Are you speaking of my father?"

I nodded mutely. Menshikov's Oranienbaum was close enough for a dawn raid. I shook with fear and tension. "Menshikov was the first to sign your father's death sentence. He, who had tutored Alexey and had every chance to form him! The Tsarevich died with Menshikov's knee on his head; he urged Father on and on. . . ." I choked and halted, crying too much to speak. I shook my head. "My half-brother was not a traitor; he was a victim. Menshikov's victim."

"What can I do?" Petrushka groaned and swayed. His shirt was stained and his dark hair stuck to his temples.

"Your father's true murderer is Menshikov." I folded my trembling hands. "The Tsar can do anything. Always."

He smashed his fist on the table, making plates and glasses topple and soaking the table linen with burgundy. "I shall show him who is Tsar!" he shouted, and then stepped up, towering over me. "If I do, will you be mine? Promise me," he slurred, holding my wrists.

"I so wish I could," I said, turning away.

Petrushka turned and kicked the table savagely, toppling it. As

I fled into the scented cool of the night garden, my heart racing at my own daring gamble, priceless porcelain shattered on the marble floor, closely followed by a rain of glass as the Tsar hurled the crystal goblets against the mirrors.

On the terrace d'Acosta waited, holding a torch, ready to accompany me to Mon Plaisir. Had he witnessed Petrushka's rough-and-tumble attentions as well as his promise? The dwarf had an uncanny knack for being in the right place at the right time, seeing it all, sealing it away for future reference.

"Off we go, d'Acosta," I said, my voice unsteady, clasping my hands in front of me to stem their trembling. It seemed impossible to split the man from the nephew, and the nephew from the Tsar. Was I summoning powers I could not master? But if I let him be, Menshikov would destroy both my Holstein nephew and me. I had no choice.

"Give me the torch, midget," Buturlin commanded, joining us. "Otherwise I'll crush you like an ant."

D'Acosta arched his eyebrows: "Daring, dashing, dead. Remember, Buturlin, that's how it goes."

Buturlin kicked out at him, but d'Acosta avoided the boot with a nimble twist, wiggled his pert backside at Buturlin, and then walked ahead, gravel crunching under his small feet. An orange harvest moon hung above the Bay of Finland, drawing a silver path on the sea's still surface. The night air was fragrant with wild roses, pungent elderflower, and the yeasty smell of the harvested fields beyond. Buturlin's anger and jealousy rippled toward me. I was careful to keep a distance between us.

"I shall see the Tsarevna to bed, not you, little man." Buturlin shoved d'Acosta once more when we reached Mon Plaisir, tearing the torch from his hand. "Vile misfit! Your mother should have drowned you on the day of your birth. Though the sea itself would have cast you out in horror."

The dwarf's voice was tinged with hurt pride when he said to me: "Tsarevna Elizabeth, be careful. Please."

"It's all right," I said, though I was not sure of it.

"If you think so, Tsarevna." D'Acosta bowed to me.

"Go before I flog you, imp!" Buturlin grabbed a fistful of gravel and chucked it after him.

"You shouldn't underestimate d'Acosta. Small does not mean powerless," I warned Buturlin once we were safely inside Mon Plaisir, surrounded by the gilt-framed mirrors in the entrance hall. I saw him reflected a dozen times over, tall, dark, and handsome, jaw set, eyes glittering.

"I am tired," I said.

"Me too." He seized my wrists. "Tired of watching you being chased by other men while I have to linger in the shadows. I adore you, Lizenka," he whispered. "I could have killed the Tsar when he touched you. I could have killed *you* when you said: 'I *so wish* I could.'"

"I am yours," I said hoarsely, excited by his rage, kissing his fingers. "But I also belong to Russia."

"And I am yours as a Russian," he swore, his eyes bright with tenderness. We kissed and made up, whispering and laughing, feeling our hearts beat to the same rhythm, wild with passion and slowing with sated desire.

50

When a slim new moon hung in the early morning October sky and the Neva's waterline was low, Major General Saltykov, a kinsman of Aunt Pasha and my cousins Ekaterina and Anna Ivanovna, landed together with a dozen armed men on Vassilyev Island, where Menshikov's palace gleamed like a pearl, the wan dawn being its oyster.

Menshikov was found asleep in the arms of a nameless mistress. The plump girl was lucky to be left unscathed, while he was forcibly restrained in a ball and chain and left kneeling on the marble floor for hours, awaiting his fate. His wife, Daria Menshikova, was dragged from her rooms, fainting twice in the corridors and then once more when she saw her husband stripped of all his power and riches. Saltykov himself tore the Imperial engagement ring—an enormous pink teardrop-shaped Siberian diamond—from Maria Menshikova's finger. It would return to the Crown, just like the rest of Menshikov's worldly goods: the coal, gold, silver, copper, and ore mines; the glass, garment, and weapons factories; the spinning mills and weaving halls; the thousands of acres of pristine Ural woodlands; the carpentry workshops; the prime arable land bearing wheat, barley, and oats; as well as his innumerable sporting estates and palaces throughout All the Russias—Menshikov could cross the realm and sleep every night under his own roof—and, last but not least, the hundreds of thousands of serfs, the unfree peasants bound to the soil they worked, the foundation of our *Matushka Rossiya*.

* * *

The Tsar refused ever to see Menshikov again. I, though, insisted on taking leave of him personally: he had bitterly betrayed too much that I loved and was loyal to for me to miss this opportunity. Inside their simple carriage with its barred windows, Maria Menshikova still wore her nightgown; her eyes were veined with red, and her dirty blonde hair straggly. Daria clung to her. Their two weeks in the confines of a dark cell of the Trubetzkoi Bastion—possibly the one where Alexey had once awaited his fate at Menshikov's hands, beside himself with terror and disbelief—had slimmed her down and pushed her to the brink of madness. Menshikov sat hunched in one corner, banging his head against the side of the carriage. He cursed and grunted, tearing at the iron chain that looped through rings at his wrists and ankles, restraining him like a tethered bear at a spring fair; it had chafed his skin sore. I saw blisters and pus. He must be in pain. Good.

"Alexander Danilovich," I said softly. I had taken great care with my appearance that day, wearing a gown of duck-egg-colored silk intricately embroidered with pearls, crystals, and a generous sprinkle of aquamarines and turquoises. It was low-cut for a day-dress, but I should see the Tsar later on. My cheeks were flushed from the first autumnal chill, and my blonde hair neatly wound in a crown around my head. Diamonds in my earlobes and at my wrists had been fashioned to match the frame of my icon of St. Nicholas.

"You!" He sucked his teeth but dared not spit at me when Buturlin and two of his regiment's soldiers stood tall behind me. They would finish him off, there and then, if he dared do anything—which might be a mercy compared to what lay ahead of him.

"Me." I checked the carriage's tattered mattress and half a dozen threadbare blankets, as well as its lack of cushions. I nodded my head, content to see it. "Are you sitting comfortably? You have a long trip ahead of you." Maria Menshikova buried her face in her hands as Daria lunged for my fingers. I crossed my hands behind my back.

"Lizenka, please! For the love of your father!" she pleaded.

"The great Tsar whom you swindled as long as he lived?" I asked.

"The friendship of your mother—" she continued.

"The Tsarina from whose dead body you tore the jewelry?" I reminded her, before adding: "And let us not forget my brother, the Tsarevich Alexey, whom your husband condemned to death and helped murder with his own hands."

I had kept my voice low, yet in the Winter Palace's enclosed courtyard, the words gained force, lifting me up. I felt like a bird, circling high above Menshikov's miserable carriage, taken higher and higher by the friendly wind. This was how Molniya my falcon felt when preparing to bring down her prey. It was exhilarating.

Daria Menshikova sank back in her seat, sobbing.

"Where are we going?" Menshikov's eyes were crazed with fear. I saw his shoulders were bruised where his fine shirt was torn. There had been nobody who cared enough to bribe the Trubetzkoi Bastion's wardens to spare him and his brethren from abuse and violence.

"A place nobody ever comes back from," I said. "If they reach it at all. Beresov in Siberia."

"Beresov! But there is nothing there!" wailed Daria Menshikova.

"That's not true. You will be there. And the Tsar in his mercy grants you this." Buturlin handed me an axe, which I lobbed into Menshikov's lap. "Pray for the Tsar's soul. With any luck you will have built your house before the snowfall is too bad." I met Alexander Danilovich's desperate eyes, steeling myself. Menshikov deserved everything he got—and more.

"It's freezing there," he screamed. "We are wearing only shirts and nightgowns. Have pity. Where are our sable coats?"

Oh, how I had waited for those words! "I still remember how

you told me your daughter liked a good sable coat, Menshikov. But then, don't we all?"

He stared at me, mute with the understanding of his complete and utter defeat.

"Good riddance, Alexander Danilovich. As you said, there is always another possibility. For whomever, whenever." The look on his face was balm to the suffering he had caused me. I knocked on the carriage's roof, giving the driver the signal to depart. A whip cracked, and the stocky ponies pulled away. The carriage jerked, hurling the Menshikovs about as they were driven from my sight forever. As they left the Winter Palace, the dark clouds above us thickened, promising thunder and lightning. It started to drizzle; soon the drops grew heavier, rain pouring down. I stood firm in the torrent and tilted back my head, opening my mouth: tears of rage and relief shook me as the rain poured down my throat. I howled into the storm, relishing its cleansing, nourishing power. Until this moment I had not realized how parched I had been. The floods eroded the walls that had held Alexey's suffering secret and captive, bricking in the memory of him. I had set his soul free, and now his name could be spoken without fear of reprisal. My family could finally heal and grow close once more.

When the Menshikovs arrived in Tver two weeks later, to be charged and sentenced, the first steady snowfall had set in. Daria Menshikova perished well before reaching Beresov. She was buried by the roadside in an unmarked grave. Maria Menshikova, the Tsar's former fiancée, who had sat clothed in silk and decked out in diamonds by Petrushka's side during his Coronation, followed her mother soon after—her grave was a ditch lost in the vastness of Siberia—dying delirious with fever and disfigured by smallpox. Menshikov himself perished within the year. Ever resourceful, he had ventured out in the Siberian night in the middle of a raging snowstorm, trying to fix the roof of the cabin he had built with his treasured axe. In the morning, when the storm abated, his frozen body was said to have stuck out from the white Siberian plain like a sore finger. I had heard that freezing to death is a painfully slow death—the limbs failing and the organs shutting down one by one—and trusted that was the truth.

51

It was as if Menshikov had never been. After his old rival and crony's fall, Count Ostermann—as wily and catlike as ever—was not to be seen at court, reportedly suffering from crippling gout, but still plying his former pupil Petrushka with letters brimming with ideas, instructions, and suggestions. The Dolgorukys' star was in the ascendant, and Ostermann stayed in hiding, taking care to be a dagger in nobody's eye, only pulling strings while safely in the wings, ready to fight for the young Tsar's soul. Reversing Father's reforms meant nothing but eternal damnation to Count Ostermann.

"Stay, Katja. Sit, Lizenka," Petrushka ordered when he and d'Acosta, Prince Alexis Dolgoruky, and Buturlin entered the Summer Palace's small library one morning, unannounced. Winter had come. Snow lay high up a sled's side, and an icy wind bit to the bone, delighting in whirling caps off heads; people swore as they chased after them, floundering knee-high in the fresh, icy swathes. Katja and I were sitting by a roaring fire, both wearing warm, unlaced house gowns and nibbling sweet *pierogi* and chestnuts, their skin split just so by the heat of the grate. The samovar bubbled away with a low hum.

We had much to talk about: a wedding date for Katja and her handsome Italian Count Melissimo had finally been set. "Alessandro has offered me bales of Chinese silk for the wedding dress," she had said, delighted. "It is the most delicious shade of *smetana*. I will wear his family's tiara of pearls, aquamarines, and diamonds." We had met to arrange dried flowers; Buturlin's first bouquet to me, that harbinger of hope, was to form the collage's heart. The faded blossoms still bore a faint scent, which dissolved in the damp draft that Petrushka brought in with him today.

He threw his splendid wolfskin cloak—which I had had made for him—at d'Acosta to catch. The dwarf tumbled underneath its weight, drowning in its folds, struggling painfully to his feet. The sight made us laugh, and he took the hint to tumble over, moving about beneath the velvet like a mole, again and again, until Petrushka said: "Enough, d'Acosta. We have business to attend to." He stooped to admire the dried blossoms. "Exquisite work, my beloved Lizenka. You have the hands of a fairy." He kissed my fingers, then winked at d'Acosta, who stood to attention, his face grave, the Imperial cloak at his feet, and one hand flat on the pocket of his gaily colored patchwork waistcoat. "But why ever are your hands so bare, Tsarevna?"

I laughed. "Well, I shall adorn myself as an Imperial Princess for the dinner tonight. I am so grateful for the remnants of my mother's jewelry that you sent me—I love colored diamonds. But here we are all cozy and private, so I thought—"

He interrupted me, keeping hold of my hand. "No. It is now, and here, that you will be adorned. Our darling friends shall be my witnesses. And all the better if you love colored diamonds." The room fell silent. Alexis Dolgoruky frowned as Petrushka pulled me to my feet. His godfather expected to be consulted upon all the Tsar's decisions. Petrushka's sudden move swiped the last of Buturlin's dried petals to the floor in a shower of dreary dust. I bit my lip with regret. Once again my past must be left behind.

The Tsar snapped his fingers at d'Acosta, who conjured up a purple velvet cushion and rummaged in the pocket of his waistcoat before placing a little jewelry case on it.

Katja gasped, "My God, Tsarevna Elizabeth! Is this really happening?"

D'Acosta's eyes did not leave my face, his gaze as deep as a wishing well. Hot fear rose from deep inside me as Petrushka smiled tenderly, saying: "Just you wait, Lizenka." Katja craned her neck, clasping her hands at her chest, beaming at me. I sat petrified while Petrushka let the lid of the delicate case snap open, revealing the Imperial engagement ring, which he had been forced to offer to Maria Menshikova, although it was snatched back once her father was disgraced. The pink teardrop-shaped diamond shone with a cyclamen-tinged fire; it was large enough to cover my finger from the first to the second knuckle.

Alexis Dolgoruky looked aghast. He knew that as Tsaritsa I would never allow him to lead Russia back into its past, as he intended to do. Katja made a strange little hiccupping sound. Buturlin, standing guard at the door, looked thunderous. Only Petrushka's dear face was openly hopeful, his eyes adoring as he offered me the ring, clasping my fingers in his.

"Lizenka," he said, "be my wife. Be my Tsaritsa of All the Russias. I shall have you crowned. Be the mother of my children, the power behind my throne." Red patches of excitement showed on his cheeks, and he started to cough. Alexis Dolgoruky steadied him, edging closer, his gaze as hard as flint, his face ashen, while Petrushka steered me toward the warmth of the fireplace. The ring mirrored the flames, trapping them in fiery prisms. "Be mine," Petrushka said, his voice pleading and warm. Desire darkened his eyes as he readied himself to place the ring on my finger.

"I could not have hoped for more, Tsarevna Elizabeth. Both of us will be happily married come the New Year. What bliss," Katja sighed.

I would have bolted then, but, of all men, Buturlin blocked the door. Petrushka was my nephew; we were too closely related to marry. I loved him as my relative but never as a man. The memory of our dinner in Peterhof still made my skin crawl. Yet the determination in his face told me that he would find a way around anything that hindered the fulfillment of his wish. Excuses would not do. He had grown into his role as Tsar of All the Russias, which I had encouraged him toward.

"I can't," I said, pushing the ring away.

"You—can't?" Alexis Dolgoruky was the first to repeat, a flash of delight in his eyes, yet sounding as incredulous as Petrushka looked. He was too stunned to speak, emotions chasing over his face like clouds across the sky. I forced myself neither to take his hand nor to embrace him. He was almost as pale as back in Tver when I had saved him from Versailles and Vienna's murderous designs. All the hurt and contempt he had suffered in the past broke through the thin veneer of adulthood; the blanket of wealth and adulation only lightly covered that suffering. My heart went out to him, yet marrying him would make everything worse.

I kneeled before him, tears in my eyes, and kissed his fingers: "My Tsar, I am deeply honored. I adore you and am forever faithful to your cause. But I love you as my nephew. I cannot be your wife. I am barren and of no service to further my house."

Tears streamed down my face then. *Barren.* How short yet finite the word was as I faced the truth. After all the careless moments with Buturlin, night after night, I had never been with child. Had it happened, I would gladly have weathered the scandal, retreating to the country. *You will be a mother but have no child.* What cruel truth had the Leshy spirit been hiding behind those words, all those years ago, in the Golosov Ravine?

Petrushka still held out the ring to me, blinking with disbelief. "Nonsense, Lizenka. Who cares? I am not the last Tsarina's son. We shall find my heirs elsewhere. I love you, and I want to be with you." His honesty twisted my heart when he added: "Also a childhood such as mine was so terrible, lonely, and deprived of love, that I do not feel the need to bring other children into the world. I can find an heir another way—Anoushka's son, maybe."

"I can't," I repeated. Petrushka was loving toward me now, but what if he changed? I dared not breathe. My life hung in the balance, but I had to be true to myself.

"Tsarevna, please." Katja held my shoulders. "Do consider it at least. This is more happiness than any woman could hope for."

I closed my eyes briefly, shutting her out, and shook my head. "No. I am to be no man's wife. Not ever," I said as I opened them and looked around. "I am grateful for the honor you do me, my nephew. But I implore you as my Tsar to find another woman and offer her this same honor and happiness—a woman who will gladly be your wife, and who can love and cherish you, as you deserve."

"Do not go against destiny," Katja warned me.

"Who knows their destiny?" I asked.

"Another woman?" Petrushka's voice broke with hurt, disappointment, and anger. "I have never been happy. And if I cannot be happy now, with you, then no one else shall be happy either."

"Don't say that," I soothed him, once more not taking him seriously.

Petrushka turned to Alexis Dolgoruky. "My *kum*—godfather. You have always been like a father to me. Are you by my side?"

"Always, my Tsar!" Prince Dolgoruky beamed, standing to attention. He was more relieved by my refusal of Petrushka's proposal than he could ever let on. "Do you need my advice? There is many a princess who would be delighted to be your wife."

Katja watched them, rapt. Her face was as bright as a jewel, so pleased was she with the honor the Tsar showed her father.

"I need more than just your advice. I need your blessing," Petrushka said, his eyes burning with hurt, his mouth set with anger. "I request your daughter Katja Alexeyevna's hand in marriage."

Surely, we had all misheard. There were so many Princesses Dolgoruky. Theirs was a vast family of varying degrees of fortune. But my friend Katja was already happily planning her wedding with a young man she loved.

"No," she gasped. "That must be a mistake. I am spoken for!

Father, please—" She stepped up to him, leaning against his shoulder, frantically seeking his hand.

Alexis Dolgoruky dared to say: "My Tsar, Katja is engaged to marry. A date is set. It is a good match, and the young people are in love."

Petrushka shrugged, his face pinched. "Engagements are meant to be broken. Dates are made to be altered. And what is love anyway? Think of Maria Menshikova." The casual threat in his words was chilling as he held out the astonishing jewel to Katja. He was growing into a real Romanov.

"Petrushka, please," I said quietly. "You can't do this."

He fought tears but turned to me and raised his chin determinedly. "Ah! Didn't you say that the Tsar could do anything, always?" He looked at Prince Dolgoruky. "Godfather Alexis, I haven't heard your answer yet."

Prince Dolgoruky bowed, his long-thwarted ambition vanquishing any fatherly concern for Katja. After all, who was Count Melissimo, a foreign diplomat, compared with the Tsar of All the Russias? Finally Dolgoruky would be in position to achieve what he longed for: to obliterate all my father's efforts. His eyes were hard when he clasped his daughter's wrist, holding her firm. "What an honor! A wise decision, my Tsar. After all, the Dolgorukys are one of Russia's foremost families. We founded Moscow, built the Kremlin—"

"Yes, yes. Don't bore me." Petrushka shrugged dismissively, while Katja struggled in her father's grip.

"No," she shouted, her voice drowning in tears. "No. Never! I will marry Alessandro!" Her father slapped her hard, making her head jerk and her lip burst open. I recoiled at the sudden violence, mute with shock. My friend gasped and felt for the cut, touching her mouth with trembling fingers.

"Give me this trinket," her father said, and twisted Count Melissimo's engagement ring off her finger. Before she could prevent him, he threw it in the flames. Katja howled and made a foolhardy dash for it, but he seized her; his iron grip forced her to kneel in front of the Tsar. Wretched with tears, her hand slack, she watched Petrushka twist the huge, heavy Imperial ring onto her slender finger.

"It fits," he said coldly, sounding pleased. In the fireplace, a furnace for Katja's love, dreams, and hopes, Count Melissimo's ring melted. Petrushka took a deep breath and bowed to peck his fiancée's cheek, next to her bleeding, trembling lip, as a brother might. "So this is it then. Do not cry, dear Katja." He touched her tangled hair, looking down at her bent head. "It will pass. Everything does. Believe me, I know. We will be happy, whatever that means. I shall not hold a grudge against you for your reception of my proposal but prefer to think that you were beside yourself with joy." He turned to Prince Dolgoruky. "Godfather Alexis, take my beautiful bride home, and, once she has calmed, let her pack. Henceforth she is to live in the Golovinsky Palace. The engagement is to be announced in a fortnight, and her title is to be Her Imperial Highness, the Bride Tsaritsa. Our wedding date will be the same as was set with Melissimo, for the sake of convenience."

Prince Dolgoruky bowed, his puffy face reflecting feelings ranging from pity to pride. His daughter stumbled to her feet, her face ravaged by grief.

"Come now," Prince Dolgoruky urged, pulling her toward the door, possibly afraid that Petrushka, or I, might think again. Yet on the threshold Katja turned to face me.

"This is your fault. Life will make you pay, if not I," she raged, shaking her fist at me.

"Don't listen to her. Katja has been secretly besotted with His Majesty for a long time. She might need bleeding after all this excitement," her father said, dragging her out.

"Father!" she sobbed in the corridor. "Don't!" We heard another slap—a hard, determined palm hitting a young face. As the sound of their steps faded, I sank into a chair, my hand to my mouth. My palm still bore the faint scent of petals. The fire devoured the last of Melissimo's ring. Petrushka gathered his gloves and adjusted the wolfskin cloak on his shoulder, looking as if he had aged a decade during the last half hour. It broke my heart to see him like this.

"So be it then, Elizabeth. I have achieved what I came for. I am engaged to marry, committed to honoring a woman and making her happy," he said, straightening his back. "But I am not quite finished with you yet." He toyed with his cloak's fastening and gave a small nod to d'Acosta. "Open the door."

To my surprise a guard of soldiers belonging to the Imperial Semyanovsky Regiment entered.

"Stay, Lizenka, my dove. And you, my friend Buturlin, as well," Petrushka said softly to us.

52

D'Acosta's face was as keen as an unsheathed blade. Petrushka stood with his hands clasped behind his back. "As it has come to this, there is something else I would like to know. How, exactly, Tsarevna Elizabeth, my unmarried virgin aunt, would you know that you are barren?"

The blood drained from my head. At the door Buturlin froze. Our eyes met; Petrushka's lips curled, but his eyes were sad. "I know how you know, my beautiful, beloved Lizenka. Because you have been whoring with my chamberlain for a year now, if Menshikov's slander is to be believed. Oh yes, he spouted the truth under torture. All through the summer months, when I thought we were courting, when I thought we were in love!" Beads of sweat were glistening on Buturlin's Tatar forehead; his eyes were wide with fear as he shook his head in denial. Petrushka spoke on: "Menshikov—whom I banished because I thought he hindered our match. And now, despite all the affection and favor I have shown you, you refuse to be mine. Buturlin, can any honorable man accept this? But then, what do you know about honor, compromising a Tsarevna as if she were a stable maid?"

"My Tsar!" Buturlin fell to his knees, his hands outstretched, prostrating himself.

"Too late." Petrushka clapped his hands, a short, sharp sound. The Semyanovsky Guard seized Buturlin, who shouted: "No! Let me explain," and put up a brief struggle, fists flying, ribs crunching, and uniform tearing, until a swing to his stomach made him

278 ᴥ ELLEN ALPSTEN

double over. He wheezed with pain. When he tried to stand, a blow to his chin sent him to the floor. Buturlin groaned, curling up, sobbing, as kicks and punches started to rain down on him. "My Tsar, believe me," he begged, his mouth bloodied.

"No. Quiet now. I have heard enough," Petrushka said, raising his hand to fend off Buturlin's pleas, squeezing his eyes shut against the sight of his former friend, battered and bloody. The Tsar breathed heavily and blinked away tears before he addressed me. "Speak. Do you love him, Lizenka? So much that you truly forsake all others? Even me? Do you wish to marry him?"

I cast a look at d'Acosta. In Russia, the tiniest hand could spin fortune's mighty wheel. "Don't, Petrushka," I pleaded. "Please. Try to understand. I had lost both my parents. Augustus died. Anoushka left. I was terrified of Menshikov. Buturlin brought light into that darkness. I am grateful for it. But I shall never be any man's wife." I reached for Petrushka's hand, but he jerked it back as if stung.

"Do not ever touch me again. Buturlin shall pay for that." Petrushka's face twisted with rage and pain.

"Have mercy. Don't kill him!" I fell to my knees, wringing my hands. "He was the only one who always spoke on my behalf."

"*I* was your friend. I shall not kill him. Yet he shall never speak again." Petrushka stood, pale and shaking, horrified himself by the events of the past hour, and watched while the guards dragged out Buturlin—the man who had been his first friend and chamberlain, loyally shadowing his every move—onto the Fontanka quay, where a sled waited to take him across the ice to the Trubetzkoi Bastion.

He shall never speak again. Such was Petrushka's sentence, and such was to be Buturlin's fate.

53

The lights and the shine of the Winter Palace's long gallery during Petrushka's second engagement feast blinded me. I felt like a prisoner emerging from the Trubetzkoi's dark cells on execution day—a cell such as the one where Buturlin now lingered. Was I the only one thinking of him? I sent Lestocq there daily, taking food and warm clothes as well as money—a lot of money!—to bribe the wardens; I could not bear the idea that he should be hurt or tortured while being interrogated or awaiting his sentence. After all, no further questions needed answering.

Thinking of him in prison made the surrounding splendor unbearable to me: thousands upon thousands of candles bathed the palace's vast spaces in light; uniform buttons gleamed, and leather boots were polished to perfection. Women floated about in their splendid gowns, looking like blossoms on a stream; jewelry like liquid fire pouring down rosy earlobes, smooth throats, and slender wrists. Almond and orange trees scented the air—in which hothouses had these been reared to bloom in the bleak midwinter?—and dark green, fragrant hedging created arbors where tables groaned under the realm's delicacies.

Wherever I walked, all conversation ceased. No one gave a kopeck for my future. There were no more suitors asking for my hand in marriage. My only option was the convent.

Katja and Petrushka received the well-wishers from a dais in the Throne Hall. The crimson velvet canopy floating above their carved and gilded thrones dwarfed them. In the two weeks since her en-gagement to the Tsar in the Summer Palace's library, Katja had lost weight. Neither her pasty makeup nor her *smetana*-colored dress, which hung from her bony shoulders, enhanced her looks, once famed for their perfection. Petrushka himself sat like a statue, his court clothes stiff with gold-thread embroidery, his gaze briefly sweeping the assembled court before looking far be-yond the crowd.

As I entered, Count Ostermann stood by the high double-winged doors. Alexis Dolgoruky kept him at bay from the Imperial couple, as one dog might another, guarding the feeding bowl. He bowed half-heartedly to me, averting his slate-tinted gaze: "Tsarevna Elizabeth. Of course. As the Tsar's closest living relative, you must be the first to congratulate him. It is your duty." If he was delighted that it was not I who sat on the throne next to Petrushka's, he hid it well. What would it take ever to shake his self-control? One day I should love to find out.

"My duty, Count Ostermann? It is my joy and my honor," I coolly said: I knew how much he had feared a possible betrothal between Petrushka and me. Had I played into Russia's and my en-emies' hands by refusing the Tsar? The thought was horrid, but I had to be true to my heart.

"The Tsarevna Elizabeth Petrovna Romanova." The Court Marshal called my name. The crimson carpet stretched endlessly ahead; the courtiers parted like the Red Sea. People busily whispered their versions of the real reason for Buturlin's disgrace. They loomed over me, lusting for my downfall. I would not do them that favor just yet, I decided, walking toward the dais. As I neared the thrones, I spotted Count Melissimo in the crowd and felt pity: for him, for Katja, for Petrushka, for me—for all of us. We were all the She-bear of Russia's cubs, tossing and tumbling, hoping to humor her and keep ourselves out of harm's way.

"Your Majesty. My sincere congratulations." I curtsied to kiss

Petrushka's hand. He bowed his head, his pallid skin blending with his white wig, immediately retracting his fingers, true to his word that I should never touch him again.

As I turned to Katja, she clenched her fist as if ready to punch me.

I stepped back.

When it was the foreign dignitaries' turns to congratulate the Tsar, Count Melissimo came forward. Had he been searched for weapons? A love as strong as theirs was bound to lead to foolishness. If he was noticeably unstable—he was unshaven, his black hair unkempt and oily—his elegant hands with their long, refined fingers shook too much for him to mount any assault; his chocolate brown eyes were red-rimmed and swollen from crying. Katja swayed on her seat, tears streaking her makeup. Petrushka watched with a basilisk stare as Melissimo was restrained from any further demonstration of his grief by two Tyrolean friends. The struggle was brief.

The Secret Office of Investigation handed Count Melissimo his laissez-passer the same day. He had no choice but to leave. His sled for Vienna departed two days later, where he arrived just in time for Yuletide.

Lestocq was by my side when Buturlin was led up the scaffold, which had been mounted next to the Saints Peter and Paul Cathedral, just a couple of days after the celebration of the Imperial engagement. He had bled me twice in the morning to calm me, in vain.

"Did you manage?" I whispered, my head spinning. "Has Buturlin been spared the worst?"

Lestocq shrugged: one could never be sure of the brutes working as wardens in the Trubetzkoi. Often they pocketed the bribes and still tortured their prisoner. I sank lower in my seat, praying soundlessly, asking for strength. The St. Nicholas icon was hidden beneath my voluminous fur collar. I dared a glance at the Imperial couple: Petrushka was bleary-eyed, yet cleanly shaven and looking splendid in the green cloth of the Preobrazhensky Regiment—clearly chosen to humiliate Buturlin further, as was the wolfskin lined with crimson velvet, which I had made him, together with the golden chain of links shaped like Imperial double-headed eagles. His fur cap tilted as he leaned in to Katja, listening to her whisper. On her throat, my mother's twelve-row pearl-and-diamond choker gleamed in the dull morning. Ostermann had sent the Imperial Guards to collect the gems from me; the last remnants of my mother's vast collection were gone. I had nothing to remember her by but my recollections of her tremendous spirit and joy in life. Had I inherited even a shred of her strength? I was not so sure any longer. My breath crystalized, and I clenched my fists inside my mink muff, as if to hold my heart too tight for it to break.

Hundreds of people had gathered around the scaffold, their stench blending with the sickening smell of roast meat, hot chestnuts, and mulled wine: at an event like this, street vendors prepared for brisk business. My stomach roiled as Buturlin's regiment lined up in double file, the men's faces set. In his shame he must walk between them. Warm breath clouded their horses' nostrils as they scraped their hooves in the ice and snow, desperate for forgotten shoots of green. The crowd silenced in anticipation as a single brief cannon shot shattered the crisp morning air. The sound had been expected yet still caught me unawares, making me shudder to my bones. A murder of crows set off in a dark cloud from the winter trees, cawing in protest and leaving the bare branches reaching into a pasty sky. The birds would return soon enough, hoping for rich pickings.

Katja looked at me: her gaze was as shiny as wet coals, her face pale behind the veil of a slow snowfall. *This is just the beginning,* her eyes said. *Just you wait.*

There was a commotion at the Bastion's Neva Gate. I clenched my fists inside the fur muff. People moved about at the prison walls like an army of ants. As Buturlin's sled approached along the frozen river, Lestocq moved closer to me. His presence was a comfort, even if he was fiddling with something: the Tarot cards that had once predicted Buturlin's future. *A fool for love.* Aware of my gaze, he slipped the cards out of sight, just as the sled appeared between the lines of soldiers. The Preobrazhensky Guards followed orders: they jeered, lashed out with their crops, and spat at Buturlin, their former officer and commander. I sank into my seat, trembling with dread and disappointment. My efforts to ease his lot had been futile, if not counterproductive: despite the freezing weather, he was stripped to the waist for all to see how savagely a whip had crisscrossed his back and shoulders, making the skin burst and each weal crust with blood. Once healed—if they ever did—the scars should chart a map of his suffering. He fell from the sled as it reached the scaffold, crashing into the snow, unable to stand. He gave a pained cry as the cool, moist flakes touched his wounds. Patches of his thick black hair had been torn out, and his shoulders were out of joint, legs broken. He groaned as wardens seized him beneath the armpits, dragging him up the scaffold's rough wooden steps to where his tormentor waited. Buturlin crashed to the planks at the hooded man's feet. A warden seized his head, hoisting him up, forcing him to see. He squinted through swollen eyes and howled with terror. The sound made my skin crawl, and I struggled to sit still and swallow my sobs.

In a smoldering coal basin lay a large pair of red-hot iron pliers. In the Kolomenskoye stables I had helped the blacksmith shoe horses with such a tool; on my father's wharves the carpenters used them to twist misplaced nails out of a ship's keel. As Buturlin shivered and sobbed, the torturer made a show of spinning the tool on its bed of coals; he held it up for all to see. The crowd sighed in fear, longing to witness suffering that for once was not their own. Through my veil of tears, their faces mercifully melted away.

The torturer twisted Buturlin's head toward the Tsar. I leaned in to Lestocq, seeking warmth and human contact, and shut my eyes in prayer. Beneath my cloak, he gripped my elbow to steady me. Nobody saw his touch, but I would not have made it through without it.

"Look, Lizenka," Petrushka called, beady-eyed, as a warden forced Buturlin's jaw open and grabbed his tongue, clutching it firmly close to its root, deep down the throat. I felt cheated: the executioner had pocketed the last of my last gold so that he should apparently satisfy the Tsar's order yet spare Buturlin the worst. But there was to be no mercy for my lover. The air sizzled as the searing pliers squeezed his tongue. A sickening scent of burned flesh rose in the clean winter air: *Uuuhhh!* went the crowd. I gagged as my lover arched and passed out with pain, hanging limp in the wardens' grip. The torturer stepped back; the people cheered. As the wardens poured a bucket of water over Buturlin, he came to, gasping, the drops freezing on his body. The torturer placed the tongs once more and gave Buturlin's tongue a short, sharp tug.

There was nothing human in either my lover's scream or the brief ripping sound, as if a trader tore silk off a bale in the *gostiny dvor*. A fleshy pink and foamy rag dangled from the pliers, a shred of bone attached to it. I tasted bile and cupped my mouth, having to watch as Buturlin—my friend, my love, once so full of courage and bravado—spouted a fountain of blood and collapsed on the scaffold boards. He lay in a puddle of russet, clutching his throat, passing out anew. The executioner threw the tongue to the hovering crows, which set upon it in a black, clamoring cloud.

"The Tsar's will be done!" Prince Alexis Dolgoruky shouted, rising from his seat, and the crowd roared, ready to scatter, eat, drink, and be merry. Petrushka led Katja to the Imperial sled; she cast me one last triumphant glance and climbed into the open vehicle, where she sat prettily wrapped in furs and velvet. Petrushka mounted the sled's back, standing as a footman would, bending down to whisper to her. She nodded as the horses set off. It hurt me to breathe; I could not fight my tears yet never tasted their salt, as they froze on my cheeks in a crystalline layer.

The snowfall shrouded the sight of the coarse sled that dragged the unconscious man away: Petrushka had demoted him to a simple soldier, sending him to Kamchatka on a posting of no return. As his regiment dispersed, some soldiers looked shaken, wiping away tears they had not been allowed to shed before the Imperial couple. The simple people of St. Petersburg, so little spoiled, living in their wooden houses and shacks that stood hidden behind the first row of palaces on the Neva's riverbank, scooped up horse droppings to dry and feed their hearths with. As I sat and regained my strength, fresh flakes hid the traces of Buturlin's suffering on the scaffold's sullied snow. The crows returned to the trees, waiting for richer pickings next time round. Even the St. Petersburg dogs, scarred, shaggy beings, stayed away. I sat, shaking and sobbing, stooped with sorrow, until the court had departed.

"Tsarevna, let us leave. It is too cold here. I shall blend you a sleeping potion," Lestocq said gently, as if talking to a child. I saw real pity in his eyes, a rare thing at that point in my life. "You have to be strong," he reminded me.

Sleep? I feared nothing more. The horror of what I had witnessed would surely blight my dreams, imprisoning me in a never-ending nightmare. I clasped his fingers as a beggar would a coin: "Strong? For what? More of that? Pain and disgrace for everyone who loves me—Augustus, Anoushka, Buturlin?"

Lestocq shook his head, snowflakes settling on his thick auburn hair. "God's bow has many arrows," he said, touching the pocket that hid the Tarot pack, as if casting a spell.

The sight made me shudder.

He led me back to the sled and tucked me in, as a father would a child, hooking the bearskin securely across my lap.

54

"Will Feofan Prokopovich conduct Petrushka's wedding service?" Alexis Dolgoruky had had the Archbishop of Novgorod, who had given Father daring counsel, placed under house arrest as soon as Petrushka came to power. Feofan, who had conducted my parents' marriage ceremony and crowned my mother, had neither crowned the young Tsar nor was he to be seen elsewhere.

It was our last evening in the Summer Palace before departing for the Tsar's wedding in Moscow. A maid packed my chest—it did not take her long, as I barely had any dresses left to choose from; whatever I had bought with the roubles Petrushka had given me, I had sold. Once more the Princess Cherkassky had proved to be a loyal customer and friend; once more she did not dare to wear what she bought but passed it on to her maids. In my rooms wind chased down the chimney, making the flames cower and wafting ashes and embers.

"Prokopovich was arrested a couple of days ago," Lestocq said. "The Secret Office of Investigation has taken him to the Trubetzkoi Bastion for questioning."

I stared at him, mute with shock. If Feofan Prokopovich could be arrested, who then was safe? We all knew what it meant to be taken to the Bastion for questioning.

"What else were you expecting? Alexis Dolgoruky fears him. Ostermann must choose new allegiances. Feofan Prokopovich was your father's closest ally," Lestocq said. "All traces of the great Tsar's work will be eradicated. Russia is stuck in a mortal struggle between the past and the future."

The Imperial Treasury blocked my funds indefinitely—no money was needed in a convent after all, Katja was overheard jesting with her ladies upon her arrival in the Kremlin. I had nothing left to sell as Lestocq and Schwartz joined me in the sled traveling from St. Petersburg to Izmailov: my last days of liberty, awaiting Petrushka's wedding, would be spent at Aunt Pasha and my Ivanovna cousins' former house. At least my monkeys' chatter and my birds shrieking in their cages would lighten the mood. I had refused to take any books. Reading had never done Anoushka any good, so what benefit would it be to me?

The sky was exhausted after a night of steady snowfall. Crows rose from the birches' bare branches, cawing and flapping, as I left the Summer Palace for what was possibly the very last time. I wished to lock the sight of the house's buttercup and crimson façade forever into my heart. Once I was confined to a cold convent cell, the memory of it would offer me solace. As I got in the sled, a rider approached on the haphazardly cleared gravel path, his horse plowing through the snowdrifts. "Tsarevna Elizabeth! Wait, please," he called, his breath clouding around him. He got off his mount and handed me a delicate, beautifully carved chest of ebony. "A gift from the Bride Tsaritsa. She gave it to me before she departed for the Kremlin." He bowed, his cheeks bright red and raw from the cold. What on earth could Katja Dolgoruky have sent me? I shook the chest, my heart in my mouth. It gave a soft thud.

"What is it?" asked Lestocq, sounding guarded.

"It feels light. I shall have a look once we are in Izmailov. Let us be off." I tucked the chest away, as I should have been surprised if Katja had sent me anything worth having. For all I knew it might be a nun's habit, cut from coarse, dark cloth.

The journey to Izmailov passed in sullen silence, my two

companions probably wondering how to present their diplomatic failure to their respective courts: all those years they had been shadowing me, championing my possible—or impossible—cause. The horses slipped many a time on the roads, their surfaces frozen hard as iron, making the sled veer violently. The air crackled with frost, and the clouds darkened with further snow. I longed for sunlight, however bleak and short-lived it might be.

My nights would soon be long enough, if not eternal: any time now.

The thought of attending Petrushka's wedding terrified me. I envied my cousin Anna Ivanovna, Duchess of Courland, whose letters pleading to join the ceremonies accompanied by her lover Biren were read out for the court's entertainment and then filed away unanswered.

Izmailov offered me no respite: the formerly lovingly cared-for palace—once a testing ground for all my Grandfather Alexis's ideas concerning Russian agriculture—had been abandoned for years. The guards had deserted as soon as their wages had gone unpaid. Serfs and farmers had plundered the larders and cellars. Beneath the snow the orchards and the fields lay fallow, and the plethora of fishponds were suffocated with weeds, turning the thick ice green with frozen lily pads. The fruit trees stooped under their load of snow. The Babylon, the maze where Anoushka and I had played hide-and-seek as girls, was almost too overgrown for me to identify. In the Wolf House, which had once been home to orphaned sable, fox, and even polar bear cubs, the rotting door creaked on its hinges; the cages were empty and soiled by rats. Bats hung from the beams, their faces scrunched up in sleep.

Everything weighed down my spirits; any endeavor, either to improve my living accommodations or to impose order on the palace grounds, felt daunting and dull. I struggled with the hopelessness that lay like lead on my mind and fettered my heart. Whichever task I started seemed pointless—be it having the baskets filled with firewood, the ponds and streams dredged, the cracked tiles replaced on the roof after too many winters of heavy snowfall, or even joining the hunters. Whatever torment Katja planned for me, Petrushka would give it his seal of approval, I knew.

I had thought to become mistress of my own fate by refusing Petrushka, moving from pawn to player. Instead he had instantly replaced me in his affections with Katja, and now I was firmly in her hands.

And just like that, the inner Ice Princess rejoined me in the solitude of Izmailov, occupying my heart where she settled at her cruel craft, shredding my soul with her icicle fingers, her frosty gaze puncturing my spirit into a sieve, all the last vestiges of my strength and happiness pouring out. She shadowed my every move; any mirror reflected only her, eyes exuding a pale fire that chilled me to the core.

I remembered Katja's parting gift only a couple of days after my arrival in Izmailov. There was no key in the chest's delicate lock, so I pried it open. As I lifted the lid, a sickly sweet, rotten smell made me recoil. I cupped my mouth and nose, eyeing the ragged thing inside: small bones poked through dark clumps of flesh and feathers. Shocked, I dropped the chest on the hard flagstones, where it shattered. I reached for the candle to peer closely at what it had contained: at my feet lay what was left of Molniya, the peregrine falcon. My beautiful bird's neck had been wrung before Petrushka's hounds had mauled her. She was a tawny mess, her once shiny, subtly spotted feathers sullied by clotted blood. As hard as I tried to steel myself, Katja's message cut straight to my heart.

It was a lonely walk through Izmailov's dark, silent corridors. In the kitchen I waved off the maid who slept in the warm ashes of the oven, guarding the fire during the night—*leave me alone!*— and shoveled some glowing embers onto a cast-iron tray. I crashed back the door's heavy bolt and slipped into a pair of heavy servant's boots that were standing on the threshold. The cold of the clear night bludgeoned me, but I forced myself forward into the darkness. I broke through thigh-high snow, struggling to balance while clutching the remains of the chest and carrying the fire tray. My fingers became numb, and every breath stabbed my lungs. If I walked too far, I should never return; for a heartbeat, the thought seemed alluring, but then I fought it. No! Not yet. Not here.

The edge of the deep, dark, frozen Izmailov forest stood before me like a wall. I reached the shelter of the first trees, scraped the icy snow aside, and hunched over, stiffly shaping a dome of frozen twigs and rimy leaves. The tinder was slow to light, but I showered it with sparks, blowing carefully until there was a first crackle. Flames danced blue and yellow, bathing me in cold light. Molniya's corpse was frozen stiff when I placed it on the pyre; for a breath or two, the fire shied away from her. As the flames finally seared her feathers, the metallic smell of her bloodied flesh was hard for me to bear. I waved it away, choked by tears: "Fly safely, my friend," I whispered, then rose to crush the last bits of Katja's accursed chest beneath my boot, finally feeding the ebony splinters to the flames. Once Molniya was gone, I kicked snow on the fire, hearing it hiss and watching it die. The ashes I ground into the frozen earth. As the last bitter smoke rose to the stars and the full moon, my beautiful bird returned where she belonged: to Mother Russia.

The day of the Imperial wedding drew closer.

Once my lonely Yuletide was over, I should have another week of liberty. The court relished being in Moscow once more: women set upon the *gostiny dvor* like a plague of locusts, while men never left the *kabaki* and the Red Square's many coffeehouses, reading newspapers; sipping the hot, bitter brew; exchanging gossip; and eyeing the endless stream of newcomers as Russians from all over the realm poured into the city. Come Epiphany, Petrushka blessed the waters of the Moskva by stripping off his cloak under the clerics' watchful eyes and dipping himself in the freezing waters through a hole drilled in the thick ice. Prince Alexis Dolgoruky applauded loudly: it seemed Russia was to return to the old ways. It was as if Father and all his hopes and endeavors for his realm had never been. I tried to make discreet inquires about Feofan Prokopovich's fate, but in vain. Was the priest and my oldest friend still alive?

That winter was colder than any other in Russia's memory. Birds fell from the sky, frozen in midflight. The Izmailov lawn was strewn with feathered corpses, hard as stone when I gathered them. The small, single mica panes in the windows' lead frames were covered in crystalline frost patterns inside and out. Rime whitened the bare flagstones—all the rugs had been stolen and sold—as well as the bare walls; Aunt Pasha had taken all the hangings when she moved to St. Petersburg. My fingers shriveled when I yanked open a window to rub my face with snow. The shock did not put an end to my waking nightmare. As cold as the house was, a deeper chill rose from deep inside me. Bleakness flowed through my veins, covering my hoary soul. I was lost in an eternal Russian winter, the beast that could still bring any enemy to his—or her!—knees.

I summed up my life so far. The men who had loved me—both Augustus and Buturlin—had been struck down because of their feelings. From now on I must stay a spinster and bear no child. In any case, in a short while I was to be sent to a convent, shackled to the void of my endless numbered days, as possibly my wrists and ankles would be to a wall. I fought the fear and instead relished the memories of the love and friendship I had shared with Augustus, as well as my love and lust for Buturlin.

I decided no regret should weigh me down further.

"You have to eat," Lestocq urged me, while clearing away my un-touched dishes: simple fare such as baked potatoes and *smetana*, sauerkraut, and kasha laced with bacon rind. This was as far as our budget stretched.

I shrugged. "Don't worry about me. It is too late. Save your-self."

"Drink at least," he insisted, lacing my *chai* with vodka and pos-sibly some laudanum: I soon slipped into a heavy sleep riddled with nightmares. Augustus was with me, inflaming my senses. Then Anoushka lit a furnace, showing me the burn marks on her arms, sparks and embers flying. In the ensuing blaze Buturlin held me tight before he faltered, melting like a tin soldier, his body a bub-bling, toxic puddle at my feet. The child Petrushka grew into a man before my eyes, his features as sharp and bird-like as Molni-ya's, his gaze a whetted blade, ready to stab me. Flames devoured the scarlet Imperial seal, the double-headed eagle crumbling away before it fell to ashes, smoke billowing in the shape of a peregrine falcon before dissolving into thin air. *Curse the Romanovs*: the Leshy spirit bared its fangs. I woke, sobbing and scared. Lestocq bled me, as I was burning with fever.

I fought him and his damned needles and knives, ordering him to leave me, but he settled close to my bed, lining up his Tarot cards, letting them dance and spiral under his deft hands. "Put those away!" I moaned, recalling the horror of their prophecy for Buturlin. Yet as I fell back weakly among the cushions, my face sweaty and my mind reeling, his eyes were still glued to the cards, a frown on his forehead.

55

Petrushka braved the cold to greet the regiments that were to stand guard over his winter wedding, thousands of men, acknowledging them one by one, like a good and gracious Tsar. In all he spent four hours on the ice. Afterward he mounted the same light sled that had carried Katja and him away from Buturlin's scaffold, standing upright behind the seat, exposed to the freeze that kept even hardy Muscovites in their homes. Katja wore a tight bodice of blue velvet adorned with golden toggles to match her sparkling eyes and display her famously full breasts; her fine-boned face was haughtier than ever. Sapphires and diamonds sparkled in her ears. Two dozen horsemen in silver livery accompanied them, musicians played, and page boys ran alongside, showering the couple with scented petals on this bleakest of midwinter days. Petrushka bowed to Katja, complimenting her on her beauty: whatever dark force had driven him to this engagement, he seemed determined to carry it through in style.

As Katja was whisked away to recuperate in a hot *banja*, Petrushka returned to the Kremlin. One hour later he complained of a searing headache. He was served steaming glasses of grog before being wrapped in heated furs. Although his fever soared, his attendants wasted hours before calling in the doctors. The Tsar's teeth chattered, his limbs trembled; he was unable either to stand or to sit for crippling backache. When diarrhoea and vomiting set in, his physicians were finally called.

Petrushka was confined to a darkened, overheated room, where he lay delirious.

As I left Izmailov, the sky hung low over the palace, ready to spit with sleet. Laden bushes and trees groaned for fear of further snow; crows' sooty wings covered the heavens. In the waiting sled, a maid placed a hot copper pan at my feet and another one beneath my blanket. She curtsied and kissed my hand, crying and taking leave for good: "God bless you, Tsarevna Elizabeth. Russia loves you and always will."

As my sled set off, the first pustules had appeared on Petrushka's young face, neck, and shoulders: searing, angry, and ruby red. Smallpox took just hours to blossom. The boils burst, spreading their vile pus, before turning scarlet and scabby. He screamed, pleading to scratch, but his physicians forced his hands into mittens and bound his wrists to the bed. They bled him and kept the room, which was stuffed with fearful courtiers, heated at *banja* level. The Tsar gasped, suffocating and begging for air, yet no one dared give the order to open the window. In the Dolgoruky Palace, Katja had been locked in her apartment, where she howled, unhinged by the news that had upended her life once more.

No one dared approach her.

I was oblivious to all this when I arrived at the Kremlin in the early morning hours, preferring to journey on through the darkest of nights rather than stay at a grubby inn, its windows nailed shut against the cold and hung with wax cloth, the straw on the floors soiled and rotten. My sled's torches ate into the inky blackness, their tar dripping into the snow and making a hissing sound, keeping wolves, bears, and highwaymen at bay. I held my whip, and Lestocq and Schwartz kept their pistols at the ready. The Kremlin's steward was sleepy and half-dazed with drink; the rooms he allotted me were much too mean for someone of my rank. My mounting dread rendered Lestocq's laudanum useless. I could not sleep even as my lids burned with fatigue. I avoided the mirror in my room: soon, I should be shorn-headed and lacking any last traces of finery. I was twenty-one years old, yet felt I had already endured enough for ten lives if I added up all my loves and losses. I paced the room, torn by fatigue and fear.

Lestocq, who had gone to make inquiries, came rushing back. "Tsarevna!" he gasped.

"What is it?" I readied myself. Had a convent been chosen? Instead he threw himself on his knees and seized both my gloved hands. "The Tsar is dying," he said, his breath hot on my wrists.

"No. This can't be," I protested.

"The smallpox is taking him," he said. "He has but hours to live. We have to be quick. This is the moment. Go and claim the throne of your father."

"The Tsar is still alive." I pulled my hands away, sickened by the memory of Augustus's suffering. Must I also lose the last adult member of my closest family to the dread illness?

"But for how much longer?" Lestocq rose to his feet, a vein throbbing in his temple. "If you do nothing, you betray your own blood."

"I should send you back to Versailles with your tongue in your hand! What do you know about loyalty?" I held my head as my thoughts raced. "Perhaps you can save the Tsar. Do something."

The flames in the grate threw tall shadows, making his face hard to read. "I can't," he said, but the real answer might well have been, *I will not.*

"But I can!" I pushed him aside and flew out into the corridor, where I seized a torch and ran. I could only remember the lonely little boy Petrushka had been, not the spurned suitor who viciously schemed to cause me misery. My steps echoed down the dark passages of the Kremlin, the torch chasing away shadows. Tar dripped from it, sizzling on the icy stones. I reached the Tsar's rooms with my ribs heaving and aching from a stitch. People blocked the corridor, some still fully dressed, some in their nightgowns, all looking bewildered. The crowd parted as I stepped toward the dim lights and hushed murmuring within the Tsar's bedroom. When I slipped past Alexis Dolgoruky, I heard him saying to Ostermann, "She *has* to sign our conditions. No signature, no crown!" He stopped short upon seeing me.

I stared at him, not sure if I had heard right.

Me?

A low moan forced my attention elsewhere.

"Petrushka!" I moved toward his bedside, bracing myself.

The Tsar lay slack-limbed upon the bed, looking as if he had been tossed there. His chin had fallen, and with each rasping breath, his lungs rattled as if drowning in liquid—a sound that was almost too painful for me to endure. D'Acosta lay curled up like a kitten at Petrushka's feet but stirred and rose when I felt for the Tsar's limp, hot hands. He did not turn his head, but his eyelids fluttered once or twice when I touched him. I so hoped that he sensed me by his side when he whispered, "Let us get the horses ready for the hunt."

"Yes, Petrushka. We shall ride in the morning," I said in a voice choked by tears. My vision blurred. I barely took in the courtiers' avid watchful faces, the fire's thick smoke, the flickering candles. I could hear whispering all around, like a flood rising against a dam. On the other side of Petrushka's bed, Count Ostermann kept close watch beside Alexis Dolgoruky, their faces gray from worry. Past and future hung in the balance. Petrushka's hand slackened in mine; the Imperial seal hung loose on his thin finger; the crimson double-headed eagle glinted like fire.

If he still felt my caress as I stroked his palm, I could not tell. His skin was parched, and his eyes rolled up, showing livid, mottled whites. His cracked lips pulled back from his gums as he grimaced in pain and then calmed, his head rolling to one side. His utter helplessness made me forget all my fear and sorrow. I dipped a crumpled silk handkerchief in a glass of water, dabbing his lips with the moist cloth. "Sip, Petrushka," I whispered, but my hand, hovering over his mouth, felt no further breath. The sudden stillness of his chest was terrifying. Droplets of water ran down Petrushka's slack jaw. On the Red Square, the clock struck three o'clock in the morning. I dropped the handkerchief and hid my face. As I looked up, my eyes met Count Ostermann's hooded gaze, for once recognizing his true feelings: deep grief, anger at fate's injustice, and utter despair.

"The Tsar is dead," I said, my voice brittle, holding on to Petrushka's purple velvet bed-curtain as I pulled myself to my feet. It was incredible the frightening precision with which fate had struck once more. Petrushka had perished the very morning he was to wed Katja Dolgoruky.

The Tsar is dead. Voices started up beyond the smoke and incense, shock and excitement rising like a wave.

"Who is to succeed? The Tsar is dead. Katja stands to inherit! She should rule, as she would have been his Tsarina. I claim the throne for my daughter!" Alexis Dolgoruky acted quickly, lacking all shame.

Ostermann snorted. "Katja? Do not be ridiculous! Not a drop of royal blood runs in her veins. And she is compromised by her dalliance with Count Melissimo."

"Watch your dirty mouth or I'll smash your teeth in," Dolgoruky growled. "My family founded Moscow. I am descended from Ivan Grozny."

"Maybe. But who knows from whom Katja is descended, pretty as she is. No. Why not get the little prince from Holstein, Tsarevna Anoushka's boy?" Ostermann suggested.

"He is a German and barely one year old. A long Regency is the last thing the country needs," Dolgoruky objected.

Ostermann looked at me, his cunning gaze never leaving my face. My heart pounded; I could not help it. Me? Was I ready now, after having passed the last time I sat at fate's gaming table?

"What about Tsar Ivan's eldest daughter, Tsarevna Ekaterina Ivanovna?" That was Dolgoruky once more.

"For her awful, estranged Mecklenburg husband to move in with her in the Winter Palace? He'd be here in a flash and Russia ruined," Ostermann dismissed the suggestion. "No. We know the way forward. We discussed it as soon as the Tsar fell ill. Let us announce the new Tsarina."

His eyes were fixed on me, gleaming like wildfire.

Me!

My head felt light, as if I were breathing among the clouds, yet I let go of the heavy curtain. In the past five years the Russian throne had been vacated three times. I looked down at my bare hands. The lack of sun in the winter months and the candlelight had turned my pale fingers to alabaster. The Imperial seal weighed heavily on any hand, I told myself, getting ready, as d'Acosta slid up to me, staying close. He had never been far away during any of the decisive moments of my life, for better and for worse. *Go and claim the throne of your father. If you do nothing, you betray your own blood.* In my mind Lestocq's words blended with the Leshy's prophecy.

Count Ostermann stepped closer to me. Surely, at this fateful moment, all our former differences were forgotten. Only time would tell if I was a deserving ruler; if I had watched and learned more than Mother had. "Pardon me," he said, and kissed the Tsar's veined hand, whispering in his former pupil's ear, caressing his sweaty hair. Tears ran down the German's stubbly, sagging cheeks. Most of the little happiness Petrushka had known in his short life, Ostermann or I had given him. If we ourselves had not seen eye to eye, I was ready to overlook our previous differences. A ruler needs wise counsel, I thought, as Ostermann eased the Imperial seal off the dead Tsar's finger: Petrushka had grown so frail during his short suffering that the seal slipped right off.

I readied myself to feel its weight on my finger. Blood raced through my veins. The courtiers fell to their knees, bowing their heads and holding their breath, awaiting the announcement as eagerly as I did. I felt their probing, fearful glances and spotted Lestocq leaning on the threshold, face pale with excitement, biting his lip. Behind him, Schwartz's face bobbed like a lantern. I read their gamblers' minds: one game was over, a new one was about to start. Ostermann closed his eyes, gathering himself, closing his fingers and hiding the gold and ruby seal from view. I felt as lonely as any ruler is once the full weight of the task settles upon him—or her.

"The Tsar is dead!" Ostermann's voice resounded through the chamber just as Tsar Ivan Grozny's Kremlin bell started to toll, low and steady. The winter wind carried the sound away into the vastness of the Empire. Was Russia ready for another Tsarina? After all, it had been my mother who had been the realm's first female ruler. Did she pave the way for me?

"Long live the Tsarina!" Ostermann bellowed.

I closed my eyes, fighting tears, my breath halting, as the court gave a single roar. Exhausted onlookers were stumbling to their feet, ready to bow once more. Lestocq straightened in anticipation, his eyes gleaming. Schwartz slapped the Frenchman's shoulder, looking delighted. I savored the moment, my heart racing. After all, I had been born for this, I would show myself worthy.

Ostermann swapped a quick glance with Prince Dolgoruky, who nodded. "Long live the Tsarina!" he repeated. "Long live Her Imperial Majesty Anna Ivanovna, widowed Duchess of Courland, second daughter of our beloved Tsar Ivan V!"

56

Russian Mountains. This is what foreign envoys called a favorite pastime among St. Petersburg residents during the long winters. Serfs piled up sky-high mountains of snow on the frozen surface of the Neva, building a steep and icy slope. We would climb up the other side, stumbling and sliding, gasping and laughing, hanging on to each other, even taking tumbles. Once we made it up to the top, there were wooden sleighs at the ready. We would feel out of breath and slightly dizzy, warm from the effort but also chilled by the icy air and the snow beneath, as well as by fear. Those who lacked courage downed a couple of glasses of vodka and then received a hearty push, careening forward while hoping for the best, which meant reaching the bottom alive. Once the first thrill had faded, the serfs poured water on the slope, making it even more breakneck. The next ride was about pure survival: on the treacherous glistening surface, the sleigh could easily spin out of control and fly into the air, the riders hanging on for dear life, screaming. Anything might happen; any run could be the last.

My life had become just that—a steep, icy, deadly slope, a Russian Mountain.

"Long live Anna Ivanovna, Tsarina of All the Russias!" Ostermann's voice echoed in my ears as silence fell over the courtiers. I saw shock in people's eyes; only Dolgoruky smiled slyly. Lestocq was pale with disbelief, while Schwartz had disappeared, more light-footed than seemed possible for a man of his weight. No doubt he was already busy coding his message to Vienna, attaching it to the foot of a pigeon schooled in avoiding the Secret Office of Investigation's hawks. Shock seeped in. Anna Ivanovna? My cousin, the derided and destitute virgin widow bride, forever begging for favors from far-flung Mitau, capital of her barren, boring duchy, and compromised by a low-born lover? *She* was to rule All the Russias? Anna Ivanovna? How?

Ostermann raised the Imperial ring high above his head, holding my gaze captive with a serpent-like stare. *Spoil him and you destroy him,* he had said to me accusingly at Petrushka's Coronation. Now it was clear he blamed me for the death of his charge, the only one to whom he had ever given love—and who in turn had loved only me.

The reckoning could last as long as his lifetime. I had pursued Menshikov while my most implacable enemy had been lurking in the shadows, biding his time, ever the perfect diplomat and statesman. Andrej Ivanovich Ostermann, Count and Vice Chancellor of Russia. All the strength drained from me as my closest companions—fear and loneliness—returned to haunt me. *You would make a spirited Tsarina,* Menshikov had sneered at me. The Privy Council—Dolgoruky and Ostermann—would not give me the chance to prove it, too intent on securing any advantage they could gain for themselves, clawing it from history. I felt a sharp tug on my little finger: when I glanced down d'Acosta's face was full of compassion. Only the little man whose wrath had made Lestocq suffer exile, whose loyalty had made Illinchaya suffer her final punishment, and whose pride had had Buturlin maimed for life, showed me that rarest of emotions.

I closed my icy hand around his.

Ostermann explained: "The throne is vacant for the third time in five years. The male line of the Romanovs has become extinct. The realm needs incontestable legitimacy and a pure bloodline. It needs stability." The slight was clearly intentional: I had been born out of wedlock; when my parents' wedding had legitimized me, making me a Tsarevna, I had been three years old. My blood started to boil. "Anna Ivanovna offers what we need. Her father Tsar Ivan V was the elder brother of our great Tsar Peter." D'Acosta wove his fingers closer with mine, silently counseling prudence and self-control. "Her mother was Tsaritsa Praskovia Saltykova, noble daughter of one of Russia's oldest families. The Duchess Anna Ivanovna's legitimacy is uncontested." The German's gaze rested on me as he relished delivering the insult. I ached to line his face further by clawing it. "Widowed shortly after her marriage, Anna Ivanovna has lived in virtue, honoring the memory of her husband in Courland."

No mention now of Herr Biren, her faithful companion and former groom, though it had been the talk of the court for more years than I could recall. Anna's husband had been a vile drunkard and gambler, suffocating in the snow on his own vomit after days of debauchery, leaving her a virgin widow, which, if Ostermann were to be believed, she still was. I would have shown him what I thought of that falsehood, but I remembered the many slights and betrayals Anna had suffered and how grateful she had once been for a bit of kindness and understanding. At least Biren seemed to be good to her. Why should I mock her for welcoming his love?

"She has all the experience needed, having ruled Courland wisely and benevolently for the past twenty years, taking counsel from her advisers," Ostermann ended his obviously well-prepared speech. Dolgoruky nodded his approval. I felt sick with sudden understanding: Anna, overwhelmed by her sudden change in station, was to be their puppet, expected to do anything they said. She would turn a blind eye while the Old Believers led Russia back into a dark past.

Lestocq had disappeared. I was lonelier than ever. Russia had a new ruler: Tsarina Anna I. The courtiers left the Tsar's rooms, stealing a last glance at Petrushka's corpse. It hurt to breathe, yet it took time for the tears to well up. Petrushka had been my last living reminder of the happiness I had once known; the last

Romanov of the direct male line. His life had been snuffed out like a candle. *Your sons shall bleed.* The Leshy's curse had come true once more. In vain had I refused to let Lestocq and Buturlin allow Petrushka to die in Tver. Even here in the Kremlin, hours ago, I would not listen to Lestocq's urging. I braced myself. There were more ways to honor my heritage than someone who wheeled and dealt like a brothel keeper could ever fathom. Anna Ivanovna's father, Tsar Ivan V, had throughout his life been so ill that his constantly twitching head had sent the Imperial crown flying; his mouth bubbled with spit. Yet he had been my father's elder half-brother. I crossed myself with three fingers, touching my forehead, chest, and shoulders in recognition of the Trinity and of the two natures of Christ, human and Divine. Petrushka's skin was as cold as marble when I closed his eyes. Ostermann had been too distraught to think of it.

"Sleep well, Petrushka," I whispered, weeping at last. Was he at peace now, united with his murdered father and the mother he had never known?

"Get some rest," d'Acosta said to me. "You have a whole life ahead of you. Who knows what fate has in store for a splendid Tsarevna such as you?" His kind words surprised me: the threat of Katja's revenge had died together with Petrushka, yet the past weeks had drained me. If my life was a Russian Mountain, then I had just survived a ride down the steepest, iciest slope possible. I had been flung off my sleigh and had neither the strength to scramble to my feet nor the courage to climb the steep slope once more.

Instinctively I fingered the icon of St. Nicholas, its gold cool against my throat.

Surely I had nothing to fear from the new Tsarina. During our last brief encounter in the Kremlin, some days after Mother's Coronation, Cousin Anna Ivanovna and I had been friends, almost as close as sisters.

57

Cannon shots marked Petrushka's funeral, smoke rising through the glassy January air. The troops—tens of thousands of them—took position in the Red Square, spilling into the surrounding alleys and roads. Eight generals lifted the long, narrow coffin onto their shoulders, as our house had no more male princes left to do so, carrying it to the Kremlin's Archangel Cathedral. Alexis Dolgoruky had broken another of my father's rules, which stipulated that under Great Peter all Romanovs were buried in St. Petersburg. Would Dolgoruky dominate Anna Ivanovna and make Moscow, this lively, sprawling city, Russia's capital once more? How could Ostermann, as my father's close adviser and a cunning politician, allow it?

The people's wails grew deafening and echoed from the Kremlin's walls, as if hordes of wolves had gathered: soldiers mingled with the onlookers, knouting anyone who did not lament loudly enough. In the midst of the mayhem stood Ostermann: a stricken figure, his narrow frame stooped with sadness. He draped the Tsar's coffin in a black velvet, ermine-trimmed Cloth of Estate, his hands shaking, tears freezing on his sagging cheeks. His little Petrushka should not suffer any cold in the Imperial vault.

Katja stood shrouded in dark veils, looking so forlorn that I forgot the bitterness between us. We were both victims here, yet she had lost the most: her former love, already engaged to another and posted to Madrid, and the prospect of being Tsarina of Russia. Life had mangled her hopes as unforgivingly as she had treated

Molniya. When I embraced her, she clung to me, sobbing, before her father led her away.

The bells tolled solemnly while the Archbishop of Moscow led the funeral procession toward the old Romanov tomb. Ostermann watched gray-faced, clasping his ebony cane, as the lead-lined coffin was lowered into the burial vault.

I did not begrudge Anna Ivanovna the crown. She was of the elder royal bloodline; chosen by God and elected as the Tsar's heiress, satisfying the law. Doubting the legitimacy of her rule was against everything I had ever been taught. Yet I hated Ostermann for the way he had humiliated me. I clenched my fist in its black kid glove, mended in several places and missing buttons. I was not able to afford a new pair for Petrushka's funeral.

It was a couple of days later that I understood the meaning of Dolgoruky's words: *"No signature, no crown!"* The Privy Council had drafted a document that severely curtailed Anna's powers as a ruler, Lestocq told me once we had returned to Izmailov.

"She agreed to *that*?"

"What wouldn't a pauper do in exchange for a great title and a life of luxury?"

"Careful! You are speaking of the Tsarina of Russia."

"Tsarina in name only following her signature. Anna agreed neither to marry, wage war, sign a peace treaty, curtail the rights of the nobility, promote to high rank, nor grant gifts of estates, without the Privy Council's seal of approval. She is also not to command a regiment—which beggars belief."

I swallowed hard. Anna Ivanovna was signing away her right to rule. Alexis Dolgoruky and his Old Believers were to run things instead, digging their claws into Russia's flesh, sucking its blood.

"What else?"

"Well, it is uncertain whether she can use the chamber pot by herself!" said my adviser, with a droll expression on his face.

I could not help but laugh before asking: "Is Ostermann in on this?"

"That's the strangest thing of all. No. Ostermann is said to have been suffering from severe gout ever since the Tsar's funeral. He has refused to sign Dolgoruky's draft document. Apparently his hands are too incapacitated." Flames crackled in the fireplace; a log crashed; embers flew. I poked the fire with an iron, pondering the news. Ostermann's gout served him well whenever he wished to keep his distance from unpopular measures. At some point he would no doubt step out of the shadows, surprising us all. Anna had signed away crucial Imperial rights, dissolving the invisible bond between Russia, her people, and their ruler. Delight at her new rank, wealth, and privilege could not excuse this. There was the future to consider for this ruler's heirs. *Her heirs.* I reined my thoughts in, as guessing who might be next in line to the throne was considered high treason. I so missed having a friend and lover to talk to about this with. At least I should have my cousin here soon, Anna Ivanovna, by God's grace, Tsarina of All the Russias.

Once the Imperial messenger had dropped to his knees in the freezing Mitau Castle, pressing his forehead to a floor bare of any rugs or furs, Tsarina Anna made fast work of leaving Courland. "*Send me ten thousand roubles for traveling expenses, as well as six pairs of the best sables for a muff and a scarf,*" she wrote to Moscow. Dolgoruky obliged—these were trifles compared to the value of her signature upon his self-serving document. Three weeks after Petrushka's death, she arrived in Vesevatiskoy, a village where the Tsars rested before their accession, to cleanse their mind for the enormous task that lay ahead.

Anna invited me to join her there: "*As fast as possible, Lizenka, my dove, little cousin sunshine!*"

I strung the icon of St. Nicholas prominently around my throat, tightening the leather straps. It had been her parting gift to me when she was my derided, near-destitute cousin. Today I wore it to welcome her back as my Tsarina. In the past five years my life had felt like a journey on a river swollen by the *ottepel*'s force, borne along by treacherous currents, dashed against boulders, and sucked into maelstroms. Anna's own knowledge of suffering might create a bond of understanding between us. Being granted her protection would be like reaching an island of warm dry sand, where I could lie in peace and regain my breath.

58

Two guards stood outside the simple country palace of Ve-sevatiskoy. Dating from my grandfather's time, and built of timber, wattle, and daub, with mullioned mica panes in its windows, it looked antiquated. The poplar trees surrounding the house lay bare, their branches crooked with snow. In the courtyard a harras of horses was being led to the stables, fine heads twitching, eyes rolling, and breath steaming up the winter air. On the porch, which in summer afforded fine views, stood a high cage securing two plump black-and-white ostriches, their long necks craning through the bars. Behind my shoddy hired sled the Privy Council's grand ornamented vehicle came into sight, iron-bound skids hissing on the hard-trodden snow. The messenger who descended from it gave me the curtest of nods; I left him in my wake. Nobody could expect to be alone with the Tsarina Elect, not even a member of her family. Yet it was my right to greet her first.

"The Tsarevna Elizabeth Petrovna Romanova," the Imperial steward announced me as I stepped into the palace's main hall. It had been lying dormant since the accession of my father and his half-brother, Tsar Ivan. The merciless winter light illuminated the dusty flagstones and rugs worn to the weave; the furnishings consisted of battered sofas and a couple of armchairs, their leather upholstery brittle and torn, fistfuls of straw showing through. No hangings adorned the whitewashed walls, and the room faintly smelled of tar, as the ceiling joists had been hastily resealed to keep the cold

and moisture at bay. A fire burned in the huge fireplace at one end
of the room, which was full of people. Their bodies made it as hot
as a *banja*, but it smelled much worse: animals roamed free. I
spotted a porcupine, its spikes almost two feet long. Birds darted
about overhead. Already the high gilt-framed mirrors were
stained with their droppings and the velvet sofas torn by their
claws; nightingales, robins, greenfinches, and yellowhammers all
vied for perches.

"There you are," my cousin Ekaterina Ivanovna said, sliding up
to me, pulling her daughter Christine behind her. With increased
age the mutilations Ekaterina had suffered showed up even more:
the ivory teeth had loosened in her shrinking gums, and her scars
were worsened by wrinkles. A splatter of bird droppings hit her
full on the chest, and Christine bit her lip so as not to laugh out
loud, lowering her dark eyes. I winked at her.

"Where is the Tsarina?" I asked.

Ekaterina Ivanovna jerked her head ill-humoredly toward the
big fireplace. I spotted Anna's broad back—she towered over them
all—but too many people surrounded her for me to see more. I
thought I heard a baby wail. I hesitated, feeling Ekaterina's dark gaze
on me, before a tall man approached, arms outstretched, greeting
me confidently, as if he were the master of the place, and cordially,
as if we were the oldest and best of friends.

"Biren!" I smiled at him. "You came along. What a nice surprise."

His ruddy coloring, broad build, and beaming smile still made
him look like an innkeeper with whom one would not mind sharing
a drink or two, having a laugh, and listening to the latest gossip.
Anna's lover's big blue eyes were still hungry for just about everything life might offer him. "How could I not? Welcome! I have forgotten neither your grace, nor your beauty and charm, Tsarevna!"
At his booming voice the Tsarina Anna Ivanovna ever so slightly
turned her head, listening in, though she still had not acknowledged me in the turmoil, and I knew I had to bide my time.

"You haven't changed either, Biren," I said, flattering him, as he had doubled in weight. "Well, a bit perhaps. For the better," I added, eyeing his fine attire. He grinned broadly, smoothing his embroidered waistcoat. Its fabric was so stiff with gold and silver thread it could have stood up on its own. "All tailored in Lyons, where they crafted the lace for my shirt, too." He made the delicate, frothy lace around his throat flutter, stretched his legs in their cream-colored silk breeches, and turned his shiny leather shoes this way and that. They looked immaculate, having certainly had no contact with snow whatsoever. "They were made in Milan. Only the finest soles shall carry me into Russia."

"How splendid!" I said admiringly, all the more aware of my own humble black attire: as usual, I had adorned it with a white collar and wore a bright sash slung around my waist. But the change in him ran deeper than met the eye. Back at Mother's Coronation I had sensed a warm animal current of energy in Biren, a willingness to engage with life. Then the court had derided Anna and him. Now, however, his charisma was unmistakable, like a river breaking through a dam in search of new territory. He carried himself like a man of breeding and power, and whoever crossed him did so at their peril.

"How good of you to accompany the Tsarina to Russia, Biren," I said.

"I should never leave Her Majesty in a moment of need," he replied, eyes sparkling.

"Whose need, I wonder?" Ekaterina Ivanovna sniggered.

"I am also not called Biren any more," he said sunnily, ignoring her. "My name is now de Biron."

"De Biron?" I frowned. "Like the French dukes?"

"Yes. I like the name and have decided to carry on their extinct line." He beamed at me. "I also adopted their coat of arms. It's quite pretty."

"Why ever not?" I felt faint. The importance of breeding and nobility had surely been instilled into Anna from an early age. Yet Biren had simply helped himself to one of Europe's oldest names. I wanted to dismiss this as the action of a simpleton, yet that would make me no better than Ekaterina Ivanovna, whose eyes bored into her sister's lover with loathing and disdain while she clenched Christine's slender wrist.

"Yes, why not indeed?" another voice said, and I looked into Feofan Prokopovich's slate-colored eyes: the Archbishop of Novgorod, whose wise words had helped my father achieve so many of his dreams. Alexis Dolgoruky had imprisoned him, and yet he lived and walked free!

"Feofan! Your Beatitude. What a joy it is to see you," I greeted him, my cheeks flushing with joy. His simple black cloak and unruly, wavy hair surrounding a clever pug's face made me feel like a child again. He had always endured my probing questions with humor and kindness. I seized his hands, delighted: "Are you going to crown the Tsarina?"

"Yes. Her widowed Majesty recalled me from, well, shall we call it retirement?"

I laughed, relieved: few were those who ever left the Trubetzkoi Bastion unscathed. Yet here he was, smiling and rosy faced, his chubby hands as always fondling the cross on his breast.

"Will you be returning to Novgorod?" His diocese was the richest in Russia, owning almost fifty thousand serfs.

"No. I am needed by Her Majesty's side. I am to be the head of the Secret Office of Investigation," he answered.

I frowned, thinking of Buturlin's brutal interrogation and what Feofan himself might have suffered in the Trubetzkoi Bastion. "How is that? You are a man of the Church."

"There will be inevitable compromises to make. But I will do anything to ensure Her widowed Majesty's safety. She has suffered enough."

"Our *widowed* Majesty." Ekaterina Ivanovna savored the words, soaking them in spite and sarcasm. "When it comes to suffering, I am surely equal in rank to my sister," she said sourly: as the eldest, she no doubt felt better entitled to be Tsarina.

"At least you have Christine," I said. My cousin's glum dark eyes glowed before she lowered her gaze. Had she learned to hide her feelings, or was she devoid of them?

"Christine? I might as well have a log for company. Sometimes I cannot believe that I gave birth to this bore." As Ekaterina raised her fist to cuff her again, Anna Ivanovna stepped up to us and seized her sister's wrist. I curtsied deeply while de Biron and Feofan bowed their heads.

"Don't," she commanded.

"Don't you tell me what to do! I am the eldest surviving child of Tsar Ivan, and I am her mother!" Ekaterina hissed.

"And I am the Tsarina." Anna raised her eyebrows. Aunt Pasha's former maid Maja slid up, keen as ever to guard the family's secrets and bar the scene from the sight of onlookers. Her cleft lip made her smile look more than ever like a snarl. I greeted her before she curtsied to Ekaterina and Christine. The girl pulled a disgusted expression and turned away, while Maja pleaded, "Tsarina, Duchess Ekaterina, please, don't quarrel—for your mother's sake."

De Biron brushed Anna's elbow. "Beloved. You should not excite yourself. And don't make the most charming guest of today wait unacknowledged." He gently nudged me forward.

Beloved. Feofan lowered his gaze. Ekaterina opened her mouth, then shut it again. Maja seized Christine's elbow, and the girl forgot to tear her arm away. A robin darted past, and the giant porcupine rustled in its straw. Anna's dark eyes smoldered in a broad face. Her cheeks were veined, they had sagged, her chin tripled. She looked more awe-inspiring than Aunt Pasha ever had: her bosom reminded me of two loaves of bread in a bag, her arms almost burst the seams of her beautiful blue silk dress, and her belly strained against her loosely laced gem-studded stomacher. Yet when she smiled, she still showed pretty dimples.

"Certainly, I shall not, if the Tsarevna Elizabeth deigns to greet me properly?" She straightened her scarlet sash of the Order of St. Catherine. I, too, had once received the order, but had judged this visit to be an informal one. The Tsarina, though, frowned at my plain appearance.

"Come closer, Lizenka. My eyesight is not what it used to be. De Biron is right. You are still as lively and beautiful as you ever were. And always in wonderfully high spirits, I hear, despite everything. You have suffered terrible losses. Yet nothing darkens your mood and abates your courage. Would you be a true Romanov woman after all?"

She gave her last words a curious weight; I remembered how Ostermann had stressed her legitimate birth when pronouncing her Tsarina. Had he trickled his poison into her ear? If so, I would not let him have his way, I decided, and raised the icon in my fingers so that her short-sighted gaze could see it. "That is because I always wore this, Your Majesty, to protect me and offer me guidance. Whatever happened."

Anna squinted harder, ostrich feathers bobbing on her piled-up hair. She wore a heavy headband set with glinting sapphires and diamonds; matching earrings brushed her shoulders. Her throat was hidden by a many-stranded pearl choker, and a dozen diamond bracelets adorned her wrists. On her ring finger the Imperial seal stood proud.

Anna frowned, touching the icon. "How nice. What is that?"

59

The gaze of her sour-cherry eyes was impenetrable. I was aware of all the people watching us. "Your Majesty gave it to me after my mother's Coronation. Don't you remember? You came into my bedroom in the morning. We spoke about Alexey."

"Ah! Alexey. The Tsarevich who was born to the great Tsar's true wife. God bless his soul." The surrounding courtiers dutifully made doleful noises. *The great Tsar's true wife*. Was she slighting my mother, who had shown her nothing but friendliness and generosity? No, it was me she was targeting with this insult.

"I really don't remember," she said with a shrug. "It suits you, in any case. A dear little bauble. It is always wise to honor the saints."

De Biron smiled welcomingly as a slight, richly dressed woman stepped up to us: her face was pockmarked, her mouth pinched. Her light eyes looked flighty as a ferret's. To my surprise, she handed Anna an infant, and a second child toddled toward her feet. Anna's face lit up as she kissed the baby boy: "Meet de Biron's wife and their sons. She stems from the same German village as dear Count Ostermann does. What a bond between us!"

Dear Count Ostermann: obviously they had been in contact. Anna heaved the baby boy higher on her hip; he twisted her splendid necklace, sucking on the pearls, looking at me with curiously dark eyes. She rummaged in the folds of her skirt and then tucked twice at his bib, as if folding something underneath, then smoothed his clothes. "Don't bite my pearls, little one. Do you think they are fake? The Tsarina of All the Russias might do many things, but she does not wear fake jewelry."

She chuckled, handing him back to de Biron's wife. De Biron himself kissed the elder boy, who had the same dark eyes as his little brother, and then turned to the door. Anna's gaze followed his as if attached by invisible ties. At the same time de Biron's scrawny wife and mewling children moved closer, making any private word with the Tsarina impossible.

"Where are you going, dearest?" Anna called after de Biron. "Don't leave me."

He gallantly bowed. "I never would. I am just checking if the messenger of the Privy Council has arrived."

Her face lit up, mirroring his mood. "Ah, yes," Anna said. "Forgive me, Lizenka. The state calls me away from where my heart would like to stay."

Dolgoruky's messenger hovered on the threshold, holding a tray of hammered bronze containing the carefully folded blue sash and diamond-framed brooch with a portrait of St. Andrew upon it. It was the realm's foremost order, yet either to wear or to grant it was another royal right that Anna had signed away.

"Your Majesty. The Council sends you this Order of St. Andrew on loan to wear at your entrance into Moscow," the messenger said. Anna fixed her gaze on the man, who quailed slightly. I felt heat rising within her as she forced a laugh: "The Council is giving me the Order of St. Andrew *on loan*? Surely this must be a mistake. It is my due." She snatched the sash and pulled it over her head, dislodging the ostrich feathers. The blue fabric twisted across her bosom and belly as she haphazardly fastened the huge, sparkling brooch of St. Andrew to her bodice. "There," she breathed. "Perfect."

"But—the conditions . . ." the messenger stammered.

She feigned surprise. "Which conditions? The weather, you mean?" She peered outside. "It doesn't look as if it will snow any more today. Also there is no bad weather in Russia, only a lack of sable coats," she chuckled. Then her face darkened. "Or are you insulting me, your widowed Tsarina? How could I be in any condition to worry about? God has never blessed me with children. Do not rub salt in those wounds."

The man fell to his knees. Did he feel his head wobble on his shoulders or his tongue coming loose from his throat? He'd better.

"No, no, Your Majesty," he stammered, his face as crimson as an autumn apple.

"Well, then," Anna said. "What are we waiting for? I am ready."

"Ready for what, my dearest?" de Biron asked, coming close to her at once, and Maja moved in as well. The Tsarina had three shadows when she announced: "I shall go and visit the Russian regiments. Do come along, de Biron."

"Where you go, I will be." He nodded at his wife, who duly gathered the boys. How strange that the children had such dark eyes, I thought, seeing both the de Birons' light, wide gaze.

"Your Majesty," the messenger dared to object: visiting the regiments without agreement from the Privy Council—or Alexis Dolgoruky—was also against the conditions of Anna's rule. Maja shook her head at him in a silent warning.

"What is it?" the Tsarina snapped. "I shall act in accordance with the will of my people. Nothing else shall be my guideline."

The dwarf d'Acosta—as ever, where he ought to be—rose from his bearskin by the fireplace, weaving his way through the courtiers. He kneeled down next to the messenger, blowing out his cheeks and aping the man's fear and confusion. Anna laughed, and all the courtiers quickly roared along with her. The sycophantic display of mirth stuck in my throat. *No signature, no crown!* I remembered Dolgoruky's words. If they had thought to have their way with Her widowed Majesty, they were mistaken. Still, she had signed Dolgoruky's clauses. How would she get out of having given her Imperial word?

De Biron waited in the doorway, now wearing a velvet and

wolfskin cloak trimmed with gold galloon, not unlike the one I had once offered Petrushka. His sour-faced wife covered the Tsarina's broad shoulders in a magnificent blue velvet cloak lined with ermine. The sellers in the *gostiny dvor* must have been working overtime to fill my cousin's wardrobe! Finally Anna pulled on kidskin gloves, the soft leather snagging on the huge Imperial seal. "Good afternoon to you all," she said, ready to leave, then turned to me once more. "Before I forget: where do you live now, Lizenka?"

"In Izmailov. The house of your childhood."

"Ah. I see. Make sure not to go anywhere else without our Imperial approval, will you? I prefer to have you close." She swept out, de Biron in her wake. The courtiers' chatter grew to a cacophony, making my parrots' morning gossip pale in comparison. Upon the Tsarina's departure there was general movement: the courtiers flocked out, de Biron's wife leading them into smaller and cosier rooms. Ekaterina Ivanovna and Christine seemed ready to return to the Kremlin. Only the birds still darted about in the hall. Even Feofan Prokopovich made his way out, brushing me as if by mistake in passing.

"Stay close, Tsarevna, I beg you," he whispered. "She wouldn't take kindly to you straying from under her eye. Whom she loves as a cousin, she ought to fear and dislike as a Tsarina." Then he spoke up, for all to hear. "Be my guest in my house in Moscow, will you? Do come as soon as possible," he added, his gaze fixed on me. Was he speaking as my family's priest or as head of the dreaded Imperial Secret Office of Investigation? My breath caught in my throat, raw with fear.

No man shall disappoint you as a woman will.

Once more, the Leshy spirit's words had come to pass.

Anna had been mistaken about the weather. As I stepped outside, the dark layers of sky shifted, and snow fell once more, the thick, wet flakes swallowing trees and houses. A sled bearing Ostermann's coat of arms had arrived, and a servant stepped out, carrying an exquisite-looking clock of German make, his gift to the new Tsarina. I tightened my squirrel-fur collar against the cold; at least I had not yet stooped so low as to wear rabbit, as Anna had done at the time of Mother's Coronation. Better be on my way back to Izmailov; the cold, lonely ride should at least allow me some respite.

I knew that once again I had slipped from the frying pan straight into the fire.

60

Beloved.

I stretched out on the mottled, sticky furs of my hired vehicle, just as the large Imperial sled floated through the stable yard's arched gateway. On each door the Imperial eagle was emblazoned, large and golden, threatening even daylight into submission; the crimson velvet curtains were drawn. The sled flew down the snowy poplar alley, silver bells ringing at the eight horses' ruby-red leather reins. I imagined Anna and de Biron sitting inside, sipping mulled wine, nibbling *blintshiki,* and discussing it all: my visit, her sister Ekaterina, and her niece Christine, surely mocking the Privy Council's messenger. They might whisper and laugh as Augustus, and then Buturlin, and I had done. The one had prepared me to love, the other had been my lover. Did de Biron combine both roles for her? What a blessing if so.

I imagined Anna Ivanovna's arrival in the regiment's barracks: the soldiers worshipped the ground beneath the Tsar's feet. They would be overjoyed to see her, cheering her, perhaps even lifting her up on their shoulders, though it would take many mightily strong men to achieve that! A change of ruler also meant a general change in fortunes: Anna knew how to play that game. I forbade myself any further grief, as it robbed me of my strength. I needed to keep my wits about me in order to survive.

My hired sled driver, who looked every inch the kind of lice-ridden, smelly thug who might rob and rape me before dropping me for dead by the roadside, stuffed some chewing tobacco beneath his upper lip. Before mounting the box, he spat out. His cherry-colored saliva splashed blood red, soiling the fresh snow, reminding me of Buturlin's fate. What was Buturlin doing in Kamchatka—deeming himself lucky to be alive, or cursing me in gargled cries, his mind broken by living a ceaseless nightmare from dawn till dusk? I could do nothing to change his lot.

"Go," I ordered the driver, swallowing my tears. His whip cracked. If he sped on, I might be in Izmailov by suppertime, where Lestocq awaited me. I knew what he was thinking: *If only you had allowed me to bleed Petrushka.* But I never would have, either back then or now if he were still with us. This was the order of things, and cursed be she who forces fate's hand. The two ponies strung in single file took the strain of the sled, and I dropped the curtains around me. Pain ground inside me like a screw driven into soft wood. *Beloved.* I placed my fingertips on my temples. What a blessing to share life with another: it meant lightening any burden and doubling any joy. Surrounded by the frosty, sleeping landscape, my heart twisted as I remembered how I had been described to the Tsarina. *Still as lively and beautiful as you ever were. And always in wonderfully high spirits.* De Biron had spoken honestly, yet all the gifts God had graced me with were wasted.

Beloved. Would anyone ever say that to me again, sharing my laughter and my tears, offering advice or holding his tongue, loving and desiring me? My hand slipped down to stroke my barren belly. I was unable to give life, while Anoushka's son grew up a stranger in Holstein. Hot tears welled up, the chilly air cooling them on my cheeks. I lifted the sled's curtain once more. The cold slapped me, making my cheeks burn and my eyes sting. Icy clods and gravel flew from the horses' hooves and the sled's runners. I ducked to avoid being hit yet remained peering out. The road was long and winding; the skies were bursting, the horizon all but swallowed up in the gathering snowstorm. It was impossible to see where we were heading. Loneliness lunged at me like wolves in winter at a solitary traveler. I sank back into the smelly, threadbare cushions. The ponies pounded on; the coachman, too, wanted to return to his *izba* before night fell. I closed my eyes. The worst was neither Anna being Tsarina, having me at her mercy, nor me being cast aside on the grounds of my illegitimate birth.

The worst was the absence from my life of that one word I doubted I should ever hear again: *Beloved.*

61

Have you heard?
      These words dominated life after Anna's arrival, making the air crackle constantly as if lightning had struck.

Have you heard? The Tsarina has given de Biron the rank of Grand Chamberlain and Count of the Empire. His family is to move into Kremlin apartments, neighboring hers. The Tsarina does not take a step, let alone a decision, without him. He is the cause of the German yoke on Russian shoulders. It is called the age of the *Bironyshkchina.*

Have you heard? The Tsarina will neither live in the Kremlin nor St. Petersburg. She will build a new palace of two, no, three, no, four hundred rooms. Or is it five hundred? It will be called Annenhof, a fine name indeed.

Have you heard? The Tsarina is now the colonel of both Imperial Regiments and the Imperial Horse Guards. The officers threw themselves at her feet, kissing the embroidered tip of her silk slipper. She offered them drinks with her own hands, handing out roubles as freely as if coins were acorns.

Have you heard? The Coronation will surpass anything we have ever seen; the crowds who gathered in Moscow for Petrushka's wedding are to stay put. Precise orders are being drafted concerning their clothes, liveries, and uniforms. Flout them at your peril!

Have you heard? The Tsarina is finally meeting the Privy Council ahead of her entrance to Moscow. She is said to have agreed to sign Dolgoruky's conditions.

Have you heard? Even Ostermann is out of bed, his right hand miraculously recovered from the attack of gout. He, too, is to attend the meeting of the Tsarina and the Privy Council.

When I heard that Ostermann was up on his feet again, ready to stand by Anna's side, I knew the game was afoot. The meeting in which the Privy Council planned to end the absolute rule of the Tsar or Tsarina in Russia was set for February 25, 1730. Whatever man decides makes for fate's merriment.

62

"Count Ostermann. Good to see you so well—your health was restored just in time," I purred, waiting outside the Kremlin's throne room for Anna's arrival. Ostermann bowed his head as perfunctorily as he could get away with, looking pale and leaning on a stick. Had he truly been ill? I was not so sure, knowing him to be not above plundering his wife's rouge or leaving it off when it suited him. I straightened myself so I could look down on him.

"Timing is indeed everything in life, Tsarevna," he said, as if talking to an indolent child. As much as I hated him, I took careful note of his every word.

"Whom are we to meet?" I asked.

"Well, *the Tsarina and I* are to meet the Privy Council, who wish to curtail the Tsarina's powers," Ostermann said. "Let us see where Dolgoruky wants to take this. He has long pondered which form of new government might be best suited to Russia."

"And what do *you* think, who owes all to the Tsar, my father, an absolute ruler?"

Ostermann gave me a probing look. "Indeed. Dolgoruky wondered if we should follow the British or the Swedish model." I knew nothing of the differences between them, but Ostermann rattled on. "The Swedish monarch is but a puppet. And as for Britain—can you imagine a parliament in which the Russian people truly have a say?" He gave a short, incredulous laugh. "A great many things are happening at the moment. I see lies, intrigue, duplicity, ambition, and self-interest wherever I look. But never—*never,* Tsarevna—

must the Russian people be allowed to rise from their stupor, or they will feed upon themselves in the cruellest way imaginable."

"Does Dolgoruky think the same?"

"I doubt it." Surely Ostermann had had a good reason for distancing himself from the Council's demands on Anna: if there was a noose when they backfired, his head would not be caught in it. I thought of de Biron's wife, who came from the same German village as Ostermann did; of Anna carefully tucking something under the baby's bib, as if hiding it; of his servant delivering the gift of a clock to the new Tsarina: a clock large enough to hide a message. Had the Privy Council really thought they could seal Anna off from *him*? Ostermann was like dirty water, always seeping back in through the tiniest of cracks, a flood that did immeasurably more damage than a roaring fire ever could.

I smiled. "Who only sees what is shown to him, and only hears what is said, misses out on the truth."

Ostermann looked at me, as surprised as a lizard that has missed a juicy fly.

Inside the Throne Hall the atmosphere was thick with suspense. The opposing forces that had reigned, clandestinely or in the open, since Petrushka's death, charged the air with tension, though emotions were hidden, expressions carefully kept in check.

I crossed the red carpet to the dais, where low gilded chairs with plump purple velvet upholstery waited behind the throne: Ekaterina Ivanovna was already seated there, her face as sour as if she had enjoyed a bottle of vinegar for breakfast. Christine twisted her fingers in her lap, her shoulders slumped. I slipped onto my seat as drumrolls and trumpets sounded in the Kremlin's corridors. Silence fell in the hall; all heads turned, expecting Anna and her ladies to sweep in, guileless and gullible.

Instead the heavy footfall of hundreds of men preceded her into the hall: the Preobrazhensky Guard. The men looked splendid in their dark green coats, cream kidskin breeches, and polished, thigh-high boots, faces set and hard. The Privy Council cowered in surprise, like wildcats facing the lash of a tamer's whip. The soldiers positioned themselves to one side of the throne as the sound of chanting began. The courtiers crossed themselves with three fingers and knelt as Feofan Prokopovich and every possible dignitary of the Church entered the hall to flank the throne's other side. Their heavy golden crosses were a reminder of the one true power. Red-cheeked choirboys accompanied them, swinging jars of smoldering myrrh and frankincense, spreading a musky scent.

Only then did Anna enter, moving through the sudden eerie silence calmly and at a measured pace. She was covered in the State jewelry, which had been piled on: a high diamond-and-emerald *kokoshnik* tiara matched her earrings, which brushed her shoulders, and the collier, which spread in a star-shape and filled out her cleavage in the low-cut dress of silver cloth. Upon spotting the Privy Council, she looked at each of the men in turn thoughtfully. Was she pondering their reward or their punishment? They swapped swift glances before bowing deeply. Only Ostermann stayed straight-backed, his hooded eyelids lowered, his face dreamy, which meant he was more alert than ever.

As Anna took the throne, her ladies-in-waiting adjusting her beautiful mustard-colored velvet train, the tiny diamonds sewn on it catching the light of the chandeliers, Alexis Dolgoruky stepped forward. He held his list of conditions in one hand, a quill dripping ink in the other.

"Yes, Prince? We listen," Anna said, but as Dolgoruky made to speak, she tutted. "Not you, Dolgoruky. I mean the Prince Cherkassky, of course."

"Cherkassky? But why?" Dolgoruky dared to object, looking alarmed. This had not been planned.

Anna ignored him as Cherkassky stepped into the middle of the hall, a small, broad man with a head that seemed too large for his neck, tilting toward his left shoulder while his belly hung to the right. He wore heels to make him look taller and more appealing, which was an unnecessary ruse since it was known that nobody was richer than the Cherkasskys. "Prince Cherkassky, I so fondly remember your visit to Courland, many moons ago. Let me listen to you, old friend," Anna said.

Dolgoruky blew out his bearded cheeks: "By what right . . ."

Anna frowned at him as Cherkassky thundered, "I have the same right to advise Her Majesty as you have to impose conditions on her—without consulting us, the army, or the Church." Anna looked from one to the other, still apparently stunned. Then she rose, looking mountainous in her Imperial splendor, hands placed on the throne's armrests. Ostermann did not take his eyes off her, as if working her like a puppet.

"What are you saying, Cherkassky?"

He bowed. "Your Most Gracious widowed Majesty. Eight hundred Russian nobles have gathered on the Red Square, imploring you not to sign these conditions. They will harm you—and thus Russia."

"Eight hundred nobles, eh? But who are they? How is this possible? I thought the Privy Council gives voice to my people's will, which I vow to obey. The will of *all* my people!"

"Your people's will? Far from that," Cherkassky spat. "This is the conspiracy of one man only: Alexis Dolgoruky."

Anna turned to Dolgoruky, her eyes wide. "Do you mean that the list of conditions you sent to Mitau were *not* approved by All the Russias?" She looked nothing short of magnificent: as tall as a man with the Imperial ermine coat cloaking her shoulders; the blue sash of the borrowed Order of St. Andrew rose and fell across her mighty bosom, diamonds and emeralds glittering on every inch of exposed flesh. Feofan crossed himself, as if horrified, and the regiments jeered. As if on a secret cue, the waiting nobles now flooded up the Red Staircase, spilling into the hall, filling up every available space.

"Were these conditions the will of my people?" Anna shouted above the commotion. "Yes or no?"

"No! They were not, Your Sovereign Majesty, and they will never be!" Cherkassky shouted triumphantly as Dolgoruky stood defeated, his shoulders slumped. Shots rang out and stucco crumbled from the ceiling. Ivan Grozny's bronze bell started to toll in its tower. The soldiers roared, and the courtiers stormed the dais, throwing themselves at the Tsarina's feet so as not to be swept away by the turning tide, cajoling and assuring her that they had always despised and doubted any conditions that limited her power.

"Silence!" Anna thundered. She had the majesty of a true ruler, and her fury reminded me of the story she had told me about Aunt Pasha punishing the man who had denounced her as an Old Believer. Anna Ivanovna the Terrible indeed, as d'Acosta had once called her. "Alexis Dolgoruky, have you lied to me?" she roared, and he fell to his knees as Cherkassky drew his own petition from his waistcoat.

"My Tsarina: sign this instead—promise to be our absolute sovereign, whose will and wisdom are governed only by God."

"Your Majesty," Dolgoruky dared to plead. "Do not make any rash decisions."

Anna hesitated as Ekaterina Ivanovna jumped up, saying: "What's this talk of rash decisions? Why should my sister deliberate over so simple a matter? Surely it is better to get it over and done with." She took Cherkassky's petition and gave it to Anna. The Tsarina signed it, ink dripping and the quill scratching, before Ostermann quickly spilled sand over the signature and then dripped hot red wax on the document. The members of the Privy Council shrank back, ready to slip away and lick their wounds, but Anna caught wind of their intention. With a flick of her wrist, she plunged the Imperial seal into the oozing mass, pressing down hard: "I request the pleasure of my Privy Council's company at dinner. Now!"

The game was up: there was no coming back from this, no further conspiracy. The Tsarina was still the absolute ruler of Russia, as the Tsars had always been. Ekaterina Ivanovna, Christine, and

I followed Anna as her ladies-in-waiting arranged the Tsarina's heavy train. Alexis Dolgoruky rose reluctantly, unable to refuse her invitation. A terrible understanding dawned in his eyes.

The same evening, the strangest lights showed in Moscow's inky sky, tearing the night apart and crisscrossing it in bold flashes of every color of the rainbow, from a riverine green to the richest crimson and vermilion. The horizon looked as if it had been dipped in blood.

63

The servant girl's high-pitched voice was to be heard through the door to the Tsarina's bedroom. I stopped to listen: "As the robbers entered the castle, they found the duchess on her window seat—"

Anna clapped her hands, delighted: "Slow down, slow down. This is my favorite part!"

"Please, Your Majesty. I am so tired. I have been telling stories since sunrise and had no food."

"Tired? One moment, let me give you something." I heard a sharp slap and then a muffled sob. Maja, who led me, shrugged and averted her eyes, so I guarded myself from making any comment. I was already sure my every move was being reported to Anna. It was only two months ago that she had seized absolute control of Russia, but already I felt exhausted by the scale of the changes in life at court.

"Lean against the screen, girl. You, d'Acosta, stand there so I need not see her leaning. Otherwise her hands and nose would be chopped off for insulting My Majesty, and we do not want that, do we?" The Tsarina's silky voice veiled her terrible threat thinly.

"As the robbers entered the castle—" the girl went on, her voice shrill with terror.

"You may enter, Tsarevna," Maja lisped. "The Tsarina is trying on robes and jewelry for her Coronation."

"Thank you, Maja. How lucky the Tsarina is to have such a loyal servant."

She blushed, unable to suppress a pleased smile, and curtsied. "I am still grateful for your generosity in my day of need, Tsarevna, back when the Tsaritsa Praskovia died. You are truly your mother's daughter."

"I was glad to honor your service to my Aunt Pasha and the family," I said.

"Not everyone would be," she said, averting her gaze.

Anna's rooms were as dusky as a dressing room in the *gostiny dvor*. A curious smell lingered in the air—flesh, sweat, the vanilla and bergamot of her perfume, spilled vodka, and another note that I could not name, resembling cooling ash. The Imperial apartment looked as if a cannonball had hit it. Robes lay everywhere, many dozens if not hundreds of them, piled on top of overskirts, stomachers, lace collars, and capes. Thick velvet and fine wool cloaks were carelessly tossed about; priceless furs had been flung to the floor; and silken stays, lacy undershirts, and tight whalebone corsets were stacked up on her bed, chairs, chaise longue, and stools; a pair of silk stockings even dangled from the screen where the young storyteller half-leaned, exhausted, with d'Acosta hovering in front of her. When he saw me, he clapped his hands, calling out, "Look! It's lovely Lizenka, visiting the enchanting Tsarina!" His voice blended with the silver bells that were tied to his ankles and wrists, and he winked at me, like an old friend, of which I had none.

"Shut up," Anna snapped, not enchanted at all but busy eyeing me, taking it all in: my fresh, flushed face after the morning ride (I needed neither crimson paint on my cheeks and lips, nor kohl to accentuate my dark lashes and arched eyebrows); at the nape of my neck the neat bun that could hardly contain my thick honey-colored hair; as well as the slim-cut, knee-length coat and tight breeches that showed off my hips and my legs in their high, mud-splattered riding boots.

"Why do you come dressed as a boy?" she asked, pushing her fists into her blue dressing gown's pockets. She wore it open and was naked underneath, a shocking sight: her breasts dangled—the nipples were large, pink, and absurdly long—and her vast, protruding belly was lacerated with white stretch marks, as if an animal had clawed her. "The masquerade is planned for after the Coronation, if I am well informed?" She beckoned me closer, unsmiling. Everything inside me quivered, on the alert. The scolding was over, though.

"Look," she breathed, sounding rapt, and pointed at a cask propped up on her bedside dressing table. It was a small chest locked by a spider's web of chains. Anna had the key dangling from a thin necklace between her breasts. "You might recognize what you will see inside here," she said, giving d'Acosta a vicious kick when he came too close. "Away, misfit! This is not for your eyes. And you, shut up!" she snapped at the storyteller, who had rattled on and now paused, gasping for breath.

"Open the curtains," Anna ordered. "I need more light."

At the windows I groped for the pulley of the heavily lined curtains but felt cold metal instead. "What's this?" I asked, recoiling: a gun was mounted on the windowsill, pointing toward the Red Square. Empty cartridges rolled at my feet, which explained the musky scent in the room. It was gunpowder.

"My gun." Anna shrugged.

"What do you do with it?"

"Well, I shoot with it, of course. Silly you!"

"Taking aim from the Kremlin's window? At the Red Square?"

"Yes."

"What's the target? Or—who?"

"Whoever walks there. They'd better do so fast. I don't really want to hit them, but sometimes it just so happens." She waved her hand at me impatiently. "Go on, open up. Don't dawdle, Lizenka."

I obeyed. It was mid-April. The sky was of that dense, clean blue that heralded the end of the *ottepel*. Spring had settled in; the hours of daylight were lengthening. The people awoke from their winter stupor, and Moscow brimmed with Russians from all over the realm, hanging around to witness Anna's accession. Yet the Red Square, normally bustling at any hour, was almost empty. Instead, throngs of people pressed along the walls beneath the arcades of the surrounding houses, ducking for cover. Clearly word of Anna's pastime had spread. I touched my icon of St. Nicholas in a silent, short prayer. "Is this better?" I asked as the crisp light flooded the room, showing the full, formidable extent of the mess.

"Better," Anna confirmed, letting the casket snap open, the chains slipping to the floor. The case's sides opened like petals. I stood mute, staring at the splendor of my mother's crown, for which Father, as a sign of his love, respect, and adoration, had paid one million roubles only seven years before. It seemed an eternity ago.

"So beautiful!" I admitted, fighting my sadness.

"Indeed. I have paid my jeweler, the little Jew Liebman, forty-five thousand roubles to improve it." Her finger brushed a newly set ruby the size of a pigeon's egg. "This stone comes from China. The new rim Liebman has added from twenty-eight new diamonds, which are the largest ever found in my Siberian mines. The other two thousand stones come from all over my Empire."

My mines. My Empire. Like sweets to be devoured, or toys to be played with. It pained me to see my mother's crown altered like this, to be placed on another woman's head. I told myself that was silly—a crown was an heirloom, intended and made to be passed on.

"The Coronation will be a feast such as All the Russias have never seen," Anna said dreamily.

"I shall be sorry to miss it," I said. "With your permission, of course."

"What?" She turned to me. "This is the first I've heard of it."

"I came to ask for leave to go on a pilgrimage. I have been planning it since before Petrushka's engagement. I have contacted the Pecharsky Monastery near Kiev and proposed that I should stay with them for a while. The Abbess there, Agatha, was a dear friend of my mother's."

"Ah, yes. My little sunshine aunt. She was the only one who deigned to answer the many pleading letters I sent from Courland."

I curtsied, anxious to please her further. "I implore you, allow me to go. My soul needs the calm and quiet of the convent. Too much has happened lately. Petrushka was the last male Romanov, and I still mourn him."

"It is true. We are vastly diminished. That is why we have to stay close, Lizenka," Anna said. "Who knows? You might enjoy the convent's routine so much that you stay for good. What do you think, Maja?"

"The Tsaritsa Praskovia always warned me not to get ahead of myself," Maja said demurely. "But the Tsarevna will surely benefit from the pilgrimage. And she shall hear all about the splendor of the celebration later, shan't she?"

"We shall miss you, dear cousin. But you are a lesser Imperial Princess, born out of wedlock. Whether you are present or not is of no real significance. By the way, Alexey's mother, your father's first and true wife, is to attend," Anna said.

"Evdokia?"

"Yes. The widowed Empress. She is still mourning Petrushka, of course. What suffering! My sister Ekaterina and my darling niece Christine will be my maids of honor, as they represent the elder Romanov bloodline."

A lesser Imperial Princess. Your father's first and true wife. The elder Romanov bloodline. My line of the family would be pushed into oblivion, if not extinction, should any ill befall my Holstein nephew.

"When are you to leave?" Anna asked.

"I am dressed to ride," I said. "Lestocq is waiting for me at the Red Staircase."

"Ah, yes. Lestocq. The hired Frenchman. Your crony paid for by Versailles. Beggars cannot be choosers, as I know myself. We all have our vain hopes, so why not also the King of France? Is he hoping that you will be named my heiress? It is possible. But make no mistake: nothing of the sort is decided yet, and my hand will not be forced." She admired the crown once more. "Safe travels, Lizenka. I have a lot to take care of."

"What is the first task of your reign? Fighting the famine?" I wondered. "Russia has suffered for too long. People lock up their children in case they are stolen and eaten. Nobody in their right mind travels unaccompanied, and peasants bake pies out of sawdust."

"The famine? What on earth are you talking about?" She looked at me sternly. "There is no famine in my realm. Never has been, never will be."

I bit my lip, yet wanted to know more about her plans. "Or is the quarrel about the Polish throne keeping you busy?" Rumor had it that Russia would soon be at war again, crushing the country with new taxes and duties.

"You are as boring as Ostermann. He, too, harps on about the Polish succession and wants the throne for the Saxon Elector, while the French of course push for their Queen's father, Stanislas Leszczyński." She cast me a mean glance. "Ah, yes. I had almost forgotten. You have a bone to pick with that line, don't you? Didn't his daughter once steal your handsome fiancé, the King of France, from you?"

I nodded mutely.

"Well, I might join the war after all. Even if it's just to avenge your slighted honor."

"Would you?"

"No. Of course not. A pretty face is not reason enough to send soldiers marching to their deaths. I am busy with other things: once crowned, I shall have a theater and an opera company to supervise. Where do we find the best company of actors?"

"D'Acosta might know," Maja suggested.

"Oh, yes. Dear d'Acosta. He really knows everything, doesn't he?"

The dwarf bowed.

I was dismissed.

Just days after I had left Moscow, Anna was crowned Tsarina of All the Russias in the Cathedral of the Assumption by Feofan Proko-povich, who blessed her face, shoulders, breast, and both sides of her hands with chrism, gently dabbing her skin dry as chant-ing rose and he murmured his prayers in her ears. Anna's strong neck supported the weight of my mother's altered crown well. The gemstone-encrusted Imperial scepter was so heavy that she had to change hands continually to support its weight; the golden orb, which measured an *arshin,* rested on a velvet cushion next to her. Anna retired early from the banquet and ball that followed to drive through the streets, where dozens of triumphal arches showed her image lit by seven thousand seven-*arshin*-high candles, which the Spanish Ambassador, the Duke of Liria, had sponsored. Their glow held the night at bay and flattered the ladies as much as it en-couraged men in their daring advances. The festivities lasted eight days, after which the waters of the Moskva were set alight by the reflection of a firework display not to be bettered anywhere else in the world.

By then I had put as many *versty* as I could between Moscow, that snake pit of a city, and me.

The ride to Kiev, oldest and holiest of the original Rus' cities, from which Grand Prince Vladimir had brought Christianity to Russia almost a thousand years earlier, spanned nine hundred *versty.* The mid-April sunshine did not last. Soon we rode through driving rain. In the fields the first green shoots drowned, their furrows filled with rain. Serfs desperately dug canals to steer the rising flood-waters away, but in vain. I made a point of praying at every village, however backward, and tried to leave a gift with the priest for the neediest of his flock—yet there were so many, it broke my heart.

"Must we?" sighed Lestocq, as I once more got off my horse to worship.

"What on this earth must we do on a pilgrimage if not this?" I countered. "I thought the French were devout Catholics?"

"Occasionally. Less so in cold and rain." He sniffed and waited for me, studying the wall-eyed virgin portrayed in the church's icon and eyeing activity in the small *mir* with disdain. The floodwater had flowed into the *izby,* spoiling furniture, food, and clothes. Drowned sheep, goats, and poultry drifted belly-up, floating toward the rivers and streams. People lay stranded, too drunk to move, on their large ovens, islands in the *izby* that had turned to ponds. There was to be no respite from the previous year's famine. How could Anna Ivanovna as Tsarina deny their plight? Loving Russia meant loving her people.

On the first dry night I chose to camp. Lestocq and I took turns guarding the fire, while the other slept on their bedroll like a proper pilgrim. The earth and the spirit of my country revived me: Anna's sickly sweet yet stinging words were suffocating me, making me feel like a wasp stuck in jam, unable to spread its wings, slowly perishing. Lestocq snored next to me, and the embers of our fire still glimmered when I sat up and listened: *truly* listened. A pair of large gray owls had built their nest in the treetops above. With nightfall the birds swooped over the countryside, their wingspan darkening the stars. They returned, sharp beaks filled with mice and other small mammals. Wild boars rustled in the bushes, poking their snouts deep into the moist ground, looking for acorns a squirrel might have buried, or better still, truffles. A lynx's yellow eyes loomed at me from behind a screen of branches, lusting for the remains of our dinner—a sinewy hare—but the creature hesitated to pounce. The forest felt like a web in which I was swallowed up. I was at peace here, wrapping my cloak tighter around me and holding my icon, and yet I could not settle. My fingers brushed the earth next to my Tatar saddle, which I used as a cushion. The grassy ground was damp with dew. I clawed up a tuft from the coarse blend of sand, gravel, and dust it was rooted in. This was the very backbone of Russia, the foundation on which my country was built. Warm and welcoming on the surface, but with a steady, steely chill lurking beneath. I hungrily stuffed the grass in my mouth, chewing on it, gulping, savoring its blue taste. Tears welled in my eyes then and streamed down my face, but they brought me comfort.

Whatever happened, I always had Russia for my bedfellow.

64

We reached Kiev by the end of May. The spring had curdled, the early summer drowned. The vastness of Russia might have turned into a lake for all I knew: I could not remember when I had last worn dry clothes. My nose felt runny, my throat sore. I shivered constantly. After weeks of travel, my body was as sinewy as the creatures we fed on, if we shot any at all. With the famine, poaching was rampant, and the forests bare of game, let alone berries and roots.

I halted my horse upon approaching the city, taking in the sight. Dusk's blue hour had begun. Kiev's golden domes rose from a slope on the Dnieper's western bank. Their splendid color gleamed in the evening sun, like a promise man might make but only God could keep. I stood briefly in my stirrups, then lost all strength, and sagged in the saddle. My vision blurred.

"Let us push on," Lestocq said, sounding worried. "Will you make it?"

My throat ached too much for me to answer, and a cough wracked my chest as I nodded.

Our horses' hooves sounded hollow on the stone paving when we approached the Pecharsky Monastery. The hour of almsgiving was long gone: no pauper was out, hungry for a last ladleful of thick pea soup; no groups of lepers lingered in corners, hoping for the impossible, such as a kind word. Shadows flitted by. Under cover of darkness a different side of life was revealed. A mother in need might leave her baby in the convent's revolving door, and pick-pockets—or worse—gathered here to plan their exploits for the night ahead.

"Let me help you," said Lestocq when I struggled to dismount from my horse. I was uncertain if my legs would support me but shook my head. Anna's scorn of him had hit home: why was he still with me—had Versailles doubled his salary, hoping that I might yet be made heiress to the throne? True loyalty in my life seemed an impossibility. I felt lonelier than ever. Yet he brushed away my objections, lifting me from the saddle with shocking ease. My jacket hung loose, and I had added some holes to my belt, tightening it more with each day. At first my fingers missed the knocker on the monastery's main door, but I clasped it at the second attempt, leaning against the doorframe, as I waited for my summons to be answered. A window set into the gate was unbolted. An eye peered suspiciously at us through the small, barred opening.

"Who asks to enter?" a voice asked sternly. Was this Abbess Agatha? She had been Mother's friend: if I had neither parents nor sister, I had her. I had decided I would not leave this place without answers to the many questions that troubled my heart. If indeed I left at all.

"Her Imperial Highness Tsarevna Elizabeth Petrovna Romanova of All the Russias," Lestocq boomed, before I could stop him. Pompous fart! I thought, a searing heat rising from my neck to my skull, setting me aflame with pain.

There was a brief silence. "How does God know you?" asked the woman behind the door, unimpressed by my title.

"Lizenka," I said, holding on to the gate, steadying myself. My voice broke and I was wracked by a choking cough.

Agatha opened the door wide and spread her arms to embrace me. "My friend the Tsarina's daughter, Lizenka. This is as I know you, too," she said. Her scratchy robe smelled of smoke and camphor; she was lined and drawn. But her blue eyes sparkled, and her smile touched my heart. I felt so relieved to have reached her.

"God, you are skin and bone!" she called. "I'll beef you up, little one. Dinner is ready to be served. You are in luck—we slaughtered a pig just yesterday. But you might want some rest first."

I shivered. "No, Mother. First, I would like to thank God for my safe arrival, if the chapel is still open?"

"It always is. Except there is someone in there now. But you should not be in each other's way. Do join us quickly. You look exhausted." She felt my forehead briefly. I took her hand and kissed it, letting it drop. The Abbess looked at Lestocq. "I have prepared a room for your physician above the stables, where it is nice and warm. Your being a Frenchman, I suppose you look forward to dinner? We have stewed apples from last autumn to go with the pork crackling, which our cook has rubbed with salt."

Lestocq patted his gaunt midriff: "Rubbed with salt? How interesting. This is what we do in Alsace, too. So who am I to say no, *Mère*?" he said, shouldering his saddlebags and smiling. "I have also heard about the quality of your beer."

The Abbess looked flattered and they chatted as she led him away. "Ah, yes. We add toasted white sugar to the barrel, letting it ferment for a week or two. It lightens the drink, I find, and makes it wonderfully frothy."

"In Champagne, too, we use an interesting method to make the wine pearly, shaking the bottles. Let me tell you all about it." As their voices disappeared down the cloister walk, I took the archway toward the chapel, walking slowly and occasionally resting my hand against the wall for support, mopping cold sweat from my brow.

Just a brief prayer, I told myself.

Nothing more.

It was cool and dusty in the chapel, its scent laced with beeswax, myrrh, and frankincense. The carved and studded timber double doors fell shut behind me. The thud they made washed up the aisle to the altar, its echo lapping at the pillars before ebbing away. A feeling of deep calm engulfed me. I dipped my fingertips into the font water, crossing myself, my spirit settling and my soul opening to the surrounding silence. The candles here would burn throughout the night. Thousands of icons framed in solid gold, silver, and gemstones covered the walls, their shine and splendor awe-inspiring. I stood still a moment to catch my breath, but my legs trembled, and my knees buckled as I stood beside one of the first pews. I grabbed hold of it, my bruised knuckles blanching with the effort. The altar blurred. Pain throbbed behind my temples. Memories of Augustus and Petrushka haunted me: merry by dawn, buried by dusk.

Gasping, I sank into the pew, shivering and fastening my cloak over my chest in a vain attempt to feel a bit warmer. My high mud-splattered boots made kneeling difficult, but I took off my flat hat, placed my gloves on the bench, and folded my bare hands, their skin hot with fever. Still my spirit would not settle; instead, I checked my limbs for red scabs, panicking. There were none. The sound of footsteps made me look up.

A man came out of the vestry hidden behind the altar. He wore a monk's dark belted cassock. He was tall, with strong shoulders and narrow hips, so far as I could tell. His dark hair fell to his shoulders, curly and unruly.

I ducked my head. I did not feel like company and wished only to pray.

A low humming sound filled the air. He stood before the altar, tuning his voice, which seemed to make the air throb around him. My hands clasped each other tighter. The sound grew, filling my ears, deep and steady. I forgot my prayer and stared at him in awe: what a gift! The man turned his face to the heavens and spread his arms, starting to sing. The flesh on my arms prickled with goose bumps. In the chapel's unsteady light his faith shone forth, that miraculous voice rising toward the dome's inner cupola in a tone as beautiful as a bronze bell's. My soul followed the sound, spiraling skyward. The golden notes poured from his throat into the stillness of the chapel. There was a river of them, soaking into the barren ground that was my soul. I pressed my fingers to my lips, tears welling at the sheer beauty of his voice. What a gift! I could not help it: I buried my face in my hands and sobbed helplessly, crying so desperately for all I had lost that I noticed neither the sudden silence nor the steps coming down the aisle toward me.

"What are you doing here so late, boy? Should you not be home for supper?" a voice inquired.

I wiped snot and tears from my burning face. The singer stood before my pew; his blue eyes were stern and his black brows furrowed. Hard lines were etched into his forehead, though he was probably not much older than I. *Boy.* My boots and breeches had fooled him. I wanted to answer, but my voice failed me. Instead, I clutched my saddlebag, the sudden movement making the candles flicker. Their flame caught the diamond-studded icon around my throat, the simple leather strings belying its value.

The singer seized my wrist, his touch cool and firm on my feverish skin. "Oh, my God! Look at yourself. You are but a child and already a vile thief! Where have you stolen that amulet? Here, from this church? I'll have your skin!"

No! I shook my head, unable to speak.

"What is hidden in that saddlebag, scoundrel? Your loot?" He grabbed me harder, making me wince. "Shame on you, stealing from the house of God! As young as you are, your soul belongs to the Devil. Let me see." He tore the saddlebag from me, unbuckled and shook it. My dearest belongings tumbled to the chapel's marble floor: a silver cup, in which my mother had served Anoushka and me hot chocolate on the rare evenings she had put us to bed; a velvet-bound book of prayers, the fabric frayed but studded with silver and precious stones, that I had inherited from Aunt Pasha; a chipped ebony-and-ivory cross from Mount Athos—Father had worn it around his neck in Poltava, where it had caught a bullet intended for him—a silk scarf, which Anoushka had embroidered when a child, the stitches large and clumsy. I saw my belongings through his eyes: of course, he took me for a common thief. The incense made me dizzy; the saints' mournful gazes spun around me.

The monk bent and picked up my belongings, scooping them into the open saddlebag with one hand, not letting go of me. "I will take you to Mother Abbess. They will bury you up to your neck and stone you!"

His handsome, stern face seemed to float among the candle flames, making him look like an avenging angel. All the strength seeped from me, leaving me limp: I hung in his grip as he shook me, dropping the saddlebag. Then his hand checked my forehead just as I began to lose consciousness. He caught me as I leaned into him, sighing: smoke, leather, and tobacco scented his cloak.

"Oh, God! You are a girl," he called incredulously. Around me silence and darkness beckoned in eternal welcome.

Yet safe in his arms I floated in a pool of light, like a feather on a lake's silver surface.

An angel will speak to you.

65

For a fortnight I was at death's door, drifting between the earthly and heavenly realms, undecided as to where I belonged. My dreams were ridden by the past, memories blurring: Anoushka and I fleeing the Golosov Ravine; Mother's tears at her failure to produce a male heir; Petrushka offering me Molniya, who fell victim to his love for me later; Anna Ivanovna offering me the icon of St. Nicholas . . . *everything comes at a price*; Father disappearing in a halo of light; Augustus holding me in the Bay of Finland; Menshikov's gaunt and frozen face; Buturlin's mouth gushing blood; Katja Dolgoruky mourning her losses; Ekaterina Ivanovna sneering; Christine smiling dully; Ostermann incalculable in his movements; Maja's cleft mouth mumbling a warning not to get ahead of myself. Once the fever abated, I fell into a deep sleep.

Finally reality regained its hold over me: Abbess Agatha slipped in and out of my cell. "No, I will not read the last rites. She will recover," she insisted to the fearful Lestocq, spoon-feeding me hot chicken broth laced with wine and *smetana*.

He checked my temperature and tapped my chest, hoisting me up to listen to my pained breathing. "There is no blood," he said when checking my phlegm, the relief in his voice palpable.

There was another presence, though, one I was unable to recognize. Someone floated alongside me, bravely, brazenly, crossing the twilight between life and death as soon as the Abbess and Lestocq had departed. Warm fingers held my hand. His touch cooled my fever; he dabbed my parched lips with a cloth soaked in water and vinegar. My soul rose to meet his fingertips as they circled my throat and neck, cleaning me with rosewater and almond milk. When I stirred, he said, "Shhh," holding me tight, as a brother would. To make me fall asleep, he sang to me, his voice a cloak that shielded me against the cold and darkness.

"Don't you dare!" I heard him warn Lestocq when the Frenchman started heating up his cursed cups on an open flame, preparing to bleed me. I felt too weak to open my eyes and protest. The stranger objected for me: "Bleed her? For what reason? She is but a young woman. How can she have bad blood?"

What might have been a fleeting memory lost at sea became an anchor holding me safe on life's ripping, roaring currents.

By midsummer I was back on my feet. Long hours of light still kept the darkness at bay, reducing the night to short, pale hours. The Abbess led me around the monastery's cloistered courtyard, linking elbows, carefully adjusting her steps to mine. Every day I walked a bit farther, soaking up the sunshine, until she led me back to my cell, where I lay and rested. Agatha also offered me a kitten from a stable cat's litter, which I spoiled with leftover *smetana*. The adorable little thing—silky black fur, three white socks, and a white belly—kept on bumping into me: it took me a while to realize that it was blind. I had to dip its nose into the cream to make it feed.

Its helplessness made me love it even more: I felt needed.

Lestocq called on me every day, whether I wished to see him or not, as if there were a future to discuss. Wherever I hid, he found me: late in June I sat in a nook of the cloister's walkway, making the kitten tumble from one palm to the other. He sneaked up on me, appearing out of the blue.

"Tsarevna Elizabeth," he said. "You look well. Soon you will be strong enough to ride again."

"Surely not." The thought of returning to court made my

stomach go cold, be it Moscow or St. Petersburg. I might be shot at during Anna's little morning practice when crossing the Red Square, or serve as fodder for her birds and stinking giant porcupines. Compared to that, staying in a convent was a sensible choice. Anna was right: as things were, I only had a hired Frenchman to count on.

To hide my despair, I held the kitten to my cheek; it purred, closing its veiled eyes with pleasure. Its warmth reminded me of how life simply carried on: the Pecharsky's grounds were teeming. Birds ruled the treetops, calling with the first light of the day, making us curse them despite the beauty of their song. Later on they flitted across the courtyard, beaks filled with grass for their nests. Ducklings and goslings waddled about, getting under everyone's feet; cygnets dotted the banks of the Dnieper. In the stables calves sucked on my thumbs; I held the lambs to be branded and even helped the blacksmith turn a foal in her mother's belly. It was born safely; we shared the mare's pride once the little one rose, unsure of its own wobbly legs. I felt like a child again, back in Kolomenskoye.

"I am not sure I will ever return to court," I said.

Lestocq stuck his hands in his pockets, weighing my words. "Of course you will. Don't you know who you are?"

"Oh, I do. Who I *am* is the problem."

"Others would be delighted."

"Well, ask them to do your bidding then."

"Are you afraid?" He bent until he was eye to eye with me. His gaze pinned me to the cloister wall; the cold of the stone seeped into my back. "Think about it. How did your father feel when the Streltsy slaughtered his family in front of his eyes? When his half-sister tried to assassinate him? When the clergy turned on him, and his realm cursed him for his reforms? What were his thoughts the night before the battle at Poltava, which was to determine the fate of Russia forever? We do not know, yet one thing is for sure: he didn't run and hide!"

"He was not a woman."

Lestocq gave me a surprisingly warm smile. "Your gender is of no importance. After all, you are the Tsarina's daughter."

"My mother had my father and the support of his cronies." I fought back tears. "I have no one. You have seen my loneliness at court."

He smiled with the same daring that had brought him, a Huguenot, to St. Petersburg in the first place, and which had convinced Mother to end his banishment to Kazan to join my retinue. "Win them over then. And take heart: you still have me."

"You mean, I have Versailles?"

He shrugged. "*Soit.* That is more than most people will ever have. You ought to return. There might be a war against the French as the quarrel about the Polish throne intensifies. But even if Versailles fights Russia in Danzig, it still wants you back at the Tsarina's side."

"When I last looked, I was a Tsarevna, not a French princess."

"Last time you looked is already much too long ago," he countered.

"What's the urgency?" I tickled the kitten's soft underbelly, smiling at its utter abandon: paws stretched, eyes closed, purring with pleasure.

"The Tsarina Anna will have to name her successor. She needs an heir. Or should that be an heiress?"

"And that would be me?"

"Who else? Sweden and France are ready to back your claim to be Crown Princess once more: Tsesarevna."

His words were high treason. "They are both enemies of Russia! What, I wonder, am I supposed to do in return? Everything comes at a price."

"Well, yes. They demand the return of the Baltics, which your father took in the Great Northern War."

I carefully placed the kitten on the floor and rose to my feet, fighting the lightness in my head. "Listen, Lestocq," I said, seizing his lapels. "If you suggest ever again that I surrender an *arshin* of land for which a drop of Russian blood has been shed, you can pack your stuff and leave."

He looked at me, at first unsure if I was serious, but then seemed surprised at my determination. "Then you'll be lonelier than ever. And penniless."

"You are the mercenary, not I. I should rather starve than be a traitor to my country. It's called honor, Lestocq, a word that must be foreign to you," I said hotly, letting go of him.

He stroked back his hair, adjusted his coat, and cleared his throat. "Well, then, return to court for Russia's sake."

"Better not let Ostermann hear those words."

"Ostermann will not live forever." Lestocq smiled. "You have to be seen at court; people must not forget your existence. A Chinese delegation is approaching Moscow. They left Peking to celebrate Petrushka's wedding but arrive for Anna's celebration of six months as Tsarina. Also the Shah of Persia is looking for a bride for his eldest son. Apparently two thousand men and sixteen elephants, laden with gifts, are also closing in on Moscow. We could do with replenishing our coffers."

"Are you serious?" I frowned. "You know my stance. I have rarely seen happiness arise from such marriages."

"It will be interesting, nevertheless. One must think ahead, at least a step or two." He might as well have poured a bucket of icy water over me.

"Even if I were ready, how is my horse?" I said, to gain time.

"It's in the stable, all fattened up, ready for the ride back to Moscow. Eventually, I mean," he added, as my face fell. "That is, soon. Very soon. The best day would have been yesterday, actually."

"I shall see for myself." I scooped up the blind kitten and placed it in Lestocq's cupped hands. "Here. Be careful it doesn't bump into the pillars, will you?" The clever thing meowed and clawed his fine, nervy physician's hand.

"Ouch!" he complained.

I would have giggled had not his words about Father already wormed their way into my mind: *he didn't run and hide.*

The June sun cast shifting shadows over the cloister's flagstones as I stepped out into the walled rose garden. The air was heavy with scent and filled with the buzzing of bees. The white gravel of the pathway was blinding. Trying to calm the anger I felt at the dressing-down Lestocq had just given me, I turned into the monastery's courtyard. Here nuns were returning from the market, the novices carrying baskets that were as full as the Mother Superior's purses: the monastery sold as much as it bought.

The air was laced with smoke as the blacksmith hammered away, shaping a hot, gleaming iron bar. A carpenter planed heaps of rough timber into smooth planks for another outhouse, pigsty, or chicken coop, while butchering the tune that he whistled. The tailor sat cross-legged at his work, his tongue sticking out between his lips and his eyes squinting as he threaded a needle. I crossed over to the stables; their rooves were freshly thatched, and their walls whitewashed with lime. A cat turned lazily on the warm cobblestones, her belly for once big not with kittens but the mice she had caught. Abbess Agatha ran a tight but happy ship. Damn Lestocq! The day I left here I would lose paradise.

At the trough outside the stable, a rider had arrived. He tethered his low, sturdy horse and pulled off his shirt to wash himself. I gasped: his back and shoulders were covered with scars from the lashes of a knotted whip. Some of them had paled and thickened, looking like bark. Others crisscrossed the shoulders like a fresh map of crime and punishment; blood and pus seeped onto the tanned skin. It reminded me of how Buturlin had looked upon leaving the Trubetzkoi Bastion. My heart was in my mouth at the memories the sight evoked.

"What happened to you?" I could not help but ask.

The man turned and gave me a ready smile. It was in stark

contrast to the deep lines on his young face. This was the man from church; the monk who had saved my life. The memory of his strong arms carrying me gave me goose bumps.

I banished the thought immediately. This man was out of bounds.

66

"Are you better, Lizenka?" He pulled a coarse sheet from his saddlebags, which were stuffed to the brim. *Lizenka.* I hesitated a split second, yet haughtiness had never been a flaw of mine. He, however, noticed my reaction. "That is what the Abbess said I should call you, but please correct me if it is wrong."

He did not know who I was, I understood: Lestocq and the Abbess had kept it a secret. What a gift! "That is indeed my name. I am much better. Thank you for carrying me out of the chapel." I smiled at him. "You saved my life."

He placed his folded shirt on the trough's edge. "It was my pleasure. You were as light as a child. Now your cheeks are round again," he said, not looking at my cheeks at all. I blushed, aware of the simple white blouse that had slipped off my shoulders to show the alabaster skin beneath. Over it I wore a bodice of unbleached linen, laced as tightly as a maid's. He averted his eyes; his sudden shyness stirred me. It contrasted with all the brazen courtiers I knew, forever looking to take advantage. Even Buturlin, for all his true desire and devotion, had not lacked ambition. "Don't thank me but God in His mercy," the man told me. He wrapped the ends of the cloth around his hands, pulling it taut, to dry his shoulders. As the rough fabric touched the wounds, he winced.

"Don't!" I was shocked to see fresh blood. "Let me do that." He hesitated, but I ordered: "Turn. You'll have to lean forward, otherwise you are too tall for me to reach." He sucked his teeth as I blotted dry the fresh wounds. "Who did this to you and why? To think that you called me a thief who needed punishment! Did the Abbess give you a knouting? Or have you chastised yourself? I thought monks were merciful and just."

"Me, a monk? God, no! Life is too short for that."

"Well, then?" I asked, dabbing some more. The number of scars spoke of years of abuse.

"My father knouted me every day of my life, for as long as I can remember, up to this morning when I took my leave."

"Why would he beat you like this?" I dropped the sheet, aghast.

"All men want their sons to follow in their footsteps."

I fell silent. My father had killed Alexey for refusing to yield to his overwhelming demands.

"Did you hear me sing in the chapel?" the man asked, his voice proud and his eyes bright, betraying a passion that was wonderfully different from simply wanting to rule or ruin others. What a blessing to know such a purpose. I was almost jealous. I was unable to think of a calling for myself that was not high treason and punishable by death.

"I did. It was unforgettable. Divine."

His face lit up. "Thank you. You see, my father thinks I should be a shepherd and a cruel drunkard, like him. In fact he opposed the Tsarina's orders."

The cloth almost slipped again from my fingers. "What sort of orders?"

"I shall tell you. But, please, go on—I like your touch," he said, little lights dancing in his eyes. "My story is proof that there is a God." He laughed, showing strong white teeth and dimples in his cheeks as he raked back his black curly hair with his fingers.

"Tell me all." I eyed him shyly. He had muscles in places I had not thought possible: his body was like an iron spring; his taut, tanned skin glistening.

"If you share my joy, it doubles." He smiled and crossed his arms on his bare chest. "Today is the last time that my father will ever beat me. I am leaving here."

"What does your mother say about that?"

"She died last year, having been brought to bed sixteen times. Of all those pregnancies, only my brother Kyril and I were to live. My father, the randy goat, killed her; I apologize if those words are not suitable for a maiden's tender ears." He bowed slightly to me. "I hope only to save my brother from him one day. Kyril is so different from me, but we understand each other perfectly."

"My elder sister and I were as different as apples from pears. Still, I miss her desperately, every day," I said. "She, too, died in childbirth. Her son grows up far away from me, a stranger."

His eyes were full of compassion when he said: "Being a woman is a punishment. I hope life will treat you better, even if you can't leave here as I can."

Leave. That word again. I felt my good spirits start to fade. "Leave? To do what?"

"The only thing I can. I will join the newly founded Imperial Choir."

"No!" I was shocked but also flooded by delight. "How did the Tsarina hear about you?"

"The village priest, who had schooled me and my voice, invited me to sing when an Imperial messenger stopped by. He was on his way to Moscow from France; the Tsarina Anna had run out of champagne and ordered another hundred thousand bottles," he said. "Apparently she bathes in it, together with her German lover. A foreigner calls the shots in Russia. I hate that."

"What a silly, nasty rumor. Nobody calls the shots but her," I said fiercely.

"How would you know, little Lizenka? Do not lower your eyes. I love them: big and blue and wonderfully lively. I shan't ever forget them." As our gazes locked my heart skipped a beat.

"So what happened after the messenger stopped by?"

"I was ordered to come to Moscow. I was thanking God for His mercy when I met you." He took the sheet from me, storing it in his saddlebag. "And thank you, too. Compassion and kindness are rare qualities in Russia."

The rarest thing in Russia was a man in whose favor the wheel of fortune spun, but pointing out his luck to him might have spoiled it. He looked at my hands: "What soft little paws you have, Lizenka. Are you waiting on a highborn lady? Did she pay that foreign quack to heal you?"

"No, no," I said hastily. "I work in the parlor, making *kefir*, cheese, and *quark*."

"Do you know how to make a creamy *pashka* pudding and *kulich*, the sweet bread?" he asked. "If so, my memory of you shall be forever sweet."

"Sure," I fibbed, longing to impress him. I was confident that if I had to, I could bake the perfect sweet Easter bread and whip up the sweet curd pudding that usually accompanied it. "Nobody makes a more delicious *kulich* than I—packed with fragrant spices, dried fruit, and even citrus peel, if I can get my hands on it. If I make *pashka* to go with it, I use only the thickest, most creamy milk for the curd, and masses of candied fruit, almonds, and whey butter instead of honey." I had watched Illinchaya at work often enough to know how she had made the delicacies.

"Is that so?" He slid back into his shirt, lacing it up, hiding his smooth chest. "That's a big claim. My mother made the best *kulich* I know."

"I'll take your wager."

My heart pounded as he weighed his answer; I so wanted him not to go when I had just found him. This was a decent man, and they seemed to be rarer than black snow. "Find me in the convent kitchen tomorrow afternoon, if you dare," I teased him, knowing he could not resist my challenge.

"So be it. You'd better get going. A good *kulich* takes time. If you do it properly, of course." He winked and lifted the heavy saddle off his gelding—a farmer's horse, thickset and low, with heavy, hairy hooves—shouldering the load with ease. He led the animal away, and I called after him: "What is your name? I only bake for men who present themselves properly."

He bowed, laughing. "You are right. Where are my manners? Alexis Razum."

"*Razum.* The mild one?"

"Indeed, Lizenka."

I smiled. "So be it then, Alexis Razumovsky."

My mare stood hidden away in the last box. Her straw was fresh; she had had good feed, and her coat was shiny. She whinnied with joy to see me. Her warm nostrils nuzzled my palm searchingly. "Sorry, I'll bring you an apple later," I promised, combing her tawny mane with my fingers, her large chestnut eyes questioning me. A blanket had been draped over her silver-gray coat—the hue of a moonlit night—to hide her Imperial brand. Abbess Agatha had gone to great lengths to keep my stay a secret, allowing me time to heal.

The thought of returning to court made the blood rush through my veins, for reasons that were entirely different from the ones I had expressed only an hour ago. But first I needed to bake the world's best *kulich*.

67

Vasilisa the cook was out at the market when I sneaked into the kitchen the next day. The maids greeted me before getting on with their work. I was glad not to encounter the mistress of the kitchen: Vasilisa was a giantess of a woman, her hands big as shovels, abundant graying hair hidden under a floral headscarf. She had a tongue even sharper than her knives and a round belly that strained against her plain robe and starched apron. She ruled the Pecharsky slaughterhouse, dairy, and bakery—as well as the fabulously stocked cellar. Its impossibly large key dangled from her belt.

I squinted as I opened a smaller storeroom: sunlight fell through a tiny window placed high up in the wall. The shelves groaned under jars of oils, vinegar and pickled beetroot, gherkins, and onions, as well as walnuts and stewed fruit to be eaten like jam on fresh warm bread. Damsons, cherries, apricots, and peaches were all delicacies of the Ukraine. Sacks of buckwheat, flour, oats, and barley were piled up next to bags of dried red, green, and white pulses. Cabbage cured in a good dozen barrels and countless bundles of dried herbs—parsley, thyme, chives, dill, bay, and sage— were strung from the ceiling. Dried forest mushrooms hung in long, knotted chains, waiting to be soaked for soups, stews, and sauces. I climbed on a footstool to reach the candied fruit that Vasilisa kept on the highest shelf—novices were renowned for their sweet tooth, and so she hid it away. Of the whey butter, which took days to thicken in the summer pastures, I naughtily took a whole bar.

My arms full, I kicked the door shut behind me and piled everything on the long kitchen table, which normally sat a good twenty people—the kitchen staff—once the nuns and their visitors had been served. Its scrubbed wood showed countless scratches from its many years of service. In the heat of the kitchen, I was grateful for my blouse's low neckline; Vasilisa had baked bread, and the oven still glowed. Loaves were resting on the far end of the table; the late-afternoon sun made their crusts shine.

Right. I had the candied fruit and the whey butter. As I had no curd to make *pashka*, I scooped the cream off the top of the bowls in the dairy, hoping to keep it as thick as possible, just as I had watched the maids doing. I whipped it stiff with a bundle of tied twigs, licking my fingertips: delicious! Now I had to get on with baking the *kulich*. I would surprise Alexis, I thought joyfully. When had I last felt *anything* as real as my excitement now?

Illinchaya, our nurse in Kolomenskoye, had hummed a song to remind herself of the recipe, and I still remembered the verse: "Two sticks butter or lard, soft not hard. Six eggs do whisk, but never too brisk. Use flour abound, it makes everything sound. Sugar on top, don't say stop." The half-dozen eggs that I had taken from the basket next to the oven lay close to hand. The monastery's chickens—silly birds that put up a terrific fight for each egg, scratching, flapping, and pecking—laid all day round. I cracked them into a large porcelain bowl, scattering the shells carelessly over the table. Next, I needed the sugar, Vasilisa's treasure. I inched it down from between sacks of pepper, mustard seeds, and saffron, and sifted heaps of it into the eggs. Vasilisa would have my hide if she knew—but she never would, so I powdered in a little bit more in a soft, even layer. I was such a master baker!

My cheeks flushed with pride as I creamed together eggs and sugar, making a foamy mess. It did not look too bad when I added the flour from my raised hands—"It needs air," Illinchaya would say—making the table look as if a snowstorm had raged around it. All the while the butter melted in a heavy cast-iron pan on the oven. Ouch! I burned my thumb lifting it clear, then poured the golden liquid into my batter before adding the flour, gently, cup by cup, so it took in air. Pails of fresh, foaming milk stood in a shady corner of the kitchen. I spooned a bit off into a bowl, adding the yeast—a blend of flour meal and water that stood fermenting close to the oven's warmth—and mixed it in well. There! Now it just needed to rise.

A couple of hours later, when Vasilisa and the maids were napping before the preparations for supper started—this task and clearing up afterward kept them up into the early hours of the morning—I was back. First I dropped the beautifully risen dough into a copper *kulich* form, smoothing the top. Then I placed it in the oven, which blazed away day and night, heating water for the samovars, roasting a couple of lambs, and baking the Abbess's favorite cookies. The bar of whey butter was still out and quite hard, so I placed it next to the oven to soften. I could not resist eating quite a bit of it before the *kulich* was almost ready.

"Here you are!"

The voice startled me, catching me with my thieving fingers in my mouth. Alexis Razumovsky stood in the doorway. I sucked my fingertips clean, seeing his eyes darken before he averted his gaze. "You are late," I said, smiling. "Typical. Men have that infallible way of arriving when all the work is done, and the food is ready. In half an hour, I promise, you shall taste the best *kulich* ever."

His presence filled the room. My cheeks burned. I moved away from the oven, but, if anything, I felt even hotter when he approached, checking on the *kulich* by opening the oven's hatch door: "I wouldn't call this ready. Show-off!"

I felt dizzy, both from the heat and his closeness. How beautiful his hands were, tanned and strong, with long, slim fingers, pronounced knuckles, and short, clean nails.

"Let us see," I said, slipping on quilted oven mittens and lifting out the mold, flames licking toward me. Wiping my damp forehead with one forearm, I placed the *kulich* on the table. I brushed my hands on my dark skirt, careful not to spoil its beautiful floral embroidery.

"You like whey butter, don't you?" he said.

I tucked a stray curl behind my ear. "How do you know?"

The open collar of his casually laced shirt showed the smooth skin of his chest. He had the wiry strength of a shepherd, accustomed to climbing rugged mountain slopes to rescue a lamb and to defending his flock from wolves and eagles. Gently he traced the curve of my upper lip. My breath stalled as my gaze became caught up in his. "You have some crumbs here," he said, his voice tender.

"Remove them."

"I can't manage with my fingers."

"Well, then." I raised my face. He lowered his. My lips parted as I felt him searching my mouth, tenderly, without haste. His breath was sweet and fresh as he kissed me once more, careful, and chaste. "Got it. It's wonderfully sweet, like you."

"Let me taste," I whispered, going on tiptoe. I saw his surprise as I kissed him hungrily. Together we stumbled backward. He lifted me to sit on the kitchen table, kissing me, cupping my face, and caressing first my hair and then my bare shoulders, where the blouse had slipped. I arched my neck, sighing, as his lips found my throat, sending flashes of lightning through my body. My quickening breath made him cup my breasts, lower his head, and taste my buds through the blouse's thin linen. The fabric was moist, clinging to my hard pink nipples, a sight which made him groan. I remembered myself at last, wriggled away, and tucked up my stray curls, trying in vain to adjust the blouse, blushing. He would think me a girl of easy virtue! He tore himself away from me, breathing heavily.

"I am sorry. This is not right," he said. "I am soon off to Moscow forever, and you are a good girl. I shall not leave you shamed.

In Kiev many a good man might wed a sweet parlormaid." He gave me a last, tender kiss before placing my palm on his pounding heart. "I knew it. You little thief."

I cleared my throat and slipped off the table. My legs shook but I steadied my voice. "How about some *kulich* now?"

"That would be lovely."

It slipped from the mold easily, all spongy and steaming. He smiled at my proud expression when I piled on the thick cream, sprinkling it with layers of candied fruit and whey butter. I chose from the block the long, blunt knife that Vasilisa used to cut cakes. "Do you want the first slice?"

"As I will be the judge of who has won our wager, gladly."

I placed a large slice on a plate. How perfectly fluffy the sweet dough was, and how stiff the cream—I felt so pleased to see him eat it. Alexis chewed—and almost choked, coughing, bringing up the *kulich,* and running to spit it out in the bucket near the fire. He was still retching when he looked up.

"What is it?" I asked, a deep blush creeping over my throat and up to my face.

"My God, Lizenka, you used salt instead of sugar!" He wiped his mouth.

"I am so sorry," I stuttered, then mirth rose from deep inside me. This was so funny! "Now I know why Vasilisa keeps the sugar next to the pepper!" I laughed and laughed, bent double and leaning against the table, holding my sides.

"Are you laughing at me? After almost poisoning a good man?" he asked.

"I am," I gasped, wiping my eyes.

"Just you wait!" He came up to me, seizing me and kissing me again. His lips sought mine with shocking passion. We devoured each other, limbs entwined, laughing and kissing even more. "You've won!" he whispered, coming up for air.

From outside we heard heavy steps and a woman cursing under her breath, fumbling with keys.

"It's Vasilisa. She'll have our hides!"

"Run! She's much too fat to catch us." He took my hand, and we darted out of the back door, racing up some steps and crossing the courtyard, only stopping once we were well beyond the stables.

"Is it soon you must leave?" I asked, catching my breath. There was no time for playing games. I fought back tears when he drew me in, holding me warm and close, cupping my face. "Tomorrow. At dawn."

I saw tears in his eyes, too, and swallowed hard: any time would have been too soon, be it now or in twenty years.

"Promise to forget me," he said, holding my hands to his chest.

"I promise," I lied, choking on tears.

"Do you? Well, I won't manage to do the same," he said, stroking my hair. "I have nothing to offer you, Lizenka. Go, meet a good man, and have a dozen strong, healthy sons who adore you. May God bless you." I let him kiss me for what we thought was the last time, deeply and desperately. I was sure the memory of this beautiful moment would stay with me forever.

When I was a child, my father took me to the Kunstkamera, his collection of nature's misfits and miracles, such as a fetus with a fishtail; a puppy with two heads; the beheaded and preserved skull of one of his mistresses, the Scotswoman Marie Hamilton; as well as the skeleton of a hunchbacked giant. What I remembered most, though, was an iron that drew another piece of metal close, irresistibly so: Father called it a magnet. I could have left things there with Alexis Razumovsky: a brief chance encounter, sweet but soon over.

Instead, still drawn to him as if magnetized, I sought out Lestocq.

Lestocq and Abbess Agatha sat in her study, sampling last autumn's ham. He spoke with his mouth full. "The smoked ham has merits over the cooked one for flavor, but I like the fleshiness of the latter."

"Let me taste it, too!" Agatha giggled, washing down each bite with a sip of fortified wine. Her cheeks were blooming. Both of them looked up guiltily when I appeared on the threshold. Lestocq rose, taking in the sight of my flushed face.

"What is it, Tsarevna?"

"I am ready to return to court."

"When, Tsarevna?" He angled for another piece of ham, filling the Abbess's glass anew while eyeing the almost empty bottle. "Do we have more of this, Abbess Agatha?"

"Lestocq!" I ordered sharply.

He sighed. "All right, all right. There is the impending war in Poland to consider. Travel is not safe. Also nobody really knows how far the Chinese have advanced. The Shah's brother might never come. Haste is the worst adviser."

"We ride at dawn," I said curtly, leaving them to it. "I have found another traveler who is going the same way."

68

Lestocq had the good grace either to fall behind Alexis and me or to canter ahead, scouting for highwaymen and other dangers. The summer had grown much too hot, making both men and animals moody and unpredictable. He was armed to the hilt, looking like a weapons dealer in the *gostiny dvor*: pistols, daggers, and blades were concealed in his jacket and waistcoat, as well as stuck in his belt and even the ribbon of his hat.

Alexis had accepted my explanation for Lestocq's presence as easily as the excuse I gave him for our journey: "How good of your Moscow cousin to send her quack to accompany you. So you will work for her? What an unexpected turn of fortune that we can ride together," he said as our horses cantered side by side. "What is Moscow like, do you think?"

"Huge. And wild. Or so I have heard. Not that I would know, of course," I added hastily, not wanting to blow my cover. "I believe that the Kremlin, where the Tsarina lives, is at its very heart."

"That is where I will work. I will sing in the Imperial chapel. Just imagine its splendor and glory."

"I wish I could." Was this taking things too far? The moment to tell him the truth was fast approaching, but I could not bring myself to alter the mood between us by telling him my real identity. I decided to trust to the same fate that had sent him my way. The right time to tell him the truth would soon be upon us. Until then. . . . He reached across, tenderly stroking my gloved hand. "I shall tell you all about it when we meet in Moscow. I pray to God that will be often."

He kissed my hand without halting his horse.

Agatha had provided us with hard cheeses, cured meats, and pickled vegetables and fruit. Alexis was a brilliant fisherman as well, so we never went hungry. While Lestocq tended to the horses and I stoked a fire with kindling, Alexis struck up our tents, then set out with his spear and returned with salmon, eel, or perch. He sliced both fish and flesh very thinly—whistling while doing so, finding happiness in the smallest of things—and we ate it raw. "Salt instead of sugar, eh?" He winked at me, chuckling. "Thank God you have plenty of other qualities!"

Lestocq ate in silence, watching us with his dark, assessing eyes.

Not far from Moscow we pitched camp for the night in a clearing. The fire was burning bright, and Alexis had spiked a fat salmon on the spit. We had finished Agatha's provisions, except for some preserved Crimea lemons; their acerbic sweetness blended with a rub of salt, pepper, and wild garlic for the fish's skin. Already there was a heavenly scent coming from the roasting fish; the salmon's glazed eyes popped, showing that it was ready to be eaten. Our last bottles of the monastery's famous beer were cooling, stuck in the muddy riverbed. The sky's silver-gray edges were darkening to charcoal. The brightest of the White Nights were over now. Our campfire lit the men's faces eerily.

"Care for a *partie*?" Lestocq asked, his gaze challenging as he flicked his Tarot cards.

Alexis, who had guarded sheep against predators since childhood, sensing their approach in the darkness, recognized the change in atmosphere between us. He frowned. "What are those? I abhor games of chance."

"Amazing that a shepherd's boy who spent time in a priest's household would know any of them," said Lestocq.

"Priests, too, are mere men. Father Gregory loved a good card game, even if we played for pieces of moldy cheese. That was the extent of the sinfulness in his household," Alexis chuckled.

"Tarot is not a game of chance, boy. It's the game of life." Lestocq fanned out his cards, looking rapt. "Choose three and turn them over," he goaded. "Let us see what fate has in store for our handsome nightingale."

Alexis picked three cards. *Do not!* I wanted to plead in sudden fear, just as he snatched them up, saying in a voice laced with contempt, "Look what I do with these cards. Devil's work!" Disgusted, he flung them into the fire. Lestocq leaped at them as the flames curled the cards' edges black and their bright colors fell to ashes.

"My voice is a gift from God." Alexis touched his throat. "What else than His blessing would I need? Send me a demon who tempts me to know my fate, and I'll kick its furry arse."

I stared at him: yes, that was what a man like him would do to the Leshy, if the evil spirit dared to show its ugly face and mutter its terrible prophecies to torment him. Crazy laughter broke from me, but Lestocq was furious. The Tarot pack was one of his greatest treasures. "How dare you, farmer's boy!" He slung his coat around his shoulders. "I am not hungry. You can eat your stolen salmon on your own." Nobody held him back, which infuriated him even more: he stomped into his tent, pitched away from the fire, facing the forest.

"Very well." Alexis shrugged with a bright smile. "How about a cold sweet beer?" Before I could answer, he slipped off his boots and waded in to retrieve a bottle. Back at the fire the golden, foaming drink matched my mood. "To fate's gifts," I toasted, and he raised a bottle, eyes gleaming. After we had feasted on the fish's pink, fat flesh, Alexis dispersed the smoldering coals. In the hot weather wildfires could spring up suddenly, devouring acres of land in no time. A full moon rose, and in the reeds a frog concert started. The fire burned down, bathing us in its warm glow.

"Your skin looks like fresh *smetana*," he said, close to me, his voice sleepy. "I wonder, will you taste as sweet?"

"Why not try? It's worth the gamble."

"Nothing to lose." He leaned in, our breaths mingling sweetly, before our lips touched. How I had longed for this. As he kissed me, a current seared me, as when I had seen lightning striking a tree, setting the brittle wood aflame. His lips were soft, and I loved his warmth. My whole being dissolved as he pushed back the collar of my riding shirt so he could kiss my throat. "Ever since that day in the kitchen, I have dreamed of doing this," he whispered. I dissolved under his tenderness and longed for his next touch.

He gently lowered me on his cloak, its fabric warm against my back. My boots and breeches came off, and I lay there offering myself to his hungry eyes. "How beautiful you are, Lizenka. Another gift that God has made me." He tasted every inch of me, sending shivers over my pale skin. I gave a muffled scream when his tongue flicked over my sweet, slippery flesh. "Shh," he cautioned with a smile, "we don't need that snooty Frenchman back here!" It was the sweetest torture: I bit my lips, helpless with lust, as he parted my thighs further and let a finger slip into me. Starlight danced in my eyes; my blood seared my veins as I came, rearing and carelessly shouting out, Lestocq or not. I sighed as he lifted me up, his hands digging into my flesh. I sat astride, slipping onto him, gasping as I felt him, bit by bit, his adoring gaze mirroring the stars above us.

"Now," I sighed. "Please—"

He let me slide backward. In the dying light of the flames—eyes closed, naked chest broad, tapering to slim hips—he looked to be molded from bronze. Desire washed over me anew as he seized me. My back arched, and my head tilted as he made me move: slowly at first, but then ruthlessly, my body stretching toward him, until he buried his face in my breasts, their skin luminous. Each of his moves made me plead for more, and I whispered words I had not thought possible, not caring what he would think. When he came, he held me pressed against him, both our skins drenched. I hung on his neck, utterly sated, until we lay, panting, our eyes closed. The earth had opened, swallowing the world as I had known it.

"Come here, Lizenka," Alexis said tenderly and wrapped me in his coat when I shivered. He sat me up by the fire, pulling me close. As we gazed at the night sky, a shooting star lit up the darkness, so bright and so big that even the fireworks at Anna Ivanovna's Coronation paled by comparison.

"Quick, make a wish," I said. "But you mustn't tell me what it is."

"I need not," he said, his gaze earnest, kissing my forehead. "You know what I wish for. I pray that this wish be granted." I snuggled up to him while he caressed the nape of my neck. I started to cry then, and he kissed the tears from my cheeks. "What is it, Lizenka?" he whispered.

"I am so happy. I never expected to live like this."

"Me neither. Ever since you poisoned the *kulich* and just laughed, I knew that you were the sweetest thing—ever."

"One question though," I said with a naughty smile.

"Yes?"

"Where does a shepherd learn to make love like that?"

His hand slid down between my thighs, brushing my pubic hair. "From the sheep." He grinned. "Their coat is just as fair and curly."

I giggled, but he said: "A question back."

"Yes?"

"Where does a sweet parlormaid learn to speak like you?"

"Oh, you know. Butter wouldn't melt and all that," I smiled.

He laughed so hard he had to wipe tears from his eyes, then he kissed my fingers. "But I do worry. We must not do this again for as long as we are not married. What if I shame you?"

I hesitated. "You won't. A doctor once told me I am barren."

There was a moment of silence. What man did not want children, and, best of all, a son? He might end things now, I feared, and braced myself for his next words.

"Good," he said instead. "My mother died in childbed. It should not happen to the woman I love."

"Love?" I whispered, wide-eyed.

He cupped my face in his hands. "Yes. I am falling in love with you, Lizenka. Deeply, truly."

"Me too."

"I will find a way for us to be together in Moscow, even when I live in the Kremlin. Trust me."

"I do," I said, knowing full well that it was I, and not he, who needed to find a way to join the court in the Kremlin. If it were up to the Tsarina, I should live isolated and shunned in Izmailov. We slept, bodies entwined, warmed by the last embers, and woke with the first light.

"Good morning." Alexis kissed the tip of my nose. "This is the first day of our new lives. If it were not for that guy in his tent, I'd show you the best way to start it."

Lestocq brewed strong coffee for us without a mention of the night before. I did not care that he knew what had happened. This was my life. As I mounted the saddle, I was sore from Alexis's lust and sought his gaze. He smiled and blew me a kiss. I could not wait for the evening. All I wanted was to lie with him forever. After a lifetime of struggling in quicksand, I had finally stepped onto firm ground.

69

We reached the Sparrow Hills two evenings later. Far beneath us Moscow stretched out along the horizon, its thousand spires piercing the skies, thin smoke rising from countless chimneys, the Kremlin a dark heart in the coiling labyrinth. Alexis looked awestruck. He was riding to meet his fate. Lestocq barely hid his delight at our parting, merely nodding to Alexis when the two of us rode off to Izmailov. I forbade myself from turning round to see him disappear; his horse's hooves retreating was the saddest sound.

Although I was ready to undertake many things, I had no idea how to reveal my identity to Alexis. Lestocq was right: if Tsarina Anna made me her heiress, things might be easier. I knew what I had to work toward. I had to be the Tsesarevna once more.

As we arrived in Izmailov we were met by a shocking scene. The orchards, in which the trees had recently been carefully pruned so as to encourage larger fruit, lay sawn down and ransacked, goats gnawing at the stumps; the branches had recently served for firewood. The neighboring fields and flower beds had been trampled, the earth deeply rutted by vehicles. Some of the cattle that had been crossbred to obtain a stronger strain were running free; the rest had ended up on the spit. The carefully cleared brooks had been turned into open sewers. Fish drifted belly up, their corpses caught in a web of wilting water lilies. The path to the once magnificent

Babylon maze was so trodden down it looked like an alleyway. All the ancient yews had been felled.

"Oh my God!" Lestocq reined in his horse. Those were as good as the first words he had spoken to me since we had parted from Alexis. I had been silent, too: fearing what might come, while smiling at what had been.

I stood in my stirrups, shielding my eyes. Izmailov Palace still rose dreamlike from its island, which was separated from the parkland by a moat and a hundred-*arshin*-long bridge. Yet all around countless tents were pitched, and fires glowed in the early evening's blue hour, tarnishing the air with smoke and the stench of cabbage or pea soup. Voices rose—laughter, squabbles, curses, songs. We rode on, toward the middle of the busy encampment, where one tall, wide tent rose proudly above the rest. Its brightly patterned flaps were stunningly embroidered and the timber posts carved. Persian rugs lay on the ground, and exquisite furniture stood carelessly dotted about: graceful marquetry desks and sofas and chairs covered with furs and velvet throws. Servants swarmed on all sides, looking like birds of paradise in their livery of silver cloth with green trimming. They served food and drink or lugged more firewood to feed the huge pit in the middle of the tent, all the while hurrying as if a stern, invisible eye were watching them.

"What is going on, Lestocq?" I had become used to him knowing everything.

"Schwartz sent me a messenger pigeon to the monastery, but I thought it was a joke! The Tsarina is camping out here until her new palace at Annenhof is finished. The building site has been ravaged by fire twice already, but the builders restarted from scratch both times."

Izmailov had been my last refuge from the madness of court. What else could she take from me? My chest tightened. I must keep Alexis safe from her.

A servant pinned back the Imperial tent's flap further, revealing

a giant birdcage complete with a man-size perch on which we saw
a human figure, dressed up as a bird. Who was that? Beyond him
courtiers in astonishing finery formed a circle, while Anna and de
Biron welcomed a group of about thirty men and women, travelers
from the look of it, since they were even dustier than we were. The
man in the cage swung on his perch, making pecking motions, while
the gossiping courtiers took absolutely no notice of our arrival.

I clicked my tongue and eased the reins. No one could ever take
the past weeks away from me. If I had been broken before, Alexis
had mended me. I owed him.

A sentry led my horse away, as servants stuck torches in cast-iron
holders before Anna's splendid tent, shedding golden light into the
gathering dusk. The guard eyed us suspiciously: Lestocq was right.
I had left it too long to make clear who I was—a Tsarevna of All the
Russias.

"Gack, gack! Gack! Chirp! Peep, peep." I took a proper look at
the giant cage and recoiled, aghast. Locked inside was Prince Alexis
Dolgoruky, whose ancestors had founded Moscow, who had survived my father's fury when he had supported the usurping Regent
Sophia's claim, as well as when he had been a staunch Old Believer
and Petrushka's godfather, seeking to promote a new form of government that might befit Russia. Yet attempting to curtail Anna
Ivanovna's powers had been pushing his luck too far. His hair had
been torn off and he lacked a couple of teeth. His face was bruised,
and his body, in its bright, feathered costume, looked withered.
I stared as he flapped his arms like wings. Then he beat his head
against a large, round mirror that dangled on a chain from the top
of the cage, sending it spinning with each movement. I was appalled by the sight. As much as I disliked him for the humiliation
that he had made me suffer, and for what he had wanted to do to
Russia and my father's legacy, there was something too sinister for
words at work here.

"Gack, gack!" Dolgoruky smacked his lips, eyes fixed on us in warning before he bent to pick at some seeds that were scattered on the cage's floor. I gave him a tight nod. Anna and de Biron had been swallowed up among the new arrivals, who spoke loudly and gesticulated. The courtiers, too, shouted as if spurring somebody on. I craned my neck: a miniature racecourse had been set up on the ground by positioning some goblets and string. Half a dozen crayfish crawled for their lives toward the crudely drawn finishing line. A young man who struck me by his pale, affected beauty—his cheeks and lips were painted crimson—observed the race, fists clenched. He roared at the top of his lungs, jumped up and punched the air, jubilant, before picking up his crayfish. "Mine won! Your wagers, please," he demanded. His footman collected the winnings from the other players, and shocking sums changed hands; gambling for such amounts made courtiers sell entire villages to pay their debts. It was a death sentence for the people in a surrendered *mir* in days of famine.

"Well done, Count Lynar," my cousin Christine called, pushing her way through the crowd, "I knew you would win!" She had blossomed: the shine of her dark braids was enhanced by strings of pearls, and her once flat chest had swollen into a perfect aristocratic handful.

"What is to happen to it?" Christine asked sweetly, pointing at the crayfish. "Shall we set it free in the ponds?"

"No need to tamper with the workings of fate." Count Lynar handed the crayfish to his servant. "Cook it for supper with a couple of dozen more. It will be delicious. Perhaps Her Highness would like to join me?" He bowed to Christine as the Tsarina and de Biron stepped up to them. Anna Ivanovna's arrival made the onlookers scatter.

"Her Highness is too busy, Count Lynar. And you should be, too. I hear you have eighteen illegitimate children at home in Saxony, whose wet nurses you also put in a condition to look after them. That should be enough to keep a man permanently occupied, I'd say."

"Eighteen illegitimate children? And their wet nurses pregnant? Really?" De Biron sounded impressed.

Count Lynar flushed and bowed, his mop of white-blond hair falling over his sled-dog eyes, cleverly hiding his utter lack of embarrassment.

"Where is Julie von Mengden, your lady-in-waiting?" Anna asked Christine, who looked dejected: how astonishingly bad at hiding her feelings she was, given that she had spent her life at court. "Count Ostermann, where is your niece when I need her?"

"Here I am, Your Majesty." A young woman curtsied. I had never heard her name before: her pointed nose and the narrow set of her gray eyes gave her the look of a pine marten. Ostermann's niece! God, there were more of them at court now, breeding faster than rabbits.

"Enough amusement for the evening. The Princess needs rest," the Tsarina decided.

Christine's gaze turned longingly to Count Lynar, but Julie von Mengden linked arms with her and led her away. I watched it all, astounded. In my short absence I had missed significant changes at court: new, foreign-sounding names risen to importance and the good Russians, whose families had served the Tsars for generations, fallen into poverty and oblivion. Behind me Dolgoruky clucked in his cage, pretending to peck at a worm, his eyes rolling.

"Lovely Lizenka has returned," de Biron said warmly as he stepped up next to Anna.

I faced a wall of bodies and disapproving glances and was made to feel like an intruder in my former home. Inside I bristled, but I curtsied as low as my breeches and riding boots allowed. Anna Ivanovna herself wore a vast, unlaced green housedress that clung to her thighs and breasts, yet she was covered in jewelry. De Biron nodded to her slightly, making her open her arms to me in welcome. Her mouth smiled, but her gaze was flinty.

"Who is this handsome stranger?" the Tsarina cooed. "Ah! It is you, Elizabeth. Forever playing at dressing up."

"My Tsarina and cousin, please do excuse my clothes, but I find it easier to ride this way."

"Granted. I appreciate that you came straight to Izmailov to be our guest," she said, hitting bull's-eye. Of course, Izmailov, which I had begun to consider my home, was hers by birthright. I was destitute once more, but took heart: soon, I should be her heiress, both by birthright and by bloodline.

"You come just in time, Elizabeth, to meet my company of actors," said Anna.

"Who are they?" And what else was going on at this frenzied court usurped by foreigners, with Russian princes pretending to be chickens, and crayfish making a dash for their lives? In the background, watching us, I saw Count Ostermann.

"Italians freshly arrived from Warsaw. The Elector of Saxony sent me one of his five troupes. Five! How could I have none?" Anna looked at the men and women whom soldiers had herded into a corner, their captain barking orders, shoving and prodding the strangers. They cowered like chickens facing a fox. "Remember? Staging an opera is my utmost priority." Anna frowned at de Biron. "Why do the actors look so disturbed?"

"They are artists!"

"What is that supposed to mean?" She looked at a loss.

"Captain Birckholtz has chased them like cattle, all the way from Warsaw. But in Italy artists are treated like indulged children. Even Augustus of Saxony caters to their every whim. Yet on their way here, their trunks were pilfered, their food stolen, and their clothes drenched. Worse, Madame Lodovica's chocolate has disappeared. Without chocolate she can't sing."

"Ah! I'll make up for it." Anna snapped her fingers. "They will stay in the Kremlin until the first performance for the Chinese delegation. Madame Lodovica will have Petrushka's apartment. Madame Cosima, Katja Dolgoruky's rooms."

"Katja?" I looked up. "Is she well?"

Anna shrugged. "Why not ask her, my dear? That might cheer

her up. A dove will only take a week or so to fly to Beresov. That's where all the Dolgorukys have been banished to hard labor."

"Beresov in Siberia?" Katja's slender, fine-boned beauty was not the type to withstand the privations and hardships of the Arctic. The thought gave me no joy, despite everything that had happened.

"Exactly. Beresov. Where you sent Menshikov."

"And all the Dolgorukys are there?" I heard the disbelief in my voice. If I was no stranger to taking revenge, a Tsarist court without this oldest of Russian noble families, who had founded Moscow and built the Kremlin, was unthinkable.

"Indeed. They went too far with their plotting against me. Katja might still be alive, but most of the others are not. Our fine bird in the cage over there was the only lucky one."

"What are you saying? The Dolgorukys are one of Russia's oldest families."

"Which does not exempt them from just punishment." A somber figure joined us then, standing between the Tsarina and de Biron: Count Ostermann.

"What happened to them?" I asked, my voice thick with fear.

"Whatever was necessary. De Biron advised me, but the decision was Ostermann's." The Tsarina smiled at him. "Beheading. Quartering. Broken on the wheel."

De Biron shrugged, looking vaguely flustered, his hair ruffled, and face flushed. Ostermann returned my gaze unblinking; if he could order the demise of one of Russia's oldest and most noble families, what else could he do?

"Are de Biron and Ostermann forming the new Privy Council then?" I kept my voice low.

"There is no more such nonsense as a Privy Council. I rule as an absolute monarch, as is my due. I am advised, though, by a Cabinet. Ostermann counseled me to let Alexis Dolgoruky live, as a fine example of what will happen to those who oppose me. My little pet here can count himself lucky." She glared at the clucking Prince Dolgoruky: "If you stop just once, Alexis Grigoryevich Dolgoruky,

I will shoot you and feed you to the pigs. They will rejoice when they find the pellets in your limbs. It's a sign of luck."

I met Lestocq's eyes, who shook his head slowly in a clear warning. If the usurper Menshikov had been fended off, and Dolgoruky sat perched in a cage, Anna was pursuing her own policy of Westernization, which would throw Russia to the wolves.

"Bang! Bang!" D'Acosta cheered, hopping forward, pretending to shoot at the prince. Then the dwarf lowered himself on all fours, scouring the floor as a pig might search for a truffle beneath rowanberries. The court roared with laughter.

Prince Dolgoruky crowed and flapped frantically.

For myself, I would have preferred a clean shot.

70

After Maja had barked at the translator and shooed the offensive Captain Birckholtz away, the actors' voices rose in happy cacophony. Any threats or hardships they had suffered were rapidly recast as adventures. Servants offered pitchers of burgundy and platters of hot, steaming *pierogi*. D'Acosta started to imitate Captain Birckholtz, which made even Anna giggle. How many Tsars had the cunning little Portuguese entertained? Four, so far. How many of their secrets did he know? Countless. I watched him, and as he turned, he met my gaze with bottomless eyes and a knowing smile.

"When is the Chinese delegation expected?" I asked. Whenever they arrived, the choir would be on stage together with the opera singers. The choir—and Alexis. My thoughts cartwheeled: I did not want to be left behind in Izmailov once Anna moved to Annenhof in Moscow. I must work toward becoming her heiress.

"Are you taking an interest in the affairs of All the Russias?" Anna asked. Count Ostermann listened intently. There was no right or wrong answer: showing no interest made me a flighty young woman, showing too much could be lethal.

"What is good for Russia is good for my Tsarina. Nothing is closer to my heart than her well-being," I said smoothly. Ostermann blinked. He appreciated a worthy opponent. Anna weighed my words, wobbling her mighty head. "So be it. And do you wish to take up residence in Izmailov again?"

"I would love nothing more than that," I lied. The court had wrecked the place: it would take years to rebuild.

"Well, you can't," Anna decided. "Once Annenhof is ready, we all move there."

I lowered my gaze, as if fighting tears, to hide my triumph. Off to Moscow I was going in the meantime, together with the court.

"The Chinese delegation shall be my first guests in Annenhof: our grandfather, and both our fathers, sent ten trade missions altogether to Peking, as well as eleven different ambassadors. Yet never—*never*—was there a delegation in return."

"How so? There is trade, isn't there?"

"Well, some. Russian merchants in China are confined to caravanserais. If they dare to wander outside, they are executed. They sit and sit, until all the food is eaten and all the vodka drunk. Then the Chinese bring them a little tea of the worst quality, even less gold, coarse porcelain, and second-rate raw silks that split after a couple of uses," Anna said with a frown.

"Sounds like they offer us their warehouse refuse?"

"Exactly. Worse still, once our merchants have packed up, no further stay in the country is permitted them. Any dawdling is prosecuted by death. But why are you interested in all this? It is me they are here to meet, not you, nosy little thing," she scolded me.

De Biron laughed, making amends: "All women are curious. By the way, the Elector of Saxony also sent a dozen Stradivari violas to accompany the choir."

The choir. *Alexis.* How I longed for him to be here, all true, tender words and strong arms. He lived a world away from the terror in Anna's tent. Was the struggle to become her heiress worth any of this? The thought alone tired me.

"Wonderful." Anna beamed. "Everybody will be amazed to listen to my choir. My messenger found me this incredibly gifted singer close to Kiev. He is to be my soloist."

Her choir. *Her* soloist.

Alexis had neither an idea of her true nature, nor a clue as to my identity. The idea of his reaction to the truth filled me with more dread than Anna's entourage ever could.

I needed advice, or more than that: the wisest and warmest counsel Russia ever had to offer.

71

"How good of you to come and see an old man, my dear child!" Feofan Prokopovich welcomed me, and I could not help but fly toward him, before kissing the *panagia* that gleamed on his simple black robe: if anyone could tell me how to save Alexis and myself, it was this man. His wisdom had enabled him to leave the Trubetzkoi Bastion unscathed. Now his enemies were dead, banished, or confined to a cage, clucking for their life, while he had turned the tables on them and was heading the dreaded Secret Office of Investigation. His clever pug's eyes sized up my simple cloak of undyed linen as well as the dark, unadorned skirt and neat white blouse. My earlobes, wrists, and fingers were bare. The only jewelry I wore was, as always, the icon of St. Nicholas.

"Welcome to my humble abode," he said, turning to indicate the vast stone house rising proudly from a walled courtyard, lit by the fading October sunshine. It was constructed with utmost care and complete disregard for cost. Anna cared as little for what Feofan spent as my father had. The courtyard was all hustle and bustle: carts arrived to restock his kitchens. Men lugged bags of oats, groats, barley, or wheat and rolled countless barrels of beer and wine toward trapdoors leading to the cellars. Feofan had many mouths to feed and countless staff, ranging from valets and cooks to craftsmen such as carpenters, clerks, and copyists, as well, of course, as equerries, coachmen, grooms, and harness-makers, not to mention his gardeners. In one corner of the courtyard, artists sat cross-legged, sketching birds who picked at carefully arranged crumbs. Two Greek Orthodox priests were about to mount their carriage; two rabbis waited for another, their long black cloaks billowing in a fresh wind. Feofan saw each group off with a farewell in their own language.

One never left Feofan without feeling a little bit better, a little bit wiser.

"You time your visit well," he said. "I have taken delivery from Novgorod." He patted his belly, frowning. "I despair at the cost of my table. Are six barrels of anchovies too much, I wonder?"

"I'd make that seven next year," I laughed. "Don't ask me. I am as greedy as you are."

"A woman who eats is a gift from God." He winked at me, comfortable in his celibacy. "I have also received wine from Italy. It's a stunning color—almost green—and it smells of cut grass." On the threshold he inquired, "Now, do you come as a Tsarevna or as a friend?"

"Both."

"Is that possible?"

"I should hope so."

"In that case there are some men who would like to meet you."

At a nod from him, a couple of soldiers rose from the courtyard's slabs, straightening their dark green uniform jackets, gold buttons and toggles gleaming in the sun. I hesitated: the presence here of soldiers of the Preobrazhensky Regiment did not bode well. Nobody was safe from sudden arrest or prosecution by them. If I could not trust Feofan, whom could I trust?

He sensed my unease: "Do not fear. These men, too, have come to see you as a Tsarevna, but also as a friend."

Buturlin had belonged to the Preobrazhensky Regiment. The soldiers dashed toward me, impatient as young colts. "Tsarevna Elizabeth, what luck!" The first of them to draw level with me kneeled to kiss my fingers and the other men followed suit.

"Once I told them you were coming, I couldn't hold them back. And as head of the Secret Office of Investigation, I need to be informed of all your meetings." Feofan winked at me. "Though as luck has it, just now I really ought to check on the kitchen."

"*Matushka!* Our Little Mother! What a pleasure to have you back," another officer greeted me. I furtively scanned the busy courtyard. *Little Mother.* That was the customary way to address the Tsarina, not an outcast such as me. Behind him lingered a groom, ears flapping. Was Feofan, the leading spy, being spied on? De Biron was no fool.

"I, too, am happy to see you here. Are your barracks still close?"

"Not any more." The man had cautiously lowered his voice.

"Let us walk." I ducked through an archway into Feofan's walled garden, a refuge from Moscow's stench and noise. Fruit trees grew next to rows of berries and vegetables. No mole stood a chance here. The crisply raked gravel cut through the thin soles of my slippers. "Why have your barracks moved?" I asked. "Yours is the foremost Imperial regiment, founded by my father."

"The Tsarina has founded a new regiment, the Izmailovsky Guard. She gave her men our barracks while we moved to make-shift buildings."

"Who is its colonel? The Tsarina herself?"

"No, upon de Biron's advice she has appointed a German, Count Loewenwolde."

A German as colonel of an Imperial regiment? What an insult to any good Russian soldier. The soldier drew closer. "*Matushka,* we come to ask for a favor from you. Already our age is known as the *Bironyshkchina,* the age of the German yoke. There are foreigners everywhere. Who has the strength to save this country? Who will be the Tsarina's heiress? You must be Tsesarevna once more."

Bironyshkchina, the age of the German yoke. The mythical bond between people and Tsar, knotted from ancient threads, was these days reduced to rags, replaced by a shiny cloth so garishly new it unraveled everything I knew, lived for, and loved. They were right: the only way to change this was to be Anna's heiress, the Crown Princess, and Tsesarevna once more.

"I have no influence," I warned.

"We want no influence. We want your love. We know who you are."

"And who is that?" I looked up at him, my heart pounding, tears welling up.

"You are Russia—the Tsar and Tsarina's daughter. We beg you: our wives have had children in the past weeks. Do us the honor of being their godmother. Then we will feel that not all is lost."

Feofan appeared at the back door of the house. One hand gripped his pectoral cross, the other shielded his eyes. His gaze was as impenetrable as God's will. Nothing here happened by chance. I held out my fingers for the soldiers to kiss once more. "It will be my greatest pleasure. Let me know when and where the christening is taking place. We shall wet the children's heads together."

Before I knew what was happening, the men had seized me and lifted me on their shoulders, spinning around and wreaking havoc on the neat gravel, shouting and laughing. I screamed, first with surprise and then with joy, and barely avoided being thrown into the air. As I pleaded for mercy, laughing, they let me down, and Feofan joined us: he gamely asked about the mothers' wishes and the children's needs. Christenings were expensive; Feofan always had an open purse and tended to forget and forgive a debt.

Generosity, I learned, was an invaluable trait in a Tsarevna.

Lunch was simple: borscht and marinated herring, served with hard cheese, sourdough bread, boiled eggs, and chives, all washed down with Italian white wine and chilled vodka. Dessert was a towering honeyed *medovik* tart, and Feofan set the samovar to boil, ready to lace the *chai* with vodka, nutmeg, and cinnamon.

"How good of the soldiers to consider me their children's godmother," I said. "Surprising that they remember me at all."

"Russia has never forgotten you," he said. "Especially not now. I see a lot of both of your parents in you."

His words were balm to my wounds. "I don't think Count Os-termann shares that opinion."

Feofan cut two generous slices of the *medovik,* its crust break-ing perfectly and honey dripping. "Oh, cranky old Ostermann. He loved but twice in his life. First your father, who adored you. Then Petrushka, who adored you even more. The German's vindictive-ness blinds him, which is astonishing for a man as levelheaded as he is. At least you are aware of his caliber."

"Father was a match for him. Peter the Great! Who dared op-pose him? But my chances against Ostermann . . ."

"Your father was not born Peter the Great. When he and I first met, Russia was in dire straits and Moscow almost under Swedish siege. He was a young man crushed by the weight of history. But he rose above that. I sense a change in you. Has something hap-pened?"

I decided to be honest. "Yes. I have met a man. I think he's the one."

"That is a tall order for any mortal. Does he feel the same?"

"Yes. Still, I don't know how to make him mine."

Feofan chuckled. "That should not be a problem for you, the most beautiful princess known to Christianity. You have the natu-ral warmth and the spirit your father adored in your mother."

I blushed. "That's not the problem. He is a soloist in the Tsa-rina's choir, brought here from Kiev when she heard of his talent. Anna has already taken Izmailov from me, so what will be his fate? Everything is done to keep me in check. I am not her heiress yet and might never be."

"Her ways are unfathomable. Moscow rules Russia. The Krem-lin rules Moscow. The Tsarina rules the Kremlin. God rules the Tsarina. How did you meet this man?"

"During my last pilgrimage. An angel spoke to me." I halted, surprised: I had used the Leshy's words with neither fear nor hes-itation.

Feofan licked the honey off his fingers, as a boy would. "God Himself has put the two of you together. Man should not presume to interfere."

"I have not seen him since moving to Annenhof," I said.

"That was only a couple of days ago. Send for him," Feofan urged.

"He doesn't know who I am. I mean, he doesn't know who I *really* am."

"Oh," he said and leaned back. "I see. And he still loves you?"

"Surprisingly enough, yes," I said, my voice small.

"If he is so good a singer, it is natural for the Tsarina to want him in her choir. Russia's best is hers by birthright."

Even the cup of hot spiced tea that Feofan placed in my hands could not fight my sudden icy fear. "I need him, Feofan," I pleaded. "I long for him every day. How can he be part of my life?"

He sipped his *chai* pensively. "In the long run it might mean that the Tsarina will not pronounce you her heiress. Everything comes at a price. Are you willing to pay it?"

"I shan't sell my soul," I told him. "Otherwise, yes."

"That is what I hoped to hear. Then, Tsarevna, there is a way to get him. But will his love for you survive what you need to do?"

"I am damned if I do and damned if I don't."

"That about sums it up," he said, eyes full of pity. His words were like bricks, walling me inside the choice I had to make.

72

Winter came suddenly. Steady snowfall shrouded the city. As all the sounds and smells of summer were suffocated, others took over: the scent of caramelized hazelnuts, roast chestnuts, and hot beeswax that dripped from costly candles filled the air. In the coffeehouses surrounding the Red Square, spiced wine was served next to hot chocolate and the house's dark sooty brew.

Feofan served up all those drinks—and more!—adding crunchy almond biscuits and moist date bread at each christening of a Preobrazhensky Regiment infant. Thanks to his generosity, I donated a golden ducat each time. "It's well invested." He smiled benignly at them all, and soon, if I was out and about in town, soldiers would jump on my sled's skids, chatting with me, joking, and hitching a ride before hopping off again, to carry on with the day's duties.

I would meet Alexis at the Inn of the Four Frigates, which was notorious among wayward couples. I hired a sled at dusk and came draped in a cloak, the hood drawn deep over my forehead. What was not clear to him—a shepherd from the Ukrainian Province—was glaringly apparent to anyone else: I was a lady of high standing who did not wish to be recognized. The innkeeper smirked when I paid for the chilly, dank room; Lestocq provided the funds more than unwillingly, but I left him no choice. I hated the situation: we were neither harlot and customer, nor husband and wife.

Yet this had to suffice for the moment, whatever the future held. Being with Alexis was the only thing that made me feel complete. I forgot all about my life's unbearable no-man's-land when I lay in his arms after the love, talking, and laughter.

As the Yuletide festivities drew close, we met one last time. The choir was practicing every day, as the Chinese delegation was expected soon after Epiphany. Winter was at a turning point as the longest night had passed. I twined my arms around Alexis's neck and shoulders like a creeper on a tree, holding him, whispering, caressing his hair. He countered my tenderness with all the sweet nothings in the world as we held each other. "I want to spend my life with you, whatever it takes," he whispered. "I want to sing your praise as long as I live. You know that nothing makes me as proud as my voice. Let me dedicate it to you."

I smiled; my body was still flushed, my face glowing, feeling both invincible and more vulnerable than ever. Had anyone ever felt like this before? I kissed him to silence him and so that I could avoid taking that vow.

He had no idea of the price I would need to make him pay for our love.

73

How garish the Kremlin must have seemed to the five Manchu envoys who had left Peking over a year ago. Delayed by Petrushka's death, they had wished to be alerted to Anna's accession officially only upon their arrival, in order to keep face. Peking's aim was Russian neutrality in its struggle with the Mongols; Ostermann hoped to institute better trading relations. He worked meticulously toward his goal, as always. Throughout the Chinese advance over Russian territory, the journal *Primechaniya* published a series on the history of China, so that people were better informed about the country and its people, and everything was at the mission's disposal: food, drink, houses, horses, and girls. As the delegation's nine carriages finally entered the Red Square, thirty-one gun salutes and the three regiments' drum corps welcomed them. Unusually, there was no delay in meeting the Tsarina. She invited them into the Great Hall immediately.

Her sister Ekaterina Ivanovna had excused herself because of a swollen stomach: she was still young enough for there to be a ripple of scandal—*Whose is it?*—so Christine and I joined the Tsarina on our own. At her behest we dressed simply, while her forty-three ladies-in-waiting dripped with diamonds and wore magnificent dresses: lace foaming on sleeves and collars, gemstones and pearls crusting stomachers. While we were waiting, Anna said to me, "Watch me well. This is something your father *never* achieved."

Trumpets sounded as the doors were flung open. The court

gawped at the gifts that were carried in—certainly no second-rate goods here, but eighteen trunks and boxes of silver sable skins, rolls of brocade, and china, as well as priceless lacquered boxes.

"T'o-Shih, head of mission of the Emperor of China, and his retinue," the chamberlain boomed. T'o-Shih entered, holding his scroll of appointment high above his head. His eyes took it all in, calmly and without discernible expression: the throne room's burgundy velvet and silver brocade tapestries patterned in petit point flowers; the ceiling groaning with frumpy gold galloon. Upon reaching the throne, the Chinese delegation kneeled: five sleek figures, dressed in severe black-and-gray heavy satin calf-length robes. Even as they bowed low, they retained their sableskin caps. Utter silence reigned as T'o-Shih climbed the steps on his knees to reach Anna's feet. He congratulated her on her succession, his speech sounding coarse and chopped to Russian ears. All five men kowtowed three times, showing utter humility. It was to be the first and only time that Chinese officials prostrated themselves before a foreign ruler. Yet I sensed they would fulfill their mission without offering much in return.

In the evening I left Annenhof to pick up Christine ahead of a Masquerade in the Kremlin. The Tsarina's new palace had been finished just in time for winter, but its vast rooms and corridors teemed with rats. The rodents spilled inside from the park and the countless canals in the vicinity linked to the River Yauza. Anna had cats set free; any servant caught feeding them was flogged. In the splendid gardens—Annenhof Grove—de Biron, as a surprise for the Tsarina, had hundreds of full-size trees planted overnight.

I was dressed up for the evening as a hunter, my curly hair adorned with feathers. On the way to the Kremlin, I sounded out the darkness inside me. My new path led me toward the light, I felt sure: Alexis had turned a key in my soul, allowing me to step into the secret room within. One I never wished to leave.

* * *

I sat snug, wrapped in furs, with hot copper pans placed at my feet. The snow danced in front of the lanterns that now also lit Moscow's streets, as they did St. Petersburg's. Coming in from Annenhof, I saw Moscow's first houses in darkness, yet the roads grew livelier, and the Red Square was teeming. People had met in the many coffeehouses ahead of the Masquerade. Officials and their ladies moved like ants toward the mighty fortress walls; at the Red Staircase, gravel and sand had been strewn to prevent anyone from slipping.

Once inside I turned away from the well-lit way leading to the state rooms. The windowless passage to Christine's apartment in the former *terem*, the women's quarters, was dusky; a couple of dim lights hung suspended from brackets, staining the corridor more than lighting it, the illumination as oppressive as the idea of locking women away. Footmen and maids flitted in and out of rooms like pigeons into their nests, bearing quickly altered robes, freshly curled hairpieces, trays of food and drink, and baskets filled with firewood.

Christine's apartment was hidden deep inside the *terem*. At her door I halted, ready to knock. Instead my hand hovered and I held my breath. Giggles and muffled voices came from inside: low but clear conversation.

"Do stay," Christine pleaded.

"I can't. As much as I wish I could," a woman answered.

"Why ever not? Are you afraid?"

"Who wouldn't be? If the Tsarina finds out about us . . ." That was a man speaking.

"She won't." Christine again.

"If so, I'll be done for."

"*We* will be done for." The woman again. "I am not sure my uncle will vouch for me once I am useless to him."

"Ostermann will not vouch for anyone but himself," Christine said.

There was a moment of silence, which allowed me to retreat

into an alcove, pulling my cloak's hood deeper over my forehead. Christine's door opened a gap, and a man slipped into the dusky corridor, pulling a woman behind him.

I pressed myself flat against the paneling. "Come. There is nobody here," Count Lynar whispered. His pale skin gleamed pearllike above a turquoise suit, and his white-blond hair formed a halo around his skull. "We'll come back later tonight."

"Please do," Christine whispered, sounding tearful. She was dressed in an Amazon warrior's elaborate costume, embroidered with pearls, crystals, and emeralds, while a wide leather belt gathered a pleated, diaphanous skirt. Ostermann's niece, Julie von Mengden, was Lynar's companion. I held my breath: was Ostermann trying to get his claws into the Tsarina's niece as well? Julie rearranged Christine's gathered top and skirt and gave her a little push. "Look at yourself. Go and fix your makeup before Elizabeth comes."

"Gently," Count Lynar told Julie, tenderly kissing her hand before stroking Christine's hair. "Julie is right, my angel. While I do not care what that illegitimate upstart thinks, I would hate to see Elizabeth looking lovelier than you. Go and powder your nose, and we will see you in the Great Hall."

"I shall," Christine promised, and closed the door.

Count Lynar and Julie stared at one another for a moment before she collapsed against his chest, muffling a giggle behind cupped hands. "Shh!" urged the Count, holding her gently and stroking her upper arms. "I wouldn't have minded staying in there with the two of you." He kissed her but then recoiled, touching his mouth in disbelief. "Ouch! You bit me!"

"Never again tell me off in front of her!" Julie hissed, grabbing him between his legs, holding him captive in her clenched fist. "If you do, I'll have your balls. Ostermann is my uncle, not yours. If we tire of you as the envoy of the Saxon Court, Christine will tire of you as a lover. Then you can return to Dresden, your wardrobe of lovely little pastel outfits in tow. Understood?"

"Understood," he said. "Let go of my cock. I still need it tonight."

Julie went on tiptoe, giving him a peck on the cheek. "We both do. Your costume is just too lovely. We shall tear it off after the Masquerade, using our teeth." She smiled and slid away from him. As her steps faded, Count Lynar leaned briefly against the wall, gathering himself. Finally he straightened his coat and patted his hair before hurrying past without seeing me.

Only then did I dare to stir, cooling my burning cheeks with my palms. I tasted bile. Illegitimate upstart? This was surely Ostermann's scornful name for me; was it fitting for those two to repeat it? Yet I also pitied Christine: was Lynar her first love and von Mengden their go-between? I thought of the warm companionship I had shared with Augustus; even my lust for Buturlin seemed straightforward in comparison to this twisted ménage. What Alexis would make of these self-indulgent people was anyone's guess.

When I finally knocked at her door, Christine's powder had been applied, and she slipped out of her room quickly to join me, linking elbows. "Lizenka, how good of you to pick me up. Let us show the Chinese how to celebrate!"

"How do you like my Masquerade?" Anna Ivanovna, who was dressed as Helen of Troy, asked the Chinese. T'o-Shih weighed his head, pensive eyes resting on Prince Alexis Dolgoruky, who wore an especially elaborate feathered costume inside his cage. The long tail fanned out like a peacock's, swaying each time he kowtowed, which he did ceaselessly, giving hoarse cries.

"Is not all here a Masquerade?" T'o-Shih asked, his answer a riddle in itself. I wondered how he would sum up his Moscow experience upon his return to the Forbidden City.

De Biron, dressed as a Friesian sailor—an insult to my father, whose costume of choice this had always been—tried to make light of the situation. "Look at the lovely ladies. Who do you think is the most beautiful?" he asked, jovially elbowing T'o-Shih. The Manchu shrank back, horrified at the physical contact, but politely considered the surrounding ladies, who chatted and compared their splendid jewelry while assessing better-dressed competitors and eyeing the men present from behind lowered lashes.

Anna smiled triumphantly. The verdict seemed a foregone conclusion to her—of course he would choose the Tsarina herself. Yet T'o-Shih bowed to me. "Well, if her eyes weren't quite so large or so blue, I'd say that the Tsarevna Elizabeth, despite looking like a man of the forest tonight, is the most beautiful."

The Tsarina gave a short, incredulous laugh. She adjusted the golden laurel-leaf circlet in her graying locks—her French hairdresser Pierre Loubry had kept adding fake curls that sent it lopsided. "Who has lent you that green jacket, Elizabeth?" Anna asked.

"The officers of the Preobrazhensky Regiment."

"Why is that? I have not made you my heiress yet. Careful."

"As a mark of their longstanding loyalty to the Imperial family," I said, thinking of the men's anger at the entirely foreign new Izmailovsky Regiment and its German Colonel, Count Loewenwolde. I had chosen my costume to attract as little attention as possible, but in that aim I had spectacularly failed. "May I?" I said, and had the interpreter ask T'o-Shih, "What is the most astonishing thing to you here in Moscow?"

Things went from bad to worse.

The Manchu smiled, his ivory skin looking like parchment. "To see a woman on the throne."

74

Anna Ivanovna went ahead with planning her opera performance, in which Alexis would sing. To me this meant only one thing: it was inevitable that he would learn the truth about me. Just the thought of it was terrifying. "I am expecting five *intermezzi*," she would say, loving the word, as it made her sound learned, even though she, too, had just learned it from Ristori, the company's director. As my father's theater inside the Kremlin had fallen into total disrepair, he had had a portable stage built in only five weeks. The skill of the Moscow carpenters, who crafted the revolving stage with their simple axes and chisels and no guidance from engineers, was miraculous.

"Do the Russian people know now what an opera is?" Anna asked de Biron. "Has the article I ordered been published in the *St. Petersburg Gazette*?"

"Yes, my dear. *'An opera is a musical composition, comparable to a comedy, sung in verse, including a number of dances and extraordinary stage effects.'*"

"Good. Count Lynar must write to Saxony right away, telling Augustus all about its success. Nobody can say I have not tried to educate my people."

Alexis had held me for the last time a week earlier: he had been full of stories about both the rehearsals and the Tsarina's secret visits. "She is a big woman, Lizenka. Handsome, I'd say, though not everyone would agree," he said. "She certainly inspires fear."

"She was called Anna Ivanovna the Terrible as a young woman," I said.

"How do you know?"

"Oh. Everybody does," I said evasively.

These days Lestocq refused to stray far from my side. "You might need me at any time," he said darkly.

The opera was scheduled for the first Friday in March. The Great Hall was bathed in candlelight, flames dancing in the dozens of full-length mirrors in their heavy, ornamented gilt frames. Six hundred people poured into the hall: foreign envoys; German, Swedish, and Baltic military; Russian aristocrats; the Chinese guests, all splendidly clad in costly finery paid for by secret sources, feigning any interest other than their true purpose for being there, which was to flatter the Tsarina. Lynar, swathed in pistachio-green brocade, chatted with Count Loewenwolde, who sported the bright red uniform of his Izmailovsky Regiment. Julie von Mengden tried to catch her uncle's every word, storing them away as a field mouse might grain, hovering about him while he ignored her. The Russian boyars, counts, and princes looked on glumly: they were not only still reeling from my father's costly reforms, but seeing their incomes dwindle even further, thanks to the new taxes levied by Anna to pay both for her buildings and the now impending Polish war: Russia was to face France in Danzig. Families were forced to sell estates to fund new liveries. To the cloth woven for Russia, gold and silver were added by the ounce in Lyons, as the Tsarina abhorred dark colors.

Even I did not wear my customary black skirts tonight: Feofan raised his glass, toasting me, when I entered the hall. He had made me a gift of a bale of lilac-colored silk, as well as yards of foaming, creamy lace to ornament the cleavage and sleeves. A touching note accompanying the fabric read, "*The soldiers of both the Russian Regiments send their beloved Tsarevna Elizabeth this cloth. Wearing this, you can face fate; any man will forgive you any deed."* I re-turned Feofan's smile: the officers' gift was daring, as I must never appear more popular than the Tsarina. Yet feeling loved made me happy; that had been a terribly rare occurrence for me.

The beginning of the opera was just moments away. I sat in the front row, next to the Tsarina and Christine, and readied myself to see Alexis. If there had been a moment to disclose my identity to him, I had missed it. The stiff bodice held me up, although I was feeling faint; my heart pounded, and the blood raced through my veins. My fingers trembled too much to hold a glass of the deli-ciously chilled champagne offered by Moorish page boys clad in red velvet. People mingled, searching for seats that allowed them to see and to be seen. The hall swirled in a maelstrom of lights, sounds, colors. Anna had swept in, followed by de Biron, d'Acosta, and her retinue. Prince Dolgoruky, who sat chained to a celebratory giant nest by the door, crowed with delight, wearing a rooster costume, making Anna say icily, "One more time, and I'll wring his neck." The court howled, complimenting the Tsarina on her wit, passing on her words. The Chinese sat in their simple dark satin gowns, faces inscrutable and posture rigid. Seeing the general amusement, they clapped their thighs and laughed hysterically. Prince Dolgoruky took great care not to make a further straw rustle. There was wis-dom in T'o-Shi's observation: *Is not all here a Masquerade?*

Alexis's voice rose from the choir to the heavens. The Tsarina sin-gled him out with her gaze, her eyes moist, applauding in between pieces or whenever she felt like it. He stood tall and handsome; his music was like one of his caresses. Even the Italian actors bowed to him at the end of each of the *intermezzi*. Anna wiped away large tears of emotion.

I, however, yawned and fiddled with my gloves and fan. At the end, as applause, shouting, and stamping rose to the stuccoed ceiling, I got up, my expression bland, as if ready to leave. Now or never. Forgive me, my love, for what I must do to you, I silently prayed, as I felt Alexis's hot gaze find me. He gave a muffled sound and recoiled in shock.

Anna turned to me in surprise, her voice stern. "Why the haste, Tsarevna Elizabeth? Were you not pleased by the rendition?"

The court fell quiet. Julie von Mengden cast an excited glance toward Ostermann. Clearly they hoped that I, the *harlot*, the *illegitimate upstart*, should utterly disgrace myself. How they would love a misstep from me! I would not do them the favor.

"It was charming enough." I shrugged, looking toward the door, as if I had a more pressing engagement.

"Charming enough? Are you then used to better?" Anna's eyes fixed on me, as if I were crossing the Red Square at dawn; an unwitting, perfect target for her shooting practice. I could hardly breathe.

Up on stage Alexis stepped to the edge so as to see me better. Any moment now he could give us away, and all would be lost. I had to pull us both through this.

"Possibly the bedbugs in Izmailov are more entertaining?" Julie giggled, relish in her eyes.

I froze. Had she spied on Alexis and me?

"I see that wit runs in your family, Fräulein von Mengden. The opera was pleasant," I said.

"Pleasant? No more than that?" Anna Ivanovna rose, her height and width more impressive than ever thanks to her ostrich feathers, state robes, and jewelry. The courtiers fell silent. *Alexis,* I thought. *Give me strength.* Yet I did not look up at the stage; I would not meet his gaze. Feofan had been clear: this was a gamble I might lose. If so, I should slice my wrists that very night. The other singers joined Alexis, curious. His gaze scalded me, as he slowly, painfully, put two and two together.

Sweat trickled down my neck. I smiled, saying casually: "No, beloved cousin. It was simply unworthy of the Russian Court. Perhaps the King of Saxony allowed himself a jest when suggesting a performance such as this one?" I locked eyes with Count Lynar, who paled more than ever. "Your dear mother, the Tsaritsa Praskovia, my aunt Pasha, taught me many things about plays and music. After all, she left her trunks full of costumes and props to me alone," I said, playing my trump card. "I feel I am able to judge music."

The Tsarina tugged on her satin evening glove. "True. I had forgotten about that."

"Your Majesty, my King would never—" Count Lynar hastened forward, his icy blue eyes popping: no wonder. Russia's favor was a saving grace for Saxony. Lynar would not want to take responsibility for any diplomatic *froideur*. Anna waved him off: who cared what the fat and greedy Elector of Saxony did? She turned to the stage. "Come forward. All of you. Now."

The Italian actors and the choir swapped anxious glances. They were exhausted; sweat glistened below their wigs and had made their thick, pasty makeup dissolve. Madame Lodovica and Signor Ristoli held hands, stepping forward.

Despite Alexis's surprise to hear my faint praise of him, he was still elated after singing, his eyes sparkling. His gift truly came straight from Heaven. He closed his eyes briefly, then opened them again, shaking his head as if waking from a dream. I ignored him, pain searing me: I had relished our love for its truthfulness. Alexis had loved *me*, not the princess I was, from the beginning. Wasn't that reason, and excuse, enough for me to try and hang on to this rarest of emotions? The next moments were crucial.

"Come on, then, Lizenka," said Anna. "Tell us. Who was best?"

"Signor Ristoli is a genius," I said. "His stage is a movable feast and his voice flawless."

The Italian bowed. Everybody clapped.

"Who was the worst performer then?" Anna tapped her folded

fan against her gloved palm. "Say it. I shall not be angry. Promise." Already her voice trembled with suppressed fury.

"To be honest, the male soloist did you no honor." I locked eyes with Alexis, who faltered as if I had swung my fist square into his stomach. "Best to return him wherever you plucked him from."

"Ha!" Anna snorted, furious with me, but she could not help flicking her wrist in a gesture of dismissal. "Away with him then."

"But you just called him to court," Ostermann said. His hooded gaze found me, the cogwheels of his gloriously sharp mind whirring into motion. "He was herding sheep close to Kiev." He limped up to de Biron's side. I had to be faster than they were.

"That was obviously a mistake, as the Tsarevna Elizabeth so kindly pointed out," Anna snapped.

"What should happen to him then?" Ostermann asked.

Julie von Mengden chirped, "What is not good enough for the Tsarina should be adequate for the Tsarevna Elizabeth, my uncle. Why not place the singer in her retinue? He shall delight her every day with his mediocrity. It takes one to know one."

"Oh, yes, it does. It does!" laughed d'Acosta, looking at me.

Anna's eyes lit up. "Wonderful idea, Fräulein von Mengden. See, Lizenka: wisdom, too, runs in that family. Take him and enjoy him."

Oh, and how I would! But I made a show of shaking my head and looking aghast. "No, really, I am not sure . . ."

"That is an order," Anna said sharply. "I do not wish to see him any more."

"Bundle him up as if this were the *gostiny dvor*," d'Acosta teased: he knew, I understood. Nothing much was hidden from the creatures who roamed the secret passages and servants' staircases of the palaces at night.

"Shut up," Anna said. "Or will you be the next one clucking on a nest?"

"Oh, if so, I promise to lay you an egg a day. D'Acosta knows how to make himself useful." He circled the Tsarina, flapping his arms. De Biron kicked him, and d'Acosta somersaulted away as the hall emptied rapidly in Anna's wake.

It was time for her birthday banquet, six hundred dishes to a course.

Alexis stood dumbstruck.

75

"What have you done?" he asked, sitting opposite me in my sled. His face was ashen and his bare knuckles white as he clutched his few possessions, pressing himself into a corner as far from me as possible. His dismissal had been instant: he still wore his embroidered costume from tonight's performance. If he had not been in shock, Lestocq would have been unable to bundle him in with us. Now the brightly painted sled flew through the Moscow night, devouring the miles out to Annenhof.

"I have saved you," I said, tearing back the curtain and sucking in the icy air. I felt I should suffocate of despair. The freezing wind bludgeoned my forehead, clearing my thoughts. Snow whirled inside, settling in our hair and clothes. "I have saved *us* and our love."

"By hiding your true self and fooling me for weeks on end? Is that what you call love? Well, no more of it, thank you very much."

"I never hid my true self. On the contrary," I said, tears in my eyes. "Only my identity. I'd hoped to be able to separate the two." I reached for him, but he recoiled as if scalded by my touch.

"I would have loved you the same had I known," he said, his whole frame sunken with sadness. Why did he speak in the past? Fear overwhelmed me. We could be together now: people would ridicule us, underestimating the strength of our bond. I did not care. Everything came at a price, but I was ready to pay. The reward would be the greater: a life together with Alexis.

"You would never have dared to meet me," I said. He shrugged, pulling his gloves up over his wrists where the wind was biting his bare skin.

"Tsarevna, please, close the curtain. Your catching a deadly cold is not the plan," Lestocq pleaded, but I would not care if I did.

Alexis sneered: "What *is* the plan then? And who are you in the first place? You hardly work for the Tsarina, or, should I say, Lizenka's wealthy and influential cousin, do you?"

"He works only for himself," I said. "And possibly for his King and country."

"That makes too many masters," Alexis mocked him.

"You are mistaken, Tsarevna. I work only for your benefit and have long done so," Lestocq said with dignity. "So, yes, I have many masters but only one mistress," he said, as the sled turned into Annenhof's poplar *allée*. At its end the illuminated palace awaited the Tsarina's return, looking like a colorful two-story cake. The sled came to a halt; the coachman got down from his box, patting the steaming animals. Footmen came running, but Lestocq waved them away. We needed no witnesses.

"*You* might have arrived. *I* need to travel further," Alexis said stiffly, climbing out of the sled. I ached for him. Oh, to hold him and to be held! *Beloved.* Without looking at me, he walked away, stepping on my heart as he withdrew from my company. I was mute with fear, shaking.

It was Lestocq who scrambled out of the sled and called after him: "Where are you off to, Razumovsky?" As I, too, stepped out, Alexis slowed and looked back at us. Snow thickened on his shoulders and hair. The sled's torchlight illuminated him as it turned up the *allée*. He clutched his bag, shivering with cold and emotion. "I am going home," he said.

"Home!" Lestocq laughed. "To be with the sheep?"

"*I* am your home. *We* are. *Our* future together is." I sobbed and wrung my hands.

"There is no *we*, and there is no future for us. I will do whatever

I can. Go and live with Father Gregory, the village priest. Help my brother."

"Don't!" I cried. "Please stay!"

He shook his head, stepping away into a darkness that would soon swallow the memory of our happiness. "Please!" I begged, shaking with tears.

He hesitated.

Lestocq was at his side in the blink of an eye. "She is asking you to stay," he said, grabbing Alexis's elbow. "Don't you hear her, man?"

Alexis shook him off, dark-eyed, snowflakes melting on his hot skin. What else could I have expected from him? He was proud. I would not have him any other way. "I have loved a different woman. The Lizenka I knew would never have done that to me."

"I am Elizabeth Petrovna Romanova. I am the Tsar and the Tsarina's daughter. Yet everything I told you is the truth: my story and my suffering."

"You are the Tsarina's daughter, but I am a free man." He backed away. "I can't stay here now even if I wanted to. What man could?" He wiped away tears. "It breaks my heart. Meeting you made me complete. I have never known such love. Tomorrow morning I shall catch a sled back home, for my father to thrash me daily and my voice to compete only with birdsong. You have robbed me of my greatest gift."

"Stay!" I begged, sinking to my knees. "I have hurt you. I know. For that I beg your forgiveness. One day, God willing, you will understand why I acted as I did." Clouds straggled across the huge, pale moon. The stars made a fleeting appearance, as brief as human happiness, while a breeze caught the imported trees' stiff branches, making the thin, glossy icicles hanging from them chime in eerie concert. An owl swooped by, its golden eyes glinting and wings wide, to settle among the beams of the palace's vaulted roof. Still Alexis hesitated. My life hung in the balance. I tasted bitter fear:

he clutched his bundle and shook his head. Still I kneeled, dumbstruck, despite the frost biting into my kneecaps.

Lestocq grabbed Alexis by his lapels, furious with him. "Your gift, you say? What are you talking about? Fool."

"My voice. My singing." Alexis tried to shake him off in vain.

The Frenchman leaned in, spittle flying as he explained matters as he saw them. "I'd beat some sense into you if I were not a gentleman, stupid shepherd boy! The greatest gift God ever made you is *her*. Your voice and your meeting the messenger who happened to hear you sing—that was all *His* plan. Can't you see that? Who are we to doubt him, Razumovsky?"

Alexis hesitated, and Lestocq swept on: "Do you think anyone—*anyone*—will ever remember you for your *voice*? Oh, you angel of naivety!" Alexis flinched in the face of Lestocq's scorn while I hiccupped in surprise. "You know the answer to that. Give or take a couple of decades, maggots will be gnawing on your precious throat soon enough. Yet if you stay tonight, I promise you, you shall not be forgotten ever. You will always be remembered *for her sake!*" Lestocq was like a hound stalking a noble beast, cornering it: if Russia needed me, then I needed Alexis—and Lestocq knew it. "Make her become who she is!" he urged. "That is the only thing *you* may be remembered for."

Make her become who she is. The night's crystalline breath froze the tears on my cheeks as the wind bit us to the bone.

"Let me pass." Alexis pushed Lestocq aside and placed his bundle on the frozen walkway. He came up to me, gravel crunching beneath his feet. "Get up, Tsarevna, or you will indeed catch a deadly cold." He helped me to rise. This might be the last time I felt his touch. "I may be a feeble and flawed man, but I do not wish your death on my conscience."

I shook with cold and emotion. I kissed his hand, not daring to ask what his decision was. Time was running out. Soon other sleds would return from the Kremlin in a snowy, glittering throng;

we would have an audience of people, hooting, screaming, and laughing.

"Go to bed, Lizenka. Let Lestocq make you a hot milk with vodka and honey. I shall sleep in the stable tonight," Alexis said.

"In the stable? But . . ." I thought of the soft bed that a maid was warming with her body for me as we spoke. If he were not to share it with me, ever again, I might as well die. "How should I sleep? What about tomorrow?"

Tears hung on Alexis's thick, dark lashes. "I do not know yet," he said, and picked up his bundle, leaving us. The Frenchman held me back from following. "Stay. Would you want him otherwise? Wait. The answer will come to you."

As the stable door closed behind Alexis, a sliver of warm light and steaming animal breath escaped into the freezing night. There was no certainty, only hope.

76

*

I do not know how long I slept, utterly spent. It was still snowing when I woke, the thick flakes drowning out the day and swathing the park's statues—delicate figures bought in Italy and Greece—with shapeless white shrouds. The paths were buried beneath feet of snow, and crows scored the sky like lead pellets. Silence clawed at my soul, and I gladly drank from the bottle of laudanum that Lestocq sent me daily. It blunted my pain.

How could I live without Alexis by my side?

Days or weeks later, I had no idea, there was a soft knock at the door—was it the hour for breakfast? Probably, though I did not care for the food—usually a silver jug filled with hot chocolate; warm bread with molten salty butter; boiled eggs, *smetana,* and caviar—nor could I abide a maid's senseless chatter. "Come in," I mumbled as a footman entered, hands full, back turned, kicking the door shut with his heel. Clumsy fool, couldn't he pay more attention? I dug myself deeper under my thick eiderdown, longing to stay hidden from the world.

The footman fussed about, turning the tray this way and that on a small table.

"Put it at the foot of my bed and be gone." I sat up.

He turned to me.

My heart stalled.

His smile revealed deep dimples, and his eyes were the dark blue of a midnight summer sky.

"God, you women are fickle. Didn't you just ask me to stay?" Alexis said, settling the tray carelessly. I leaped up and flung my arms around his neck, soaking his collar with my tears.

"Was the stable no good?" I laughed and cried.

"No," he said. "Not good enough." I noticed the dark shadows underneath his eyes.

"No sheep there, I gather?" I teased.

"No sheep. And no parlormaid either to feed me salty *kulich*. Or would that be caviar?" he asked, pointing to the tray.

"Never mind the caviar." I embraced him, out of breath with happiness. "I'll have you."

77

The Chinese delegation left before the *ottepel* when travel on the still-icy roads was swift. Upon their return Peking dispatched a gift loaded into five hundred chests to be carried across Siberia. Hundreds of gemstones and six thousand silver pieces; thousands of rolls of satin, silk, and brocade; as well as thousands of gowns, dresses, and costumes; plus skeins of untwisted and twisted silk were heaped at Anna's feet. The letter called the gifts: "*a sign of gratitude to the lesser classes of the Russian people, who welcomed the five Manchu so kindly.*" Anna laughed, as delighted as a girl, seizing as much as she could hold in both her hands before de Biron took his share. When she invited her closest family to take their pick, her sister Ekaterina Ivanovna was unable to attend. All ideas of an illicit affair had been forgotten as her stomach had now swollen to the size of a cushion; then, suddenly, she could keep down no food. The illness stripped all the flesh from her bones. My cousin writhed in pain, almost squashing my fingers as I held her hand for the sake of that sunny day in Peterhof, ten years and a world away, when Anoushka and I had been made Tsesarevny.

Christine had to be forced to her mother's bedside. She cupped her mouth and nose, barely concealing her relief and hatred. Even when dying, Ekaterina Ivanovna refused to remove her fake ivory teeth. Twice she almost suffocated on the yellowed pieces, which had come loose from her shrinking gums. When I could stand the sight of her suffering no more, Lestocq dosed her with so much laudanum and vodka that she died sighing and smiling, her spirit easing into a better place.

78

Twice a week the Tsarina ordered the *damy* of the Court to the Countess de Biron's apartments, where we embroidered an enormous tapestry together. The fire burned high, the sweets provided were delicious—crisp pastry filled with curd, nuts, and candied fruit—and the *chai* intoxicating, so no one much cared how quickly the work proceeded. As I entered, one day in December, two years after Alexis had stayed for good—my new way of, reckoning time—the Tsarina was kneeling with the de Birons' sons close to the tapestry frame, spinning a colorful wooden top. The children clapped for joy as I stood mesmerized, seeing the three figures' eerily similar smiles. Anna greeted me with a nod: I was keenly aware that every day more foreigners arrived in Moscow, ready to make their fortune—and I was still not her official heiress.

"Catch it," Anna said, pushing a hoop down the hall, and the boys chased after, laughing. The Tsarina watched them, enchanted, then sat down by the fire. The Countess de Biron, too, looked on. Was she pregnant again? She, like the Tsarina, wore her dress unlaced.

"You come in time for our last session here, Lizenka," the Tsarina said casually, as we both took up needles, thread, and the bright, colorful silks that had been part of Peking's gift. "The court is moving."

"Where to?"

"Back to St. Petersburg. De Biron wants a proper riding school.

In Moscow there is no good spot for it." She turned to Mrs. Rondeau, wife of the British envoy. "As an Englishwoman, you know the value of a good riding school, don't you? I have such an earnest desire to make your Queen's acquaintance that I might even travel to meet her halfway. In St. Petersburg, that is almost the case."

St Petersburg! When had I last seen my city, the symbol of everything Father had given his country: a strong new thread in Russia's sacred tissue? But I took great care to hide my joy. "Your wish is our command," I said gamely.

"Indeed." Anna frowned at the last, botched stitches. "Twenty-three years ago, I left St. Petersburg as a bride to my beloved husband the Duke." Her ladies duly dabbed their eyes and made sobbing sounds as Anna said sternly: "You know nothing of the joys of marriage, dear Lizenka." Despite living with de Biron, she was eager to keep face: her court was to be known as a virtuous one. "A woman needs a husband, and Russia needs heirs. Anything that results from your relationship with that shepherd-singer—oh, yes, I know, of course I do!—can't be either." She cast a brief glance at the Countess de Biron, who gathered to her the two boys with their raven Saltykov hair.

Russia needs heirs. Never before had Anna alluded to making me her heiress or to me bearing Russia children. The air crackled. Maja watched me, her face tense. Julie von Mengden looked up, alarmed. Word would reach Count Ostermann tonight, I was sure. Mrs. Rondeau made a mental note to tell her husband later on: if I were to be Tsesarevna once more, London would start courting me immediately. I touched the icon of St. Nicholas, finding Augustus's leather strings brittle from wear. "If I only ever do half as well for Russia as you, my Tsarina, I am blessed."

She had to be pleased with my answer. My heart raced. I would be Tsesarevna. And this time I would rule.

A couple of weeks later, the Countess de Biron gave birth to a daughter. She paraded little Hedwig around, a buxom German wet nurse in tow. The Tsarina was not to be seen for a week or two until she appeared at court again, smiling, her dress still unlaced. She smothered Hedwig with love, as if she were her own daughter.

The court was in shock at the discomfort and expense of the move back to St. Petersburg. As my sled left Annenhof shortly after Epiphany, I turned back to look one last time. It was the best example ever of the Russian art of *skorodom,* by which a timber structure of any size could be made and moved to wherever it was desired. Russian carpenters would have spirited the palace along for Anna, raising it anew on the Neva if she had wished. Yet Annenhof was left behind, uninhabited, amid its luscious park and placid canals and sparkling fountains. Guards and sentries took position, ready to desert the place once their pay ran out, which would be in a couple of weeks, given de Biron's grand St. Petersburg riding school plans. Soon vagrants would join owls, bats, foxes, and badgers in the vast, vacant halls, warming themselves on a little fire and a little more vodka, falling asleep in a stupor. One night stray sparks set the splendor alight; Annenhof, the timber palace, was lost in an almighty blaze; a fire so fierce that not even the Domovoi's river of tears at the loss of so much timber could quench the flames.

Although it had been neglected during the past five years, St. Petersburg had grown; too much had been achieved here for the city to revert to marshland. The city embodied my father's vision and willpower; its inhabitants prospered on this inheritance.

"What is this habit of keeping the carriage windows open?" Lestocq moaned, looking up from the game of dice he was playing with Alexis. The night in Annenhof, when we bared our souls, had changed things between us. We felt linked by destiny.

"I want to see everything," I laughed excitedly.

"I think you are the only one who has been looking forward to returning to St. Petersburg, Lizenka," Alexis said, casually shaking the cup, sending the dice rattling, and tossing a brilliant throw. He waved Lestocq away as the Frenchman reached for his purse, sour-faced. "The courtiers moan like children."

"You don't say." Lestocq collected the dice. "I wonder how many of my possessions will arrive safely this time. Will only fifty, or possibly all, my champagne bottles break? At least I was never ordered to build in this swamp. Elsewhere age might make ruins; in St. Petersburg they are made to order."

"So watch out, Alexis. And you, Lestocq, should mind your tongue," I said. "Tomorrow we will be home." I fell back into the plump cushions and toasted the men with some of the splendidly chilled champagne Lestocq had conjured from his bags. At least this one bottle had survived unscathed. Herr Schwartz drank the most, refilling his glass again and again.

"I see it!" The next morning, I tore aside the curtain at the sled's window. "Look, just look!" I pointed to the brightly gilded, pointed spire of the Cathedral of Saints Peter and Paul, relishing its contrast with the bulbous Byzantine cupolas found everywhere else in Russia. Seagulls pierced the sky with their cries, diving down in the Neva's glitter, making the horizon and the waters blend in a sudden splash. I held Alexis's hands. "I am looking forward to showing you all of this," I said. "It was my father's finest hour when he built St. Petersburg."

"More like a million finest hours," Alexis said, and Lestocq crossed himself.

"And a million souls buried in its foundations."

"Lestocq!" I said sharply. "Careful. I am not joking."

"I apologize. I wish for the city one day to witness your finest hour as well. It can't be long now, can it?" We all knew what he spoke about, yet merciless whipping was the mildest punishment that Anna's Secret Office of Investigation could mete out for any comments that were made about her accession, my right to the throne, or the state of Russia in general. I struggled to reconcile Feofan's role in the Secret Office of Investigation with his calling as a man of God; he passed the sentences but left the dirty work to others, hidden in the confines of the Trubetzkoi Bastion.

In the Winter Palace the plumbing was gone, the roof leaked, and gusts of icy wind ripped open the windows where panes were broken. Still, eighty people sat down with the Tsarina for dinner, and following the banquet, we rose for a ball. The court's gaze was upon me. Did the return to my father's city also herald my rise to the role of heiress to the throne of All the Russias? I danced, wearing a pale pink dress encrusted with pearls and rhinestones that Lestocq had offered me, and ended the night in Alexis's arms: he did not even take the time to undress me or unlace my stockings. As the sun rose over St. Petersburg, my glorious, beautiful city, I could not have been happier: yet who among us has never mistaken dusk for dawn?

79

It was the fourth year of Anna's reign. Had Russia changed, or had I? Possibly both of us: in St. Petersburg, Alexis gave me the calm and the strength not only to look, but to see, as if for the first time ever: *"Make her become who she is."* What sort of country was I to inherit?

The question was almost as dangerous as the answer was distressing.

My return to St. Petersburg started inauspiciously. At a ball shortly after our arrival, Anna set the sky alight with a glorious firework display. People were often injured or maimed by wayward rockets, but this time one crashed through the palace windows, causing shards to fly, gashing my forehead deep above my right eye. The pain was like a lightning bolt; a gush of blood blinded me. I tumbled and fell; it was de Biron who caught me and cleaned my face.

Alexis kissed the bandage that Lestocq had placed on my forehead. "It doesn't mar your beauty. Nothing ever could, even if you live to be a hundred." Yet I read in his eyes that he, too, was shocked.

The incident was the worst possible omen. Julie von Mengden had said loudly for anyone to hear, "This can mean only one thing. Bloodshed for Russia! Beware of the Tsarevna Elizabeth!"

Her words rang true, though her insight was unwitting. A letter from Mr. Rondeau, the British envoy, was intercepted by the secret police. It read: *"The Masquerade is at the door, and the court's talk is only about amusement at a time when the common people have tears in their eyes. We are on the eve of some sad extremity; the misery increases from day to day. . . ."* Feofan read it to me, once the cut to my forehead had healed into a neat and, as Alexis said, charming little scar in the shape of a half moon. We spent a couple of days out at Feofan's dacha, as the city's summer heat was stifling. The ride to the house in Nadykino—a large estate lying between Peterhof and Menshikov's Oranienbaum—was an insight into all of Russia's woes, and it broke my heart. No animals were to be seen in the villages or fields, neither mice nor rats, and no cats, dogs, or horses, let alone proper livestock. The people were skin and bone, lying listlessly in the shade of their miserable *izby*. Earlier in the year, an unusually strong spring sun had drained what floods the *ottepel* had brought, and a couple of months later, the scorching heat set the corn in the fields alight, kindling walls of fire and blinding people with smoke, rendering them unable to fight the flames. The famine that followed was more devastating than any that had scourged my country throughout her history. Travelers only moved in groups for fear of ending up in a stew. Children were sold by the roadside. People made it to Moscow with the last of their strength, dropping dead in the streets, attracting wolves and bears to come into the city and feast on the corpses. More than a hundred thousand people had starved to death already.

"Does the Tsarina do nothing about this?" I asked, sitting at Feofan's table.

He cast a warning glance over to the footman. "The Secret Office of Investigation has slit noses, torn out tongues, and knouted people senseless for lesser questions."

"Who should ask if not I?" I countered. Alexis gave a proud smile.

Feofan sighed. "She tries. She recognizes the problems but fails to follow through and solve them. She ordered both Church and Court to allow their serfs access to streams and to provide them with seeds. In vain. Her cousin Saltykov was to distribute bread to beggars; all five thousand loaves ended up in the bellies of noble families." He shook his head. "Russia's enemies are our own hesitation, our laziness, inefficiency, and dishonesty."

"What will come of this?" I asked, chasing away the memory of Julie's remark—*Bloodshed for Russia!*—while the servant ladled chilled borscht into my bowl of beautiful Meissen porcelain. The ruby-colored soup shone like blood through the delicate rim. My stomach churned.

"Good intentions are in vain if nobody sees them through. Candles that were to be handed out to inmates in prisons, now light de Biron's riding school instead, all night long," Feofan said, sounding short of breath. "Listen to this extract from a letter sent home by the Prussian envoy. *'Discontentment could not be any greater, but there is no rebel leader. This humble nation is so accustomed to slavery, and fear is so great: nothing will happen during this Tsarina's lifetime, whose rule can be likened to that of Ivan the Terrible.'*" He rummaged in his pocket. "I have lost the letter from the Spanish envoy, but I know his words by heart. *'Everything here is ripe for revolution. The revenues of the Crown lands have fallen, trade is languishing, the exchange rate is sinking steadily—'*"

"This is awful! What can be done to change things?"

"Very little. We have to wait and see. When, for example, did you last hear anything good about the war?"

I looked up, surprised. "Which war?"

"Exactly. Russia is now fully involved in the Polish War of Succession, championing the useless Elector of Saxony. Yet the fighting might as well be going on in the Americas instead of in Poland, right next door, as it is. When there are victories to report, parades are held, and church bells rung. Silence buries what lies in between. Be assured that the ordinary Russian in a far-flung *mir* knows nothing of the terrible suffering of our soldiers."

I shifted uncomfortably. This talk was treason. Feofan had

achieved everything he could expect to and might now be ready to go. I and Russia, though, still had so much to live for, and so I weighed my words carefully. "What is happening? I heard nothing when I visited the barracks yesterday." I tried to sound informed: politics and statesmanship were a perpetual dance in which I must demonstrate my skills.

"Well done. Keep the regiments close, that is what I always say. But what would your father have made of a conflict that cost millions of roubles and almost a hundred thousand young soldiers' lives, without gaining Russia an *arshin* of ground? Anna's forces were slaughtered like cattle. Soon Russia will have no sons left. The big estates are deserted, the nobility impoverished."

"Can things get worse?"

"My dear, things can always get worse." Feofan looked up expectantly as his servants brought in a whole suckling pig, its crackling all shiny and dripping, served with kale, stewed apples, and buckwheat pancakes. His gnarled fingers, their skin parched from hours spent in his library, enclosed mine. "Let us pray, Lizenka."

Things could always get worse: through treachery, threat, and the disbursement of bribes, the former groom Ernst Biren, styled Count de Biron of the Russian Empire at Anna Ivanovna's accession, was legally elected Duke of Courland. He was then dubbed His Royal Highness, a Sovereign Prince, taking up residence in the Winter Palace adjacent to Anna's rooms. His household and plate impressed even Lestocq, who tended to view our kitchens as being provincial and barbaric. The Countess henceforward stayed seated in the Tsarina's presence, just as Christine and I would, and her diamonds made even Anna Ivanovna raise her eyebrows. Their carriage was drawn by eight raven-colored horses and accompanied by twenty-four footmen, eight running page boys, and four crude Cossack heyducks as guards. Nobody in the history of Russia had ever been so hated as de Biron had become; wherever his cavalcade appeared, people had to be whipped into cheering. The *Bironyshkchina,* the German yoke, weighed heavier than ever on Russia's shoulders—shoulders that were beginning to stoop.

Harrowing fires devastated Russia's capitals, old and new. In June half of Moscow had burned to the ground, including the Mint and the Arsenal, which furnished the army with cloth, weapons, ammunition, and a huge amount of ready money. Thirty thousand dwellings were reduced to ashes, their inhabitants burned as on a gigantic pyre. A month later St. Petersburg was aflame: the fire consumed around a thousand houses and palaces, among them my own, in which I had once lived with Aunt Pasha and Anoushka. The English envoy's lady, Mrs. Rondeau, had all her furniture dragged out of her flaming house; most of it was damaged beyond repair, so she used it for firewood in her makeshift new quarters.

De Biron, the new Duke of Courland, seemed oblivious to all this, too busy inaugurating his riding school on Nevsky Prospect, a miracle of gilded façades and glittering windows. Nobody in Russia lived as splendidly as his horses did. Each of the two dozen finest thoroughbreds occupied a stall identified with the animal's haughty name engraved on a solid gold plate; the stone slabs of the ground floor were imported from Solnhofen in Bavaria. Observation galleries were placed at first and second floors, their stucco walls adorned with paintings of the horses by the finest European masters. An entire ministry was created to look after de Biron's brood mares and stallions. Anyone wishing to watch the Tsarina exercise her horses on Mondays had to wear a special uniform: a yellow buffalo jerkin embroidered in silver galloon, with a blue vest and trimmings to match.

It was the age of disasters. As fires ravaged the cities, I suffered an unspeakable loss, the depth of which I could barely describe—not even to Alexis. Feofan Prokopovich was out for a walk one day after lunch when his heart failed him. He was felled like a

tree, dying within seconds in his garden, where he walked holding a book, checking on the pruning going ahead to prepare his
orchards for winter. His soul rose toward Russia's endless sky. His
death left me reeling and lost. The last tow securing me to my past
had been severed and I feared to go adrift. How could I do his
memory justice, or face a future without his guidance and advice?
At least his funeral honored this unique man: after the rites, I invited the officers of the Russian regiments for a drink; Lestocq
footed the bill. The soldiers emptied the innkeeper's cellar and
then danced the polka on the empty tables, falling off, shouting,
crying with pain and laughter. Swaying, they used the empty barrels for target practice, the bullets making them spin and somer-
sault. It was the night of the first heavy snowfall; the officers and I
climbed up on the icy roof, slid down it, and fell headfirst into the
drifts below. I laughed so much, my cheeks and sides hurt. Feofan
would have approved. Yet his death caused me a physical sense of
loss. He had been the last living link to my past, and his wisdom
had been endless. I would not forget the words he had read to me:
Nothing will happen during this Tsarina's lifetime. What about the
next Tsarina then? I wondered.

Another of Feofan's wise words gave me solace: *I see a lot of
both of your parents in you.* If Russia should ask for me, I had my
answer at the ready.

Shortly before Yuletide, when Anna Ivanovna was about to enter
the eighth year of her reign, she summoned me to a private audience.

80

The morning after the messenger came, I spent an hour deep in prayer. Russia could only be governed with God's help. My cousin Christine's problem was her Protestant faith, making her vulnerable to the advances of Ostermann's niece and Count Lynar. Ekaterina Ivanovna had never welcomed her only child into the Russian Church, as she had been careless about so many things. No wonder Christine was being led astray.

Days before, in preparation for the meeting, I decided to watch the Tsarina exercise her horses at de Biron's riding school. As I set off, the air was so brittle with frost it felt as if it might crack; icicles as shiny as glass hung from roofs and windowsills, mirroring the city's glory. Snow crunched underneath my sled's runners, and every breath of air I took further cleansed my spirit. Beggars were everywhere: in *my* Empire, the loaves of bread should reach the needy. Forced laborers toiled, their noses slit, threatened with death by knouting should they try to escape. I planned to ban capital punishment—no drop of Russian blood should be spilled on my account. At street corners shadows met and parted: young people up to no good in order to survive. It broke my heart. No child should starve: was Russia not fertile enough to fill her barns with plenty?

"Tsarevna Elizabeth!" A group of Preobrazhensky officers spotted me—they ran alongside my sled, hopping on the skids, asking myriad questions.

"Have you recovered from Feofan's funeral?"

"Are you off to see the Tsarina? Don't forget us in this hour of your grace."

"My wife will give birth soon. Will you be godmother to another of our babies?"

And so on.

On Nevsky Prospect sentries opened the riding school's gilded timber doors for me. A marble staircase led to the upper reaches. I passed the first-floor gallery from which the manège could be viewed. A flash of color there caught my eye. I halted, shrinking alongside the staircase wall.

"Come with me," Julie von Mengden commanded, pulling Christine out of a door and down the corridor. "I know where to go." The two of them hastened off, skirts flying, in fits of giggles, exchanging hushed whispers, furtive embraces, and even quick kisses. At the door leading down to the stables, however, Julie cupped Christine's face and kissed her, slowly and scandalously, tousling her dark hair. Then they both slipped out of sight.

I remained still, my heart racing. It took me a while to calm down: Christine was free to love a woman—to each their own. But she was falling prey to some carefully laid plans, I felt sure. I emerged on the second gallery. The warmth of the animals' bodies and the sharp, clean smell of the sawdust drifted up, bringing me back to my senses. The gallery's benches were filled with German and Baltic officers, all of them wearing shiny new Izmailovsky uniforms.

"He rides them well," one joked, glancing down into the school where Count Lynar exercised a beautiful fox-red steed, looking cool and composed in his lilac jacket. "I hear he uses the pomade, which he spreads on his face each night, to smooth other things as well," one of the brothers Loewenwolde added, vulgar words that made the other men roar with laughter. His brother, Colonel of the hated Izmailovsky Regiment, frowned though.

"Count Lynar might be too much of a stud for his own good. If Ostermann catches wind of this little story, Lynar's in a pickle. We are talking about a royal brood mare."

"Two mares have never produced a filly," a third man chuckled.

How low had things sunk when foreigners could speak unpunished like that about Christine, an Imperial Princess?

Loewenwolde jested, "He certainly has a hold over all his mares," as down in the school, Count Lynar made his steed rise with expert hands so that she walked on her hind legs. I saw his lips move as he spoke to her, encouraging her softly and ever so lightly brushing her with his crop. My ears burned. I wanted to slap and kick these foreigners out of my country.

My meeting with Anna Ivanovna was more urgent than ever.

I saw no one but Alexis in the days remaining before I called on the Tsarina. We went for walks in the Summer Palace's snowy garden, where all the statues had been removed to prevent them from cracking in the cold, their pedestals left bare. In spring the gardeners put them back together as they thought fit: Venus's torso on a Centaur's feet; Paris with his strong male body on display above the pleated skirts of Athena. Seeing the palace's simple façade, which had witnessed so many important hours of my life, strengthened and saddened me alike: I would not live here when I was Tsesarevna once more.

The appointed hour finally came. Dusk was falling when I arrived at the Winter Palace. I had dressed carefully, wearing the lilac dress that the regiments had offered me for the Chinese reception.

I followed the Tsarina's gentleman of the bedchamber—who had replaced the Duke of Courland in his official duties—up Rastrelli's huge marble staircase, trying to appear calm and composed. Upon our knock the Princess Cherkassky, the Tsarina's principal lady-in-waiting, opened the door, greeting me with a warm smile and curtsying. She had always been a friend to me.

In the Tsarina's room d'Acosta hunched next to a screen, and Count Ostermann had settled by the fire, the warmth alleviating his gout. The flames cowered under the chimney's draft, drawing on the wall frightful shadows that looked like witches' fingers. I steeled myself: neither the vile Leshy nor her crazed prophecies were welcome memories here. I had been victorious, a true Princess of Poltava.

Ostermann bowed his head to me ever so slightly. Opposite him sat the Duke and Duchess of Courland, and next to them stood a fourth man. He had a bristling mustache under a gleaming bald head. One elbow rested casually on the mantelpiece, but the tiny eyes that he turned on me were deep-set and dangerous, making him look like a snake. Russian and foreign medals covered his dark green uniform jacket. This was General Ushakov, since Feofan Prokopovich's death the all-powerful military head of the Secret Office of Investigation. The sight of him frightened me, as it would any Russian—it was all too easy to fall afoul of any written or unwritten legislation and find yourself tortured, hanged, and drawn. Then I relaxed. Of course, my investiture was a matter of the highest importance to the State. No wonder Ushakov was here.

"Tsarevna Elizabeth," he said, and bowed to me just as the doors leading to the Tsarina's bedroom flew open. I turned, wanting to smile—and froze.

Anna Ivanovna stood on the threshold, holding the doorframe to either side, furious of face and looking like a majestic mountain of Imperial green velvet, gold galloon, and lace. Emeralds shone in her earlobes and around her neck. Behind her, her gun was propped up at the open window, its curtains open, ready for her target practice on the people of St. Petersburg. She stormed forward, gasping for breath: her face was twisted with rage, but ashen and clammy. Maja caught up with her and steadied Anna by the elbow when she winced and held her side with one hand, as if in pain. In the other hand, though, she held a small book, which she flung at me, hitting me hard in the chest. I exclaimed, winded by pain and shock.

Ostermann gave a small, sly smile while de Biron turned his head to look at the flames.

"How dare you, vile, treacherous creature?" Anna screamed, coming for me anew, shoving me hard. I stumbled backward and almost fell but caught myself on her desk. She shouted: "You are a viper in my bosom. Read this and explain yourself. If not, I will have you arrested and tortured until you confess."

"Confess to what?" I stammered.

"Besmirching the face of Mother Russia by conspiring against her with foreign powers." She hurled this terrible accusation at me before screeching: "That is high treason! Worse than anything the Tsarevich Alexey ever did."

I stood petrified. The little book lay facedown, pages splayed.

D'Acosta picked it up, pity flashing in his eyes as he handed it to me. "Take it," he said calmly, and I obeyed, not knowing what to make of this.

"Traitor!" Anna wheezed. Maja gave her some smelling salts and led the Tsarina to her chaise longue, whispering reassurances. The fire crackled. I sensed a whiff of sulfur, as from the poisonous geyser that had bubbled away at the Leshy's feet. The Tsarina rose once more: "Think of what happened to your half-brother and double his pain. That will be your punishment!"

"Read, Tsarevna," General Ushakov said coldly. "Read and explain yourself. We are all listening." His voice rasped like the sound of silk tearing, blended with a hint of excitement. I had heard rumors of what happened to women who fell into his clutches. My blood ran cold, yet I would be damned if I showed that bloodhound my fear. My fingers trembled when I read the book's title on its spine. *Lettres Muscovites* was thinly embossed in gold on the blood-red calfskin binding.

"Read!" Anna Ivanovna gasped, sweat pearling on her forehead. She swayed, steadying herself on de Biron, but clenched her fists, ready to punch me. I opened the book where a page was marked by a folded corner. Fear shot through me, red hot, like an iron struck on an anvil, as I read the first words, which doomed me. Every letter printed in the book, criticizing Russia's domestic policy, made it look as if I conspired with foreign powers to besmirch Russia's image abroad.

What a fool I had been.

Today Tsarina Anna Ivanovna was not going to decide if I was to be her heiress; she was going to decide if I was to live or die.

81

My voice was faint as I read aloud the words that someone, probably Ostermann, had marked with a line of
ink: "'*What must we think about those foreigners who abuse the
confidence of the best of PRINCESSES? Their whole aim is to fill
their own coffers and to screen themselves against any future event.
Rightly so: how will they escape the storm if ever the illustrious
PRINCESS, who has an incontestable right to that crown, accedes
to the throne?*'"

I halted, my throat parched, voice shaking. Anna circled me,
screeching: "Now, who could that best of Princesses possibly be,
Cousin Lizenka? Viper! A nunnery is too good for you. Once you
have read this, I shall tear out your forked tongue! To think of the
patience and bounty I have shown to you. And you collaborate like
a rat with foreign scum."

I bit my lip. Foreign scum! Well, she knew all about *that*. Yet I
was too scared to think straight: her menacing shadow on the wall
was reaching toward me, fingers extended ready to claw and tear,
just like the Leshy's, demanding her payment—my soul. I wanted
to run away with Alexis and hide in a little *izba* somewhere. But I
knew I had to stand firm.

"Read on! That is nothing to what follows, you treacherous
creature," Anna howled. "With whom have you been working?
Whom have you been feeding with your lies about Mother Russia and all I do for my realm? You besmirch your family, country,
history—"

"I have never collaborated with anyone. I would never speak against either you or Russia," I dared defend myself.

"Don't exert yourself, my dear." De Biron forced Anna to sit. She gasped for air, pressing her hands to her painful side. He turned to me. "Read, Tsarevna Elizabeth, please." Even in this situation he treated me with courtesy.

I struggled for composure but continued. "*'The manner in which the Princess Elizabeth is treated cries aloud for vengeance'*"—here Ostermann snorted, his gaze scalding—"*'for instead of respecting her as the presumptive heir to a vast Empire, they do not even allow her the wherewithal to support her dignity. Her loyal* domestiques *rather linger in misery than to quit her service. She is kept in bondage, which deters anyone from making their court to her; she is abandoned by the whole world—'*" Here I halted, unable to read further. It was the truth, even if the words were not mine. This was how I had lived for almost a decade. Somebody had noticed: I was not alone! The thought was a relief, even if I had no clue how this information had left Russia, come to be published, and was widely circulated and read in Europe. The damage it did to Russia's reputation abroad was immense. How could Anna Ivanovna not blame me? I sensed a last trap. All they needed to get rid of me was a good reason. Yet were there right or wrong answers to any question they might ask? My ordeal was far from finished.

"Yes, do listen, my Tsarina," said Ostermann. "The best is yet to come."

"Spare me," I pleaded, tears streaming down my face. "This is unbearable." I was reading my own death sentence. Of course, nobody believed that this was the first I knew of the book. Instead of leaving the room as Anna's heiress, I should go straight to the Trubetzkoi Bastion. Both Maja and d'Acosta sat hunched, leaning against the screen, as peasants would. The dwarf pressed his fists to his eyes. I met Ostermann's gaze: my time was up. But something in his eyes—his sheer glee—steeled me. *Your father was not born Peter the Great,* Feofan had reminded me. I would show them how the Tsar's daughter behaved. I read on, my voice strangled: "'*This Foreign Ministry who excludes the PRINCESS will meet the fate it deserves once the native Muscovites give her their support.*'"

The threat in that conclusion was as clear as it was true: once I became Tsarina, the fat days of the foreigners in Russia would be over.

"Which fate would that be then?" Ostermann asked, adding snidely, "Princess?"

This was more than I could bear. Yet he was not the one I needed to convince. The Tsarina and I were of one blood; we were Romanovs, both of us.

"Your Majesty." I threw myself at Anna's feet. "Beloved cousin. For all that links us—"

"What would that be?" she screamed, furious once more, her face tear-stained, wringing her hands. Each chubby finger was adorned with two or three rings up to the knuckles. They ground together.

"By the blood of the Tsar Alexis, our grandfather, that runs in the veins of us both!" I gasped.

"Who knows who your father really is?" Anna shouted. "Perhaps you were justly left illegitimate for so long?" I quailed under the weight of that insult while she sank back on her chaise longue sobbing, her chest heaving with irregular breaths. She was like a massive tree fighting not to be felled.

"How can you say that?" I wailed, clawing her skirts and burying my face in their folds, sobbing helplessly. "For the love of my father, Tsar Peter, your father-uncle, and my mother, Tsarina Catherine Alexeyevna, your little sunshine aunt—"

"Who both made me lead a beggar's life in Mitau, where I was ridiculed by my own courtiers!" She, too, was crying uncontrollably. Maja rose and dabbed Anna's cheeks with a lace handkerchief as the Tsarina said: "For anything I needed, I had to send a dozen pleading letters, which gathered dust unanswered in some drawer."

"I knew none of this. I swear it by the sacred icon you once gave me in the Kremlin!" I clutched the icon of St. Nicholas, so hard that Augustus's leather strings tore. I stared at the damage, then dropped them to the floor and fervently kissed the icon. "St. Nicholas is the patron saint of Russia. Ever since you offered this to me, it has been my dearest possession. I have sold all my worldly goods to survive, but never this icon. You see, after all, not everything has its price."

Anna shook her head and hung on Maja's arm, weeping and shivering as if she were a child again, the least favorite of her mother's daughters, the family's black sheep. I clutched her fingers and looked up at her. "By everything the two of us have survived, I swear: I would never commit treason against Russia."

She hesitated, but Ostermann sniped: "Not Russia, perhaps, but against the Tsarina?"

I shook the St. Nicholas at him, as if warding off the evil eye. "Count Ostermann. You, who owe everything to my parents, do not ever—ever!—dare suggest the like again to my face, or I shall scratch your eyes out, for want of another weapon. The Tsarina *is* Russia! She and her people are linked by an indissoluble bond. If you doubt the loyalty of a Russian toward Russia, it is you who are the traitor!"

He held my gaze "The lust for power does strange things to people, Tsarevna."

"You should know," I spat. "You might kill off the Dolgorukys. But, my Tsarina, what can of worms might you open if he is allowed to spill Romanov blood? It's a dangerous precedent."

Anna's gaze went from Ostermann to me and back, unsure. Yet I felt that I was gaining ground when he met my eyes full on, revealing his hatred and contempt. The most dangerous man in Russia was my enemy. I had to fight his cold cunning with the best weapon at my disposal: hot, true passion. If this trap did not finish me, his next would. I picked the book up and flung it to the parquet floor anew; then I stamped on it. "This is what I do to traitors to Russia!" I said. "Where did you unearth this rubbish?"

"Prince Antioch Kantemir, my Ambassador to England, sent it. It circulates all over Europe. The editor claims to have found the manuscript, written in invisible ink, in a trunk washed ashore on a beach, the property of a writer lost at sea."

"What nonsense!" seethed Ostermann: I was escaping his and Ushakov's clutches. So what? He could add the book to his long list of imaginary grievances, tear out its pages, and use them when he went to relieve himself for all I cared.

"Indeed," de Biron said. "It's actually written by an Italian, Locatelli. As he never mentions anyone by name, we can't accuse him of libel."

"We could give him a hiding, though," the Tsarina suggested.

"Already done, my dove," de Biron said. "I hired a gang of thugs who beat the villain up. Properly."

There was a moment of silence. The fire crackled, and logs crashed, sending up sparks. I felt cold sweat drying on my neck. My heartbeat steadied. Yet this was still not over and done with. Anna turned to me, frowning deeply. "I have decided against all better advice to trust you one last time. Which does not mean that I have decided what to do with you. Marry you off—"

"Never!" I cried.

"Never indeed. But not by your choice, Elizabeth," she taunted me. "Who would want you now? Your reputation is as destroyed as any princess's has ever been. You leave me with only one choice."

My heartbeat stumbled. The blood rushed from my head. "The convent," I whispered.

She turned her back on me. "General Ushakov, you are free to leave. The Tsarevna Elizabeth is exonerated from suspicion of high treason. For now, at least." Once Russia's foremost torturer had left, the room seemed warmer and the air clearer. Anna leaned on Maja and wheezed: "Let us proceed. All of you shall accompany me to my private chapel. Now. You are to be witnesses."

Witnesses of what? She might shear my hair immediately, ready to send me to a dank, dark cell in a far-flung retreat. I panicked: I was to see neither daylight nor Alexis again. My throat tightened until I could hardly breathe. No one would ever know what had happened to me; there was nowhere for me to hide.

The Duke and Duchess of Courland smoothed their garments as Ostermann struggled to his feet. His face was expressionless, though I felt his fury. I still had not escaped his clutches. Maja and de Biron supported the Tsarina by the elbows, leading her down the private corridor that lay behind a secret door concealed under a tapestry. She winced with pain at every step, and her breathing rattled like a blacksmith's bellows.

On leaden feet I followed them out of the Imperial apartments, on the way to the Tsarina's small private chapel. These were possibly my last steps as a free woman.

Still, I walked as tall as I could.

82

The Imperial chapel was unchanged: here there were none of Rastrelli's soaring domes, organs with a plethora of pipes, or rainbow-colored marble floors. It was a reminder of what our faith and our country had once been like, before Old Believers and Reformers started tearing it apart. Myriad gilt-framed, gem-studded icons' eyes followed me as I walked up the aisle, the bare flagstones icy beneath my slippers. A priest waited next to the baptismal font, standing beneath a simple cross. The whole chapel was bathed in candlelight. Anna had not called us here on a whim: it all had been well planned and prepared.

I startled as a group of men rose from the front pew. They were strangers, looking rugged and sweaty as if they were just off their horses' backs. All three of them—two grown men and one blond-haired younger man—bowed deeply to Anna. Was this the guard who would take me to the convent? My heartbeat tripped. Anna Ivanovna sank down in her pew, short of breath, sweat glistening on her forehead, before she greeted the men with a wave of her hand. The huge ruby seal on her finger gleamed in the soft light, a dire reminder of her absolute power over all of us. I buried my face in my hands, breathing deeply so as not to faint. Whatever the Tsarina did, she was guided by God, I reminded myself.

Which convent had been chosen for me: Susdal, where Evdokia had lingered, or gruesome Solovetsky, where Peter Tolstoy had perished within weeks of his arrival? I expected neither pity nor kindness. The youngest of the three strangers stepped over to the

Tsarina, and to my surprise Anna embraced him while she stayed seated.

De Biron asked, "Are we ready?"

"Better ask: is *she* ready?" Anna replied, casting a dark glance at me.

"I have no doubt of it," Ostermann purred, his gaze also on me. "She has had time enough to prepare."

I sat up straight, my breath searing my lungs with fear. I had nothing more to say. Was there ever enough time to prepare for a living death?

"Let us get on with things," said Anna, sighing and holding her side at a sudden stab of pain. I settled behind her, next to de Biron's wife and Maja, who furtively brushed my fingers with hers, her gaze impenetrable. Ostermann lowered himself into the pew next to the young stranger the Tsarina had embraced. Despite the tense moment it struck me how ugly the lad was: with his big head and skinny body, he looked like a tadpole, and his face was covered with red, knotty pimples. Possibly age would become him better.

The priest stepped up, looking solemn. "Let us not worry but rejoice. Leave behind what was and embrace the new. This is a joyful and well-worn path, a journey that many souls have made. 'Come and see,' said Philip to Nathaniel. 'Come and see. Come alive!'" He sought my eyes as he intoned the text. I swallowed back tears, already feeling my scalp shorn, coarse cloth for my dress, a barred door enclosing me forever. It was too late for me.

The priest raised his palms as the chapel doors were flung open once more.

I turned around, my breath stalling.

83

Christine, Princess of Mecklenburg, daughter of my cousin Ekaterina Ivanovna, entered the chapel with slow and measured steps, meeting no one's eye. Swathed in black silk and lace, her pale face veiled, she cut a regal figure. Julie von Mengden carried her long, dark train, carefully adapting her steps to Christine's pace. Upon reaching the font, my cousin curtsied to the Tsarina and then faced the priest.

"Welcome," he said. "Just as we pray that God's will be done, we shall embrace His faith in God's time." He bowed his head as Christine sank to her knees before the Cross, folding her hands in prayer, and then looked up to the Lord.

In their pew the three strangers exchanged contented glances, nodding to each other, discreetly and proudly clapping the young tadpole on the shoulder. Ostermann smiled at them all. The priest's voice carried through the tiny chapel. "Conversion means living the one true faith. It means belief and acceptance in Jesus Christ, the Savior of the world. It does not happen at once. Nothing ever happens at once. You must convert every day anew if you desire your soul to be saved. Are you ready?"

"I am, so help me God," mumbled Christine. I sensed her urge to look at Julie; yet Ostermann stared at his niece, his cold gaze keeping even her in check.

The priest never took his eyes off Christine. "There is no salvation without repentance. You must repent all sins, both voluntary and involuntary. Sins of thought, of deed, of word. Repentance is the way to forgiveness and the Kingdom of Heaven. Do you repent?"

Christine's voice quavered, "I repent all sins."

"You have to acknowledge Our Lord as the One who is truly the Christ, the Son of the living God. He who came into the world to save us sinners."

"I acknowledge Him." Christine's voice was muffled by her veil.

The priest raised his palms, asking the heavens for their blessing. His voice carried through the chapel, resounding like a bell. The hairs on the back of my neck rose; my skin tingled with a sudden rush of blood. "Rise then, Princess Christine von Mecklenburg, and become Tsesarevna Anna Leopoldovna Romanova, heiress to All the Russias. Become the adopted daughter of your aunt, Her Majesty the Tsarina Anna Ivanovna. May God grant the Tsarina a long life; may He guide you with His wisdom."

What? I felt faint. My cousin Christine, the plain and abused child, had been baptized in the Russian Orthodox Faith and renamed Anna Leopoldovna Romanova? Worse still, she had been made Tsesarevna? My knuckles turned white as I clutched my hands together in prayer.

The priest dipped his fingers into the font, blessing Christine's forehead three times, making the Sign of the Cross on her face, chest, and navel in token of the holy Christian Trinity. My chest hurt, and breathing was painful. Russia was worth a Mass: Christine sobbed aloud, and, once again, the three strangers exchanged contented glances, whatever their business here might be. If they wanted to lock me away in a nunnery, the way was clear. Russia had an heir. The chapel spun around me, and I clutched the pew in front, shaken to the core. I could not even take leave of Alexis, the greatest gift fate had bestowed on me.

"My darling child, welcome to the one true belief!" Tears streamed down Anna Ivanovna's face as she opened her arms to her niece. "I will struggle to call you by your new name, so to me you will stay Christine," the Tsarina said.

Choked by sobs, the heiress flung herself into her aunt's embrace. For all her display of tears and mercy to me only minutes ago, Anna Ivanovna had ensured that the throne stayed with the older Romanov bloodline of Tsar Ivan V, my father's half-brother. She was fully entitled to do so. Yet I felt as if I had survived a mock execution when I met Ostermann's eyes. This was his doing.

Anna embraced Christine, kissing her hair and forehead, moistening her face with her tears. Only then did she push de Biron forward. He bowed to my cousin, kissing her white, bare fingers, but Christine pulled her hand away as quickly as possible from his pursed lips. Then it was Ostermann's turn, and finally the new Tsesarevna turned to me, smiling in triumph. I was raw with humiliation. Once more my heritage had been ignored and my bloodline insulted. I had no choice but to curtsy deeply and kiss Christine's hand. "Tsesarevna," I mumbled.

Julie looked at me unblinkingly. *Illegitimate upstart,* her gaze said.

Christine, as I would always think of her, was now the Tsesarevna Anna Leopoldovna Romanova, so named in honor of her rapist, wife-beating, twice-divorced, and debt-ridden father, Charles Leopold von Mecklenburg. She awaited the Tsarina's command for her to leave, but Anna Ivanovna had not finished yet. The Tsarina clasped her hands and announced joyfully, "For an Empire as vast as Russia, one heiress is not enough. My dearest child, we have considered all possible options in this matter to come up with the best solution."

Christine was taken off guard, looking at Julie, who gave a tiny, questioning shrug.

"Prince Anthony of Brunswick." The Tsarina smiled. "Step forward."

Ostermann seized Julie's elbow, holding it firmly, and pulled her away from her friend as the tadpole stepped forward. Prince Anthony of Brunswick was smaller than Christine, who had inherited Aunt Pasha's height. While walking, his big head wobbled on his gawky neck, as if fitted with an invisible spring. He slung back his dark coat, showing a couple of military medals that looked suspiciously shiny; how could a man of his youth possibly gain such distinction? Christine was unable to hide her instant revulsion. Her appalled expression was echoed in his eyes; he had just seen himself as she did.

"My dear adopted daughter." The Tsarina smiled encouragingly at her. "Christine—or rather, Anna Leopoldovna—meet your cousin, Prince Anthony, Duke of Brunswick. He has asked for your hand in marriage. I hesitated, given my deep love for you, and searched my heart. But Anthony has already proved himself in the Crimean War. His page boy was shot dead in battle; the colonel next to him was wounded in the head. Yet Divine Providence led Anthony safely home. It is a sign of God's intent for him. I have agreed to your engagement today."

Christine looked aghast. Julie reeled. Had Ostermann not held her so firmly, she would have rushed forward, giving away their secret.

"No, I can't. I mean—" Christine stammered, casting about for help where none was to be had. Her gaze fixed on Julie, who shut down her face as a shopkeeper might his premises at dusk. "A Duke of Brunswick . . . Is that good enough for the Tsesarevna of All the Russias? I am a Romanov now." It was her last, futile attempt to evade her fate.

"Prince Anthony is cousin to the Crown Princess in Vienna, Maria Theresa. Our beloved Petrushka was another direct cousin—their mothers were all sisters. Russia can't ask for a better bloodline," Anna said.

"I don't know him at all!"

"There is time for that once you are married." The Tsarina shrugged. "I had only met my beloved husband once before Tsar Peter walked me up the aisle."

My thoughts raced. All I longed for was Lestocq's loyal counsel. Would he even remain by my side after Christine's appointment was made public? I was further away than ever from the throne. Surely by now Versailles had had enough; their funding of me would cease. The thought of losing Lestocq was harrowing. Time had done its wondrous work, our common cause welding us together. Without him I would be devoid of any wise counsel.

"So be it!" Christine sobbed, and Anna Ivanovna cheered: "I knew that love would prevail! As you stand to inherit an Empire of ice and snow, let us have your wedding reflect that."

The Tsarina was forever resourceful, and the resources at her disposal were endless. An ice wedding of unimaginable beauty and horror it was to be.

84

The sky over St. Petersburg looked like a badly wrung dish-cloth, the clouds hanging low in a shade of stained yellow. Russia and I were lost. Christine's engagement meant German Tsars for all eternity, rulers who were Romanov in name only. I bowed to Anna Ivanovna's decision to adopt Christine and to change her name to Anna Leopoldovna Romanova, while my heart was inwardly bleeding. There was nothing I could do about it, short of committing treason. Alexis looked after me, guarding me in my sleep, his unshaven face growing a salt-and-pepper stubble, his eyes red-rimmed and bleary. Without him I would not have made it through. In vain had I been born on the day of the Poltava parade, the December stars singling me out as a Wolverine. My struggle with the Leshy spirit's dreadful prophecy had been futile.

After Christine's adoption, Russia, the sole reason for my existence, was lost to me for all eternity.

That winter was the coldest in the memory of humankind, colder even than the days of my birth. According to Lestocq, in Versailles brandy bottles burst, and wine froze in drinking glasses. All over Europe rivers froze over. Shopkeepers set up booths and roasted whole oxen on the ice, people flocking to the fairs in droves. In Russia things were less joyful: people choked on the breath freezing in their throats.

When Lestocq came to see me one day, his Tarot cards dancing in his hands, it was three o'clock in the afternoon. The sky was swollen with the threat of more snow. The early, dense darkness matched my mindset. I hid, curled up on a chaise longue in the library—the same room in which Katja Dolgoruky had been forced to accept Petrushka's proposal—my feet in Alexis's lap. He massaged my toes, making the minute bones crack. For the first time I noticed the onslaught of gray on Lestocq's auburn hair. He was so pale that his freckles showed up like poppy seeds on a white bun. Today even his wide mouth found little to smile about.

"How are you?" he asked me.

I shrugged sullenly.

"Perhaps I can entertain you with some tidbits about the Tsesarevna's wedding," he said glumly. "Christine said she'd rather slice her wrists than marry Anthony of Brunswick. During the engagement ceremony, she hung on her aunt's neck, crying so much that the Tsarina sobbed as well."

I looked up. "Does Christine hate her bridegroom, the Tadpole?"

"Worse. She is full of contempt for him. No man can overcome that."

"And the Tsarina?"

"She pushes for a speedy wedding, as she wants another heir. That is the main reason for Christine's elevation."

"So why are you still here?" I asked Lestocq, sitting up. Alexis's hands stopped caressing my bare feet. "Versailles must have found better investments than me."

"No. I convinced them to keep going with you. Not all is lost."

"In what way?"

Lestocq eyed his Tarot cards. The sight of them made me shiver. He frowned. "The country is unstable."

"How so?"

"There was an uprising in Ukraine. A man there pretended to be your half-brother Alexey. The desperate people believed him, calling for a ruler with Russian blood. Villages emptied as he went by. When de Biron heard of it, he had the man impaled, together with all his followers. Hundreds, if not thousands of them. A forest of bleeding bodies, dying on the ungreased stake. Anna Ivanovna in her clemency pardoned his village but razed the houses in mid-winter."

"Her *clemency!*" Truly Russia had fallen prey to wolves.

Lestocq walked over to the window, pulling back the lined Dutch brocade curtains. I winced at the draft and squinted through the dim, dirty light outside. "At least the Tsarina's clemency is also keeping her handymen busy. Come and look, Tsarevna," Lestocq said. To my surprise Alexis rose and reached out his hand, "Yes. Do come and look, Lizenka. It's a sight to behold."

The pale sun bounced off the snowdrifts, its rays magnified. Among the Neva's waves frozen in mid-ripple, where ships' hulls rose like gigantic skeletons from the white surface, the ice wedding was in full preparation. Men, horses, oxen, and donkey carts were dragging thousands of blocks of ice up toward the Winter Palace. Guards shouted at them as they crawled like ants, their bodies in stark contrast to the bluish ice. Each block was cut to be identical to the last, to precise measurements; cranes stacked them on top of each other. Serfs poured water over the growing walls, making the glittering edifice look as if it were hewn from a single glassy piece of ice. They were a good ninety feet long and at least thirty feet high.

"What are they building?" I asked.

"An ice palace. It costs a thousand roubles a square *arshin*. Small change given the scale of Christine's marriage celebrations. She is the Tsesarevna Anna Leopoldovna, after all. The Tsarina has loosened all purse strings."

"But Christine and Anthony are not actually getting married in there?"

"No." Lestocq chuckled, a short and joyless sound. "But Prince Alexis Dolgoruky is. He will be freed from his cage to wed the Tsarina's Kalmuck dwarf, Buzhenina."

"Buzhenina. Isn't that the name of a recipe?"

"The Tsarina's favorite stew of roast pork with spiced vinegar and onion sauce, to be precise. Once they are done, it will be Christine's turn."

As the Austrian Emperor in Vienna was the highest-ranking relative of Christine's groom, Prince Anthony of Brunswick, his ambassador, the Marquis de Botta, formally asked for her hand in marriage. At the ceremony fresh tears ruined the paint on her face. She covered her mouth in disgust when Anthony pranced into the room, his white satin suit embroidered with gold, his long fair hair curled with tongs like a girl's. As Anna made them exchange rings, Christine shook with rage, her eyes constantly seeking Julie's. I understood and pitied her: she was truly in love. Yet this marriage was the price to be paid for her adoption and elevation to Anna Leopoldovna Romanova, Tsesarevna of All the Russias.

Alexis and I followed the Tsarina's retinue through the Ice Palace: Anna Ivanovna pointed out this and that, delighting in the sheer beauty of the building, its finesse, and its stunning details. A life-size elephant hewn from ice greeted us, spouting a twenty-four-foot jet of water. At nighttime this would be changed to petroleum and set aflame. As I walked around the sculpture, a horrid sound scared the wits out of me. I jumped, but Alexis caught me, laughing: a man blowing a trumpet sat inside the frozen beast. The palace's façade was marbled in green paint, and at either end rose thirty-foot trees, hewn from ice and painted to look like the real thing—down to the ice birds nesting in their branches. Above the elaborately carved entrance, a dozen fat little angels floated. De Biron referred to them as putti, looking knowledgeable and pretending to speak Italian. Inside, windowpanes fashioned from slivers of sheet ice allowed the wan daylight to flood this wonder.

"Where shall we go first?" Alexis asked, in awe, breath clouding from his lips. The Imperial retinue had moved on without us, and we were like children discovering a new world.

"How about here?" I laughed. "It must be a drawing room." An ornate ice table surrounded by a dozen ice chairs was topped by an ice clock, glassy enough to show its works. Frozen to the surface of the table lay real cards and counters. Shelves carried ice books; a sideboard groaned with ice replicas of dishes from all over the world, painted in their natural tint, next to a tea service, goblets, and glasses, all shiny and frozen.

"What is upstairs, do you think?" Alexis pulled his fur coat tighter.

"The bedroom, I suppose." I thought of Alexis Dolgoruky: was his fate of being a figure of utter ridicule truly better than his family's demise in Beresov?

"Come," Alexis said, pulling me up the vast ice staircase to the marital chamber, where Dolgoruky would bed his dwarf tonight, the Tsarina and her court watching, roaring with laughter. We saw an elaborately carved and curtained bed. Even a nightcap had been chiseled with icy precision; on a stool I spotted two pairs of glossy, frosty slippers. In the fireplace opposite, ice logs were waiting to be set alight using petroleum, as were ice-sculpted candlesticks. Above a dressing table's perfectly copied bottles and jars hung a splendid mirror of silvery ice, reflecting our astonished faces.

Prince Anthony of Brunswick arrived at the cathedral with pomp and ceremony, accompanied by the de Biron family: ten footmen in livery walked ahead and behind them, while Moors dressed in black velvet, wearing brilliantly colored feathers in their silk turbans, ran alongside. When Christine stepped from her carriage, the gray sea of watchful, ragged people fell silent, staring at the spectacle. They looked like the walking dead: protruding jawlines, bodies skeletal, hungry eyes popping with disbelief from dark sockets. The bride entered the cathedral as reluctantly as if she mounted a scaffold, wearing a silver dress with a stomacher sparkling with diamonds. An exquisite gemstone-encrusted coronet was secured upon her shiny, dark Ivanovna curls. While Count Ostermann sat in the Imperial Loge, Christine's lover Julie von Mengden had been told to excuse herself on health grounds.

At the Ice Palace, in the meantime, riotous mirth and outrageous joy foamed over like a shaken champagne bottle. Three hundred couples from all over Russia—Finns, Lapps, Kirgiz, Bashkirs, Kalmucks, Tartars, Cossacks, Samoyeds, and many more—had gathered to welcome Dolgoruky and his bride, who sat perched on the back of a real elephant. After a dinner in de Biron's riding school—during which Dolgoruky was violently sick, as by now he was only used to his bird diet of seeds, grains, and the odd worm—candles were lit inside the Ice Palace. It shone like a giant lantern of terrifying beauty. The prince and his new princess were put to bed—Dolgoruky groping the Kalmuck woman Buzhenina, who lay back obediently—as the ice elephant roared, and the guests and the court howled with laughter. The couple only survived the night because Buzhenina, thinking on her feet, traded her string of pearls for one of the guards' goatskin coats.

Christine fled her wedding bed, appalled by Anthony's clammy hands and clumsy, rough-and-tumble attentions. Instead she spent the first night of her married life in Julie's rooms, where Count Lynar joined them. When Anna heard about this, she slapped Christine so hard, and so many times, that the girl cowered at her feet, covering her head and begging for mercy. Maja gleefully spread word of it, taking revenge on Christine for years of unceasing scorn and unkindness.

"The Empire needs an heir," Anna had screeched, yanking up Christine's head by the hair, scaring the girl witless. "Spread your thighs. More is not required of you."

The next evening, Prince Anthony was led into Christine's bedroom for all to see. A couple of hours into the night, Julie von

Mengden escorted him away, letting Christine melt into her and Count Lynar's arms. Soon afterward, my cousin's pregnancy was announced.

Come the month of May, the Ice Palace had melted away. By now the Tsarina could hardly move for pain. She had her bed placed by the window, taking aim from there; furious at her failing strength, she shot whatever or whomever she could.

In late August Christine was delivered of a son, Prince Ivan, an uncommonly fair and handsome boy. De Biron pretended to be overjoyed, emptying all the coins he had about him into the messenger's hat. I pawned some exquisite Meissen I found in the Summer Palace's pantry to buy Ivan a present, praying for his health and strength at my little altar on the morning of his baptism. When I was admitted to his nursery before his Christening, it took but one look for me to be smitten.

"How can anything be so perfect as you?" I cooed, delighted by the way his fingers clasped mine and by the inquisitive expression in his huge blue eyes. I felt like choking. "May I?" I asked pleadingly. Before I could help myself, I reached out for him.

Christine looked at Julie von Mengden, who had been appointed Imperial nurse; she in turn checked with Ostermann, who shrugged. The wet nurse handed me the infant from his solid golden cradle, which was lined in black fox fur.

"Oh!" I gasped, overcome by this sweetest possible weight in my arms. Instinctively I rocked him, and he gave a little sound of delight, an adorable chuckle, that bowled me over. I rocked him a bit more and sought for his little feet beneath his swaddling, tickling them. He squealed, a sound that burst from him like a soap bubble in the bath. His smile of purest joy filled the deep void inside me.

I felt tears welling up as I looked around. "God, I could spend my days doing this."

While Christine smiled at me for once, Ostermann nodded to Julie. She stepped up and took Ivan from me. "Good that you know what you are missing, Tsarevna," the Vice Chancellor said.

My adoration for Ivan could not hide the bitter truth: "His birth as official heir to Christine—or the Tsesarevna Anna Leopoldovna, as I have to call her in my dispatches to Versailles, though that makes my quill curl in disgust—removes you not once, but twice and thrice, and thus forever, from the Russian succession," Lestocq said darkly, seeing the prospect of the Palace revolution he had hoped for since joining my service slipping inexorably further away.

"He is my family!" I said, though I reeled from Lestocq's warning. He was right: Russia was doomed to be ruled by Tsars of German blood. But I had taken Ostermann's bait: love for Ivan buried itself in my heart with barbed hooks.

85

It was a stormy night shortly after Ivan's birth in the ninth year of Anna's reign. There had been neither a golden autumn, nor an abundant harvest to fill the Russian barns. Only rage ruled as nature preyed on people's distress. Winds whipped across the city's prospects, making the Neva flood the quays. Once the waters had retreated, St. Petersburg smelled like a sea chest flung open after years stashed in a ship's hull.

A raging thunderstorm almost drowned out the sound of fists hammering against the doors of the Summer Palace. It was too late for visitors. We sat by the fire, sipping hot, spicy *chai*, which Alexis had laced with more than one shot of vodka, listening to a story that Lestocq read to us. Schwartz plucked at his violoncello's strings. Our companionship felt like a small flame burning in the face of darkness.

"Who can that be?" I looked up, my heart pounding.

The knocking resumed, purposeful and determined. Schwartz's fingers hovered on his strings. Lestocq halted mid-sentence. Alexis rose. "Let me see who it is, shall I?" he said.

I followed him. Ever since I had felt General Ushakov's flinty gaze on me, I had been dreading just such a moment. Uncertainty was a punishment in itself, expertly applied by Ostermann.

Only Alexis's strength of spirit and my belief in God's will still anchored me.

"Don't face them alone," I insisted, knowing the brutality of Ushakov's men: I could negotiate Alexis's safety if I gave myself up.

In the freezing corridor the draft almost snuffed out my light. I held my breath as Alexis unlatched and drew the bolt. The door opened with a whine. I raised the light, letting its feeble glow contest the darkness, rain, and cold. I saw nothing—but heard quiet laughter.

"Down here, Tsarevna." D'Acosta looked up at me, his eyes sad. He looked as wrinkled as a pair of unused bellows; clearly he had not shaved for days. White whiskers sprouted above his lip to match his thick snowy curls.

"D'Acosta!" I opened the door wider. "Is everything all right with the Tsarina?"

"Yes, Her Majesty lives." He turned his head as if to summon a companion. Into the light stepped Maja. Her white hair was undone and spread like a spider's web over the simple dark woolen shawl that had been hastily looped around her shoulders. Behind them a hired carriage disappeared into the darkness, leaving d'Acosta and Maja stranded.

"Come in," I said, opening my door wide. Hospitality was sacred, even if I was being spied on more than ever these days. What could Maja, the Tsarina's most trusted aide, want here?

"God bless you, Tsarevna," she cried, and slid in, clutching a bundle.

"What has happened?"

D'Acosta shook himself as a dog might after a wet evening walk. He looked to be in dire need of a drink. "The Tsarina has taken Ivan away from his mother. The boy is to be raised by her. Christine may see her son for five minutes only every week, and never on her own. I dislike the Tsesarevna, but the poor woman was beside herself, screaming and scratching the soldiers who came to collect the infant. It took both Lynar and von Mengden to prevent her from harming herself or the boy. They convinced her to relent. Any refusal would have looked as if she doubted the Tsarina's capacity as a mother. Yet Christine made one condition."

"Which was?" I asked.

D'Acosta touched Maja's arm. "Forgive me, my friend. But Christine said, 'My son is never to see the monster Maja.'"

The servant's face melted into a mask of misery. "After all I have done for them! My mistress cast me out there and then. I was not even allowed to hold the baby once. De Biron, the swine, even kept the bag of gold the Tsarina wanted to give me," she cried. "I don't know where to turn. You have always been good to me, Tsarevna Elizabeth. Have a heart."

"She is not to enter the palace ever again," d'Acosta added, seeing me hesitate.

"You may both stay," I decided. "Take your pick of the maids' chambers close to the kitchen, they are the warmest. All my staff have left, so you may have a different room every night of the week. I can't afford to pay you, but I can at least feed and house you."

"I would not have expected anything else. God bless you, Tsarevna." Maja fell to her knees, kissing my fingers. I felt pity for her, but also for Christine, who had suffered through long hours of labor only to have little Ivan taken from her. She had been but a means to an end; Anna would raise Ivan as her own son, the true heir to the Empire.

"Are you sure that you are doing the right thing?" Alexis asked me, his voice hushed, when d'Acosta walked Maja away to the kitchens.

In the following weeks Ostermann refused to leave his house, claiming his gout was worse than ever, making him unable to move. It was a sign of great change and danger looming ahead. A month later Anna Ivanovna's condition worsened such that Ostermann had himself carried to the Winter Palace for a meeting with de Biron in the Tsarina's antechamber. Anna Ivanovna was in such pain and screaming so loudly that the men could hardly hear themselves discussing the future of the Empire. Twenty-four hours passed without her being able to relieve herself. She lay bloated, writhing in agony. When de Biron finally sent the Imperial sled to take me to my last audience with her, Maja saw me off, her pale face blending with the empty sky. "Take leave for me, too. The Tsarina is the last of My Lady the Tsaritsa Praskovia's daughters. I always kept my promise to guard them well for her. It was the Tsarina who sent me away."

86

Tsarina Anna Ivanovna died on a wet October evening in 1740.

Eight horses carried me through a moonless St. Petersburg night. The palace was hushed, yet I sensed onlookers lurking everywhere. Three times over I had witnessed a Tsar dying; Russia was on its knees, praying. Even the city's bells lay silent, waiting. The Tsarina's rooms were filled with soldiers, government officials, and nobles of every rank. In his cage Dolgoruky sat tightly gagged; eyes bulging, cheeks suffused, unable to crow. His arms, too, were bound, so that he would not flap them. Breathing close to Anna Ivanovna's bedstead left me gasping: the stench of sweat, pus, and gangrene was suffocating. I silently prayed, touching the icon of St. Nicholas at my throat, where I had secured it with leather strings once more.

The Tsarina lay in state well before her death, wearing a white lace dressing gown. Despite being so close to her end, she was adorned with jewels—the gems catching the candlelight, shining in a ghostly nimbus. "Lizenka," she whispered to me, attempting a smile. I dropped to my knees as Christine entered the chamber, her hair loose, wearing a velvet dressing gown. Since Ivan had been taken away, she refused to dress and spent hours in bed, reading soppy novels and making love with either Julie or Lynar: it was the talk of the town.

Christine sank down on Anna's far side, taking her aunt's other hand. She squeezed the fingers as hard as she could, grinding the rings painfully into the Tsarina's swollen flesh. There was a look of sheer hatred in her dark eyes.

De Biron caressed the Tsarina's hair. Ostermann cowered in a chair, waiting and watching. Ivan's wet nurse, a buxom German woman, held the fretful infant; it was way past his bedtime. Milk glistened on his full lips; the candlelight turned his unusually fair complexion pearly white. I crossed my arms to stop myself from reaching out for him. Christine avoided looking at her son altogether. I could only imagine her pain.

Anna turned her head, gasping: "Ivan." The wet nurse held the terrified infant toward her. "Ivan is to be my heir. He is the next Tsar, Ivan VI." The Tsarina arched with pain as a cramp seized her.

"Am I being kept only to breed?" Christine shrieked. Her spirit surprised me, then I remembered the strength that Augustus's friendship, Buturlin's adoration, and Alexis's love gave me. Did Julie and Lynar's presences do the same for her? De Biron's icy stare was meant to silence her bravado, but Christine hid neither her hatred nor her contempt of him: over the nine years of Anna's rule—a run of absolute power for him—the once tall, lean, and muscular man had grown massive, his paunch barely contained by a masterfully cut crimson velvet waistcoat. The once alluring, animal gleam in his eyes had morphed into a steady, relentless glare. "Who will be Regent for Ivan then?" she asked. "I am his mother. And I hope I have not changed my name to Anna Leopoldovna, as well as my faith, for nothing?"

Ostermann slipped two papers from his waistcoat and pressed a quill into Anna's fingers, where the Imperial seal had settled deep in her flesh. The ring would need to be cut in half before it was removed and forged anew. Twice the quill slipped from her grip. In the end Ostermann guided her hand as she made the two-month-old Ivan the next Tsar of All the Russias.

Ostermann held out a second scroll. "And here is the declaration of Regency. It will be a while until the Tsarevich is fit to rule."

"Perfect. This is for me then finally?" Christine snatched the scroll from Ostermann. De Biron scrutinized Christine as if presented with a mare he found wanting, then he stooped and tenderly kissed the Tsarina's fingers. But Anna Ivanovna's last look sought and found me. "*Ne boisya*," she mumbled. "*Ne boisya*." Never fear.

"I won't," said de Biron, who for one last time was allowed to assume that everything was about him. Just days later the de Birons would be dragged naked from their beds, beaten into submission with musket butts and arrested. They handed over all their possessions—gold plate and jewelry—in order to be spared torture. Accused of usurping the Imperial power and embezzling public funds, the de Birons were sentenced to be drawn and quartered; the punishment was, however, muted to lifelong exile in Siberia.

When I took my Oath of Allegiance to the infant Tsar Ivan VI, I nibbled the boy's pinkie, making him squeal with delight. I was thirty years old. Any younger and I would not have been ready for what was to come next.

87

Anna Ivanovna's open coffin was placed on a sleigh drawn by eight horses, their raven coats groomed to a mirror shine, reins studded with gemstones, black feathers bouncing on their headbands. The Tsarina's corpse had been dressed in a cloth-of-silver court costume; in her hair gleamed her favorite diamond crown. The funeral procession took three hours to complete a couple of hundred steps, the church bells' dull, steady call setting the rhythm for the thousands of spectators shuffling forward. After a decade in which wearing black had been banned, the court was back in funeral attire. The only hint of white in my mourner's weeds, with their heavy nine-foot train, came from wide linen bands attached to my neck and cuffs so that I could wipe the tears from my eyes. Following the funeral the cloth was crusty with salt. I had cried partly out of a real sense of mourning for Anna Ivanovna, who had at one time offered me her friendship, for whatever reason. During the eulogy my gaze met the vixen eyes of Julie von Mengden, who together with her uncle Count Ostermann shielded Christine from anyone's attempts to speak to her.

"*Ne boisya*," Anna Ivanovna had advised me: Never fear.

Easier said than done.

Christine was named Regent Anna Leopoldovna for her infant son Tsar Ivan, but Count Ostermann reigned in all but name. My cousin was happy to retire to her apartments, floating about in sheer lacey nightgowns, playing cards, reading soppy novels, nibbling on honey pastry, and spending her days and nights with Julie and Count Lynar. To keep up appearances the Saxon envoy became engaged to Ostermann's niece, and they took turns standing guard while the Regent lay with one or the other of them. If her husband, Prince Anthony of Brunswick, came to his wife's door, he was chased away like a dog. Come summer, the court moved to Peterhof, leaving me behind; the Summer Palace's furniture, crockery, and cutlery had been loaded onto carts, leaving me to live in an empty shell of a house. On the way out to Peterhof, a sudden downpour ruined the lot. Christine dumped the priceless furniture by the roadside and ordered everything to be bought anew in Paris, London, and Amsterdam.

I was not even asked to join Tsar Ivan's first birthday celebrations. Instead I found joy in the love shown to me by the people of St. Petersburg: the food seller who forced a bag of hot *pierogi* into my hands, refusing to take payment; the Parisian finery shop that consistently forgot to charge me for my orders; the women who asked me to bless their babies when I was out and about; the soldiers who never failed to greet me, joining me for *chai* and dinner.

Soon the bloodhound Ostermann scented my growing popularity. Count Lynar was to leave for Saxony to prepare for his wedding to Julie. Before he left whispers reached me that he was overheard advising Christine to "deal with Elizabeth."

The uncertainty of what this might mean drove me mad with dread. Count Lynar departed from St. Petersburg on the eve of St. Nicholas's Day, when Russia honors its patron saint. He is protector of the weak, savior of the oppressed; he gives to the poor without harming the rich. St. Nicholas is the kindest of all Russian saints, a true hero of the disadvantaged.

Fate could have chosen no better moment.

88

On the evening of December 5, I sat together with Alexis in the Summer Palace's small library, lights burning low and a fire crackling. Still, I did not feel warm. Only some of the furniture Christine had looted had been replaced. Thumb-sized gaps showed between the floorboards; moisture crept inside, trickling down the bare walls; the windowpanes shook from drafts. Lestocq rushed in, brushing snow off his sleeves and head. He made no attempt at civility. "Tsarevna Elizabeth—we have no time to lose. Ostermann has ordered the regiments to leave town and to join the front within twenty-four hours."

"What does that mean?" I rose from my chair.

"You will be defenseless. Once they are gone, you will be arrested for planning a coup, tried, and possibly executed. Go, Tsarevna. Take what is yours. The palace and the power."

I crossed my arms, trying to stem my fear. "I will never go against the oath I have sworn to my cousin Ivan, the rightful Tsar. I am no traitor to my house."

"Your house? If only," Lestocq said, smiling lopsidedly like an actor who had been given a better cue than he could ever expect. "You have believed that for far too long." He stepped aside: on the threshold, Maja cowered next to d'Acosta, her face swollen with tears, white hair wild. Alexis stepped behind me, placing his hands on my shoulders.

"Speak now, woman." D'Acosta shoved Maja forward. "Pay your debts to the Tsarevna."

Maja crossed herself: "I swear by the soul of the Tsaritsa Prasko-via, your aunt Pasha, that Christine has brought this upon herself. The Regent—" she spat out, hugging her arms around her shaking body. "Her viciousness relieves me of any oath I took."

My fingers sought Alexis. I leaned into him, feeling faint: "Speak!" I said.

Maja shivered. "The Tsaritsa Praskovia never lay with Tsar Ivan; she could not bear the thought. My lady was the most beauti-ful maiden ever, as dark and sweet as a blackberry, and they threw her to this man, this—" She stopped short of insulting my uncle, Tsar Ivan. "On her wedding night, she was beside herself with fear, threatening to slice her wrists. So I helped her. Every evening I gave Tsar Ivan the milk of paradise to drink, so he lay passed out. Year after year I harvested the poppy fields around Moscow. He never, ever consummated the marriage."

"But how—" I started to say. The enormity of Maja's confes-sion overwhelmed me. She held her arms over her head.

"Don't ask any more!" she pleaded, wiping away snot and tears.

"Speak!" d'Acosta hissed, pulling at her pitilessly. She shrieked; the sound made me freeze with terror. D'Acosta shook her with sur-prising force, making her teeth chatter. "Say it."

"She lay with a gentleman of the bedchamber instead. Neither of the Tsaritsa Praskovia's daughters were fathered by Tsar Ivan. Neither of them was a Romanova," Maja sobbed. D'Acosta let go of her, crossing his arms.

I sank against Alexis, buckling under the weight of Maja's words. Cheating on a Romanov was one thing, fooling All the Russias quite another. Aunt Pasha's position had been one of honor—the Tsar's wife—and being wed to him was an outcome that any noble-man's daughter would desire, however unprepossessing the groom. I was too stunned to think, let alone speak, as Schwartz rose from his corner seat, setting his cello aside carelessly. The three men's eyes locked: they were not friends, yet at that moment a powerful current of understanding passed between them. Alexis, Lestocq, and Schwartz stood united, for Russia and for me.

Lestocq placed his Tarot pack on the small table in front of me, fanning out the cards, laying them upside down. "Take three cards."

"This is not the time!" I objected. The world had just come tumbling down. Why should I play cards?

"When if not now?" Alexis said to my surprise. "Please, Lizenka. Do it."

I chose randomly, laying three cards face down on the gaming table's green felt. "Have a look!" Lestocq urged me. Alexis leaned in. Schwartz went on tiptoes.

My hand hovered.

"Turn them, Lizenka," Alexis said tenderly.

I did.

89

The world was in upheaval after Maja's revelation. Clouds hung heavy with ice, sleet, and snow. The moon presided momentarily over the prospects, making the ice on the Neva shine like black starlight before plunging the city into darkness once more. The windows in the high, flat façades of the houses and palaces were unlit; intense cold made the sentries before the palaces retreat inside, where only a spell by the brazier and a sip of vodka kept them alive.

Alexis had helped me dress in the uniform of the Preobrazhensky Regiment; the Imperial green jacket was too tight and the breeches stiff with cold. We slipped silently into the night, as the Summer Palace was certainly surrounded by spies. Away from the trodden paths, I sank thigh-deep into the snow but pressed on: we had to reach the barracks! The cold air stung my lungs and made me gasp with pain. "Let me help you," Schwartz said, linking our elbows and dragging me on as if I weighed nothing at all. Alexis and Lestocq also took turns in supporting me.

In the forced march through the city, every breath seared my lungs, black stars lit my gaze, and my thoughts were hazy from exhaustion. Just when I thought we should never reach the barracks, their lights and din pierced the darkness, parting the veil of snow. The quarters of the two old Imperial Russian regiments teemed with life, despite the night hour. Everywhere soldiers dragged saddles, clothes, arms, and food rations to the stables; all goods were loaded onto mules, horses, and sleds, destined for the front. The men shouted, laughed, pushed each other, happy to escape the city's oppressive atmosphere and their exclusion from court where any task of importance was awarded to the purely German and Baltic Izmailovsky Regiment.

Were these men ready to assist me? I could not be sure, but just the sight of them made my spirits soar. I was doing what I was destined to do, by Divine Law. I was fulfilling my duty toward Russia. "Let us go, boys!" I called, leaving the cover of darkness and stepping into the light. My heart pounded: how would the regiments welcome me? No explanations were needed. The soldiers dropped everything they carried and ceased whatever they were doing when they saw me. They kneeled in the driving snow. "*Matushka Rossiya! Matushka Rossiya!*" they called as one, beating their chests with their fists. Was there ever a greater show of love? Little Mother Russia. At any other time they called our country that. Their words spurred me on. It all fell into place: *you will be a mother, but you will have no child.*

I was in awe: the Leshy's prophecy had never harmed but only prepared me. What had seemed like a threat, in truth had been a saving grace, readying me for what lay ahead.

"Rise, men, and follow me!" I called. "We have no time to waste!"

We hurried ahead toward the building, sure of the common soldiers' support. The door to the officers' mess was closed. I clenched my fists. These were the men I had to convince, the leaders of the troops. What if their Oath of Allegiance to the infant Tsar Ivan bound them tighter than their love for me and Russia? I gave Schwartz a terse nod, and he kicked the door open: it struck the wall behind. The men turned, rising from the tables, hands on daggers and pistols.

I stood in the doorway: my cheeks were flushed, my blonde hair tumbled from my fur hat, and the green regimental jacket molded my body, showing my rosy skin where I had opened it so I could breathe more easily. The icon of St. Nicholas sparkled at my throat.

My legs in their thigh-high leather boots were planted firmly on the threshold. There was a moment of stunned silence before they shouted a welcome: it was a single roar, a dark green sea of officers rising to acclaim me, gold uniform buttons dancing like starlight on dark waves.

No explanations were needed. They knew why I was here. The common soldiers, too, spilled into the mess. Tonight destinies were to be forged, fortunes made or lost. Fate held its breath.

"Do you know whose daughter I am?" I shouted as two officers seized me and hoisted me on their shoulders. The atmosphere was charged with expectation. A sea of faces was turned to me, adoring and hopeful. Glasses were brandished in the air, vodka splashing.

"Yes! You are the Tsar's daughter! The great Tsar Peter!"

I raised my hands, bathing in the warmth of their affection. "Yes. But I am also the Tsarina's daughter. My moment has come. *Our* moment has come. Help me take my throne! I will reward you royally, as only I can. Tomorrow morning the city shall wake to a new Tsarina of All the Russias. Follow me to the Winter Palace!"

"Yes, to the Palace! Let us kill them all!" the men cheered, seizing muskets, bayonets, daggers, swords, and sabers.

"No!" I shouted, clenching my fists. "No, no, and no! If you plan to murder, I shall not come. No drop of Russian blood is to be spilled on my account. But hand me a sword!" I held the weapon high, its blade flashing in the light of the officers' mess like a beacon. "Follow me—for Russia. *Matushka Rossiya!*"

A tidal wave of soldiers swept me up, flooding out of the mess, seizing their weapons, taking on the night of St. Nicholas. Anna Ivanovna might have been right when she said that a pretty face was not enough to send soldiers marching. But I was the Wolverine, the Tsarevna born under the December stars on the day of celebration for Russia's greatest victory, the Princess of Poltava.

We made slow but steady progress. My friend the Russian winter muffled our footsteps. At every mansion belonging to the Regent's supporters, I placed pickets, ready for the morning arrests. Once we reached the Admiralty, I ordered Ostermann himself to be arrested. It was sad that I would not see his face when it happened, but I should witness his punishment later, whatever judgment my court should pass. He had obstructed my hereditary rights for too long. God willing, Russia was to wake to Russian rule on St. Nicholas's Day.

Yet the Devil never rests. My boots were soaked, and every breath split my chest with icy pain. The bells struck again, marking another hour lost. I fell behind, exhausted. My sight blurred as I saw the backs of the men storming ahead, snow swallowing them and drowning out my shouts.

"Hurry, Tsarevna!" Lestocq tried to help me up.

"I can't!" I gasped, tormented by a violent stitch in my side.

"Yes, you can, my love!" Alexis, too, tried to pull me to my feet. Snow hid the path ahead. My heart hurt, my limbs burned, my boots were too heavy for me to take one more step. I stumbled anew, falling into the snow on my hands and knees. I broke through its surface, feeling the icy bite on my shoulders, belly, and chin. I was soaked to the skin. I stifled a sob but said: "Let us press on." I plunged into another drift, this time disappearing up to my thighs. It was hopeless. For God's sake, even chubby Schwartz managed better!

"Schwartz," I coughed, longing for his bear-like strength.

"The Tsarevna Elizabeth!" he yelled and yanked me up, carrying me in his arms. "She's falling behind."

"Go!" I pleaded, gulping for air.

"Never," Alexis shouted. "We go nowhere without you." Schwartz gave a sharp whistle, and two officers came running back. Cheering, they hoisted me on their shoulders, galloping ahead. Alexis laughed and ran with us, relishing the adventure, as we stormed through driving snow to the Winter Palace.

The vast building lay in darkness: its shutters were closed, the courtyard deserted. I held my breath, counting the dark windows, trying to make out Christine's bedroom and the royal nursery. The sentries at the entrance gate, who had been warming themselves at a brazier, laid down their weapons immediately, kneeled, and begged for their lives, swearing the Oath of Allegiance. "Take me to the guards' room!" I commanded. There the men on duty jumped up at sight of me, unsure what to do. "I don't want any bloodshed. I am here to claim what is rightfully mine: I am the Tsarevna Elizabeth Petrovna Romanova. Lay down your arms and follow me," I called, raising my sword.

"What on earth?" their captain said, but Herr Schwartz seized the man by the collar with one hand only and flung him against the wall, winding him.

"How did you do that?" I asked admiringly, laughing and feeling exhilarated.

He flexed his mighty muscles and grinned. "I always told you: practice makes perfect!"

My regiment flooded the room, taking command, as the palace guards were outnumbered by three hundred or more men— and one woman. "Go!" I urged them on, slashing the taut skin of the guards' drums. The leather split with a wonderfully ugly sound, a hiss like a wildcat ready to pounce. Nobody would be able to raise the alarm with this. "A thousand roubles for each man who is with me when the morning dawns," I called.

There was no further hesitation. The Imperial Guard followed us as we swarmed all over the sleeping palace like angry bees, ready to sting. "Up here!" I took two marble steps of the grand staircase at a time, turning toward the northwest wing of the building. Our steps echoed along the high gallery and long corridors as we stormed ahead; the lights and torches in our hands cast ghostly reflections on the mirrored walls. Nothing was an effort anymore. My blood was a red-hot current racing to my heart, setting my mind aflame. I took only what was my due: the men's devotion and Russia's love carried me.

Outside gilded double doors we halted.

I caught my breath: the high European-style handle pressed lightly against my palm. Behind lay an antechamber, I knew, in which a dozen or more ladies-in-waiting were crammed together to sleep. They guarded the bedroom of my cousin Christine—Russia's Regent Anna Leopoldovna.

"This is it," I said, my voice tight with apprehension. I opened the door and slipped inside. As my men poured after me, the ladies and their maids woke and shrieked, covering themselves and begging for their lives.

"Take them to the kitchens," I ordered, as the women were bundled out into the corridor. "No rape and no molestation or I'll have your skins." I strode over the golden parquet, patterned with ash and ebony, and pushed open another set of double doors. The room had not been aired for a while; the air was as sticky as in the Izmailov Wolf House. I raised my light: Christine slept in Julie's arms. Both women were naked, limbs laced together, their long hair spilling over the white starched linen. In her sleep Julie's hand lay slack on the Regent's lower belly. I could see the stretch marks where Christine had borne my darling Ivan. Behind me the soldiers gawped: so the scandalous rumors were true!

Julie stirred as the light from the lanterns pierced her sleep, the commotion and excitement all around swamping her dreams. Before she could say anything, I shook Christine by the shoulder, waking her. She opened her eyes drowsily, then blinked and sat up. "Lizenka, what on earth?" She stopped short when she saw the soldiers' weapons, as well as my flushed cheeks, my uniform, the smile that made my eyes sparkle.

"Wake up, little sister," I said merrily. "It is time to rise!"

"Have mercy!" she begged while Julie sobbed. In vain she tried to cover her nakedness. They embraced one another, but the soldiers tore them apart, wrapping them in sheets. "Whatever you do, don't harm Julie," Christine pleaded, as she stood next to her bed, shivering.

"Don't worry, I won't."

"What are you doing then?" Christine clutched the sheet in front of her.

I steeled myself. "Now? I am going to see Ivan."

Understanding dawned in her eyes; fear filled her plain face. "Oh, Lizenka! Please don't hurt him!"

There were no words for the feelings that warred inside me then. I had been led to believe that this woman was my cousin, yet she was no blood relative at all. For a decade she and her brethren had obstructed my hereditary rights. Anything worth calling a life would cease for her and hers, this very night. I should end it with my own hands.

So I went to see sweet Ivan, my beloved boy, the infant Tsar, in his nursery.

90

IN THE WINTER PALACE, ST. NICHOLAS'S DAY
DECEMBER 6, 1741

The lightest load will be your greatest burden.

As the Leshy spirit's last prophecy comes to pass, the soldiers pour in, elation on their faces, the captain of the Preobrazhensky regiment storming ahead. His men and he have put their destiny in my hands by following me. The nursery's dusk is brightened by flaming torchlight, hours before the morning is due. As the wet nurse stirs, she is dragged out before she can scream. I lift Ivan out of his cradle and nuzzle his cheek, drinking in his sweet scent of milk, as well as the lavender in which his sheets are stored. I must remember this moment. If my half-brother Alexey's death at our father's hands once cursed the family, then handing Ivan to the soldiers will save the Romanovs—and Russia. I force myself to remember that not a drop of our blood flows in his veins.

"Shhh. It is me, Aunt Lizenka," I whisper, and kiss him; a smile buds, spreading sunshine over his little face. His hair is so fair; his eyes so big and blue; an uncommonly handsome boy. I loosen his swaddling.

"Enka," Ivan coos, as the captain approaches like a tomcat on the prowl, his excitement and impatience filling the room. Within hours lives are destroyed and made, riches are lost, fortunes won. He reaches out for Ivan. "Please hand me the Ts—"

I raise my eyebrows in a silent warning, and he corrects

himself. "Forgive me, Your Majesty. Please hand me Ivan Antonov," he says.

Your Majesty. It seems I took the decision about Ivan's fate when I left the Summer Palace for the barracks—or perhaps even earlier, when I decided to live up to the Leshy spirit's prophecy. I hand him over, my heart breaking. Any further delay is impossible.

"Don't drop him!" I do not know what else to say.

"I shan't. Let us go, Ivan Antonov," says the soldier, his chin and cheek darkly stubbled. Ivan rubs his hands on it, while the captain looks at me questioningly.

Let us go. I taste the bitter sting of tears. What I must do is unforgivable, yet it is the only way forward. The choice that I take to surrender Ivan is for the benefit of Russia. Who am I in comparison with that? A mere tool. My country can only have one ruler. I have earned the right to reign as much as I have inherited it. "Take the family of Anthony of Brunswick to the Summer Palace," I say. "They are to be placed under house arrest."

"And Ivan Antonov himself?" The soldier rocks the babe.

"You are to await further orders," I tell him, turning away to hide the tears welling in my eyes.

Further orders. These two words are the midwife to the most monstrous, unavoidable decision. Ivan will become Prisoner Number One of All the Russias, condemned to a living death. I will lock him away in the dark, dank Schlüsselburg for all eternity, or until the end of his days—whichever comes first. Father's conquest of this water fortress on the Neva estuary—a wasteland of swamps and thick mists—had made the founding of St. Petersburg possible. As Ivan's prison, it will be a constant reminder of what it took and takes to rule Russia. If there is any attempt to free him—and there will be, because there always is—Ivan will be killed immediately. I kiss his little hand one last time; his fingers, which will never again hold a toy, or a quill, let alone the orb and scepter.

While Ivan sacrifices his body and mind to Russia, I add my immortal soul to that grisly offering, giving my realm the Holy

Trinity that it deserves. It makes me join Ivan in a prison of sorts: the Winter Palace, where I shall forever fear dusk and the night that follows. Any night. What if another heir apparent storms along the Neva embankment toward the Tsarina's residence? For me no sleep will be taken in the same room two nights running, to confuse a possible enemy. Alexis and my court will keep me entertained with festivities lasting until dawn, when fatigue overwhelms me. Nobody will dare attack and usurp me in broad daylight.

"Poor Ivan Antonov," I say, my voice quivering. "It's not his fault. His parents are to blame."

"At your orders, Tsarina." The captain's eyes commiserate, but his soldier's stance is resolute. *Tsarina.* I am grateful for the tears that blur my vision. My throat burns, and my heart is spiked by lead as the captain leaves with Ivan in his arms; the ringing of boots against the marble floor drowns out the boy's sweet prattle.

I am not to see Ivan ever again.

Nobody is.

The palace is awake even though the morning of St. Nicholas's Day has not yet broken. Passages and staircases are swarming with people, hastening to swear their allegiance and secure their good fortune. I have become their fate. Yet I need to be on my own, to marvel at the enormity, as well as at the ease, of the events of the night. I shut the door but resist the urge to turn the key. The room is deserted—the cradle empty, the now obsolete toys scattered, the seat still warm from the wet nurse's ample bottom—and will remain so for years to come. I am *Matushka Rossiya* and my children are millionfold. My vastest and richest of all realms will shelter them. The thought floors me. My knees buckle, and I sit for a long time, leaning against the door, crying helplessly. The pain stretches away from my heart. It thins and lengthens, twisting like a threadworm before it sinks its barb into my guts.

When did I hear the knock?

I rise, wipe my eyes and my nose, turn the key and open the

door. It is Alexis, the only man I can bear to share this moment with. He embraces me, holds and rocks me, as if I were the baby. I need not explain; he knows what I have done; he understands why I had to do it. He does not judge.

"The soldiers who arrested Ostermann brought me this," he whispers tenderly, and opens his hand. On his palm gleams the Imperial seal. The double-headed eagle seems alive, rising from the gemstone's fire. The bird veers toward me, claws sharp, beak shiny, wings vast.

"Put it on," Alexis says.

I slip it onto my ring finger, where it hangs loose. The gold band has been snipped with pliers to release it from Anna Ivanovna's swollen limb. It will be properly fitted onto mine in good time.

"Come," Alexis says. Gently he leads me to the window and pulls the drapes aside. "Look," he says softly, holding me so close that I feel his heartbeat. I am grateful, as I still feel faint when I think of Ivan and the life—or rather, existence—he is to lead. My doubt and remorse will be submerged during the days to come. They pass in a deluge of adoration while I am introduced to my new life of privilege and duty, reigning over an enormous Empire. But for now Alexis loves me, despite what I have done. No, on the contrary: he loves me *for* what I have done. It is morning, and the storm has abated. Light floods the room, hitting me like icy water sloshed in a drunkard's face.

I look, and I see.

The snowfall has ceased. The sky is the palest shade of blue, like the duck eggs hidden in the reeds at Kolomenskoye. Thin clouds are strung across it, like tightropes to the heavens. The houses gleam, rainbows caught in stone. St. Petersburg is still, floating eerily in the crisp air, like a bauble in a bell jar. As I open the window, the morning tastes as sharp as chilled vodka. Soon the church bells will give tongue, their sound swelling to the heavens, telling Russia about its new Tsarina—I have saved my country and my people.

For this no price is too high to pay.

The city is asleep, yet I catch a movement over on Menshikov's Vassilyev Island. I squint—and my breath stalls. Something slides from the shadows on the riverbank into the sunshine. The creature stands and returns my gaze, a slight figure in a cloak of mottled gray. With a twist and a turn, swirls of silver fur blend with its own tresses. The light catches a face and a smile that shows the flash of fangs.

"Alexis, did you see?" I gasp.

"What is it?" He draws me back against his chest.

On the opposite bank the Leshy dissolves into thin air.

"Nothing." I swallow. "It's a glorious morning."

"It is, Tsarina Elizabeth." My love is the first to call me by this bold shining name, the one that history will remember me by. Tenderly he kisses my hair.

The Neva's ice is as blank as a mirror, a sheet of silver gleaming in the morning sun. It will keep its promise to carry me: safely, forever.

Me.

AUTHOR'S NOTE

Elizabeth Petrovna Romanova, Peter the Great's only surviving child, seized power in a palace coup and declared herself Tsarina of All the Russias on the morning of December 6, 1741.

The reigning infant **Tsar Ivan VI** was imprisoned in the Schlüsselburg where he lingered for more than two decades. During a conspiracy to reinstate him at the beginning of the reign of Catherine the Great (Catherine II of Russia), he was stabbed by his guards. His parents and siblings were kept under house arrest; once released and allowed to leave Russia, they were unable to resume a normal life. Elizabeth ruled Russia for twenty years as a contemporary of Frederick the Great in Prussia and Maria Theresa of Austria.

Count Andrej Ivanovich Ostermann, a priest's son from the German town of Bochum and Vice Chancellor of Russia, was condemned first to be broken on the wheel and then beheaded, yet, true to her promise never to sign a death warrant, Elizabeth spared his life, instead subjecting him to the horror and humiliation of a mock execution. His only sign of emotion on the scaffold was a slight tremor in his hands as he readjusted his wig. He and his family were exiled to Beresov in Siberia, where he died six years later, in 1747.

Ekaterina (Katja) Alexeyevna Dolgoruky survived her banishment to Siberia. In 1741 Elizabeth appointed her as a lady-in-waiting. In 1745 she married Lieutenant General Count Alexander Romanovich Bruce. She died of a cold in 1747.

Ernst Biren, the groom turned Count turned sovereign Duke of Courland, escaped the jaws of the great She-bear of Russia: Elizabeth recalled him from Pelym in Siberia, offering him an estate and serfs. Biren reemerged in 1762, when the Germanophile Peter III of Russia summoned him back to court. In 1763 Catherine the Great reestablished him in his Duchy of Courland. The last years of his rule there were just, if somewhat autocratic. He died in his palace in Mitau in 1772. The princely family of Biron of Courland prospers to this day.

Moritz Karl, Count Lynar, was about to commit to being the full-time lover of Regent Anna Leopoldovna—Elizabeth's cousin Christine—when Elizabeth's coup cut short his ambition. His link to Russia remained: the descriptions of him as an "utter fop," worried about his fair complexion, impregnating countless women, and always clad in pastel shades, are taken from Catherine the Great's diary. Lynar died without a legitimate heir.

Julie von Mengden, a Livonian baroness, was the lady-in-waiting and lover of the Regent Anna Leopoldovna and the fiancée of Count Lynar to hide their scandalous *ménage à trois*. She devotedly followed Regent Anna Leopoldovna into house arrest and imprisonment but was released in 1762. She followed the Regent to Denmark.

Alexander Borisovich Buturlin, Elizabeth's supposed first lover, is here merged with Alexis Shubin, another of her passionate affairs, who was first brutally maimed, then stationed in Kamchatka. At her accession Elizabeth recalled Shubin; he lived a long, prosperous life on a vast estate. Buturlin went on to be a general in her army.

The character of the Prince **Alexis Dolgoruky**, the godfather of Petrushka—young Tsar Peter II—is an amalgam of several princes of this vast, conniving family, which was left almost extinct by Tsarina Anna Ivanovna and Count Ostermann. Added to the blend is Prince Mikhail Golitsyn, who suffered as a birdman in a cage for the better part of a decade, and who was the groom at

Empress Anna Ivanovna's notorious Ice Palace wedding. His Kalmuck wife and he had several children together.

Jan d'Acosta was a Portuguese Jew and court jester, "thanks to a funny figure, knowledge of many European languages, and a gift to make fun of all and everything," as the historian Shubinsky writes. D'Acosta's fate beyond Anna Ivanovna's reign is unknown.

Jean-Armand de Lestocq, the French physician and adventurer, went on to wield enormous influence on foreign policy during Elizabeth's early reign. In 1748, however, he was accused of plotting in favor of the imprisoned, deposed Tsar Ivan VI. Lestocq was tortured and sentenced to death. Elizabeth, however, spared him and had him exiled. Only upon her death was Lestocq restored to his estates and allowed to return to the Russian capital.

Despite supposedly secretly tying the knot with the love of her life, **Alexis Razumovsky**, Elizabeth remained officially unmarried and never had children. Instead she named her German nephew, Karl Peter von Holstein (Peter III), Anoushka's son, Tsarevich. He abhorred Russia and would have preferred the Swedish throne, to which he was also entitled. As a staunch supporter of Frederick the Great, he was happy to be engaged to a young German princess: Sophie Friederike von Anhalt-Zerbst. Elizabeth baptized her in the Orthodox faith as Catherine Alexeyevna. She was later to usurp her husband's throne and rule Russia as Catherine the Great.

The **Golosov Ravine**, located near the Moscow River and the former Tsarist palace of Kolomenskoye, has several springs and a brook running through it. It is home to a neo-pagan shrine and is associated with legends about time travel and magical woodland creatures.

ACKNOWLEDGMENTS

The Tsarina's Daughter had big shoes to fill. If it takes one author to write a novel, it takes a global village of an outstanding team of publishers, editors, and agents to make Elizabeth's development from ingénue to a woman who does not shy away from making a hard—if not the hardest!—decision, come to pass. So many people were involved in helping me to write the best novel I could. Many thanks to everybody involved at Curtis Brown: my agent, the amazing Alice Lutyens, for whom nothing is ever too much and who always finds the right encouraging word while keeping her eye on the pie, as well as tech-savvy and fun Sophia Macaskill, and the energetic foreign rights team, Sarah Harvey and Jodi Fabbri. In New York, I am grateful to the elegant and capable Deborah Schneider of Gelfman Schneider/ICM Partners for her patience and belief in *The Tsarina's Daughter*. My gratitude goes to the team at Bloomsbury London—my intuitive, passionate, and wise publisher Faiza Khan, who is as much in love with strong women and the early Romanov era as I am, as well as the enthusiastic and organized managing editor Lauren Whybrow and the eagle-eyed copyeditor Lynn Curtis. Also I know that once more Philippa Cotton, Laura Meyer, and Rachel Wilkie will do their publicity and marketing magic for "my girl" Elizabeth. In New York, thank you to the team at St. Martin's Press, above all Charles Spicer with his knack for adding conflict and drama to a manuscript; Sarah Grill for her steady, spirited support; and Dori Weintraub and Marissa

Sangiacomo for their "haute couture" attitude to marketing and publicity. Thank you, too, to literary scout Daniela Schlingmann, a woman of the first hour, for spreading the word further. Thank you to the Petersham Writers Circle, in particular my fellow author Emma Curtis, as well as editor Patrick Newman, who reliably keeps the "Germanometer" of any first draft as low as humanly possible. Last, but not least, thank you to my sons, Linus, Caspar, and Gustav, who adopted Elizabeth Petrovna Romanova as their honorary sister for more than a year, even though they have yet to read one of my novels. Thank you, Tobias, for stoically taking any quips about "lots of method writing happening in this household!"

ABOUT THE AUTHOR

ELLEN ALPSTEN was born and raised in the Kenyan highlands. Upon graduating from L'Institut d'Études Politiques de Paris, she worked as a news anchor for Bloomberg TV London. While working gruesome night shifts on breakfast TV, she started to write in earnest, every day, after work and a nap. Today, Ellen works as an author and as a journalist for international publications such as *Vogue, Standpoint,* and *CN Traveller.* She lives in London with her husband, three sons, and a moody fox red Labrador.

THE TSARINA'S DAUGHTER
by Ellen Alpsten

About the Author

• A Conversation with Ellen Alpsten

Keep On Reading

• Recommended Reading

• Reading Group Questions

Also available as an audiobook
from Macmillan Audio

For more reading group suggestions
visit www.readinggroupgold.com.

 **ST. MARTIN'S GRIFFIN**

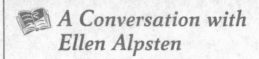

A Conversation with Ellen Alpsten

Could you tell us a little bit about your background, and when you decided that you wanted to lead a literary life?

I was born in the highlands of Northern Kenya, at the foot of mystical Mount Elgon, where life glows in Technicolor. My father is a vet, my mother taught at a local school. We had no TV, but a big garden, plenty of pets—a wounded serval cat, a grumpy polo pony called Calypso, and at times even a baby crocodile—and lots of books: my godmother sent me a monthly book parcel. I read, I drew, I wrote in my diary (recording things like: This morning there was a nine-foot python curled up in the tree above my swing). While my two older brothers were away at boarding school, I dressed up my four dogs and three cats and told them stories. Storytelling has a huge tradition in Africa, transcending age, race, and gender. I love reading the new, female gritty voices coming from Africa, especially Nigeria, such as *His Only Wife* or *The Girl with the Louding Voice*. Aged eighteen, I moved to Paris, from the savannah to the salons of the 16th arrondissement. I was lucky to be admitted to the IEP de Paris, which had schooled such great, diverse minds as Christian Dior, Alexandre Jardin, and Emanuel Macron. I walked the city's roads endlessly and wrote long diary entries. I also won my Grande Ecole's short story competition with the novella "Meeting Mr. Gandhi." This encouraged me to continue honing my craft, living a literary life.

Is there a book that most influenced your life?

That must be a very early read—*The Brothers Lionheart* by Swedish author Astrid Lindgren, the

most brilliant children's book, combining a faultless plot teeming with the big motives of storytelling—Good vs. Evil, Overcoming the Monster, a Quest, Cinderella, and Voyage and Return—with a deep spirituality, offering faith, hope, and theories of an afterlife. When my eleven-year-old read it recently, he came into my study afterward, welling up in tears, saying: "I have finished *Brothers Lionheart*." Knowing what that meant, we hugged, long and in silence. The book challenged me to make my writing consequential; our lives have become so crowded that a reader gives me their most valuable commodity—not money, but attention, time, and thought. I want to thank them for that.

Or inspired you to become a writer?

Entering high school, my teacher asked me to write a theater piece together with her. Thankfully, it is lost, and I have no recollection of its subject. But I had done it—plotting and finishing a literary piece, a formative experience that shows what a good teacher can do! I had long and lonely teenage years. My only salvation was going to the library, wiping clean shelves of books into a washing basket (literally!) —mostly historical fiction, which offers the triple E of entertainment, education, and escapism.

How did you become a writer?

Upon graduating, I moved to London for a graduate trainee program in a PR agency. I hardly earned any money and I had few friends. So, after years of dreaming and dabbling, I started writing for real, in the evening, ensconced in my little room. Very soon, I even wrote shamelessly during work hours as well—not surprisingly, I was the only graduate who was not offered a job come the end of that year. I started to write my debut, *Tsarina*, the first book in a planned quartet of books and the first-ever novel about the rise of Catherine I of Russia from serf to empress—the world's most astonishing Cinderella story. *The Tsarina's Daughter* is book two, but you can read it as a stand-alone. I wrote while working gruesome night shifts for Bloomberg TV, as a producer and an anchor. My neighbor thought I was an escort, as I cantered down the stairs at any ungodly hour. It was exhausting, and I was ill for three months with anxiety and depression after I had finished *Tsarina*. Today, I manage my resources much better.

Would you care to share any writing tips?

Getting published is artistically the hardest task. You judge a painting in a second. You listen to a song in three minutes. But reading a six-hundred-page tome about a forgotten Russian empress as my debut *Tsarina* was? Well...

So, here we go: watch the market, but don't follow it. Write what you love reading; tread that fine line between inspiration and imitation. Remember that *Fifty Shades of Grey* started out as *Twilight* fan fiction? Your book will never end how it started—give it a go. Make sure to resource yourself—writing a diary helps to develop an inner voice. Delve into your thoughts and emotions. Keep on going. Make space for it in your day—even if this means rising at 5 A.M. It's a privilege to be on your own with your morning tea and your characters. Check your work and enjoy that feeling when the "lid" lifts and the story comes, such as a golden

flow. Be serious about your writing, and be proud
of your progress. Set yourself a goal for, say, 1,500
to 2,000 words a day. Read, read, read.

And, most important, enjoy the ride.

For getting published, I investigated which
publishers published the best historical fiction—
my writing could have no better home in the US
than St. Martin's Press! I also did my homework
to determine which agents represented similar
books. After watching top UK agent Jonny Geller's
TED talk on agenting, I decided to submit to him
despite all warnings to debut novelists not to. After
two days of silence, the morning of Valentine's
Day, a heron settled in my garden. I took it as a
sign. The same evening, my phone pinged with a
new email: Geller's assistant asked me to send the
full manuscript. This was the first contact with my
agency, Curtis Brown, where today Alice Lutyens is
my agent. In the US, I am lucky to be represented
by Deborah Schneider. Once *Tsarina* was offered
it was sold on a global scale within three days.
We can't help but be fascinated by Russia and the
Romanovs.

You, too, can find your fabulous, unique, and
touching subject!

What was the inspiration for this novel?

The Tsarina's Daughter is a roller coaster called
Romanov! Elizabeth, the only surviving sibling
among Peter the Great's fifteen sons and daughters,
was dubbed "the world's loveliest princess" (on
an early portrait done by Caravaque she looks
like a young Marilyn Monroe, all dewy-eyed and
rosy cheeked) before falling from unimaginable
riches to rags, to then gather her strength and

rise from rags to Romanov. I can't believe my luck that once more this is the first novel proper about the metamorphosis of Empress Elizabeth of Russia from spoiled young girl to strong, savvy survivor, who defies the expectations of her time and makes hard decisions to rise to the challenge of her heritage and her fate. A free-spirited, brave, modern woman in a stunning, shocking, strange, sensuous setting:

How could I resist?

Can you tell us about what research, if any, you did before writing this novel?

The research is providing a frame to an author's picture painted by the imagination. I read divers oeuvres ranging from Tolstoy, Pushkin, Gogol, and Dostoyevsky to sociological studies such as the deeply disturbing but very important *The Unwomanly Face of War* by Svetlana Alexeyevich and *Young Stalin* by Simon Sebag Montefiore. I have watched Russian movies such as *Battleship Potemkin* and the experimental *Russian Ark*. Even though my Russian is patchy at best, there are original and of course secondary sources galore, and infinitely fascinating ones: early travel descriptions, such as the German merchant Adam Olearius visiting Tsar Mikhail Romanov, letters of foreigners at the Russian Court such as Mrs. Rondeau, Robert Massie's and Henri Troyat's biographies about Peter the Great, and, last but not least, the *fabulous* tome by Professor Lindsey Hughes (of the London School of Slavonic Studies) *Russia in the Time of Peter the Great*. This turned out to be my bible as I slid deeper and deeper into the strange, shocking, sensuous world

that is the Russian history and the Russian soul. In the end, I read for almost a year, immersing myself completely into the Russian baroque. I even read Russian fairy tales, which disclose *so* much about the imagination of a people. This allows me to attempt an answer to the question: So, what were my hitherto hidden historical heroines' lives really like? The journey from fact to fiction is thrilling and arduous, like weaving a tapestry on a thousand-strand loom, ending up with a work large enough to fill the walls of the Winter Palace!

Doing all that research made me realize why there was no novel about Elizabeth's rise from tsarina's daughter to ruler of Russia: we are facing one of the most complex phases in Russian history, which is so rich in complications. It took a long process of patient plotting to get things straight, comprehensible, and most important, captivating!

Do you have firsthand experience with its subject?

I have visited Russia and the Germano-Russian ambivalence runs straight through my family: my father grew up in the GDR, still remembering the people's terror when the US tanks withdrew one morning, and the Soviets rolled in after renewed territorial negotiations. As a surgeon's son, he was not allowed to study and fled one night at age sixteen through a forest, his passport and some warm clothes his sole luggage. Today, it takes him three cognacs and two cigars to sing the Soviet national anthem. On the other hand, my cousin owns a high-brow publishing house that publishes nothing but latter-day Russian intellectuals.

Did you base any of the characters on people from your own life?

Elizabeth's faithful hired Frenchman Jean Armand de L'Estoque is an amalgam of the many playful, surprising, food-loving, and individualistic Parisians I've met! My favorite character though is the dwarf D'Acosta, who so effortlessly slides between worlds, seeing it all, knowing it all. His is the smallest hand which tips fate's mighty scales in the end.

What is the most interesting or surprising thing you learned as you set out to tell your story?

Both researching and writing *The Tsarina's Daughter* made me think a lot about women. People often speak of the "good old days," thinking of social cohesion and man's limited horizons, which made for a simpler life, but for women those were frankly terrible days, offering no education other than household chores, early marriage to a man who suited your parents, annual childbirth, no privacy, no dreams, your frustrated husband probably turning violent with drink, just toiling, toiling, toiling from dawn till dusk. Life was marginally better for women of high standing and the Petrine laws of inheritance changed their situation; as always, war was also a harbinger of progress. If all men are out in the field, the women have to run the shops. If all sons fall in battle, an unmarried eldest daughter must be allowed to inherit, while a widow will have property. If in the story of *Tsarina* we witness a milestone in female emancipation and empowerment, *The Tsarina's Daughter* takes things a step further, defying all expectations living her choices, emboldened by a big, impossible love story.

Are you currently working on another book?

After initial second-novel jitters, I was surprised
to see that many reviewers and readers in the UK
preferred *The Tsarina's Daughter* to *Tsarina*. While
the first book was written using heart blood instead
of ink, *The Tsarina's Daughter* is a more mature,
carefully planned, and certainly "softer" novel. I am
now writing book three of the series—its subject will
surprise everybody!—and am once more infatuated
by my heroines. Once more, this will be the first
novel about an incredible woman who sets the stage
for a unique century of female reign in Russia. So,
after Marta/Catherine and the Empress Elizabeth,
I am adding two more "girls" to my coop of hidden
historical heroines. I feel so lucky!

And if so, can you tell us what it's about?

Unfortunately, no. It's top secret at the moment,
but as they say, watch this spot and *thank you* for
bearing with me!

Recommended Reading

Top Tips for Reading Novels About Hidden Historical Heroines

Ever since I discovered the leading ladies of my Tsarina series I have been determined to never walk a trodden path. Among the hidden heroines of historical fiction, the following novels feature women who morph from ingenue to strong survivor—I love Cinderella, don't you?

Child of the Morning by Pauline Gedge

Who would have thought that one of the most important rulers of Egypt's powerful eighteenth dynasty was a woman who eclipsed them all—Gedge's brilliant novel about Pharaoh Hatshepsut spawned my life-long passion for ancient Egypt.

Desiree by Annemarie Selinko

The world's second-bestselling historical novel, after *Gone with the Wind*. A Marseilles silk merchant's daughter gets engaged to a destitute Corsican cadet, who ditches her in favor of Josephine de Beauharnais and goes on to become Napoleon, emperor of France. She marries one of his generals, who is later voted king of Sweden. Imagine a sensuous, female, wonderful twist on the *Sharpe* saga!

The Other Boleyn Girl by Philippa Gregory

How lucky was Philippa Gregory to give Marie-Rose Tudor her long overdue moment in the limelight. The other Boleyn girl had been always there, yet hidden in plain sight, overshadowed by her fascinating and more forthcoming sister. Gregory does a great job in accentuating both

women's characters and how their hands were forced—or not! There is a great movie based on it, too, which doesn't harm.

Innocent Traitor by Alison Weir

Ah, those Tudors. Lady Jane Grey is not that hidden in history; she merely had no time, no time at all!—to make her mark. Books about England's most unknown queen are few and far between, which makes this novel by Alison Weir, an ambitious writer, such a delight. Grey's fate is filled with tantalizing questions: What sort of queen would she have been, once she shed the shackles her ambitious family placed her in?

Wild Swans by Jung Chang

The memory of this "novel"—which crosses the line to biography for some—still gives me heartache. It offers the most fascinating insight into the demise of an empire and the brutal, ruthless making of a communist nation, in which nothing is as superfluous and as expendable as human life. As such, it is reminiscent of the Tsarina series. However, I left the last pages of *Wild Swans* unturned, as descriptions of the inhuman suffering so casually imposed on women were unbearable to read.

Sashenka by Simon Sebag Montefiore

For a heartbreaking, and more contemporary, historical-fiction read on Russia, *Sashenka* introduces the reader to witness the transformation of Russia to the shocking, brutal, and utterly self-serving Stalinist regime that terrorized millions.

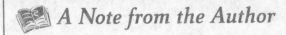
A Note from the Author

1. Is Elizabeth a sympathetic heroine, and if not, do we always understand her decisions?

2. For history buffs: Is it justified to call her "The Other Elizabeth," comparing her to Elizabeth I of England?

3. What are the turning points for Elizabeth's character, moments that make her mature from ingenue to victim to strong survivor?

4. *I was barely twenty and had lived enough for three lives.* Discuss this sentence, comparing Lizenka to a modern twenty-year-old.

5. What did you know about the early Romanovs—either from your own studies, or as portrayed in popular film/television adaptations—before reading this novel?

6. How, if at all, did it teach you about, or change your impression of, this important moment— the making of the Russian nation?

7. To what extent do you think the author took artistic liberties with this work? What does it take for a novelist to bring a "real" woman to life?

8. Who, apart from Lizenka, is your favorite character in the book and why?

9. Whom would you like to cast as the tsarina's daughter if there were a TV or movie adaptation?

10. We are taught, as young readers, that every story has a "moral." Is there a moral to this novel?

11. What can we learn about our world—and ourselves—from Lizenka's story?